OLIVIA DADE grew up an [...] the world around her as she read any book she could find. Her favorites, though, were always, always romances. As an adult, she earned an MA in American history and worked in a variety of jobs that required the donning of actual pants: Colonial Williamsburg interpreter, high school teacher, academic tutor, and (of course) librarian. Now, however, she has finally achieved her lifelong goal of wearing pajamas all day as a hermit-like writer and enthusiastic hag. She currently lives outside Stockholm with her delightful family and their ever-burgeoning collection of books.

Also by Olivia Dade

Spoiler Alert
All the Feels
Ship Wrecked

LOVE UNSCRIPTED SERIES
Desire and the Deep Blue Sea
Tiny House, Big Love

THERE'S SOMETHING ABOUT MARYSBURG SERIES
Teach Me
40-Love
Sweetest in the Gale: A Marysburg Story Collection

AT FIRST SPITE

SPITE

A Harlot's Bay Novel

OLIVIA DADE

PIATKUS

PIATKUS

First published in the US in 2024 by Avon,
An imprint of HarperCollins Publishers
Published in Great Britain in 2024 by Piatkus

1 3 5 7 9 10 8 6 4 2

A CIP catalogue record for this book
is available from the British Library.

ISBN 978-0-349-43375-2

Printed and bound in Great Britain by
Clays Ltd, Elcograf S.p.A.

Papers used by Piatkus are from well-managed forests
and other responsible sources.

Piatkus
An imprint of
Little, Brown Book Group
Carmelite House
50 Victoria Embankment
London EC4Y 0DZ

An Hachette UK Company
www.hachette.co.uk

www.littlebrown.co.uk

For my caring, whip-smart therapists, past and present: Wendy, Cathy, and Katie, I'm endlessly grateful to you and for you.

And for my husband, who climbed into the shower with me, grabbed the soap, and helped take care of me when I couldn't take care of myself. Jag älskar dig så mycket, min piffiga man.

AT FIRST SPITE

Author's Note

*I*f you're a reader who appreciates learning about sensitive content ahead of time, this note is for you. Otherwise, please skip ahead to the prologue!

. . .

. . .

Still here? All right, this is what you should know:

At First Spite addresses grief and clinical depression. It also mentions the accidental death of a young child, although that death does not occur on the page. If you're sensitive to any of those topics, please read with care, and please know that I've done my best to balance the painful bits of the book with lots of laughter and love.

For more detailed content guidance concerning this book and all my books, please visit my website: oliviadade.com/books /content-guidance.

Hugs and ♥,
Olivia

Prologue

After exchanging generic, polite greetings with an older couple and accepting their congratulations on her engagement, Athena retreated to a dimly lit corner of the museum, pushed her glasses to the top of her head, and produced her phone from her dress's deep pocket.

Finally. Ever since she'd driven over the tall, windswept, god-forsaken bridge that led to this island, the question had been niggling at her.

Abbott Island Bridge Maryland, she discreetly typed into Professor Google's search box. *Safety issues*.

A few link-clicks later, she had her answer.

Very few vehicles had hurtled over the narrow crossing's low barriers and sunk into the dark river far, far below. Which surprised her, since that wide riverbed should be bristling with rusted-out trucks and submerged SUVs. Like a reef, only with fewer rainbow-hued fish and more bumper stickers proclaiming proud parentage of schoolchildren.

Reluctantly, she slid her phone back in her pocket and perched her glasses back on the bridge of her nose.

In general, she didn't try to hide her search-engine inquiries—curiosity isn't a polite hunger, content to be fed at convenient, socially acceptable intervals—but even she knew better than to conduct research during her own damn engagement party. If the guests at this gathering noticed her in the corner, discreetly tapping at the screen of her cell, they might interpret the sight as boredom, rather than what it was: an insatiable need for information.

To be fair, also a certain amount of boredom.

But to be fair to *her*, her boredom stemmed from entirely justifiable causes. Everyone in attendance seemed to know each other already, and after introducing themselves to her, they'd immediately clustered in insular little groups. Her pediatrician fiancé, Dr. Johnny Vine, had vanished into one of those groups half an hour ago, swallowed headfirst by crowds of friends and well-wishers. No surprise there. Johnny could charm a tree out of its growth rings, and he'd been born and bred in this area.

Harlot's Bay, the water-steeped southeastern Maryland town that had raised her fiancé, lay just over that too-narrow bridge. It was the nearest community to Abbott Island, whose small but elegant art museum was hosting their happy event.

Her own friends were celebrating the holidays in Virginia with their families. Her parents were at a cardiology conference, she was an only child, and her remaining relatives lived too far away to attend, so . . . there would be no familial backup that evening either. Not for her, anyway. Eventually, Johnny's older brother—Matthew, who co-owned the pediatrics practice where both men worked—would arrive from an after-hours appointment that ran late, but she neither knew nor liked the man.

Thank goodness for Professor Google, tireless purveyor of information, dependable provider of undemanding company.

With a sigh, Athena lovingly patted her phone-filled pocket. Then she girded her loins, or whatever part of her contained her willingness and ability to generate small talk. Crowds didn't normally bother her, and she wasn't shy. Johnny or no Johnny, she needed to make an effort.

Emerging from her tucked-away corner of the room, she approached a nearby couple. The two women appeared to be in their late thirties, close to Athena's own age, and they smiled in welcome as she drew near. Smiling back, she shook their hands, introduced herself, and thanked them for coming to the party.

"Well, we heard there was an open bar," the taller woman said dryly. She winced as her companion elbowed her in the ribs. "We also wanted to support Johnny and welcome you to the community, obviously. I'm Yvonna, Matthew's friend and business partner. A pleasure to make your acquaintance, Athena."

Athena did her best to keep smiling.

Ugh. Matthew.

She wouldn't know her fiancé's brother from Adam. They'd never met, and she'd never seen a photo of him either, not even on Johnny's cell. Which she'd normally consider a bit odd, since the brothers lived in the same town and worked together, but her romance with Johnny could accurately be termed *whirlwind*. He'd proposed only two months after they'd first met. Even following their engagement, between the three-hour driving distance separating their homes and her packed teaching schedule, she'd only been able to visit Harlot's Bay twice before today.

Matthew's schedule hadn't accommodated a meeting. Either time. Johnny had blamed that on his brother's workaholic tendencies, but she knew better. Matthew had been criticizing her to Johnny, sight unseen, ever since they'd gotten engaged in October. Frankly, he sounded awful. Rigid. Judgmental. Controlling.

But she'd do her best not to hold that against Yvonna, his friend.

The museum's soft lighting set the other woman's smooth ebony skin aglow, and her black-coffee eyes were sharply focused on Athena, friendly but assessing. Her partner, a bespectacled woman with a tawny complexion and a glorious Afro, was watching Athena too, curiosity bright in her warm, golden-brown gaze.

"I'm Jackie, and I work at the university library," she told Athena. "What my wife meant to say is: We're delighted to celebrate your engagement, and we wish you and Johnny a lifetime of happiness." She paused. "I don't care about the open bar. The buffet, however . . ."

Athena grinned. "I'm a high school teacher, so I get it. Offer us soggy deli subs and limp potato chips, and we'll all trample one another to attend mind-numbing, endless after-school staff meetings."

Heaven help everyone if a cookie tray made an appearance. Then it was basically Black Friday at Walmart, only with more stapler-based weaponry.

Jackie laughed. "Librarians are exactly the same. By the way, we've been admiring your lovely dress all evening. Is that silk?"

"Yes." When Athena gave them a little twirl, the dress floated around her in a bell. "Thank you so much. It's new, and I love it."

Her wardrobe was simple. Flowing cotton dresses in pretty patterns and colors that she wore with or without a cardigan and leggings, depending on the weather. Tonight, however, her flowing dress in a pretty little strawberry print was indeed made of *silk*, and her crimson cardigan was *cashmere*, because that was how you could tell it was *fancy*. She'd even made an effort with her grooming: red lipstick, black winged eyeliner, hair blown straight.

She was still wearing her usual Keds, though. Her best pair, bright white and unscuffed. As Emily Dickinson—and later, Selena Gomez—had informed them all: The heart wants what it wants. As did the feet, Athena had discovered.

"We hear you're moving to Harlot's Bay next summer," Yvonna said. "Do you know how our town got its name?"

Of course Athena knew. Five seconds after Johnny had mentioned the town where he lived and worked, she'd feverishly consulted Herr Professor, because *Harlot's Bay*?

She wanted to move to Johnny's hometown for so many reasons, most of them selfish beyond words, but the siren song of that name would have drawn her there no matter what. And when he'd told her the name of his practice, Strumpet Square Pediatrics—*Strumpet. Freakin'. Square!*—she'd nearly burst with joy, like a gleeful human glitter-bomb.

So, yes, suffice it to say that she'd done her research. Nevertheless, she shook her head, in hopes of prolonging the easiest conversation she'd had all night.

"If you want all the details, come visit me at the library's archives," Jackie said, and the invitation sounded sincere. "This is just a quick overview."

"Quick. Right." Yvonna snorted again. "I've heard you tell this story a dozen times, and it usually requires hours."

Jackie's eyes narrowed as she regarded her wife. "I can be quick."

"About some things, maybe. Not history."

"Watch me." Jackie turned back to Athena. "In its current iteration, the town was founded in the late 1690s by two runaway women, Sarah Marshall and Eleanor Abbott, in cooperation with the remaining Piscataway inhabitants. And at some point—"

"They became a couple," Yvonna interrupted. "Even though, until just recently, historians and biographers kept insisting they were simply friends. Friends who spent decades living with one another, slept in the same bed, and wrote letters that were the colonial equivalent of sexting whenever one of them traveled."

Jackie's head tipped to the side. "I thought you wanted this explanation to be quick."

Yvonna raised a shoulder. "Sue me."

"*Anyway.*" Jackie returned her attention to Athena. "Somehow, word got around about the tiny new settlement, and other desperate and runaway women began arriving. At first, they called their town Ladywright, because of a local shipyard. Then, in the 1760s, the British colonial governor changed the name to Harlot's Bay, in condemnation of the town's founders and citizenry."

"But the joke was on him, because apparently everyone living there liked the change," Yvonna concluded. "That's been our name ever since."

Jackie nodded. "And to this day, Harlot's Bay contains more than its fair share of people, especially women, who've moved there to start over after burning down their lives somehow."

"It's our thing. We attract hot messes of all genders." Yvonna smiled. "But you're still welcome in our town, Athena, even though you have your life together."

Athena almost choked on thin air. Shit, if only they knew. She might have a fiancé and a home waiting for her in Harlot's Bay, but as far as work . . .

Well, there were probably sentient mold colonies who had their professional lives more together than she did. Once the school year ended and she moved, she had no further plans. No plans and no clue what to do next.

"That's an amazing story," Athena told the two women, and she meant it. "Thank you for telling me, and thank you for welcoming me to Harlot's Bay."

"What do you know about our local spite house?" A new gleam lit Jackie's clear brown eyes. "Because if you haven't heard the story, you should. It's—"

"Dearest." Yvonna smiled down at her spouse. "Athena's engaged to Johnny, who shares an actual wall with the Spite House. I'm sure she knows the story."

Yvonna was right. Athena had already seen the bizarrely narrow row home—hard to avoid it, since it was attached to her fiancé's house like a ten-foot-wide, four-story-high barnacle—and heard about its colorful history. Johnny had shared the tale during her first visit to Harlot's Bay, then discussed the house at regular intervals since then.

"The next time the Spite House is for sale, I want to buy it," he'd mused on multiple occasions. "Just think how amazing it would be to tear down the dividing wall and have all that extra space and sunlight."

"I know the basics, but I'd love to hear the perspective of an archivist, Jackie," Athena said. "It can be hard to separate speculation from facts actually confirmed by surviving documentation."

"The next time we meet, I'll set Jackie loose on you." Yvonna ducked her head and planted a consoling kiss on her wife's temple. "But for now, we've monopolized the poor bride-to-be long enough. Let's eat some mini-crabcakes and claim our free booze."

Jackie heaved a clearly fake sigh. "Fine. For the sake of mini-crabcakes, I'll go. Athena, it's been a pleasure, and I look forward to chatting with you again once you've settled into your new home."

"Have Johnny give you our numbers," Yvonna said with a firm nod. "Nice meeting you, Athena. Best of luck with your move."

After a few more words of farewell, the couple turned toward the buffet, and Athena was alone again. Alone and—after all that talk of crabcakes—increasingly hungry.

Well, her parents had paid for the food. She shouldn't waste their generosity.

Along her path to the hors d'oeuvres table, she stopped for casual chitchat with other guests. She didn't linger, though, because . . . there they were, at long last. The centerpiece of the entire event, as far as she was concerned. Crispy potato medallions topped with chive-flecked smoked salmon and crème fraîche. Most had already disappeared, and she didn't intend to wait any longer for her share of the bounty.

From a potato crisp's perspective, the rest of this evening was about to become Agatha Christie's *And Then There Were None*.

To her left, another guest stood perusing the offerings. When she glanced his way, she couldn't quite recall whether they'd already met, probably because he was kind of . . . generic. A be-suited, tie-clad white guy, maybe in his late thirties. Medium height. Dark hair cut short. Lean. Pale. A few crinkles at the corners of his equally dark eyes, probably from frowning rather than smiling, since he looked like the solemn sort.

Hmmm. If they'd already met, introducing herself again would tell him she didn't remember him, and that was rude. Better to proceed as if they'd already encountered each other at least once before.

"When the Romans talked about the ambrosia of the gods, they clearly meant fried potatoes." She popped a medallion in her mouth and considered the matter as she chewed. Once she'd swallowed, she added, "Although I'm not actually sure whether Europe had potatoes back then. It's not a question I've ever posed to Professor Google. Do you happen to know?"

The stranger swiveled to face her, blinking.

Then . . . he smiled, and good *gravy*.

That man wasn't generic. Not in the slightest.

Freed from what seemed to be a habitual frown, his lower lip turned full and soft, and the planes of his face transformed from severe to finely sculpted. His eyes, when lit with amusement, weren't merely dark, but the warm brown of a beer bottle held to the light.

"I'm not certain," he said, his voice low. Velvety. "And now that you've raised the question, not knowing the answer will bother me all night. We should look it up."

It was her turn to blink at him.

Johnny, bless his heart, only cared about exactitude when it came to medicine. Any other topic, he was more than willing to throw out his best guess, usually based on nothing.

The evening they'd first met—she was visiting her parents in Bethesda; he'd been invited to the informal reception they always held after the annual pediatrics conference in D.C.—Johnny had joined her in the kitchen, studied her childhood home and its sleekly curved, simple teak furnishings, and confidently complimented her family on their elegant art deco aesthetic.

"Midcentury modern," she'd told him flatly.

He'd grinned, entirely unrepentant. "What's a few decades between friends?"

They weren't friends. They weren't even acquaintances. But by the end of the night, he'd coaxed her into giving him her number. Soon enough, he'd coaxed her into giving him much, much more than that.

And from the very beginning, from that very evening, his careless imprecision had driven her to distraction. Her occasional soliloquies sharing the results of a rendezvous with Professor Google did the same to him, though, so fair enough.

It wasn't that she wanted to change her fiancé. Just that . . . she wouldn't mind him displaying a bit more curiosity about their world. More of a preference for factual reality over conjecture. But he was so young still, thirty to her thirty-six, and maybe that made a difference.

The man beside her now, his lean form clad in a slightly-too-loose navy suit and subtly striped tie, looked close to her own age. Possibly even a year or two older. Not that it mattered.

She swallowed before belatedly responding to him, her throat suddenly drier than a staff meeting on attendance policies. "We should definitely look it up. To save you from further emotional distress, if for no other reason."

"You're a true humanitarian." His smile widened into a near-grin. "While I'm a shameless pedant, as my brother frequently informs me. My apologies."

She frowned in exaggerated puzzlement. "I don't see what's pedantic about discovering the geographical origins and historical spread of a very important staple crop via a consultation with Professor Google."

"During a party," he added wryly. "The natural setting for research concerning ancient Roman agriculture."

"What better time and place to celebrate the acquisition of new knowledge?"

He actually laughed then, the sound halting and rusty but . . . warm. So warm. "Touché. We really have no choice, then, do we?"

Her cheeks heated with the pleasure of it. The playfulness. The shared desire for information, not because it might serve some practical purpose, but for its own sake.

She hadn't become high school valedictorian or graduated summa cum laude from college because she'd dreamed of harnessing one single aspect of her education and putting it to work. She'd just . . . loved learning. Surrounded by boundless fields of knowledge, she'd soaked up information and bloomed, a sunflower turning its face to the bright sky.

Which was all well and good. It had served her admirably in the classroom. Outside academia . . . not so much. But that was a problem for Future Athena, once she was comfortably settled in Harlot's Bay and her new life.

Right now, she intended to enjoy this conversation with her dark-haired stranger.

"Correct." She smiled back at him. "We *have* to figure out whether Caesar ate spuds."

"Well, then. Let's check with . . . um, Professor Google, wasn't it?" Producing his phone from a back pocket, he slanted her a sidelong glance of amusement.

"You're a man after my own heart," she told him, with more sincerity than she'd have wished. "But I don't want to be rude, so despite the appropriateness of celebrating information acquisition at a party, I'm trying not to take out my phone where anyone can see."

A strand of her long bangs fell in front of her glasses, and she pushed it aside.

"Fair point," he conceded, then hesitated. "We could find a quiet spot for our research, if you'd like?"

"I know just where to go."

He followed her to the dimly lit corner she'd occupied earlier that night, drawing closer as they passed a particularly rowdy group. Without touching her, he extended his arm between her and the partygoers, ensuring she didn't get jostled. And fuck, something about that . . .

The way the fine hairs on her body stood at attention, he might have been a conductor on his dais, orchestrating her physical responses with a single, controlled sweep of his hand.

Then they were standing alone in that shadowed corner, halfway behind a stunning statue. A pale marble depiction of a veiled woman, her head turned sharply to one side, as if in disgust or horror. Still clutching her plate in one hand, Athena pushed back her bangs again and studied the stranger consulting his phone.

"Let's see . . ." he murmured. "Were there potatoes in ancient Rome? Instruct me, Professor Google."

After setting her plate on a nearby bench, she conducted her own research and quickly received a definitive answer from a trustworthy website.

"Nope," they said in unison.

Looking up, he smiled at her again, and this time she felt it like an electric bolt. A searing flash of heat and light that could incinerate her if she weren't very, very careful.

"Evidently, ancient Romans led empty, sad lives of deprivation, unaware that crispy potatoes even existed." He nodded toward her phone. "That's what you discovered too?"

"Yes," she whispered, then cleared her throat in an attempt to speak more normally. "Yes. Unfortunately for them."

Nudging aside her stubborn hank of bangs once more, she wavered.

A wise woman would leave. Just *go*, rudeness be damned, because she shouldn't be feeling this way when—

"Which raises another question." His smile had faded, but his eyes remained warm, and they rested on her with a gentleness she couldn't resist. "What *was* ambrosia, really?"

"I wondered that too." It seemed like something she should know. A matter of cultural literacy, one might say. "Was it an entirely fictional invention, or something based, however loosely, on a real substance?"

So she stayed. Five minutes more. Ten. Fifteen.

They talked about ambrosia. They talked about the statue. They talked about that damn bridge, which he considered not just worrisomely narrow, but actively terrifying.

Heavens to Betsy, he was smart, and not in a careless, tossed-off kind of way. His intelligence was born of patience, of information painstakingly gathered and evaluated.

He was so very careful. With his words. With his gestures. With her.

Which was why she was so very startled when, before she could brush aside her rebellious lock of hair for the umpteenth time, he did it for her, his fingertips grazing her temple in the lightest possible caress.

His breath audibly hitched. So did hers.

He didn't linger over the contact. His arm dropped to his side immediately afterward.

Their eyes locked, and her mouth parted to say—something. Hopefully *goodbye*.

And that was when Johnny found them.

"Athena! So this is where you've been!" He wrapped an arm around her stiff shoulders and gave her an enthusiastic squeeze, then offered a fist-bump to her companion, who returned the gesture very, very slowly. "Obviously, you've already met Matthew. Good, good. Glad to see you two getting along so well."

It landed like a punch to her diaphragm.

Johnny's brother. Matthew.

Her intelligent, charming, dark-haired stranger was going to become her brother-in-law in August, after he served as best man for her fiancé. Even though, as he'd repeatedly told Johnny, he thought she sounded irresponsible and questioned whether she'd make his brother a decent wife.

"Have you tried the crabcakes yet, bro? Because they're fucking *delicious*. Just enough Old Bay, and not much filler. Athena planned the menu, and—"

Johnny continued talking, but the insistent, rhythmic rush of blood in her ears obscured his actual words. He sounded slightly tipsy, that much she could tell, which was probably to her benefit, since her face felt kind of funny. Somehow numb and hot and oversensitive, all at the same time.

Any hint of a smile had disappeared from Matthew's lips, as if it had never existed at all. He'd turned bone-white, the jut of his facial bones sharp enough to wound.

Now that she'd seen them together, of course they were brothers. Of course.

Johnny was the more handsome of the two men. They had the same dark hair, the same dark eyes, but the younger Vine was taller, more muscular, his skin lightly bronzed by the sun, his haircut and clothing more modern and stylish.

He was also less of an asshole than his older brother, no matter how the last fifteen minutes might have temporarily misled her.

"Athena?" Johnny's familiar voice prodded. His hand on her upper arm squeezed a little tighter. "Babe?"

Apparently her fiancé had finished speaking, because both men were looking at her now.

Mouth drawn into a thin, firm line, Matthew extended his hand. "Nice to officially meet you, Athena."

"The pleasure is all mine," she said, although she still couldn't hear much over the rapid thud of her heartbeat. "Johnny has said so many good things about you."

There. Her words were polite beyond reproach.

Their handshake was fleeting. Rushed. Her sweaty palm, his

ice-cold fingers, a lackluster grip. How such minimal, unpleasant contact sent a jolt down her spine anyway, she had no clue.

It was an unmistakable insult, how quickly he released her hand. How fervently he wiped his own hand against his pants leg. How grimly he frowned in her general direction. How assiduously he avoided further eye contact with her.

Brother-in-law? More like jackass-in-law.

The three of them talked about the wedding for a few awkward minutes. Athena remained civil and tried to summon her usual enthusiasm for all the details—the lovely, intricate DIY centerpieces she hoped would save her parents some money; the weight of card stock she'd chosen for the simple but elegant invitations; the dozen or so catering companies she was currently considering for the reception—with limited success. Johnny interjected occasionally, and Matthew simply stood there like a suit-clad monolith, silent and stony.

After a while, he turned to his younger brother during a pause in the conversation.

"Johnny." With two knuckles, he rubbed at the hinge of his jaw. "Could we speak privately for a minute?"

She waved the men off, grateful for a reprieve. Hungry for distance from both of them while she regained her footing in a world suddenly tipped topsy-turvy for reasons she didn't want to ponder.

So she wouldn't. Over the past year or so, she'd become very skilled at avoiding unpleasant or difficult thoughts. Keeping very, very busy helped. So did reading, watching television, and imagining her new, magical existence in Harlot's Bay.

Harlot's Bay. Where Matthew also lived.

Fuck.

The bathroom. She should find a distant, unoccupied bathroom, run some cold water over her wrists, and get her shit together.

Only . . . when she followed the security guard's directions and neared that far-away bathroom, she heard voices around a corner in the hallway. Men's voices. Two men's voices, to be exact.

And there they were, all of a sudden. The Vine brothers. Huddled together, their backs to her. Their voices quiet, but not quiet enough.

She should have left. Right then. Either that, or let them know she was a half dozen steps away from them. One of those two options.

She stayed instead. She listened.

"—not what you say she is," Johnny whispered a touch too loudly. "You're not being fair to her, Matthew."

Shit, she thought, *not this again*.

According to Johnny, his brother had opposed their engagement from the start, and she'd heard all about Matthew's doubts before. Still, his criticism would probably sting more now that they'd actually met face-to-face. After they'd talked and . . . connected. Or so she'd thought.

Matthew dug his fingers into his jaw again, posture stiff. "She's a thirty-six-year-old who's never held the same job for more than three years. Isn't that right?"

Shame heated her cheeks, her ears, scorching her from the inside out.

"Three and a half," Johnny muttered. "She's had her current job for three and a half years now."

"And she wants to leave that one too, once you get married."

Quietly, she retreated just around the corner, where she could still hear them, but they couldn't see her. It was a bad decision, sure to hurt her horribly, but she had to know. Anyone who'd do otherwise either deserved sainthood or had been body-snatched by an alien.

"Stop me if I get something wrong." Matthew sounded weary beyond words. "Her parents have financially supported her all this time. They covered her tuition and living costs while she earned her degrees. They're paying for the wedding. Hell, they sprung for this damn party, even knowing they'd be out of the country while it happened, because their daughter wanted to have it over the holidays."

At that, Johnny's voice turned impatient. "Don't be an ass, Matthew. She needed to schedule it while she was on break, because she can't take much time off during the school year. My asking for the party to be held near me, rather than in Virginia, made finding a good time even harder, and her parents said they didn't mind."

A moment of vindication. It almost stopped her hands from shaking. Almost.

Matthew made a dismissive noise. "From the beginning, I thought she sounded . . ." An audible sigh. "Careless, I guess. And maybe she's a good person, but that doesn't mean she'd make a good spouse. At some point, if you're an adult, you have to take responsibility for yourself, and she hasn't, Johnny. She just . . . hasn't."

Her chest contracted violently, and she bent at the waist, trying to absorb that gut punch of a condemnation. Her eyes prickled and filled.

Why was she doing this to herself? He wasn't saying anything she didn't already know, so why listen to it?

Why couldn't she seem to leave?

"I get why it sounds that way," Johnny said with an edge to his tone, "but you've met her now. You've talked with her. Does she seem irresponsible to you? Does she seem careless or spoiled or . . . whatever you're accusing her of?"

No response.

She held her breath and didn't even know why.

Then Matthew said, "She's too intense about the wedding."

The wall was cool against her wet cheek as she sagged against it.

"Who cares?" Johnny snorted. "Bridezillas are a stereotype for a reason, bro."

"It's not that." Frustration dripped from Matthew's every word. "I don't think she'd bully the people around her or become unpleasant. But when she was talking about the ceremony and reception earlier, her focus on all the details seemed a bit too . . ."

"What?"

"I don't know." He hesitated. "Desperate, maybe. Like she's more interested in the wedding than a marriage. And the wedding is one day, but a marriage is meant to be forever."

For the past few months, she'd immersed herself in wedding and honeymoon plans, mostly because her preoccupation allowed her to forget what came after Hawaii. A new town. A new home. A career path even the world's best satellite GPS couldn't locate for her.

Desperate was a bit harsh, but it was fair. Shit, it was fair.

Johnny snapped, "She wants *me*, Matthew. Not just a wedding."

"Hmmm." It wasn't a hum of agreement. "You two haven't really spent much time together. Just a few hurried weekends and six days over Thanksgiving. So tell me: How well do you actually know her? Once she leaves her job and moves here, are you prepared to have her entirely dependent on you?"

Athena counted out a full minute before her fiancé responded to that.

Every second that passed was another small cut. By the time he spoke again, she half expected to look down and see her dress soaked in a thousand individual droplets of blood.

"It'll be fine. I love her, she loves me, and we'll be good." Johnny didn't sound certain anymore. More like a man trying to ape certainty. "Enough, Matthew. I need to get back to the party."

Silently, she retreated to a different hallway, a different bathroom, before they could spot her.

Fixing her tear-ravaged makeup took a few minutes, but she managed. When she returned to the party, the music had begun, and she arrowed straight through the crowds, directly to her fiancé. He laughed as she tugged him onto the dance floor, wrapping her in his strong arms and whirling her around the marble floors in dizzying, slightly unsteady sweeps as she tried not to stumble.

Eventually they passed Matthew, where he sat all alone at a table, still rubbing his jaw, an untouched plate of food set in front of him. She stared at him over Johnny's shoulder, willing him to look up. To meet her eyes.

He did.

The smile she gave him should have drawn blood. He flinched, and she was glad, glad, glad. Then Johnny whisked her into another turn, and she laughed loudly enough for the sound to carry to the most distant tables as she danced far away from Matthew.

If living well was the best revenge, as George Herbert had advised back in the sixteenth century, she intended to be the most joyful woman alive. Contented. Successful. In passionate, enduring love with Matthew's brother.

And all her happiness?

She hoped Dr. Matthew Vine the Fucking Third choked on it.

1

Eight months later

So far, Athena's first-ever real estate purchase was not living up to her entirely reasonable expectations.

To her mind, the owner of a spite house should spend her days reclining upon a sleek settee. One upholstered in satin, or possibly velvet brocade. Whichever fabric most clearly told observers *I am a woman of both ineffable power and ineffable pettiness, and thus bought a fancy elongated chair-thing.*

Sadly, Athena's double-parked moving van contained precisely zero Settees of Indeterminate Upholstery. She did not, in fact, currently own any furniture that hadn't been sold to her along with the property, and she didn't have the money to buy—anything, really. But even without an intimidating divan, a spite house owner should be stretched out *somewhere*, relaxed and basking in her well-earned vengeance. *Dripping* with malicious glee over her property-related machinations.

Athena was dripping with something, all right. Sweat, most noticeably. Despite an intermittent breeze from the waterfront, the mid-August afternoon in Harlot's Bay shimmered with heat. And given the charcoal-tinted clouds now roiling overhead, she figured she'd be dripping with rainwater soon too. As would the many cardboard boxes of books she'd refused to sell or donate, even knowing they'd prove a major pain in her ass when she moved.

Speaking of pain: Her back ached from hauling previous boxes of books. Her thighs ached from repeatedly climbing up and down three ludicrously narrow flights of stairs. Her scraped elbow ached from when she'd inadvertently slammed it against an interior brick wall, because *not* hitting things in a home that narrow was essentially impossible for someone her size.

Her heart ached from . . . well, everything.

She might be the not-so-proud new owner of a nineteenth-century spite house, a brick-and-mortar celebration of revenge upon one's enemies. But as the clouds above loosed their first splattering drops, she couldn't help but feel the universe was spiting *her* instead.

"I heard someone had bought this place." A pause. "Wow, that's a lot of books."

Athena was bent over at the waist, stretching to reach another box—labeled, yes, Books—in the back of the van, when the unexpected commentary made her jerk in surprise and straighten. Last she'd noticed, no one had been nearby or walking her way. The brewing storm had cleared the streets, sending tourists back to their cars and her new neighbors scurrying into their homes.

"At a glance, they seem to be—what? Eighty percent of your belongings?" The crisp voice sounded thoughtful. Considering. As if the stranger were calmly doing calculations in her head, untroubled by the imminent downpour. "Clearly, you're living the dream, and I can only applaud your life choices."

That made one of them.

When she turned around, there was a woman standing a foot or two away, peering into the van with evident interest and approval. An edgy, elegant, Asian Audrey Hepburn, wearing a full-skirted dandelion-yellow dress that perfectly complemented the colorful tattoos swirling down both bare, golden-brown arms.

"My book collection was procured through devious means, sadly." Athena leaned her hip against the van's back edge, willing to ignore the approaching storm if Audrey was. "I robbed the Beast before fleeing the castle. Somewhere, a talking candlestick is calling me *that yellow-skirted bitch* and cursing my ancestry."

"Ah. You must be Beauty. I'd thought so." Audrey's dark brown eyes twinkled. "You managed to successfully flee with an entire library's worth of books in tow? Even more impressive."

"Thank you, my good lady." She curtsied. "If only my fellow villagers looked upon me so kindly."

The other woman laughed, then held out a slim, long-fingered hand.

"I'm Victoria Nguyen." Nice, firm grip, released at the perfect moment. "Lovely to meet you . . ."

"Athena? Athena Greydon?" inquired another unexpected voice from the sidewalk, at the precise moment the leaden skies above her inevitably opened and released torrents of driving rain. And this newcomer—damnation, this one she knew.

His low, controlled voice shouldn't be instantly recognizable to her, not after a single, disastrous meeting over half a year ago. But it was.

She stilled as the pounding rain soaked through her tee and shorts. Took a deep, deep breath before swiveling in his direction.

"Dr. Matthew Vine," she said, then raised a mocking eyebrow. "The Third. How wonderful."

Victoria snapped open a small umbrella and offered it to Athena, but didn't argue when Athena declined to take it. Instead, Victoria positioned it over her own head and gave it a little twirl.

"Hey, Matthew." After flicking her damp bangs away from her face with her forefinger, she offered Matthew a smile, while Athena fought the urge to offer him an entirely different finger. "You two already know each other?"

"Yes," Matthew confirmed with a deep, deep frown.

Athena offered Victoria a saucy wink. "Much to our mutual delight."

Her ex-fiancé's older brother hadn't changed much since the engagement party last December. At first glance, he was still a generic white guy in a suit, one with a few crinkles at the corners of his eyes.

Not from smiling. Somehow she'd known that, even before she'd known who he was.

She'd made him smile, though, hadn't she? Hell, she'd even made him laugh once or twice. At least, until he'd found out who *she* was.

Back then, a second glance had revealed more. Enough to make him memorable. Appealing, even. That thick, dark hair, trying so hard to curl despite the severity of his cut. Those warm brown eyes, the color softer than was fitting for someone like him.

She should have ignored his eyes and paid attention to his bone structure instead. Should have heeded those distinct and brutal lines, taken warning from the hollows beneath his high cheekbones. In a movie, he would play either the hardened spy or the archvillain: Someone powerful and dangerous and without pity. Someone unafraid to hurt others.

Someone unafraid to hurt her.

"Listen, unless you want some help unloading the van, Athena, I should probably . . . go?"

Oh goodness, she'd forgotten about Victoria.

When Athena turned back toward the other woman, Victoria was watching an increasingly waterlogged Matthew from under her umbrella, her eyes bright and curious.

"Thank you, but I'm good," Athena lied. "That said, you don't have to g—"

"Victoria's boyfriend, Akio, is a CPNP in my practice." At Athena's blank expression, Matthew clarified, "Certified pediatric nurse practitioner. He's the triage nurse who answers panicked calls from parents."

"I'm told his voice is the aural equivalent of an Ativan." Victoria's lips tipped upward, her affection for her boyfriend unhidden.

"He's the best," Matthew said simply. "Have a great weekend, Victoria. Stay dry."

With that sort of finality in his tone, he might as well have said: *My conversation with you is done now. Please leave.*

Did he actually believe he had the right to simply . . . *dismiss* company Athena had been keeping and enjoying? At least, while she still remembered she had company?

"Victoria . . ." she began apologetically, then couldn't seem to find the words to continue.

"You too, Matthew." The younger woman offered Athena an oddly conspiratorial smirk. "I'm sure I'll see you again soon, Beauty. Take care, and welcome to Harlot's Bay."

Then Victoria was gone, and Athena was left with—him.

Dr. Matthew Vine the Fucking Third.

His hometown wasn't *that* small. Why was he even here, on his brother's street? Was he caring for Johnny's empty house, watering plants and whatnot, or had Matthew somehow known where and when to find her?

And why wasn't he saying anything? Welcoming her to Harlot's Bay too, or apologizing for the destruction he and his brother had wrought in her life, or taking the opportunity to insult her again, this time face-to-face?

He simply stood there, rigid and sodden, head slightly tipped as he studied her. His deep frown carved vertical creases above the inner edge of each dark eyebrow. With his mouth pressed into such a stern line, his lower lip thinned and hardened. If she hadn't met him before, she'd never have guessed the soft fullness of that lower lip when he allowed himself to relax.

There was nothing, absolutely nothing, soft about him now. He might have been a Michelin-starred chef spotting a roach in an otherwise immaculate kitchen. A seventeenth-century judge pronouncing her a witch and ordering her dragged in shackles to the nearest stake.

It was the same look he'd had after Johnny introduced her as his fiancée.

Fine. If he wouldn't say anything, she'd do the honors.

"Why are you wearing a suit?" She flicked a hand at his clothing. "It's a million degrees outside and a Saturday, for cripes' sake. Do you spend your weekends crashing other people's weddings, so you can object and ruin everything for them too?"

Stifling a sigh, she scratched a wet mosquito bite on her arm.

Upon moving to Harlot's Bay, she'd understood that a confrontation with both brothers was inevitable. That said, she hadn't meant to reveal her resentment quite that openly or quickly, because even broke, betrayed women had their pride.

But . . . whatevs. Matthew had earned that resentment. Now it was his to handle.

Slowly, he closed his eyes, exhaling a long breath through his nose. Then he gave a little nod and looked at her once more. "Johnny told you about our conversation."

"Which one?"

There were so many to choose from, really. The museum incident last December, of course. The final, decisive confrontation a month ago, where Matthew had broken his brother's resistance by suggesting he might move from Harlot's Bay if the wedding went ahead.

Even apart from those two conversations, Johnny had suffered through—and told her about—a dozen additional discussions with Matthew concerning her unsuitability as a wife. No doubt Matthew had impugned her character on various other occasions too. On holidays and weekends and on Mondays, just for funsies.

"Which . . . one?" He flinched a little, and a surge of vicious satisfaction eased her aches. "Please tell me he didn't . . ."

"What?" she prodded when he didn't continue. "He didn't what?"

Falling silent again, he tipped his face to the sky and let the downpour wash over him. Unwillingly, she noted the dark hollows under his eyes and wondered why his suit still fit a bit too loosely, except where it stretched across his broad shoulders.

He looked tired. Nearly pared down to the bone.

Well, that made two of them. She was a music box wound so tightly, even a quarter turn more would damage the spring irreparably, but she had no choice. She had to stay poised only a small twist away from complete failure, because if she allowed herself to wind down, she didn't know if she'd ever make a sound again.

A mere four weeks ago, she'd had a fiancé. A future. The promise of a comfortable home and the time and space and financial cushion she needed to figure out her next step.

Now she had a practical joke of a house she'd bought as a wedding gift for a husband-to-be who became a husband-who-wasn't. She had a nearly empty savings account and the shame of having wasted her parents' money yet again. She had a minimum-wage job at a local bakery starting on Monday morning, because she had no time to rest or settle in or unwind even a fraction of a turn. COBRA and mortgage payments weren't fucking cheap, and she couldn't afford to wait.

And he'd done that to her. The unspeaking, rain-slicked man in front of her.

Dr. Matthew Vine the fucking *Third*.

If only he'd been this silent about her wedding with Johnny.

The ceremony would have happened two days ago. Thursday evening, exactly one year after she'd first met Johnny in her parents' home. She'd have boarded a plane with her new husband yesterday morning and arrived in Honolulu in the early afternoon, Hawaiian time, then flown to Maui. Right now, they'd be returning from an excursion she'd booked, a trip to the summit of Haleakalā at sunrise, and—and—

Johnny was there. This very second. Fresh from having watched the world renew itself in paradise, blithely enjoying the honeymoon of her dreams. One planned in its entirety by her in full faith they'd experience it together.

Instead, she was here. Dripping and hurting and moving into a ten-foot-wide home that shared a wall with his, because row houses were a thing in Harlot's Bay. Talking to the man who'd convinced Johnny to abandon her a month before their wedding.

Or, rather, *not* talking to him. That statuary garden on Abbott

Island, at the art museum where they'd held her engagement party, had contained more voluble sculptures. At least the ones with fountains *burbled*, for heaven's sake.

At long last, he set his hands on his lean hips and met her stare. "Why are you in Harlot's Bay, Athena?"

"You know why," she told him, unwilling to let him evade his responsibility for forcing her here, to this place, to this despair.

His eyes narrowed, and that distinctive shade of brown no longer appeared warm or soft. Not light through a bottle, but the bottle itself, broken into sharp, jagged shards.

He moved a step closer, then two, and his height might not be noteworthy in general, but the man clearly knew how to loom menacingly. "Are you hoping to reconcile with Johnny? Is that why you came? Because—"

When she began laughing—bitterly, hysterically—he cut himself off and waited.

"I never . . ." Another paroxysm of hilarity shook through her. "I never want to see him again. If I had a choice, I'd never see *either* of you again."

He was studying her face, in search of a lie that didn't exist. She wouldn't waste her breath trying to convince him. He'd believe what he wanted to believe. That much, at least, she knew about him.

"All right." His voice was the tonal equivalent of beige. Offensively neutral. "In that case, I'm not sure I understand what's happening."

"It's not that hard, Dr. Matthew Vine the Third." A sweep of her wet arm indicated the van behind her. "I'm moving in. It's pouring. I'm double-parked. The van is due back in an hour, and I can't afford parking tickets or late fees. I'm done with this conversation, so either bring stuff inside or leave."

She turned her back and reached into the van, not even waiting for him to walk away, because she had work to do and he wasn't going to help her. No one was. In large part because she hadn't told the people who *would* actually offer help—her parents, her friends in Virginia, even Victoria—that she needed it.

Pride might be cold comfort, but it was all she had left. Other than, of course, a ridiculously narrow row house built for fraternal vengeance.

A crack of thunder ripped through the air, and she straightened again, incredulous. Really? *Really?* A biblical deluge wasn't enough?

She raised both middle fingers high to the heavens. "Fuck you too, universe."

The universe answered with visible lightning in the distance, then another ground-shaking rumble of thunder.

"So help me, I'll go Ben Franklin on your ass," she told the sky. "Don't try me."

As she studied the worsening storm, drops of rain caught in her lashes and blurred her vision, and no amount of blinking seemed to resolve the issue. Clearing her throat, she swiped her eyes with her knuckles.

That was when large, warm hands clasped her shoulders gently but firmly and moved her aside. After climbing nimbly into the van, Dr. Matthew Vine the Third scooped a box of books under each arm. He eased himself back to the ground and started toward her house without saying a single word.

She stared after him, flabbergasted. Too stunned to even follow him.

When lightning struck somewhere nearby, the roar of thunder almost simultaneous, he jumped and gave a little yelp, his shoulders hunching. His progress toward her front door—which wasn't really a front door at all, because it opened onto the four-foot-wide alley separating her row of houses from the next one—hastened abruptly.

Depositing the boxes inside took only moments. He re-emerged into the alley, then jerked violently at the next blinding flash and earsplitting crash. After a quick glance in her direction, he stepped to the side of the alleyway, up against the brick wall of her new home.

Out of her sight.

Until she moved a few feet to the left, anyway.

There he stood, where he thought she couldn't see him. Eyes closed, hands clenched at his sides. Chest rising and falling as he took several very, very deep breaths. Then, expression impassive once more, he strode back her way. Another thunderous roar from the heavens barely caused a hitch in his stride.

Those hands, though. Those hands were fisted tight enough that his knuckles jutted white and sharp against his dark suit trousers.

He was trying his best to hide it, but he was terrified. Of this storm, or maybe storms in general. He was helping her anyway.

Probably in an attempt to assuage his well-earned guilt or shame her for the grudge she held, or maybe because her double-parking offended his rigid sense of order, but fine. Under the circumstances, she wouldn't quibble. Even if he stopped at two boxes, that was two boxes she wouldn't have to move herself.

Slipping off her rain-streaked glasses, she hung them on her collar and pretended she'd seen nothing. For all her manifold, grievous faults, the thought of mocking someone—anyone; even him—for their fears turned her stomach. Especially since she . . .

Well, she got it.

Her own fears were as plentiful as her flaws, and much better hidden.

"What now?" he asked calmly when he'd returned to the back of the van.

Okay, then. Apparently he *wasn't* going to stop at two boxes.

She said, "Can you climb inside the van again and move all the remaining boxes within arm's reach? I'll carry them into the house."

Because she might be angry, she might despise him, but he was assisting her, and she wouldn't let the Vine brothers turn her cruel. If the storm distressed him, she wouldn't make him endure it without some kind of shelter.

"I . . ." He trailed off, brow crinkled. "Are you sure?"

"Yes."

She rarely said anything she didn't mean, other than *It's fine; I'm fine; I don't need help, thank you very much.*

"I can carry more than you with each load," he informed her, as if she didn't already know that.

He stripped off his dripping suit jacket and tie and set both atop a nearby plastic storage bin. Next, he unfastened the cuffs and the top two buttons of his white shirt and rolled his saturated sleeves to the elbow. Each movement of his long, agile fingers was unfussy but precise.

Not that she was staring, but he could *definitely* carry more than her. Heck, those strong, hair-dusted forearms alone, his lean muscles shifting beneath the skin—

Shame on you, she told her id. *Now is not the time, and sakes alive, this is* not *the man.*

"I think you underestimate the strength of my arsenal." When confusion creased his face, she flexed one of her biceps, then the other. "I hate to brag, but my guns are fully loaded and ready for action."

In reality, they'd run out of ammunition about a dozen boxes ago, and they hadn't accommodated an especially high caliber of bullets to begin with, but whatever.

Assuming a bodybuilder's pose, twisted and bent slightly at the waist, she flexed again.

"And the crowd goes wild!" she proclaimed in the authoritative tones of an announcer, then approximated the sound of a cheering audience. "Yaaaaaaay."

She could have sworn his lips twitched before he rolled them between his teeth.

When he lifted a hand to scratch the back of his head, his soaked shirt clung to the hard muscles of his chest, and dammit, her id needed to *calm the fuck down already*.

"I don't suppose you'd let me handle any late fees or parking tickets," he finally said. "We could wait out the storm inside."

"Nope." She popped the *p*, hoping it made her sound jaunty. Not racked with longing simply to dump all her problems in his lap—*anyone's* lap—and take a nap for a year or two. "But you should head home or wherever you were originally going. It's dangerous being outside in weather like this."

If he left her to finish the job alone, she wouldn't blame him. For so much else, yes, but not that. She didn't mind gambling with her own safety, because *nothing* was safe anymore, and she just couldn't bring herself to care about one more stupid risk. But Matthew . . .

He might be a pompous ass, but people would miss him. He had a place. A purpose.

After studying her a beat too long, he inclined his head. "Let's get this done, then."

She should argue with him. Insist he put his own safety, his own comfort, before her convenience. But she didn't. She simply let him climb into the van again and continue helping her, and it was another red mark in her life's ledger.

Thunder shook the ground as she gathered her next load and trudged toward the house. Did tires still adequately ground a lightning-struck vehicle and its occupants when said vehicle had its doors open? She hoped so, for Matthew's sake. Yet another question to pose to Professor Google when they were done.

A few loads later, he'd finished shifting all the boxes within the van, but the storm hadn't abated. When she suggested he duck inside the house while she finished up, though, he ignored her. Slinging his jacket and tie over his shoulder, he hefted a huge box of her clothing and ventured back into the tempest. And with two of them depositing her possessions all over the increasingly crowded kitchen and dining room, they completed the job in mere minutes.

"My office is two blocks away, on the Square. We see patients Saturday mornings, because some parents work during our normal office hours on weekdays," he quietly told her as they stacked the last several boxes on the scarred kitchen counter. When she frowned at him in confusion, he clarified, "Thus the suit."

Ah. He hadn't forgotten her earlier question.

"That explains it." She bit her lip, then forced the grudging words out. "Thank you for your help."

He nodded again, solemn as ever.

She didn't want to be grateful to a man she hated, so he wasn't taking any more risks on her behalf. She'd make sure of it. "Did you walk to work? Or are you parked nearby?"

Was his brow ever *not* furrowed? "I walked."

"I can drive you home after I return the van, then." The storm's intensity might be waning now, but the danger hadn't fully passed yet. She wouldn't leave him outside and unprotected. "I'll be back in half an hour. Sit wherever you'd like."

He could settle at the dining room table, if she helped him clear a path there. Hell, she didn't care if he claimed the overstuffed two-seater couch on the second floor or the reading chair on the third floor, assuming he could reach the stairs.

The furnishings had come with the house since, as one of the previous owners explained, taking everything out would be too much of a pain in the ass.

Before buying anything, you have to measure it a million times to make sure it'll fit, the guy told her. *Then either use brute force to get it inside or disassemble it and put it back together wherever you want it. I'm not a masochist, so I have zero desire to revisit that process in reverse. Enjoy the furniture and appliances in good health, Ms. Greydon.*

That had been a lucky break for her, since she'd already sold her own furniture and appliances in preparation for moving into Johnny's home. Which stood approximately five feet to her left, through a single brick wall.

The creases above Matthew's inner eyebrows had only deepened. "You don't know."

She should ask for clarification, but frankly, exhaustion had her sagging against the kitchen counter. She wanted him gone. Besides, the world was downright *teeming* with things she didn't know, and today's list of queries for Professor Google was already extensive.

"Thank you for the offer. That's not necessary, however," he said after a few moments of silence. "I'll go."

No, she really didn't want to spend more time with him. But

before he exited her life again—hopefully for good—she had to share one last story. Because the man she'd first met at the engagement party would have appreciated it, even if that man had only existed in her imagination. Because, during a very difficult hour, he'd helped when he hadn't needed to lift a finger on her behalf.

Because she had no one else to tell. Her parents and her friends back in Virginia would listen, but if she talked about where she was living and why to anyone remotely sympathetic, she'd cry, and she was done crying in company.

When she was alone, there didn't seem to be an end to her tears.

The limit does not exist, she thought, and made a mental note to research the origins of that phrase too, because she couldn't quite remember. Math, right? And maybe a movie?

Wait. She was supposed to be doing something. Telling one last story to Imaginary Matthew Who Once Smiled at Me.

"The dude who used to live here said he and his husband had to fold their mattress in half to get it to the third floor," she said. "But try as they might, they couldn't maneuver it up the spiral stairs to the fourth-floor bedroom. So they rigged it with a rope, hauled it out the third-floor window, and had a friend hoist it up and squeeze it through a window on the fourth floor. To fit the box spring, they had to—"

"Saw it in half diagonally," he finished for her, his voice calm and sure.

It was her turn to frown. "How did you know that? Did Johnny tell you?"

"I watched it happen."

Of course he did. Heaven forbid she have something to offer him, even something as small and insignificant as a story.

She narrowed her eyes at him, aggravated enough to demand an explanation. "Were you the friend? Or were you visiting Johnny when it happened?"

"Not . . . exactly. I can't believe Johnny didn't—" Matthew cut himself off suddenly, as if some internal fuse had tripped. A trickle of water bisected his forehead, but instead of wiping it away, he took a moment to straighten several nearby stacks of boxes. He re-donned his dripping suit jacket and loosely knotted his limp tie. Then, at long last, he swiveled on his heel and made his way to the door. "Good luck, Athena."

Well, that was unnecessarily opaque and abrupt.

When she followed him outside, he waited while she checked her purse for keys, ID, and credit card. Yup. All there. Satisfied, she settled her glasses on her nose and locked the door behind them.

Unable to stop herself, she opened her mouth to remind him to find shelter if the storm worsened again. But before she could utter a word, he walked away.

From her doorway, he turned crisply to the left and quickly reached the mouth of the alley separating the two rows of homes. If he turned left again, a half dozen strides would take him past the front of her house and all the way to Johnny's welcome mat.

Instead, Matthew turned right. Took one step. Two. Three.

Then he produced his own keys from his pocket and unlocked the door of the home directly across the alleyway from hers. The first residence in the neighboring cluster of row houses.

The alleyway was narrow as hell. If she stretched out her arms, she could easily touch both sides at once. Which meant she had a single wall separating her from one Vine brother, and—at most—four . . . fucking . . . feet between her and the *other* Vine brother.

No, this wasn't blithe indifference. This was sheer malice on the part of the fates.

As she stood there, mouth still agape, frozen in shock, Matthew cleared his throat, seemingly poised to say something. But in the end, he simply raised a hand in a gesture of farewell, stepped into his home, and shut the door.

Beyond words, she thrust her arms high and raised her middle fingers to the cloud-choked sky once more. And when the weakening storm produced a last vicious bolt of lightning in response, she wasn't at all surprised.

2

*M*atthew had no idea what time it was in Hawaii. Calling now might interrupt a guided tour or even wake Johnny from a sound hotel-room sleep. A good brother would text first.

For once, he couldn't bring himself to care. If that made him a bad brother, so be it.

When Johnny answered after three rings, voice alert but relaxed, Matthew didn't bother with small talk. "Did you know that Athena bought the Spite House?"

Matthew had realized it was for sale, of course. Joaquin and Wade, the previous owners, had been complaining about the endless stair-climbing for months, and after Wade's second knee replacement, they'd had enough.

So Matthew had braced for new strangers in close proximity. He should have braced—battened down his hatches, lashed himself to the nearest metaphorical mast—for Hurricane Athena instead. Because, unbelievably, she'd spent good money on a home where only a lone brick wall would separate her from her ex-fiancé. She'd uprooted herself entirely from her former life and moved from Virginia to Maryland. To Harlot's Bay, a city where Matthew was reasonably certain she knew not a single soul. At least, not a single soul without *Vine* as a last name.

Matthew's question—one of many—was *why*.

He'd never expected to see her again, and he'd certainly never expected her to move next door to the man who'd jilted her.

Who *did* that?

Was she a stalker, obsessed with the one who got away? Should he have already contacted the authorities and filed for a restraining order?

After two short conversations with her, he couldn't accurately judge her emotional stability or predict her behavior. Only one person in his contacts list could possibly do that.

"Hey, Matthew." Johnny sounded noticeably less relaxed than he had in his initial greeting. "Sorry, the reception here isn't great. You're asking if I knew Athena had purchased the Spite House?"

The call quality sounded fine to Matthew. "Yes."

There was a long silence as Johnny considered what to say, and that was one question answered. Matthew just hoped his brother wouldn't outright lie to him.

"You knew," he said.

"Yeah." In an audible rush of air, Johnny let out a slow breath. "It was . . . it was supposed to be her wedding gift to me. The closing was maybe . . . two weeks before we broke up?"

Matthew placed his pointer finger in the middle of his forehead and pressed hard on the spot where his brain hurt.

"For whatever reason, it's never been designated a historic structure, so I could knock out the wall separating the two homes," Johnny had told Matthew over dinner one night, soon after Wade and Joaquin listed their house for sale. "I'd give myself more room, better light, and some decent cross-ventilation in one fell swoop."

"Athena too," Matthew had responded without thinking.

Johnny chewed his bite of pizza and swallowed. "What?"

"You wouldn't just give all that to yourself. You'd be giving it to Athena too."

Matthew wasn't even engaged to the woman, and he seemed to think about her more than her actual fiancé.

That night, he and Johnny had talked through the pros and cons of purchasing the Spite House and merging it with Granny's home, which Johnny had inherited upon her death. During the conversation, Johnny's hope that Matthew would provide the down payment and contribute money toward the renovations had become increasingly evident. Between paying off half of Johnny's med school loans every month and financing the honeymoon as a wedding gift, though, Matthew had no surplus savings. And Johnny had only completed his pediatric residency less than two years before, so he didn't have much in the bank either. Especially not after buying Athena a flashy engagement ring.

So in the end, Johnny hadn't bought the Spite House. But Athena had. Because she knew her husband-to-be really wanted the property, and she'd given it to him, on a teacher's salary. Then found herself without a husband-to-be after all.

"I think, uh." His brother sounded as if he were shrinking into himself, and Matthew couldn't locate even a smidgen of sympathy. "I think she used pretty much all her savings for the down payment."

How much money had she spent? How much, precisely, did she have left?

"I gave her back my key, obviously," Johnny said, before adding swiftly, "I don't think she'll ever actually live there. I mean, her family—"

"She's living there. She moved in today."

Without his conscious volition, she appeared behind Matthew's closed eyelids. Athena, her fine blond hair plastered to her skull, exhausted and soaked to the skin but flexing her biceps, the bright defiance in her stare almost—but not quite—hiding her distress.

He'd told himself to walk away, but how was he supposed to leave her rain-drenched and hauling boxes alone during a freaking thunderstorm? How was he supposed to abandon her when she was fighting tears, flipping off the churning sky, and issuing unclear but kind of hilarious threats—ones invoking a Founding Father, for goodness' sake—to nature itself?

"Oh." Johnny's voice was quiet. "Did she—did it go all right?"

"I suppose. By the time I saw her, she was almost done."

Apparently she didn't own much. Even so, moves were always stressful. Why hadn't anyone helped her? Where was her family? Where were her friends? And why the hell was he worrying about any of that when he still didn't know whether she was stalking Johnny?

"Why didn't you tell me she was buying the house?" No, that was a stupid question. He'd answer it himself. "Because you knew I wouldn't be happy about it. I would have argued with you and tried to prevent it. And once you broke the engagement, you hoped she'd quietly sell the property and I'd never have to know what happened."

"Yeah. All of that." His brother sounded tired now. "Matthew—"

He didn't want to hear it. "Why come here, though? Why not stay in Virginia or move in with her parents while she put the house up for sale again?"

"I don't know about her parents. But as far as staying in Virginia, I guess . . ." Each word wavered a little, suffused with what Matthew could only interpret as shame. "I told you she resigned from her teaching position at the end of the school year, because she was moving to Harlot's Bay before the fall. I thought—I thought she could get her job back after the engagement ended. But . . . maybe not."

Matthew laid the phone on his kitchen counter, put it on speaker, and covered his face with both hands.

Johnny sounded muffled, as if he were scrubbing a hand over his own face. "She gave up her condo too. Sold all her furniture since she was moving in with me, and my stuff was better."

Fuck. This just got worse and worse, didn't it? "What about the ring? Couldn't selling that have bought her some time while she got rid of the house?"

"She gave it back. Said she didn't . . . uh, didn't want any reminder of me."

Was that *hurt* in Johnny's voice? Because from what Matthew could tell, his brother didn't have the goddamn right to feel ill used. Shit.

Something in his right jaw popped, and when he opened his mouth wide to test the joint, it felt odd. Gritty. Next time he saw her, his dentist was going to stop mildly suggesting a mouthguard and simply shove that unpleasant putty between his teeth to make a mold, like it or not.

He bent over the counter and summed up the situation as efficiently as possible. "So, assuming she can't or won't live with her parents, Athena has nowhere else to go. She doesn't have the money to rent and furnish a new place, since she's unemployed, handling a mortgage without a cushion of savings, and probably making COBRA payments to keep her health insurance. All because of your desire to own the Spite House."

For the first time, a hint of sulkiness colored Johnny's tone. "I don't know, Matthew. I haven't talked to her since the engagement ended. You said it should be a clean break."

Since the engagement ended. Not *Since I ended the engagement.*

"The situation wasn't clear to me when I said that, and we both know why." Because his brother hadn't wanted to admit responsibility for the entire mess. Hadn't wanted to acknowledge the damage he'd done, however inadvertently. "Athena hasn't called you since then? Even once?"

"No."

"Texted you?"

"No."

"Emailed?"

"No."

"Sent carrier pigeons to your doorstep? Hired a singing telegram or skywriters to declare her enduring love for you?"

"Don't be flippant."

Because apparently only one of them was allowed that luxury. Only one of them was allowed to be funny or thoughtless or frivolous. And it wasn't Matthew.

Carefully, he loosened his jaw once more, and ignored the sandy feeling in the joint. "So Athena isn't stalking you. If she had the choice, she truly wouldn't see either of us again."

"Correct." Johnny paused. "I mean, maybe she still misses me sometimes. We *were* engaged, after all, and all that affection and commitment doesn't simply—"

"Why didn't she know I lived so close to you?" Maybe that wasn't a crucial question, but she'd visited Johnny several times in Harlot's Bay. How in the world hadn't she known?

Sure, the three of them had never successfully scheduled a joint outing. Frankly, Matthew had wanted to avoid the painful awkwardness of the entire situation, and if Johnny took time off to be with her, someone had to pick up the slack at work. No doubt

Johnny hadn't wanted to subject Athena to Matthew's scrutiny either. Or maybe he'd simply wanted her all to himself whenever he saw her.

Matthew couldn't blame him for that.

Still, why hadn't Johnny simply pointed to the neighboring row of houses during any one of those visits, indicated the home on the end, and said, "My brother lives there"?

"I was afraid if I told her, she might not want to live so close to . . . Well, Athena wasn't . . ." Johnny cleared his throat. "It's possible Athena wasn't your biggest fan. From pretty early on."

Matthew surged upright, shocked.

"What?" He understood why she didn't like him now, since she obviously knew he'd played a crucial part in her broken engagement, but back then— "Why?"

At that art museum on Abbott Island, before Johnny introduced the two of them, they'd gotten on, as his granny would have put it, like a house afire. It was the best conversation with a stranger he'd had in his entire life. Ever. Despite his general distaste for parties and his discomfort with the specific occasion. And once he'd found out she was Johnny's fiancée, maybe he'd turned uncomfortable around her, but . . . what had he done to cause active dislike?

He'd stayed polite, hadn't he? Quiet, maybe, but not rude. So what in heaven's name—

Johnny sighed. "At the engagement party, she overheard our conversation in the hall outside the bathrooms."

Matthew's head dropped to his chest. Fuck.

Johnny told you about our conversation, he'd surmised earlier that day.

Athena's soft mouth had curled into a sneer. *Which one?*

God. *God.*

He'd earned her dislike, then. With his lack of discretion. His decision to discuss such a fraught, sensitive topic in a public place, no matter how deserted and far away from the party he'd thought that hallway was.

Not to mention his insults.

"And I might have . . ." Another clearing of Johnny's throat. "I might have talked to Athena sometimes about you, even before the party. Told her what you said about the engagement and . . . about her."

"Johnny."

"She was my fucking *fiancée*, bro." All his brother's uncertainty, all his shame, had suddenly vanished, as if he'd somehow managed to pass the entire bundle of unpleasant emotions to Matthew over the phone. "We're *supposed* to share our troubles."

"Yeah, but—" Matthew tore a hand through his damp hair. "Didn't you want to shield her from awkwardness? Make sure her feelings didn't get hurt?"

Johnny's laughter didn't sound particularly amused. "No wonder you've been single forever. You have no idea how reciprocity in a relationship works, do you?"

And you have no idea how to care for someone you claim to love. Bro.

The bitterness of his own thoughts shocked him. He'd never, ever struggled with this kind of anger toward his brother before. Not even when Johnny had boarded the plane to Honolulu on Friday and left Matthew and Yvonna shouldering the work of three doctors for an entire month. All so Johnny could claim the honeymoon for a wedding that hadn't happened and *take some* me *time to think and grieve*, as he'd put it.

Matthew's jaw made an unsettling *crunch*.

He needed to calm the hell down.

Every time he blinked, though, there Athena was again. Purplish circles beneath her red-rimmed eyes. Scraped elbow she hadn't bandaged and probably hadn't washed clean. Middle fingers to the sky as she blithely dared lightning to strike her.

She was responsible for her own life. Her own choices. To say otherwise would strip her of her agency, and if he tried that, he figured she'd rightfully aim those upturned middle fingers his way.

That said, Johnny should have convinced her not to buy the fucking house in the first place. Later, with that terrible decision already made and the engagement ended, he should have insisted she keep and sell the ring. Should have offered his own money—or, hell, borrowed money from Matthew—to pay the mortgage until she got the Spite House sold to someone else. Should have found other ways to smooth her path and take care of her.

She'd probably have refused her ex-fiancé's offer of help. But it apparently hadn't even occurred to him to make the offer, and he certainly hadn't bothered telling Matthew what was going on with her. So, yeah, whether Johnny wanted to admit it or not, a goodly portion of the blame for her situation fell on him too.

But what about Matthew? How much blame did he deserve?

He'd convinced Johnny to leave her but hadn't even fucking asked what it would mean for her life and her future. He hadn't pressed his younger brother for more information, despite knowing how reluctant Johnny would be to acknowledge any wreckage left in his wake.

Matthew had wanted to ask. He'd come within a breath of asking, dozens of times. Hundreds. But speaking her name hurt both of them, so he'd kept his mouth shut and done his best to forget her.

Yeah. A share of this clusterfuck was Matthew's as well.

His uncharacteristic anger toward his brother flamed out. It turned to embers as he swallowed it. As he absorbed it within himself, even though it burned.

Johnny was both right and wrong. Matthew probably *didn't* know how to have a relationship of reciprocity with someone he loved. But that wasn't the main reason he'd remained single all these years.

Since before his brother's first birthday, Matthew had done his best to take the place of their heartbroken and distant mother, their grieving and helpless father, their lost sibling, and everyone else Johnny lacked. At eight years of age, Matthew had started raising his baby brother, and over three decades later, he didn't think he'd ever stopped.

Coupled first with school, and then work, parenting his brother had left no room in his life for loving anyone else. His patients and Johnny got all his attention.

He didn't expect gratitude, because it was his choice. It had always been his choice. But it stung to be criticized for shortcomings he'd acquired because he was caring as best he could for his critic. Especially when he was currently busting his butt and alienating his closest friend and colleague to give that critic everything he wanted.

"I'm sorry, Matty," his little brother said.

Matthew blinked in surprise. Apologies from Johnny were rare. And when was the last time he'd used that nickname? At least ten years. Maybe twenty.

"It's okay." Matthew didn't tend to hold grudges. Possibly because he never had the spare energy to keep them alive and well fed, and possibly because anger didn't come naturally to him in the first place.

"I shouldn't have said that. You didn't deserve it." A muffled sound of frustration, and then Johnny spoke again, each word halting. "About . . . Athena . . . her situation . . ."

For once, Matthew had no clue what his brother would say next.

"I, uh . . ." Johnny paused. "I fucked up. Didn't I?"

Nope, Matthew wouldn't have predicted that admission. Not even if he'd been given a thousand guesses. The unexpected remorse in his brother's voice tugged at his chest, but he wouldn't lie to provide solace. Not when Athena alone was paying the full price for decisions made jointly.

"We both did," Matthew told him, then waited out an extended silence.

"Look, I'd better go." A door slammed, and the sound of other people's chatter filled the background. "I have a lei-making class starting on the hour. I'll FaceTime or text in a few days."

The call abruptly ended before Matthew could respond or say goodbye.

He was left staring at his phone, wondering when and why the ground had turned so damn shaky beneath his feet. And when he looked up, he experienced another earth-trembling jolt.

Somehow the implications hadn't occurred to him, even after so many years living across from the Spite House, but—most of his windows looked directly into Athena's. From only four feet away. Including the window above his sink.

She'd turned on the overhead light. She was sitting at the box-strewn dining room table, one elbow propped, forehead in her palm, shoulders rounded.

Rounded and shaking.

It was a violation of her privacy. She wouldn't want him to see her like this. He might not know a lot about her—even less than he'd thought he knew an hour before—but he understood that much.

So he stood, flicked on his own kitchen lights as a mute warning, and walked away, wondering what the hell he was going to do next.

THAT NIGHT, FOR the first time in weeks, he dreamed of the art museum.

Normally he couldn't remember his dreams, but the different iterations of this one always clung to him stubbornly, even after he was fully awake and in ostensible control of himself.

They didn't accurately depict his first meeting with Athena, of course.

In reality, he only touched her once. After a brief conversation by the hors d'oeuvres table, where he found himself smiling before he quite knew what was happening, they shifted to a quiet corner of the room and talked for maybe fifteen minutes. All the while, her long bangs kept swinging in front of those bright, lively hazel eyes, and she brushed them aside again and again, until he finally reached out and did it for her.

He'd had no idea what his brother's fiancée looked like. Johnny had never been much of a picture-taker, and Matthew was trying to convince his brother to leave her, so he hadn't wanted to see her face. The less he knew about her, the less guilt he felt.

Foolishly, he didn't even glance at her ring finger before touching her, because a complete stranger's marital status had never mattered to him before. Not for personal reasons. It was merely background information on a medical chart. *Madison's parents divorced 3 yrs. Joint custody.*

One touch—just one—and her cool hair and warm skin hitched his breath. Made his fingertips tingle as if they'd been deprived of blood flow for far too long.

The prickles hurt, but they felt good too. Necessary. Like heat and life returning to a limb on the verge of permanent tissue damage. He dropped his hand to his side with the full intention of touching her again. Soon.

In reality, that was when Johnny found them. Introduced them. The end.

But in his dreams . . . that was when everything started.

Some things remained the same. She looked exactly as she had that night. A bonbon of a woman, gorgeously round and delicious. Snub-nosed, with slightly golden skin and sleek honey-blond hair cut in a bob that brushed her soft jaw. Relatively short in stature, her lush body clad in flowing silk, her glossy fire-engine-red lipstick precisely matching the color of the adorable little strawberries printed all over her milk-pale dress. Wearing black-framed, cat-eye glasses, her equally black eyeliner precise and thick and winged.

She had on Keds. Without socks. At, as he later knew, her own engagement party.

Dimly, as he'd absorbed the gut punch of Johnny's introduction, he'd admired that. Duty- and rule-bound as he'd always been, steeped in fresh misery as he was, averse to the wedding as he remained, he'd admired that.

So that part of his sleeping fantasies was familiar and true.

But from there, from a single touch of her hair, his mind meandered along various shadowy, lust-strewn paths to the same inevitable conclusion, and none of those paths corresponded to the world he inhabited during the day.

In tonight's dream, as always, he didn't stop with a single touch. Instead, his fingertips lingered on her skin. He carefully smoothed away her stubborn lock of silky hair, then slid his thumb along her temple, her jaw, down her throat. He leaned forward and pressed the tip of his tongue against that irresistible beauty mark on the crest of her flushed cheek. Her soft, soft breast filled his palm, and her eyes drifted shut as she sighed and arched in pleasure. In need.

They stole out to the sculpture garden, cloaked in privacy by the velvety night. Lit by stars, he slowly gathered her skirt in his fists. Leaned her against marble. Dropped to his knees.

Then he found out whether she tasted like the strawberries on her dress.

As ever, Johnny was nowhere to be seen. In the dream, he might never have existed at all. Maybe, in the end, that part shamed Matthew the most.

When he woke agonizingly hard, loneliness a tearing ache in his chest and throat, it felt like the punishment he deserved.

He might have wanted Athena then. He might want her still.

But what he wanted was, as ever, the least of his concerns.

3

Ridiculously early on a dark, quiet Monday morning, Athena shuffled onto her doorstep, locked the deadbolt, and checked her purse to make sure she had everything she needed for her first shift at her new job.

House key. Wallet. ID. Phone.

No need for car keys, and no need to waste valuable gas money. The bakery stood within easy walking distance, and getting there on foot was safe enough. Harlot's Bay apparently had zero crime.

At least, it *used* to have zero crime.

Although what she was considering wasn't truly a crime, was it? A misdemeanor, at worst. Or whatever was more minor than that. A peccadillo? A shenanigan?

Still, she shouldn't. She really shouldn't, no matter how badly Dr. Matthew Vine the Third deserved a bit of payback.

Only . . . damn, it would feel *so good*, and these days, almost *nothing* made her feel good. Besides, one bad decision deserved another. Wasn't that how the saying went? Or how it should go, anyway?

Surrendering to temptation, she drifted silently across the alleyway to her neighbor's house, tiptoed up his front steps, and tweaked the brass numbers beside his door, the ones indicating his address. She adjusted them just a little. Just enough to leave them noticeably askew but still easily readable. Then she backed up two paces, surveyed the results of her efforts, and slowly smiled.

She'd be willing to bet five of her few remaining dollars that Dr. Matthew Vine the Third, tidy fusspot extraordinaire, was going to notice his numbers' disarray immediately. Notice and fucking *hate* it.

When she carefully eased down his steps, a board groaned beneath her left Ked. Freezing in place, she waited for a light to come on. The door to open. His calm, low voice to condemn her once more.

Nothing. The predawn morning remained still and peaceful.

At last, something had gone right.

She admired the crooked numbers a final time. Then, whistling soundlessly, she ambled off into the darkness.

As it turned out, Karl—the grim, introverted man toiling away in the back room of Grounds and Grains, the bakery he owned— listened to monster-fucking audiobooks. Loudly, so as to be heard over the roaring clatter of industrial stand mixers and the sizzle of fat-popping fryers. At five o'clock in the morning.

This came as a surprise, frankly. After less than an hour on the job, Athena would already have pegged him for a true-crime enthusiast, given the murderous glint in his eyes whenever someone interrupted his labors to request necessary paperwork.

But nope. As Bez, the friendly Latina scheduled as Karl's other early-morning clerk, bustled around the bakery and showed Athena the normal preopening routine, some wide-eyed, widely spread chick was getting railed by a surprisingly articulate spider-dude with a bulbed arachnocock. Athena wasn't quite sure she fully understood the anatomy involved, but the girl getting vigorously bulbed approved. Several times. There were bondage-capable webs involved, as well as fangs dripping venom that served as a homemade aphrodisiac. An *artisanal* aphrodisiac, one might say. Fang-crafted with care. Trademark symbol.

No doubt many—most?—people would be horrified. Dr. Matthew Vine the Third, for example. Given that stick up his irritatingly fine ass, he likely disapproved of fiction featuring bulbed spider-cocks going up *other* people's asses.

Athena, though? She liked the freaky cut of this author's jib.

"Please, Bez. Please tell me Karl leaves his audiobooks playing after we open." She folded a pile of white bakery boxes, coaxing them into their new three-dimensional shape, since she hadn't yet been initiated into the mysteries of coffee-grinding and espresso-machine maintenance. "He wouldn't have to pay me. I would literally pay *him* to watch that."

Not that she'd be giving up all that much money with her hourly earnings. For the first time since her teenage years, she was back to minimum-wage work. Given Ladywright College's close proximity, she was competing with student labor, and students tended to work cheaply.

She was fortunate even to have a low-paid job. If the online listings she'd desperately checked every day post-breakup were any indication, most local businesses and organizations simply weren't hiring right now. Even better: At Grounds and Grains, all employees working at least twenty hours a week got benefits. That was crucial, since her COBRA payments were murdering her in much the same way Karl seemingly yearned to do. According to Bez, he also raised wages quickly past the probation period, once he'd confirmed an employee's reliability.

None of the other retail jobs available had offered benefits. If one of Karl's two early-morning clerks hadn't unexpectedly quit last week, when most students were still on their summer break, Athena would have been shit out of luck.

"Sorry, Athena." Bez's bouncy ponytail flicked from side to side when she shook her head. "No monster-fucking in front of customers. Once we open, it's soft jazz until closing."

Karl emerged from the back room and rolled a tall cart entirely filled with silver sheet pans behind the counter. Meticulously arranged on every parchment-covered tray, various pastries steamed as they cooled: doughnuts with different glazes, icings, and fillings; streusel-topped cheese, fruit, and nut Danishes; sticky buns; cinnamon buns; and much, much more.

Everything smelled absolutely amazing. Too bad Athena didn't actually have much of a sweet tooth.

Once he wordlessly departed, Bez whispered, "At first, he tried listening to the audiobooks with earbuds, but he couldn't hear when his timers went off. He burnt every loaf of English muffin bread one day, and the next morning, a satyr was loudly fucking a priest while we filled all the preorders."

Athena snorted and moved the freshly baked items into the glass display cases, as previously instructed, then relocated her stack of boxes closer to the back-room entrance, so she wouldn't miss a key plot point.

"Oh, Emil! Your bulbs!" the narrator gasped, in the breathy voice she used for the heroine's dialogue. "Are they . . . are they *pulsing*?"

Bez paused in the middle of Windexing the front display case. "Generally, I'm not a huge fan of spiders, but . . ."

Athena nodded emphatically. "No, I get it. Does the author offer specially shaped dildos and vibrators as merch? Because if they don't, they totally should."

This time, even whispering wasn't discreet enough. Bez scooted right up next to her and spoke in a bare thread of sound. "It's always the same author. *Always*. Sadie Brazen. I asked Karl once why he didn't branch out and try other writers, and he just looked at me. Another time, I asked if he knew her or something, and he retreated to the back room and didn't speak for the rest of the day."

"*Brazen?*" Athena raised her brows. "That has to be a pen name."

"Well, yeah." Bez resumed her smudge-removal duties, her volume normal once more. "You know, I went to one of Fawn's open houses this spring and saw your new home. You've heard the story, right? Why it's called the Spite House?"

"Yep." Athena's back audibly cracked when she stretched. "It's a good story."

According to local legend——and who knew whether it was true or not——two brothers had jointly inherited the land containing what was now Johnny's home and the Spite House. When one of the brothers left to fight against the Confederacy, the other had snatched the opportunity to build a home that occupied the lion's share of that land, leaving his poor soldier sibling a mere sliver. A skinny rectangle of property only ten feet in width and essentially worthless, because who'd build a house that narrow?

No one, that was who. Unless, of course, that someone was unbelievably *pissed*.

Pissed, for example, because he'd fought in a war and then returned to discover his brother's betrayal. A man in that situation, bursting with rage and raring for revenge, might in fact decide to build a house on his remaining land. Especially since the house, attached as it was to his brother's, would largely deprive that brother of sunlight, ruin much of his view, and restrict his airflow.

Thus: Spite House.

In the end, Athena's home purchase had been all too fitting. Yes, she'd wanted to offer Johnny his dream—but she'd also wanted to spite his brother. The brother who didn't think buying the house would be wise, just as he didn't think marrying her was wise. The brother whose hushed words in a white, marble-floored bathroom hallway shadowed the corners of her brain whenever she didn't feverishly distract herself with work and wedding planning.

When she'd signed all those papers at closing, she hadn't been thinking of Johnny.

She'd scrawled her name with a flourish and a wide, satisfied smirk, because she'd managed to circumvent Dr. Matthew Vine the Third's pronouncements about what was smart and good and reasonable. She'd gotten some of her own back, at last. She'd *won*.

Two weeks later, she'd found herself weeping alone in her childhood bedroom and asking Professor Google to confirm the exact etymology of the phrase *Pyrrhic victory*.

"You've gotta admire a dude who's willing to build and inhabit a ten-foot-wide house for the sole purpose of telling his brother to go fuck himself." Bez shook her head appreciatively. "Now *that's* commitment."

Would someone who bought the same house for much the same reason be considered admirable too? Or simply . . . foolish?

Athena knew which side she came down on.

"I wonder if he kept torturing his brother afterward," Bez said. "Because if something like that happened now, soldier dude would definitely buy a drum kit and practice at two in the morning, directly next to his brother's bedroom."

Apparently Bez found petty payback entertaining, at least in the abstract. Which was heartening, honestly, given what Athena had done as she'd left for the bakery that morning.

"Then he'd go to various political campaigns' websites and sign his brother up for their newsletters," Athena suggested. "Donate a dollar each to the good ones, agree to further contact, and enter his brother's cell number, email address, and physical address."

"Have pizzas delivered to his brother's home nonstop."

"Create a Reddit post about the situation, thus prompting the entire internet to declare his brother 'the Asshole.'"

"Put pre-chewed wads of gum on his brother's doorstep every morning."

"Contact local representatives of multilevel marketing companies using his brother's name, tell them he wanted to learn more about hosting parties, and request that they call, text, email, and/or stop by his house to discuss his options."

Bez whistled, low and long. "Shit, Athena. Remind me not to piss you off. Wow."

When Athena swept an exaggerated bow, Bez applauded with seemingly genuine approval, and they continued brainstorming increasingly elaborate revenge scenarios as they completed their last few preopening tasks.

At some point, Athena realized she was smiling again.

No, this wasn't the work of her dreams. But here she was, gainfully employed with benefits, chatting with a fun coworker, and listening to a young woman without an apparent gag reflex weep tears of joy during a transformative arachnorgasm. All before five thirty in the morning on her second full day in town.

Things could definitely be worse.

SADLY, ABOUT AN hour and a half later, things *got* worse.

Dr. Matthew Vine the Third appeared in the doorway, frowning at something on his phone as he entered the bakery. Then he raised his head.

He halted in his tracks, his gaze steady on her.

Shit. Did he have a doorbell camera? Had he watched her adjust his house numbers through a window?

He didn't appear angry, though. Solemn and exhausted, yes, but not accusing. So maybe he hadn't arrived to confront her after all. But if not, why was he staring at her so intently?

No one else—not the other customers at the cash register, not Bez—seemed to notice his arrival, and Athena didn't understand. The man might not be a giant, and he might be wearing a dark, unremarkable suit, but his focused intensity lit him from within. She couldn't look away.

He was the plasma globe she'd had as a kid. Diffuse, sparking power safely, sternly contained. Electricity that gathered in a bright, powerful current at the slightest touch, arcing toward the conductive body pressed against his curved glass surface.

But that glass barrier would always remain, she reminded herself. At best, she was a simple conducting object to him, an interruption of his optimal energy flow. Nothing more. The whiff of ozone, the beauty of all that power focused on her, had deceived her for a quarter hour at a small, elegant art museum, but she knew better now.

Her plasma globe had probably despised her too. Resented her disruption of its preferred conductive paths. Informed its globe brethren she was too dependent. Too intense. Too messy and unsettled to stay with forever.

Deliberately, she broke their stare and severed that arc of current connecting them.

After a moment, he stepped up to the counter.

She greeted him with false cheer, teeth bared in what the unwary might consider a grin, as if she'd never met him before. "Good morning, sir. What can I get you?"

If that was a flinch, he recovered from it with lightning speed.

"You . . ." He was frowning again. *Quelle surprise.* "You didn't give yourself a few days to rest and get settled after moving?"

Apparently he hadn't come to demand an apology for her early-morning adventures. Good. She could skip the fake remorse, then, in favor of fresh irritation at his question. Her desperation for a quick paycheck might be his fault, but it was none of his fucking beeswax.

Her smile grew wider. Displayed even more teeth. "What can I get you, sir?"

He hesitated. Then, lips pressed tight, he gave a little nod and turned his attention to the display cases. "I'll have a dozen caramel-iced buns, a dozen assorted filled doughnuts, a dozen assorted Danishes, and a half dozen assorted scones. Thank you."

Her mouth fell open a little.

"It's a lot. I know." He sounded apologetic, and she hated how charming she found that sheepish tone. "But there are twelve of us working in the office. Well, eleven, with—" His frown deepened. "Eleven today. The next few weeks are going to be especially busy for everyone, and I want to acknowledge that and express my appreciation, so . . ."

He lifted a shoulder, and it was the most casual gesture she'd ever seen him make.

Damn her insatiable curiosity. There was no one behind him in line, so she had to ask.

"You own your own practice, right?" When he dipped his chin

in confirmation, she continued, "Which means you make your own hours. Why in the world would you report to work at seven in the morning if you didn't have to?"

It wasn't her business. It was quite literally his.

Still, he answered readily. "Before I head to the office this morning, I'm going to the hospital nursery. My—uh, one of the other doctors has a brand-new patient there."

An infant. He was visiting an infant. A tiny human poised at the intersection of nature and nurture. A fresh spark of life, almost incomprehensibly vulnerable.

She didn't want a child of her own, but the thought of a sleepy, sweet-smelling baby cradled in his sensitive hands, resting in the crook of his arm . . .

Well, it wasn't the worst mental image she'd ever had.

"Her parents emailed us some photos last night, and she has this one little tuft of hair right"—he swirled his fingers over the crown of his head—"*here* that always sticks up. In every single picture. Like a mohawk."

Then, for the first time since last December, Dr. Matthew Vine the Third graced her with a small, tired smile. It was the sunrise pushing aside darkness, a soft glow edging above the horizon, and she was stricken by its beauty. The corners of his eyes crinkled, and his irises lightened to the sweet, warm brown of root beer. The hollows of his cheeks filled. His lips—

Never mind about his lips.

After one glimpse of that smile, some of his teenage patients probably formed agonizing crushes on him and found themselves desperate to know *precisely* how old you could be and still see a pediatrician. Which was a fair question, since Athena didn't know either.

She made a mental note: *Ask Professor Google about maximum pediatrician patient age*.

"I'm going to visit the nursery, do an exam, write in her chart, talk to her parents if they're around and awake, and *then* go to the office. Thus my early-morning baked goods run." That mesmerizing curve of his mouth disappeared, collapsing into his normal frown. "I should get coffee too. The biggest cup size you have, please. And, uh . . ."

His gaze flickered to the display case, and maybe someday a lover would view her with that intensity of longing.

He sighed and surrendered to passion. "One extra cheese Danish, bagged separately." As she nodded and reached for a sheet of waxed paper to transfer the goodies, he sighed again. "And an orange-caramel crunch scone. In the same bag."

"Your bag. Not for general office consumption." It wasn't a question.

"Yes, well . . ." He'd been kind of leaning one hip against the case, but now he jerked upright, into his usual ramrod posture. "Do you need me to repeat my order?"

"Nope." Her memory had always been sharp. It'd served her well in school.

As she grabbed one of the boxes she'd folded earlier, filled it with various doughnuts, and passed it to Bez at the register, she marveled. A sweet tooth. Who'd have thought lean, mean Dr. Matthew Vine the Third had a sweet tooth?

Anyone who'd seen that small, secret smile, probably.

There was no more chitchat as she continued filling his order, but his eyes followed her as she worked, and . . .

There it was again. All that current, coalescing into a single stream. Flowing toward the palm of her hand, only to disperse over the interior surface of the globe before she could reach it. Before it ran up her arm, through her body, and set her alight too.

Enough. *Enough*.

No more shared glances. No more smiles. She needed to stop touching his fucking glass.

His remaining time in the bakery, she ignored the current. Ignored him. Even when the bell on the door jingled upon his departure, she simply continued folding her pile of boxes.

A minute later, Bez gasped. "Oh, wow. Dr. Vine usually leaves a decent tip, but . . ." Her eager hand dove down into the tip jar, and she held up three crisp bills. No, four. "He left us *eighty fucking dollars*, Athena."

Pity money. But Athena would take it anyway. She'd willingly swallow down the bitter humiliation of his charity, because she desperately needed the cash.

Or maybe it wasn't pity money at all. Maybe it was Matthew's attempt at kindness.

Was she even capable of recognizing kindness anymore? Of differentiating it from pity? Especially from him?

Didn't matter, really. The money had been a final gesture. A farewell of sorts. Now that he knew she was working at his regular bakery, he'd never come back, which was exactly what she wanted. No doubt about it.

Well . . . maybe one or two doubts.

4

Athena had half her body outside one of her third-floor windows, her face flushed and damp and tipped high in apparent hopes of catching a breeze. Since her eyes were closed, she hadn't witnessed Matthew's arrival in his home office. I.e., the room directly across from her current location.

Someday, he'd manage to save enough money to install central air in his childhood home without ruining its historic charm, but it wasn't happening this summer. As usual, he'd make do with fans, a window AC unit in his bedroom, and, yes, all his other windows open for cross-ventilation.

Insects weren't a problem near them—maybe the wind from the waterfront whisked them away?—so they didn't need screens. The lack of even that insubstantial barrier only underlined the nearness of the two houses. Emphasized the unwilling intimacy of their proximity.

He could literally reach out and touch her. Replay the start of his dreams by smoothing a stray lock of her hair back into place.

Tonight's rebellious strand, wavy and dark with perspiration, clung to her cheek. Much the same way her sweaty tank top clung to her chest. To her breasts, which were soft and heavy and unbound, responding predictably—beautifully—to gravity as she bent over.

The view was . . .

Never mind that. However she might look, her current position was making him very, very nervous. Up this high, he didn't even poke his head outside unless absolutely necessary.

When he cleared his throat, alerting her to his presence, he recognized his mistake immediately. She jerked, eyes flying open in startlement, and with so much of her already hanging outside the low window, she had to frantically slap her hands against the sides of the frame to keep herself from teetering.

He'd lunged for his own window as soon as he understood what he'd done, but he would have been far too late. From that height, a fall onto the brick alleyway . . .

He squeezed his eyes shut and waited for his parasympathetic nervous system to take care of all the epinephrine and cortisol that had just flooded his bloodstream. Hyperarousal. Acute stress response. Fight-or-flight response. Whatever he chose to call it, it left his hands shaking and his pulse far too rapid.

"Just a harmless little bobble." Her voice was calm. Soothing. "I only grabbed the frame out of instinct. You're not getting rid of me that easily, Dr. Matthew Vine the Third."

When he could reason past the desperate *thud-thud* of his heart, her expression came into focus. Concern for him, only partially masked by flippancy. Her lips were pale and soft, not drawn tightly into that wide, rigid, toothy smile she'd offered him at the bakery every morning for the past week.

"I apologize." He met Athena's gaze directly. "I didn't mean to startle you."

One corner of her mouth twitched, and the rush of pleasure he experienced rivaled the first bite of a streusel-topped cheese Danish. "Yes. Your near cardiac arrest when I shifted maybe an extra millimeter out the window told me that."

If she didn't already know how quickly, how easily, the fragile vessel of her body could suffer irreparable damage, he certainly wouldn't burden her with the information. He understood the stakes very well, however. A single moment of carelessness, a single danger ignored, and . . . disaster.

Every night since she'd moved in, she'd spent time hanging out this particular window in hopes of cooling off. Which he wished he didn't know, for various reasons. It worried him. It also wasn't good for him to see her this much, or to see so much of her. But he had no choice when it came to their proximity. Not in his home, and not outside it either.

After the first morning he'd encountered Athena at the bakery, he'd called Karl. His old friend had grumpily assured him that clerks kept their tips—"What, you thought I was going to take their fucking money, dude? Jesus"—and split them evenly after each joint shift. So Matthew had been making daily pilgrimages there ever since.

His colleagues at the practice were both delighted by the continual bounty of pastries and understandably confused as to its cause. And any day now, his bank's ATM was going to spit out a receipt that said: *You haven't needed this much cash since 2007, Account #558347-ab72x. What's going on? If this is a strip club thing, wouldn't smaller bills be preferable?*

Not that he'd ever been to a strip club. His ATM should know that.

Hell, he probably wouldn't even notice a random naked woman planted directly in front of him, not with all his thoughts so firmly anchored to Athena. Which was . . . troubling.

He'd found himself unwillingly keeping track of her slow, slow progress in unpacking whenever he was home. In a week, she'd managed to fully empty maybe a half dozen containers. Most, she simply opened, stared at, divested of one or two items, then shoved to the side as best she could in such a narrow space.

Those boxes and partially filled plastic bins were killing him. He wanted to unpack for her. Get her comfortably settled. She could simply lounge somewhere and tell him where everything went, and voilà! An entire move, accomplished.

And while he was imagining things that'd never happen: After he put her belongings away, they'd go buy her an AC unit, and she'd let him pay without an argument, and then she'd look at him the same way she had last December, in that final moment before Johnny appeared.

Though . . . maybe part of his fantasy could come true. He had to try, anyway.

"I truly didn't know you'd bought the Spite House until I saw you moving in last week," he told her, "and I don't know what your current financial situation is. But I'm guessing it's not what you might have wanted under other circumstances, and I assume my brother and I have played a key role in any difficulties you might be experiencing. If that's the case, I apologize, Athena. And if you're willing to accept assistance, I'd be happy to support you however I can."

It was stiff and formal and unnecessarily wordy, but at least he'd finally tendered his long-overdue apology and shared his desire to remedy the problems he'd helped create.

She nodded, but she didn't say whether she believed him, she didn't accept his offer of assistance, and she didn't offer her forgiveness. Only a fool would have expected a different response. The simple fact she hadn't slammed her window shut on him constituted a victory.

Unfortunately, he still had one more tricky subject to raise.

While Karl had ensured his bakery employees got benefits, the pay started out low, and Matthew didn't think Athena could handle her mortgage and still live comfortably on her remaining income.

She needed a different job. If not a better one, at least a better-*paying* one. And even though he wasn't exactly a social butterfly, he'd grown up in Harlot's Bay and knew most everyone. Given a day or two, he could track down whatever work openings were currently available.

He cleared his throat. "Please tell me about your educational achievements and your professional history. From"—*what Johnny told me*—"my understanding, you have two master's degrees? Is that correct?"

Shit. Even to his own ears, that sounded pompous beyond belief. But how was he supposed to find her another position without knowing more about her academic background and job qualifications?

"Do you require résumés from everyone on this street? Or am I the only one whose neighborly fitness is in question?" Her tone was understandably tart. After a moment, though, she sighed. "Whatever. It's not like it's a secret. If you asked your brother, he'd know, assuming he didn't have me erased from his brain, *Eternal Sunshine*-style. Although I'm not sure he ever engaged deeply enough with what I said to effectively encode it into his long-term memory, so maybe his mind is spotless either way."

Around Athena, he should really carry a notebook to jot down the many questions a conversation with her raised. From what he could tell, she knew at least a little about everything and *a lot* about topics of particular interest.

Talking with her dizzied him, challenged him. Delighted him.

Even when she looked at him like . . . that. Like his absence from this planet would improve her existence immeasurably.

"I have a BS and MS in psychology and an MAEd in curriculum and instruction," she listed dully. "I've had retail jobs, checked tickets at a living history museum, and worked children's reference at a library. Most recently, I taught introductory and AP psychology for four years at a Virginia high school. Is that sufficient, Dr. Vine? Do I pass muster?"

The wide, toothy smile she offered him didn't contain an ounce of friendliness or joy. It was a baring of teeth, and he hated it.

When she'd last given him a true smile—a smile bright enough to light a dim museum corner—she hadn't even opened her mouth. Her lips had curved sweetly, softly, without a single tooth in sight. Her cheeks had rounded, and her green-and-brown gaze had sparkled.

With her current rictus grin, he might have been staring into a doll's eyes.

"This isn't about passing muster." One particular spot on his forehead always seemed to hurt these days, and he rubbed it with his fingertips. "Just . . . are you looking for a teaching job?"

If anything, her smile widened, and he had to look away. "No. I'm not subbing either, since being a high school substitute teacher is like voluntarily wearing a 'Kick Me' sign on your ass. Also, subs don't get benefits."

He nodded, staring blankly at the piles of boxes surrounding her as he considered who might hire someone with her background.

"Oh, I'm so sorry. Is my mess bothering you?" Athena's voice was like the Diet Coke she continually drank at home: fake sugar. Sweet with a bitter aftertaste. Corrosive. "My sincere apologies, Dr. Vine. I know how you value order. Everything in its place, right?"

Okay, so he kept his home somewhat . . . regimented, which

she'd obviously noted through their windows. But important things slipped through the cracks in a chaotic home, as he well knew, and the consequences could be life-altering. Life-*ending*.

"I'm just fine with messiness," he said with hearty good cheer. "Mess is . . . uh, fine. No, it's *great*."

Pinocchio's lies were less obvious than his. Dammit.

"Are you *sure* you're a pediatrician?" She crinkled her nose at him. "Because working with kids means dealing with messes. Why aren't you, like, a plastic surgeon to the stars instead?"

Is that how she saw him? As someone who'd enjoy surgically removing ostensible flaws in pursuit of ostensible perfection?

"Or if you're determined to work with kiddos," she continued, ducking back inside the window and resting her forearms on the sill, "why not become a specialist? A pediatric cardiologist, like my parents, or an endocrinologist? I'm pretty sure they don't have to slosh through children's various bodily fluids every day at work. No hip waders necessary."

While it was true he encountered his share of wet, sticky, and smelly substances on a daily basis—"I don't have to *wade*. Besides, my patients can't help it. I don't mind."

He didn't. He might be . . . order-oriented? . . . but he wasn't squeamish.

"Sure, Jan."

"What?" Who was Jan?

"Never mind. Forget my skillful deployment of archaic internet memes." She set her chin on the back of her wrist. "Okay, let's say you truly don't mind horrifying substances erupting out of multiple orifices. You still don't seem like a kid person. Don't they find you intimidating?"

That stung, for reasons she couldn't possibly comprehend.

He swallowed past an odd sort of thickness in his throat and tried to pay attention, because she was still talking.

"—always pictured you in a lab coat frowning severely at misbehaving samples under a microscope," she was saying. "Or harnessing your penetrating glowers as a nonradioactive x-ray alternative, possibly whilst lecturing your cowlick for its impertinence."

Automatically, his hand lifted to smooth down the rebellious patch of hair above his left temple. Then, catching himself, he lowered his arm to his side.

That tiny smirk indenting the corners of her mouth wasn't as bad as her Toothy Smile of Aggression. But it didn't contain the warm amusement of a teasing friend, either. It chilled him, even on such a muggy August night.

"I like kids." He could state it more eloquently, using more sophisticated language, but that was the crux of the matter. "I like helping them stay safe and healthy. I like watching them grow up."

She stared at him then. Directly at him, her gaze *present* as it had so rarely been during their recent encounters. The inner tips of her eyebrows rose as her smirk died.

All at once, her eyes closed, and her head bowed.

"Athena?" Okay, yes, maybe he was indeed frowning severely, but only out of concern. "Are you well?"

"Matthew, I'm—" She rubbed both hands over her face, shoulders slumped. "I didn't . . ."

He waited, but instead of finishing her thought, she kept rubbing. And when she spoke again, her statement had absolutely no connection to their previous conversation.

"'The limit does not exist' is a mathematical determination involving functions. Also a *Mean Girls* reference."

The words were muffled by her fingers, but easily understood. Or at least easily heard, if not easily comprehended.

"And a vehicle's frame is what protects you from lightning, rather than the rubber tires," she added. "The frame evidently becomes a metal cage that conducts the electricity around you safely into the ground, as long as you're not touching anything metal that connects to the cage."

Somehow they'd veered off a comprehensible conversational path. He couldn't say what mean girls had to do with mathematical limits. Or, harkening back to their earlier discussion, what sunlight—however eternal—had to do with memories. And he certainly had no earthly idea why they were now discussing lightning.

He wouldn't quibble, though. He owed her payback. If she wanted to insult him and talk about Faraday cages, fine. Done. Besides, the topic interested him, given his lifelong, unshakable fear of storms.

"Okay," he said cautiously. "Which things shouldn't you touch?"

She raised her head and lowered her hands. "If you're in a vehicle during a lightning storm, you should stay away from door handles, the steering wheel, the radio, and so forth, and you should have all your doors and windows closed."

Huh. Good to know.

"Sorry about that," she said inexplicably.

Perhaps, once this perplexing conversation was over, he'd spend a few minutes with Professor Google to figure out the sunshine and mean girls allusions, along with the importance of someone named Jan.

Quick as one of those lightning bolts, she was already on to something else.

"How old can you be and still see a pediatrician?" Her elbows now propped on the window frame, hands folded one over the other, she tipped her head. "Is it truly twenty-five? I thought you had to switch to a regular doctor once you turned eighteen."

Again, random, but at least he had a clear answer for her. "Twenty-five. It used to be eighteen, but our better understanding of human brain development led to the change."

"Ah." She nodded. "The prefrontal cortex. Still developing well into our twenties."

Her psychology background at work, or maybe just her native intelligence and curiosity. Either way, it was impressive. Under other circumstances, maybe even—

No, not *hot*. Not *arousing*. Not anything.

"Yes. Most patients stop seeing their pediatricians well before then, however."

"Hmmm." Her mouth opened in a wide yawn, and she didn't bother to cover it.

He let the silence spin out, but she'd apparently reached the end of her odd succession of topics. Which meant he could finally ask more questions. Two, to be exact. "What brought up all those topics for you? Why were you thinking about them?"

Her answer came slowly. "I'm just . . . curious. About everything, really. I like to understand things, and I don't like uncertainty. I want to know how the world works."

He made an affirming sound. A sort of hum he employed to tell patients and parents, *I'm listening to you. I'm interested in what you're saying. I'm not impatient. Keep talking, please.*

"During the course of a day, a lot of random thoughts occur to me," she added after a moment. "If a question pops into my head and I'm not sure of the answer, I add it to the list I keep on my phone, and every night before bed, I consult Professor Google. You just heard a report of some recent findings."

She looked away from him. Shrugged.

"Sorry. I know Jo—" *Johnny.* She'd cut herself off before finishing his brother's name, but even that first syllable felt like an intrusion. "I know no one wants to listen to a soliloquy about random shit. I apologize for boring you."

"I wasn't bored." If he hadn't been so damn tired, he would have stopped there. He didn't. "You've never bored me. Not for a fraction of an instant."

"Thanks, but I'm sure that's not true." With a shake of her head, she dismissed his claim as empty flattery. "I don't know why I thought you'd be interested."

"Don't you?" His voice was low. Hoarse.

He'd lost control. Of his tongue, of this conversation, of his brain.

When their eyes met, he was back in that cool museum with white marble floors, contemplating the history of potatoes. Researching the topic on his phone, to their mutual pleasure and satisfaction. Hoping for more non-potato-related pleasure and satisfaction to come.

And he could swear she was right there with him.

Her face was soft and stricken, her gaze searching and . . . open.

"Athena," he said quietly. Gently. "Please tell me why you don't want a teaching job here in Maryland."

If he kept pushing, she'd push back. So he let his patience, his sincere interest, work its own persuasion instead.

And in the stillness of the dark, humid night, a miracle appeared before him. An unearned moment of grace. With a long, tired exhalation, Athena laid down her weapons and shed her armor.

"Teaching, to me, felt like climbing a mountain." She rested her cheek on her arm, her voice abstracted and dreamy. Without a single sharp edge. "One of the giants. Everest or K2. It was this endless march upward, scrambling over groaning crevasses and beneath seracs that could topple at any moment. The summers were only brief stops at base camps. And the longer and higher I climbed, the thinner the air became. I was always running behind schedule, always gasping for breath. Only there was no summit anywhere in sight."

He could picture her, shivering even as her cheeks burned under the too-close sun, increasingly frantic for oxygen but pressing upward and upward again, and the image pierced his heart.

That night at the museum, he'd noted her affinity for metaphor and simile. When she spoke, breathtakingly vivid worlds opened to him, unexpected escape paths from the confines of his daily routines and duties. With Athena, his thoughts transformed from prose to poetry.

Once, for a quarter hour, he'd thought that was a gift beyond price. Now, he knew it for what it truly was: a curse.

She wasn't his. She'd never be his.

Once she had her feet back under her, she'd return to Virginia. Even if she didn't, he couldn't hurt Johnny that way. Even if he could, she loathed him.

Their time together was a crumb from a banquet he couldn't attend, no matter how he starved.

"I always had more planning and grading to do." Her eyes had closed, and he didn't know whether she still registered his presence. Maybe he was simply an anonymous confessor now. An empty container for her thoughts and memories, so she didn't have to carry them alone. "More meetings to attend. More paperwork to complete. More kids to worry about. I tried to give those kids whatever I had, because so many of them deserved so much more than they'd ever gotten."

He almost laughed at the irony, because what she'd just described? Apart from the grading, she might have been explaining his own recent workdays.

"Here's the thing, though." With a ragged nail, she scratched the tip of her nose, eyes still shut. "You can't linger in the death zone indefinitely. There's not enough oxygen to sustain life there. It gets harder and harder to make good decisions and save yourself from disaster. And maybe if I knew how to half-ass things, maybe if I'd taught for a few more years and had all my preps nailed down, the oxygen levels would have been higher. But I'm not good at half measures, and sooner or later, my department was going to need me to fill in as a geography teacher or whatever, and then there'd be an entirely new mountain looming, one even harder to climb because its terrain was so unfamiliar to me. I couldn't—I—"

She'd been talking faster and faster, her words tumbling over one another, until suddenly she stopped. Took a shaky breath.

When she spoke again, each word was slow. Precise.

She said, "I loved teaching, but it was killing me."

Her eyes opened. She stared into his.

"When your brother proposed, when he asked me to move to Harlot's Bay, it felt like the first real lungful of oxygen I'd had in years. And he told me—" She audibly gulped back . . . something. A sob, maybe. "He told me it was okay. I didn't have to keep climbing. I didn't have to know what to do next. He'd support me while I rested and recovered. I could take a month. A year, even. However much time I needed. If I wanted to, I could go back to school for something else, something that would make me happy, and he'd pay."

If Matthew could have looked away, he would have.

He'd known his brother had pledged to support Athena as she established herself in her new home, but the breadth of Johnny's promises, their sweeping, romantic grandeur . . .

Had his brother ever actually considered the practical implications? Had those promises ever been a matter of serious intent, rather than the careless, romantic vows of someone who never expected to have to follow through? At least, not on his own?

Because as always, Johnny had made promises he'd rely on Matthew to keep.

It was, at least at the beginning, the fundamental reason Matthew had opposed the marriage. After moving to Harlot's Bay, Athena was going to be dependent on Johnny to an enormous extent—emotionally, socially, financially—and Matthew's brother simply wasn't dependable. Which meant Matthew would end up with yet more responsibilities, and his own oxygen had started getting pretty damn thin a few years back.

"Teaching . . ." She was wringing restless, trembling hands. "Teaching is the closest I've come to something sustainable career-wise, because I loved those damn kids. I loved teaching. But I couldn't get enough oxygen, so no, I do *not* plan on teaching here in Maryland, because I genuinely think I might not survive it."

Okay. Okay.

If teaching wasn't an option, he could find her something else. Maybe if they revisited her work history, looking for a previous job that wasn't so incredibly demanding—

Her sweet face twisted in a way that hurt to witness. "Sounds like a simple case of burnout, right? But here's my big secret, Matthew. Something I never even told your brother."

His heart jolted at that.

He wanted to collect her secrets. Hoard them. Especially the ones Johnny had never learned.

"All my other jobs? By the time I quit, they had me gasping for breath too." Her voice was rough now, shredded by raw emotion. "Maybe I was bored instead of overworked. Maybe my supervisors wanted instant, unquestioning obedience, or I didn't fit in with my coworkers. Whatever the reason, I couldn't hack it. Two or three years after starting the job, I was out. Every. Single. Time."

He couldn't imagine that kind of regular upheaval in his life. Couldn't picture not knowing where he belonged, at least when it came to work.

Those lovely, pained eyes had turned overly bright. "I'm a mess, Matthew. And except when it comes to your patients, you don't tolerate messes. No wonder you didn't want your brother to marry me."

Jesus. She might as well have kicked him in the stomach.

He had a million ways to respond. A million things he wanted to tell her, not all of which would be wise to share.

But in the end, he only managed to say, "I'm sorry, Athena. I raised a man who makes promises he can't keep, and I apologize."

"You should only apologize for your offenses, not his. Your brother is thirty-one years old, and he'll need to make his own amends." She paused. "I mean, at some point, you have to take responsibility for yourself, right?"

Full of judgment, the final sentence rang with special emphasis. Special bitterness.

He recognized that statement. He remembered it.

Her awful, unamused smirk reappeared. "You should know that, Dr. Matthew Vine the Third. After all, isn't that what you said about me?"

Parting shot launched, she clambered stiffly to her feet and left—the window, the room, him—without waiting to see whether she'd scored a direct hit.

She was named after a war goddess. She had. Of course she had.

5

"eems to me you could be employing compliance strategies," Athena informed a glowering Karl. "Techniques for getting other people to do what you want. In our case, convincing customers to buy more coffee and baked goods."

He grunted, angled away from her, and glared down at the dough he was shaping.

The man was in his late thirties, like her. By this point, he really should have mastered the concept of object permanence. If he couldn't see her, that didn't mean she'd somehow gone *poof* and disappeared into the ether. Even sugar-addled toddlers knew better than that.

"Norms of reciprocity. We need to take advantage of them." Oh, it felt good to revisit some of the knowledge she'd gleaned from her studies and her teaching. "When you do something nice for someone, they tend to think they should do something nice for you in return. Which is one of the reasons offering samples at the counter should raise sales. It would give people a chance to try new pastries or coffee concoctions they might want to buy in the future, but it would also make them feel beholden. Like they owed you something. For instance, their hard-earned money at the cash register."

"Shouldn't you be prepping the store for opening, Greydon? Or doing something—*anything*—other than being a goddamn pain in my ass?" His eyes narrowed in homicidal menace. "I am your boss, you know. I could make your life *veeeery* fucking difficult. Also, I have knives. Lots of knives."

She grinned cheerfully at him. "I'm good."

She and Bez had their routine down now. Everything in the front was ready for their first morning customers. And after more than two weeks working at Grounds and Grains, Karl's fulminating scowl no longer intimidated her. He was a marshmallow that had been thrust carelessly into a campfire, his charred, bitter shell covering a center of sweet goo.

Karl muttered to himself. Or, more accurately, continued muttering to himself.

She stood there as he finished with the dough and portioned it into waiting loaf pans. A stubborn goat he might be, but he wasn't a fool. If she gave him a minute to reconcile himself to the prospect of change—however minor—he'd come to see the benefits of her suggestion.

"It's not the worst idea ever," he finally, begrudgingly allowed. "I suppose I could spare some brownies this afternoon. Those are easy to cut into smaller pieces."

When she pumped a fist in triumph, he snorted and even smiled a little.

Sadly for him, Athena had never met a bit of luck she couldn't push. "And have you given any more consideration to making potato bread? Because it's September now, and potatoes are very autumnal, so—"

Just as he was raising his head from his work yet again, in all likelihood to inform her precisely where she could shove her beloved potatoes, a young white woman entered the back room. Not a customer, obviously, since they weren't open yet and Bez must have let her inside, but not a coworker either, as far as Athena knew. A friend of Karl's, maybe?

"Can . . . can we talk?" The woman spoke to Karl in a near whisper, her shoulders rounded, her hands clenched together. "Privately?"

Karl's chest hitched in a slow, huge breath, and . . . why was he looking at Athena instead of their visitor? And not with his usual murder-y gleam, either, but an expression of—was that reluctance? Sadness?

It didn't matter. Athena might not fully understand what was happening, but the two of them obviously needed time alone together.

"I'll go," she said.

Wordlessly, Karl turned and trudged for his office, his visitor following with her blond head bowed. When Athena pushed open the swinging door to the front, Bez was waiting behind the counter, maybe a foot away.

Why was she giving Athena that same look? Sadness and regret?

A burst of sobbing drifted from the back of the store. Hiccupped breaths and loud, uncontainable despair. Athena was far too familiar with that particular keening grief, although it sounded different coming from someone else's throat. Hers ached in sympathy.

She caught Bez's eye and kept her voice to a whisper. "Who is that?"

"The clerk you replaced. Charlotte." Bez bit her lip. "She keeps trying to make things work with her children's father in Baltimore, but she always ends up back in Harlot's Bay. And she's sort of Karl's surrogate daughter."

That was . . . troubling.

But Bez said nothing more, even though Athena waited. So she pinched her mouth shut too, despite her rampant curiosity and growing anxiety. If Bez wanted to talk about what was happening, she would. Athena shouldn't force her.

After that late-night conversation with Matthew a week or so ago, she'd vowed to tread a bit more carefully when it came to the feelings of everyone around her. She might be in pain, but that didn't give her leave to hurt others. Not even when they might, arguably, deserve it.

And she *had* hurt his feelings, even though she'd thought—she'd told herself—he didn't actually have any. When she'd questioned his suitability as a pediatrician, implying his patients would be scared of him, he'd just sat there and . . . taken it, without protest or interruption. But everything about him had sort of sagged as he swayed subtly away from her. Like he'd absorbed a blow but was too tired and beaten up to bother dodging the next one.

She didn't want to be someone who continued punching a man after he'd conceded the match. Especially when she didn't understand why he was already down for the count before she even entered the ring.

But she also hadn't been able to make herself apologize, not when she remained so incandescently angry from being given an impromptu, late-night job interview at her own damn *window*, by a man who'd evaluated her so many times before and found her lacking each and every time.

So instead of an apology, she'd offered up her best bits of random knowledge in recompense for her meanness. Because she didn't know much about him, but she'd intuited from the first moment of their very first meeting that he liked accurate, specific information almost as much as she did.

And then . . . her lingering guilt had led her into foolish honesty. Into baring a vulnerability of her own in penance for wounding one of his.

It was—what? Their third real conversation, ever?

Yet somehow she'd shared more about her four years of teaching than she'd ever confessed to anyone else. She'd told her family and friends she was stressed. Unsure if she wanted to continue. Had she told them she was slowly, agonizingly suffocating? No.

Apart from her, Matthew was the only sentient being on this planet who knew that. Just as he was now the only other person who fully understood the root of all her professional woes.

How did the saying go? Something like: *If you meet an asshole, you met an asshole. If* everyone *you meet is an asshole,* you're *the asshole.*

She'd left a prestigious doctoral program before completing her dissertation, then taken her parents' money to earn yet another graduate degree she was no longer using in any substantive way. Between and after those degrees, she'd worked at a panoply of jobs other people seemed content to have. And if every single one of those possible career paths had led nowhere, if every single one of those professional options left her gasping for breath, there was only one common denominator.

She was the asshole. There was something fundamentally wrong with her.

Maybe he'd seen that in her from the beginning. Now, though, he knew for sure. She'd basically admitted it outright.

They hadn't had a real conversation since that night, although he'd continued his daily visits to the bakery and continued leaving his pity money in the jar. In turn, she'd continued adjusting the numbers beside his door every morning—which he would straighten over the course of the day, inevitably—because that wasn't hurtful, just irritating. Much like the song request she'd phoned into a local radio station last night. According to Victoria and Akio, who also stopped by the bakery some mornings and graciously answered her seemingly random questions without asking for further context, it was the station Strumpet Square Pediatrics played every day. Every. Single. Day.

And every evening, no matter how often she told herself to ignore her alleyway windows, she . . . didn't. She couldn't.

Spying on his orderly, predictable nighttime rituals had become comforting to her at some point. Seeing him put everything in its place, watching him frown down at paperwork or medical journals, and following his progress as he methodically washed his dishes soothed her somehow.

In the rare moments when he wasn't accomplishing anything in particular, he was still a pleasure to study. As handsome as his brother, if less flagrant about it, with more magnetic intensity. And the times she'd talked with him . . . whenever he'd kept his judgments to himself, she'd kind of enjoyed their conversations. He was interesting. Interested.

If she let herself, she could like him. Possibly a lot. Even after all he'd said and done.

The unwelcomeness of that fact didn't make it any less true.

The door to the back room swung open. Charlotte entered the front of the shop, head still bowed. Right before their frail visitor reached the entry door, she turned and looked up. Directly, bafflingly, at Athena.

"I'm so sorry," she whispered, then left.

Five minutes later, Karl called Athena into his office, voice low and gruff and pained.

Ten minutes later, Athena no longer had a job or benefits.

"WILL IT HURT, Dr. Vine?" Felicity whispered, the five-year-old's big brown eyes worried.

Matthew had reached the end of her yearly physical, and the most difficult part couldn't be delayed any longer. Normally he relied on one of the CPNPs to administer routine shots, but Johnny's absence was running them all ragged. And since he was the one who'd approved his brother's extended leave—over Yvonna's objections—he was trying to spare his coworkers as much extra work as possible.

His patient kicked her little sneakered feet as she sat at the padded exam table, peering up at him in concern as he prepared to give her the necessary prekindergarten vaccinations. Her mother was eyeing him with trepidation as well.

To be honest, Ms. Mortenson had been giving him that same look during the entire appointment, which reminded him unpleasantly of what Athena had asked him the other night. *Don't they find you intimidating?*

Sometimes, yes. On the whole, patients and parents *did* consider Johnny warmer than Matthew. Easier to talk to, at least initially. More playful. More fun. Why wouldn't they? His little brother was charming in a way Matthew hadn't ever been, either because charm had never been part of his basic personality or because he'd never had the opportunity to cultivate it.

But when Johnny's patients—including Felicity—needed to be seen after hours or in his absence, when parents had a hard time getting a referral to a particular specialist, and when a newborn arrived in the hospital nursery, Johnny wasn't the doctor who helped them.

Matthew bore much of the burden but received none of the adoration.

No, that wasn't fair. Johnny truly did care about his patients. During office hours, at least, he worked hard. And Matthew's own patients and parents might not consider him fun, but they trusted him. They believed in his expertise and his heartfelt desire to heal children and protect them from harm.

He might not charm them, but he didn't intimidate them. He had to believe that.

Even if Athena didn't.

Preparations completed, he set aside everything he needed on his tray. Then he sat on his stool to position himself at Felicity's eye level, rolled closer to her, and told her the truth.

"You'll be getting two shots today, Felicity." He kept his voice gentle and calm, his expression reassuring. "The first one will protect you from the measles, mumps, rubella, and varicella. Varicella is what most people call chicken pox. That one will sting a little. The second shot will protect you from diphtheria, tetanus, pertussis, and polio. That one will sting a bit more, unfortunately."

The little girl cringed at his words, and her mother glared, but Matthew wouldn't lie. If he did, if he assured Felicity the shots wouldn't hurt when they actually did, she'd never again trust his or Johnny's—or possibly any other doctor's—word when they informed her truthfully that something wouldn't cause her pain.

"Believe me, though: Having one of those diseases is much, much worse than getting a shot. I came down with chicken pox when I was little, and you would not *believe* the itching." Eyes wide, he played up the horror of it all. "I had bumps everywhere. *Everywhere.*"

Felicity looked intrigued. "Like, on your butt?"

"Felicity!" her mother chided, but Matthew laughed.

Putting a hand next to his mouth, theatrically blocking Ms.

Mortenson from seeing his lips, he whispered loudly, "On my butt. And when I itched there, my dad said I was being rude."

As Felicity giggled, her arms unwound from her middle and relaxed to her sides.

"That sounds bad." Her nose wrinkled. "I don't want an itchy butt."

"It's the worst," he agreed. "I don't want you to have an itchy butt either, so let's get you protected. I'll make it as quick and easy as possible, and your mom will help you feel better as soon as we're done. Okay?"

The little girl nodded in acceptance. "Okay."

"Would you like to sit on your mom's lap while I give you the shots?" After Felicity nodded again, he waited until Ms. Mortenson had settled her daughter and gathered her close.

A minute later, the deed was done. Felicity's bottom lip quivered, but the Mirabel bandages on her upper arms cheered her immensely, as did the prospect of stickers at the checkout desk. As he talked to her mother, she began flipping through one of the picture books he stocked in his exam rooms.

He passed a paper to Ms. Mortenson, who'd finally stopped regarding him with suspicion, and explained what to do if Felicity experienced side effects. Also what *not* to do. I.e., give her aspirin.

Kids weren't simply small adults. Their bodies reacted differently to many common medications, and that reaction could be harmful or even deadly.

Every one of his parents and guardians knew that. He made very, very sure of it.

"Got it." Felicity's mom scanned the paper. "Thank you for seeing us at the last minute, Dr. Vine. When I looked at the calendar this morning and realized she wouldn't be able to start school if I didn't get this done, I kind of panicked."

"No problem," he lied. There'd be no lunch break today. Again. Between his overpacked schedule and the precious minutes it took to straighten the too-loose numbers beside his front door for the umpteenth freaking time before leaving for work, he hadn't even been able to visit the bakery that morning. He was missing his daily not-at-all-recommended allowance of caramel-iced buns. Worse, he worried that Athena might need the money he hadn't tipped her. "Contact our office if you have any concerns or questions. After hours, you'll reach our call service, and one of our doctors will get back to you within half an hour."

By *one of our doctors*, he meant . . . himself. Because it should have been Johnny's turn.

Squatting, he tapped the top edge of Felicity's book. When she looked up, he told her, "Thank you for trusting me, and congratulations on having a non-itchy butt, now and in your future."

She grinned at him. "You're silly."

That was news to him. Maybe repeated exposure to Athena was causing unexpected side effects of his own.

When he stood, Ms. Mortenson smiled at him too, then turned to her daughter. "Felicity, it's time to go, sweet pea. Please say goodbye to Dr. Vine."

"Bye, Dr. Itchy Butt!" the little girl shrieked happily, leaping to her feet, and Matthew laughed along with her mother.

Once the duo left for the checkout desk and its promised box of stickers, he did some hasty charting and dedicated the remaining fifteen minutes of his lunch break to a conversation with Yvonna. Before he could walk to her office, though, he heard something . . . odd.

Since one of the CPNPs was married to the local radio station's manager, the staff had collectively agreed to pipe the station throughout the office in a gesture of support, despite its eye-rolling tagline: "W-Triple-X, the only station that can satisfy Harlot's . . . Bay with the *hottest* eighties and nineties hits." During the practice's normal lunch hour, the DJ always took listener requests, which Matthew didn't usually pay much attention to, except . . .

Had he just heard his name?

"—caller didn't identify herself. So if you're listening, Dr. Matthew V, enjoy this next song, dedicated to you by a very secret admirer. Or possibly a very secret troll."

Yacht Rock Dana Block, as the DJ bafflingly chose to call herself, snickered. Then a vaguely familiar tune began to play, and he listened carefully.

Was the song truly dedicated to him? Because he didn't know of any other Dr. Matthew Vs in the Harlot's Bay area, but . . . who would do that? *Why* would they do it? And why had they chosen this song in particular?

The music was undeniably catchy, and the singer's deep voice was pleasing enough. That said, Matthew found the assertion that no other guy would offer the woman in question a full commitment rather insulting. No number of promises about never giving her up, letting her down, running around, deserting her, making her cry, et cetera, et cetera, really compensated for such dismissive rudeness.

He stood just outside his office door and contemplated the matter, entirely mystified, as the song continued to play.

Was the dedication a romantic overture of some sort? And why the reference to trolls? Was this a *Lord of the Rings* thing?

"My condolences on the Rickrolling, dude," Akio said in passing, his lips twitching. He thumped Matthew's shoulder in seeming sympathy before disappearing into an exam room.

Rickrolling? What did that even *mean*?

Did Tolkien have a character named Rick?

Before Matthew could puzzle out the mystery, his phone vibrated in his front pocket. Karl had texted with typical brevity. *Call me.*

That was not a request Karl made often. Or . . . ever, really. Postponing his search for Yvonna yet again and mentally throwing his hands in the air about the whole song-dedication incident, Matthew went back into his office, closed the door, and phoned his friend.

"Had to fire Athena this morning." Karl was blunt, as always, but Matthew could hear the regret through the gruffness. "Charlotte's back. Both women need the money and benefits, but only one of them feeds toddlers. I made my choice. Don't care if you think I was wrong."

Shit. *Shit.*

In typical Karl fashion, the worse he felt about something, the angrier he sounded. But this wasn't their first go-round, or even their twentieth. So Matthew just stretched his clenched jaw, pressed two fingers against the aching spot in his skull, and waited for his friend's defensiveness to ease.

After a minute, Karl added more quietly, "Athena was a good fucking employee, Matthew. Hard worker. Funny. Smart. Good ideas. Wish I could afford to keep both of them." He took a long, deep, audible breath, then another. "When I told her . . ."

Another pause.

"This sort of shit is the worst part of owning my own business. Even worse than all the fucking paperwork." His voice had turned the slightest bit hoarse. "When I told her, she went blank on me. Dead-eyed. Fuck if it wasn't worse than watching her cry. So tell me you've got this, Matthew. Make this shitty morning bearable for me."

Matthew knew that dead-eyed look. Maybe it wouldn't be

gut-wrenching on its own, but after someone had seen her incandescent with curiosity, throwing sparks like a human firecracker with her lively intelligence and humor, the contrast *killed*.

How anyone could spend any length of time around Athena and not adore her, not hurt at the sight of her pain, if only a little, he simply couldn't fathom.

"I'll try my best." The only promise he could make. He didn't lie to his friends either, and how much of his assistance Athena would accept was yet to be determined. "I was already planning to ask Yvonna today if she knew about any job openings."

"Good." Karl cleared his throat. "Athena's finishing out the week, then she's done. Probably won't feel like talking to me before she leaves. Tell her I'm sorry, and from now on, her money's no good here. Free coffee and whatever else she fucking wants, for as long as she fucking wants it."

"She won't take free coffee or food from you, Karl."

Not unless she didn't actually need it. That proud defiance of hers wouldn't let her. Hell, she had to force herself to even accept Matthew's tips. Every time he visited the bakery, she stared at those ATM-crisp bills with both longing *and* loathing whenever she thought he wasn't watching.

"I know she won't," his friend said heavily, then disconnected the call.

For a minute, Matthew simply sat there and kept rubbing his forehead.

Based on what she'd told him, she'd be qualified to work any number of jobs. But she didn't want to substitute or look for a permanent teaching position, and he wouldn't push her to keep climbing through the death zone of her particular mountain. Local libraries and Historic Harlot's Bay were probably her best bets for nearby employers who paid living wages and offered benefits.

Luckily, Yvonna's wife, Jackie, worked at the university library, and her brother Terence guided tour groups at HHB.

Heaving himself up from his desk chair, Matthew trudged down the hall to her office.

They hadn't talked much recently. His fault. The way he'd disregarded her entirely reasonable reservations and pushed her to approve Johnny's honeymoon leave despite the canceled wedding had understandably angered Yvonna. It had also left both their schedules so overpacked, there was no time for idle chitchat or even sharing a table in the lounge as they ate their lunches.

Frankly, though, Matthew hadn't had much time for socializing even before the honeymoon. Not since Johnny had finished his pediatric residency and joined their practice two years ago, and Matthew had begun supervising his younger brother through the first few years of practicing medicine.

Yvonna's door was half open, but he knocked on the frame anyway.

"Come in," she called.

The sun slanting through her office window momentarily blinded him, but as soon as he moved out of the glare, he had to wince at the sight of her.

His best friend was as beautiful as ever, of course. Her hair, dyed rose-gold and cropped close to her scalp, sparkled in the light, and with her bold features and innate sense of style, she'd be gorgeous and glamorous even on her absolute worst day.

She looked damn tired, though. They both knew who deserved the blame for that.

As soon as she glanced up from her laptop, she shook her head at him. "You're lucky I love you, Matthew."

"I know," he said sincerely.

"If I keep working these kinds of hours, Jackie is going to divorce my ass, and you'll be paying the alimony for me, my friend." Drumming her gleaming nails on her marble desktop, she sighed. "The only reason I'm not one-hundred-percent pissed is because I know you're working even harder than I am. You look like death warmed over, allowed to recool and wither in the back of a refrigerator crisper drawer for a year or two, then trotted out in a boring suit and tie from the Brooks Brothers Zombie Collection."

Well, that was vivid.

Unable to quibble with her description of his current state, he glanced down at his clothing. "I can't afford Brooks Brothers. I also prefer to call my suits *classic* rather than *boring*."

"You can prefer whatever you want. Doesn't change the reality of the situation." With a graceful flick of her hand, she invited him into the upholstered armchair across the desk from her. "What do you need, Matthew? I should be charting instead of chatting, and I don't have long before my next appointment."

Even prior to Johnny's lengthy absence, she'd boasted a full roster of patients. Parents adored her clear, confident medical expertise, as well as her easy rapport with the children she treated. And now . . . now she was being run ragged because of responsibilities that should be Matthew's alone, and he hated that. Even as he couldn't quite picture himself having done anything differently.

"I won't keep you." He closed the door behind him but remained standing, mostly because if he sat down he might never get back up. "I just wanted to ask a quick favor."

She arched a single immaculate brow, and it expressed everything. Her curiosity, since he rarely asked for favors from her or anyone. Her disbelief that he was requesting more from her when his decisions were already straining her tolerance and her marriage. Her mute demand for him to cut to the chase already.

"Could you check with Jackie about possible job openings at the library and find out from Terence whether there are positions available at Historic Harlot's Bay?" When she tipped her head in confusion, he clarified, "Not for me, obviously. For Athena. Athena Greydon."

This time, both her brows reached lofty heights. "Athena Greydon, Johnny's ex-fiancée? The woman I met at their engagement party? The woman you had him dump a mere month before their wedding?"

That was *not* how he'd phrase it. Athena wasn't a worn-out ottoman or irreparably stained Tupperware, and she hadn't been carelessly tossed in a junk heap. She simply hadn't been the right woman for his brother, and Johnny had come to realize that with . . . uh, a certain amount of assistance. From Matthew. Repeated assistance.

So they'd cut ties with her. And after that, neither of them had ever checked on her again until she'd moved next door.

Which, dammit, did resemble carelessly tossing her in a junk heap and walking away.

"Yes." No point in defensiveness. He faced ugly truths every day. This was simply another to bear.

"Huh. Athena Greydon." Leaning back in her chair, Yvonna steepled her fingers and pinned him with her sharp brown eyes. "The same woman you mentioned, if only in passing, during every single conversation we had for months after their engagement party."

He scoffed. "That's an exaggeration."

"Sure, Jan."

What the hell was up with this Jan person? He really did need to clarify that.

"Doesn't she live in Virginia?" Yvonna watched him unblinkingly.

"Not anymore," he said. "I'll explain the whole situation some other time, but can you please talk to Jackie and Terence? Athena has her MS in psychology, as well as a graduate degree in teaching. More importantly, she's done children's reference at a public library and checked tickets at a living history museum. She's a hard worker, she desperately needs a paycheck right now, and the situation she's in is partially my fault."

Yvonna drummed her fingertips, still regarding him thoughtfully. "So you want to help her because you feel responsible for her. That's all."

Well, obviously. Given their fraught history, what else could exist between them but responsibility and obligation? His feelings, his dreams, were irrelevant.

"Yes," he said again, and wondered why that basic truth sounded like a lie.

"Hmmm." After studying his face for another few moments, she nodded. "Okay. I'll ask. On one condition."

He didn't hesitate, despite his trepidation. "Name it."

"Tell me what you think of these." She aimed her chin toward one shoulder, then the other, displaying new, sharply delineated lines shaved into the sides of her hair. "I call them my racing stripes."

Oh, thank goodness.

"That's new." He scratched his chin in feigned contemplation. "Do they make you more aerodynamic?"

The pen she threw barely missed his head. When he grinned at her, she grinned back, much to his relief.

She was the only person he'd ever teased. Maybe because they were equals, and his responsibilities toward her—as her friend, as her business partner—were substantial and serious but also finite. He loved her, and he'd work to make her life easier or offer his advice if she wanted to hear it, but he wasn't her brother, her spouse, or her parent.

For two decades now, she'd insisted that he make room in his life for friendship. For fun. For her. So many others had given up on him over the years, frustrated by his solemnity or the way he constantly declined their invitations. But she never had. Never even seemed close to it.

Until recently.

"I've missed you," he told her.

Her posture softened subtly. "I've missed you too. I'll talk to Jackie and Terence tonight about job openings."

"Thank you, Yvonna." He reached for the door handle. "Sorry to bother you. I'll leave you in peace now."

"Matthew?"

"Yes?"

She offered him a rueful, affectionate smile. "I'll forgive you eventually. Probably sooner than I should."

"I hope so," he said, then left before he betrayed the sudden tightness in his throat.

6

The next day, Athena finished her shift at the bakery, grabbed her purse from the back room without quite making eye contact with Karl, and pushed out the front door after saying goodbye to Bez.

Then she stood there on the brick sidewalk, paralyzed by her choices. Unsure where to go next, her granular uncertainty neatly matching her macro-indecisiveness.

She didn't want to head home yet. The cramped, chaotic, half-unpacked confines of the Spite House unsettled and embarrassed her, and she couldn't seem to muster enough energy to tackle the mess. Unfortunately, she had no spare money for a movie ticket or a lingering café meal either, or to go anywhere she'd actually be comfortable.

A not-insignificant part of her longed to drive to her parents' house in Bethesda, huddle beneath the covers of her childhood bed, and let them fix everything for her, but her pride wouldn't allow her. Her shame wouldn't allow her. Matthew's voice saying *at some point, if you're an adult, you have to take responsibility for yourself, and she hasn't* wouldn't allow her.

Surely there was something that still brought her joy or even a smidgen of peace, apart from reading and potato products. Something that made her feel settled. Something *free*.

In the distance, between two buildings, a ripple of blue caught her attention. Roundheel River. It would be a pretty spot on a day like today. The actual water might be brackish and brown, but it reflected the cerulean afternoon sky, and the shoreline breeze would cut through the continuing muggy heat of September.

Good enough.

Idly batting away the flour that dusted the front of her dress, she drifted toward the waterfront. As she turned a corner, a large, old-fashioned wooden ship came into view, bobbing gently and attached by ropes to a pier. One of Historic Harlot's Bay's exhibits, if she remembered correctly. The *Maryland Virago*.

She squinted against the baking sunlight as she wandered closer and studied the masts, the rigging, the schoolchildren being herded along the deck by patient chaperones and costumed interpreters. The kids' excited chatter carried over the water, and she couldn't help but smile. Children that age had so much *energy*.

She wished she could borrow even a little from them. Some days she couldn't remember what it felt like to move through the world without bone-deep exhaustion dogging her every step. Like she was trudging on the surface of Jupiter while everyone else skipped over the Earth's crust instead, bound by less than half the gravity she fought daily.

With a sigh, she flopped down onto a wooden bench near the shore and stretched out her aching legs as she continued examining the *Maryland Virago*. Only to startle at the sound of a politely clearing throat.

Somehow she knew. She knew before she even turned her head.

Beside her sat Dr. Matthew Vine the Third, all dark-shadowed eyes, rumpled hair, and too-sharp cheekbones. The man she couldn't help but watch from her windows at night, even as she ordered herself to look away. The man she told herself she despised, even as she wondered whether that was actually true anymore. The man she'd insulted and secretly needled with petty pranks, even as he was subsidizing her daily existence without asking for a word of gratitude.

The man who'd apologized for his own misdeeds and offered to make amends. The man who'd listened to her so patiently, so attentively from across a moonlit alleyway. The man to whom she'd confessed one of her most raw, painful secrets, trusting him to keep it.

The man who looked every bit as tired as she felt.

She'd already seen him that morning. Two hours after she'd crept through the predawn darkness to his house and halfheartedly nudged his front-door wreath until it hung cockeyed, he'd ordered three dozen peanut butter–iced brownies and dropped two hundred damn dollars into the tip jar. Once he'd left, Bez had held up the bills like sacred relics, wide-eyed, while Athena fought tears of relief and gratitude and humiliation.

She didn't want to fight him anymore. She didn't even want to irritate him with her pranks. Not unless he gave her fresh cause.

"I can leave." His voice barely carried over the gentle lapping of waves against the pier. "My lunch break ends soon anyway."

His voice was careful, his offer thoughtful.

He should really stop making it so easy to forgive him.

She should really get up and walk away before her cesspool of anger and spite drained away entirely, leaving her without even that tainted source of motivation and energy.

"It's fine," she said instead, staring out over the water. "Stay."

He'd gathered his feet beneath him in preparation to stand, but her words froze him in place. After a moment, he settled back onto the bench and extended his legs until they were parallel to hers.

They sat quietly for a while. It was surprisingly comfortable.

Then he turned to face her. His brows drew together when she met his eyes, but it didn't seem like a frown exactly. More . . . an expression of careful thought and consideration. Maybe he too feared saying something that would puncture this fleeting bubble of calm companionship.

Heaven knew, there were a million fraught subjects to avoid. If he asked about money, work, his brother, or even her parents—

"What's Rickrolling?" A thoughtful scratch of his chin produced a faint scraping sound. "Do you know?"

Oh hell. Was he trying to wring a confession out of her? "Why do you ask?"

"Someone dedicated a song to me on the radio yesterday, and my colleague mentioned Rickrolling. Whatever that is." His tie fluttered in a gentle gust of wind, and he smoothed the silky fabric down with an absent hand. "Who's Rick? Is he a hobbit?"

A . . . hobbit? What the Tolkien fuck was he talking about?

"No," she said slowly. "Rick Astley is not a hobbit. I mean, I don't know his life. Maybe he is in fact inhabiting a hobbit-hole in the Shire, eating elevenses, and trying to dodge troublemaking wizards. But probably not."

"He's a real person?"

She nodded. "A pop star from the 1980s, most famous—some would say infamous—for the song you heard yesterday."

The lines above his eyebrows deepened. "Why infamous?"

"Because a few years back, people"—uncomfortable, regretful people, in this particular instance—"began pranking each other using his song, probably because it's so instantly recognizable and such an incredible earworm." At his look of incomprehension, she explained, "It sticks in your head once you hear it, and you can't get rid of it unless you listen to, say, 'Tubthumping' by Chumbawamba on repeat."

He opened his mouth, then closed it again, clearly deciding to let that one go. "So dedicating the song to me was a joke rather than a declaration of romantic interest?"

She almost choked. "Trust me, Matthew. It was *not* a declaration of romantic interest."

"Huh." His face tipped to the sky, and his near-black eyelashes dusted those stunning cheekbones as he closed his eyes against the glare. "In that case, one of my coworkers probably called in the dedication."

"I'm sure somebody just wanted to"—*give you a hard time for increasingly unclear reasons*—"make you laugh and assumed you knew what Rickrolling was."

"Thank you for explaining. I'm glad it wasn't a romantic overture," he said after a moment, "especially given the offensive lyrics."

Sheesh. How puritanical did someone have to be to find "Never Gonna Give You Up," of all songs, objectionable? Shouldn't a person that easily offended by innocuous pop culture be busy growing a chest-length beard and churning butter somewhere amidst his beet fields, rather than living in *Harlot's Bay*, of all places?

Jeez, he was *such* a judgy asshole.

As he settled back against the bench, eyes still closed, familiar resentment and wounded pride began gathering within her like roiling storm clouds. And then . . .

Then they dissipated, bit by bit, broken apart by the gentle breeze of a peaceful, sunlit day. Warmth and light baked into her bones, momentarily banishing all the chilly darkness she seemed to carry within her these days.

"Offensive in what way?" she heard herself ask calmly.

His eyes opened, bright with intelligence and conviction as they met hers.

"He's making his case for a romantic relationship with someone, right?" That was evidently a rhetorical question, as he continued without waiting for an answer. "Let's assume a woman. But basically the first thing he says is that no *other* guy would fully commit to her. He's arguing that she has no other choice but him if she wants a loyal partner. Which is controlling and enormously insulting and . . . yes, *offensive*."

If she'd ever considered the lyrics that closely, she'd have thought the exact same thing.

Holy crap. He was . . . right?

"A man who'd say that to a woman he claims to care about might not run around or desert her, but he *will* let her down and hurt her." He shook his head, lips thin with disapproval. "Which is why I'm especially relieved the song wasn't a romantic overture, even apart from the main issue."

Angling her knees toward Matthew, she studied him curiously. "Which is . . . ?"

The world's smallest, quietest sigh escaped him. "The only adults I really talk to are my coworkers and my patients' parents, none of whom interest me that way and none of whom I'd feel free to date even if they *did* interest me that way."

She was about to be egregiously nosy and ask whether he dated at all, ever, when she noticed just how pink the tips of his ears had become. Never mind, then. She wouldn't embarrass him, no matter how much she suddenly wanted the answer to that particular question.

"I agree with your analysis of the lyrics." What she'd identified as lofty disdain on his part was instead justifiable outrage, and what a relief that she didn't have to hate him again. "That line is definitely negging, which is always gross."

Before he could ask, she clarified. "*Negging* is insulting someone so they'll be more receptive to, uh, romantic overtures."

He looked lost. "Why would an insult make anyone more receptive?"

"When your self-confidence is shot, you sometimes forget you could do better."

His nose wrinkled. "That *is* gross."

"Yep. Really, really gross." Off in the distance, the telltale arch of Abbott Island Bridge rose high above the water, only to disappear into the afternoon haze. Which reminded her . . . "You know, if I were Abbott Island, I'd continually bitch to the river about how boring my name was in comparison to Harlot's Bay and how I should have been called something else instead. Something more interesting. More salacious." She paused to consider the many delightful alternatives. "Like Floozy Atoll or—"

"Dubious Virtue Shoals," he offered with twitching lips.

She snickered, surprised and pleased. "Slattern Sands."

"That's No Lady, That's My Island."

"Just a Little Bit Trampy Shores."

He laughed outright then, and the stark beauty of his humor-lit face squeezed her heart like a fist. It blanked her brain. If she'd intended to give another alternative island name, she couldn't remember it now.

She couldn't remember much of anything. Certainly not why she disliked him.

As she tried to gather her scattered wits, he spoke again. "What have you been researching with Professor Google lately?"

"Oh, come on." She huffed out a little half laugh. "You don't really want to hear about all the random shit I've been looking up at night, Matthew. Not again."

His mouth curved sweetly. "Try me."

"Um . . . okay." Her cheeks hotter than the September sun, she fixed her gaze to the tall ship gently undulating atop the waves. "Let the record show that you asked for it."

Out of the corner of her eye, she saw him jot an invisible addendum on an invisible memo using an invisible pen. "So noted."

The gesture was so unexpectedly *playful*, she couldn't help but smile too.

Fine, then. Where to start?

"No entirely hairless big cats exist." Turning toward him on the bench, she rested her elbow on its back. "If you want a naked feline, only domesticated kitties need apply. Specifically, the sphynx breed or various Russian hairless breeds. And much to my shock . . ."

She paused for dramatic effect.

He grinned at her, and she could have sworn the sun shone brighter. "Yes?"

"Hairless breeds aren't necessarily hypoallergenic, because people are allergic to a protein found in feline saliva and sebaceous glands, rather than cat hair itself." When he simply nodded instead of seeming surprised, she frowned at him. "Wait. Did you already know that?"

He waggled his hand, palm down, in a *sort of* gesture. "The origin of cat allergies I already understood, because it intersects with my job. The rest I didn't know." After pondering the matter for a moment, he tipped his head to the side and pondered her instead. "What made you research that particular topic?"

"I live in a spite house," she began.

His voice was bone dry. "I'd noticed."

"Smartass." She flicked his forearm lightly, doing her best not to stare at the taut muscles shifting beneath that pale, hair-dusted skin. "Anyway, it seemed to me that the owner of a spite house should spend a good portion of her time arrayed upon a settee, cackling delightedly at the discomfiture of her enemies whilst stroking a hairless feline. Preferably a leopard or tiger, if at all possible, for maximum badassery."

The man really shouldn't roll his sleeves up to his elbows. It gave him an unfair advantage over those susceptible to forearm porn, of which she was evidently one.

He traced a fingertip over the spot where she'd flicked him. "But then you wondered whether hairless leopards and tigers actually existed, consulted Professor Google, and went down the hairless cat rabbit hole."

She snorted. "That was an unnecessarily confusing choice of idioms, Vine."

"My apologies, Greydon." The warm amusement in his voice was liquid honey, so soothing and sweet she wanted to guzzle it by the gallon. "Out of curiosity, *do* you spend a good portion of your time cackling on a settee? Even without a hairless kitty to stroke?"

Wow. Just that quickly, her mind dropped into the gutter.

"I, uh, don't have a settee." *Don't say it, Athena. Don't—* "No comment on whether or not I regularly stroke my kitty. Also whether that kitty's hairless."

Dammit.

"Um . . ." The tips of his ears abruptly pinkened again, and he cleared his throat once. Twice. "What—what other topics have you researched?"

When he shifted to face her more directly, the brush of their knees might have been the flick of a match against an abrasive strip. Instant flame.

He didn't pull away.

Neither did she.

"You know what plasma globes are?" When he nodded, she said, "If you break one——"

An insistent beeping began.

He squeezed his eyes shut, then reached for his cell. A single tap silenced the alarm.

Slowly, tiredly, he rose to his feet. "I'm sorry. I need to get back to the office before my next appointment."

"I understand." As she stared out over the water, gravity returned. Doubled. She was back on Jupiter, and it was a lonely, lonely place to be. "Take care of yourself, Matthew."

To her surprise, she even meant it.

"Athena . . ." He stood directly in front of her, waiting to continue until she met his eyes again. "Karl is an old friend of mine. He's genuinely sorry to let you go."

Of *course* he knew Karl. Of *course* he knew she'd been fired from her minimum-wage job after less than a month. Jeez, that wasn't humiliating at *all*.

"If another position opens up, you'll be first on his list. Also, he asked me to tell you . . ." Matthew exhaled audibly. "Coffee and baked goods are on the house from now on."

When she opened her mouth, he held up a hand. "I already told him not to hold his breath waiting for you to take advantage of the offer."

If he knew that much about her, he couldn't think she was a *total* leech, right? She supposed that was a small victory. "Thank you."

"I, uh . . ." He shoved his hands in his pockets, expression grave once more. "I have a feeling something will turn up for you soon, Athena. Don't lose heart."

Then he walked away, leaving her alone once more on a distant, cold planet.

As it happened, something *did* turn up for her soon. Only forty-eight hours after Matthew made that prediction, a two-week temp position at the college library fell into Athena's lap like Newton's famous apple, and she didn't quite understand how or why.

It wasn't just her imagination, though. The head of circulation at the Eleanor M. Abbott Library and Archives really did call her out of seeming nowhere and ask if she was available to work the latter half of September. Whereupon she simply stared at her cell, because . . . huh? She'd never even *applied* for a position at the library. There'd been no openings publicly listed.

Was this a small-town thing? Did a new resident's job history and current need for work seep into the groundwater somehow or become known through a type of weird, effortless community osmosis? Had sweet Bez or fake curmudgeon Karl put out a good word for her?

Did it matter?

No. No, it did not.

"Oh, I'm available," she assured Bunny, the head of circ. "Just tell me where to be and when."

Now here she was, back at work after only a week of joblessness. It wasn't optimal, to be honest. Two weeks' pay without benefits wouldn't keep her solvent for long, and scanning and shelving books didn't exactly thrill her. She missed Bez, the smell of fresh bread, and even Karl's homicidal scowls. She missed her tip money, however humiliating she'd found Matthew's near-daily contributions to that fund. She missed the dulcet tones of Sadie Brazen's audiobook narrator and wondered what had become of that exceedingly open-minded, open-legged young woman and her sexy guppy-man from *Desire, Unfiltered*.

All that said, she was so relieved to have even short-term work that she could cry. She *had* cried, after getting off the phone with Bunny. And maybe, if she showed them what an asset she could be to their library, they might think of her for future, more permanent openings.

Shelving might not require much thought, but it was fine. Kind of soothing, actually.

After she'd slid a few books into their rightful places in the stacks, she spotted an Ann Rule paperback tucked neatly beside *The Joy of Sex*. Which was confusing, since true crime belonged in the 300s, not the 600s. Was this a sympathetic message from the universe? Because, truly, her distinct lack of recent dick—guppy-man or otherwise—*was* criminal.

"Athena! There you are!"

When she turned around, two people stood before her, both of whom she unexpectedly recognized. Victoria, tall and elegant and more Audrey-esque than ever. Jackie, curvy and lovely, her brown eyes warm behind her glasses.

Both women were smiling at her with such sweet sincerity, Athena almost wept again as she waved hello.

"I'd heard you were working with us for a few days, and I was so excited." Victoria's pixie hair shone in the sun streaming through a window. "I wish you were assigned to the reference department instead of circ, though. I wanted to hear your tips on escaping the Beast and/or a mob of pitchfork-wielding villagers."

Jackie slowly turned to stare up at her coworker.

"Anyway, great to see you again." Victoria pointed to her companion. "This is Jackie Wells, who works in the library archives.

She's married to Yvonna Green, Matthew Vine's best friend and the co-owner of their medical practice. FYI, she knows you were introduced to her before, but she figures you saw a lot of new faces that night and might not remember."

There was no escaping the man. When they were both home, Athena couldn't stop obsessing over his brooding presence through their windows; during her time at the bakery, he'd bought a truckload of pastries made by his good friend Karl virtually every day; the one time she'd gone wandering to the waterfront, she'd found him waiting for her; and now he evidently had close ties to at least two of her new coworkers.

Yeesh. For such a quiet man, Dr. Matthew Vine the Third certainly got around.

"Hi, Athena." Jackie's grip was cool and firm. "Wonderful to meet you a second time. How are you doing? Are you settling in well?"

"I'm fine. Fantastic, actually," she lied.

Victoria's gaze landed on something over Athena's shoulder, and she winced. "Bunny's giving us the evil eye, so we'd better let you shelve in peace. Can you come by the second-floor reference desk on your break, though? We have an invitation for you."

Then the two women swept off to . . . wherever they were going, and Athena was left wondering what her first-ever Harlot's Bay invitation would involve. A session at the local escape room? Drinks at a bar? What did librarians do for fun around here?

Two hours later, she discovered the answer: Apparently, much like Karl, they read about monster-fucking.

It was her fault. Or maybe her greatest triumph? Either way, when she got invited to an upcoming meeting of Victoria and

Jackie's very specific, very delightful book club and Victoria asked for suggestions as to the theme, only one answer seemed right.

"There's satyr dick." Athena began ticking off some of the many possibilities, speaking as quietly as possible. "Lake-monster dick. Dragon-alien-creature dick. Spider-dude dick. Mothman dick. Minotaur dick. Frankenstein-y dick. Orc dick. Kraken . . . uh, dick-tacles."

Victoria snickered softly.

"There are lots of sapphic monster-fucking options too, especially if you're into Gorgons, banshees, or demonesses," Athena continued. "We can find monster-fucking for any and all preferences. Consider that my solemn promise to you."

By that point, something of a crowd had gathered around the reference desk. All coworkers, and all members of the Nasty Wenches book club, which exclusively read erotic romance and was in no way officially sanctioned by or affiliated with the library.

Harlot's Bay was truly, spectacularly living up to its name.

"That's an interesting suggestion," Jackie said slowly. "Huh."

According to Bethany, a timid-looking, fiftysomething white woman from circ, all previous book club picks had featured humans. Clearly, it was time to spread their metaphorical wings and read about monsters spreading *other* things. Notably, legs. But also sometimes actual wings, depending on the creatures involved. Either way, spreading was occurring, and Athena was assisting with said spreading.

Unless . . . dammit. "I'm sorry if I offended anyone."

Victoria's brow crinkled. "Why would we be offended?"

"Because of my language." Her apologetic grimace hurt her

face. "Or, just for example, my suggestion of monster-fucking as a book club theme."

Jackie rolled her eyes. "We belong to an erotic-romance-reading book club and call ourselves the Nasty Wenches. We're not easily offended."

"Gargoyle dick," Bethany whispered, straightening her cardigan and smoothing her flowered dress. "Don't forget about gargoyle dick."

Athena sagged in relief.

"May I invite Bez and Karl from the bakery?" She didn't want to overstep. That said, she had pretty solid evidence both her former coworkers would appreciate the meeting's theme. "I know you're the Nasty Wenches and Karl is a guy, but . . ."

As she'd spoken, a quiet explosion of mirth had occurred among the librarians.

"All genders are welcome in the book club." Jackie's voice quivered with hilarity, but her tone brooked no opposition.

"Of course Bez and Karl can both come, but . . ." Victoria paused, then choked out, "You want Karl . . . to socialize?"

Bethany had visibly perked up. "Is he the big guy from the bakery? If so, he makes the most delicious muffins. Maybe he could bring some as his chosen snack."

"He is indeed." Athena couldn't resist. "Bethany, do you know the muffin man?"

Victoria didn't hesitate. "The muffin man?"

"The muffin man," Athena affirmed.

"Yes, I know the muffin man." Bethany snickered, and her glee transformed her entire face. "He lives on Harridan Lane. Or his store does, anyway."

More hushed laughter led to more discreet shushing among the group.

After one last giggle, Athena got back on topic. "I think I could get Karl to come. I mean, maybe he wouldn't be comfortable with *every* meeting's theme, but—"

"Oh, themes aren't the problem." Victoria's graceful hand wave dismissed that concern. "The problem is that he's a cranky-ass hermit, and if you can persuade him to attend our meeting, I'll . . . what will I do, Jackie?"

"Buy her dinner and drinks at the pub." Jackie tipped her head as she considered further. "And I'll treat her to a café lunch. Or maybe we can hit the tearoom? Those little scones and triangular sandwiches are fucking delicious."

"All right, wenches. Enough chitchat. We have incoming." Victoria raised her hand to get their attention and spoke softly. "Monster-fucking as the chosen theme. All in favor, say aye."

"Aye," the book club members whispered in unison, before scattering to their separate departments as a college student approached the reference desk.

Once again, Athena was left blinking after them. Then, after checking the time on her phone, she hurried back down the stairs to retrieve another shelving cart.

By the end of her shift, she'd neatly placed an untold number of books in their correct slots, washed her hands at least ten times after encountering mysterious sticky and/or slippery substances on book-drop items, and acquired a good half dozen possible friends-to-be.

Not bad for a day's work.

Whatever had led to this job—Karl or Bez's intervention;

small-town gossip; whatever, she didn't care—she was grateful. So very grateful.

For her future paycheck.

For her new acquaintances.

For the Ann Rule paperback she planned to read tonight.

For another day where she didn't have to think about what came next.

SCRUBBING A HAND over his face, Matthew sat up in bed and attempted to stay awake as Johnny described his amazing Hawaiian adventures, his delicious Hawaiian meals, the breathtaking Hawaiian scenery, and the humbling warmth of Hawaiian hospitality.

Matthew wanted to know how his brother was doing. Really, he did, but *fuck*. Fuck, he was so tired. Envious too. But mostly tired.

And then, all at once, alertness was no longer an issue.

"Matty, I . . . I'd like to stay here two more weeks, if at all possible," Johnny told him without any sort of preamble. "Until the end of the month."

Earlier that evening, Matthew had read up on techniques to help him stop clenching his jaw. According to his research, if he said one particular letter aloud, it would keep the top and bottom teeth from touching and, as one website headline put it, PREVENT THE CLENCH.

He had a feeling this conversation was going to be brought to him by the letter *N*.

"That"—he took a moment to mouth *nine* silently—"would mean a lot of extra work for everyone at the practice. The front-desk staff would have to reschedule your appointments for the rest of September and handle angry parents. Yvonna, the CPNPs, and I would have to deal with your patients, your on-call shifts, your nursery visits, and everything else you were scheduled to do, when we've already been struggling to cover for your original absence."

Ninny. Nein. Ninnifer.

"I know, I know. I'm sorry. It's just . . ." Johnny was apparently on the move. In the background, there was now a *whoosh* of wind and the rhythmic crash of waves to fill his hesitation. "I don't think I realized, Matty."

Why were his brother's words so small? So unsure? "Realized what?"

Automatically, Dad Voice had emerged from his own throat. Gentle and calm, but authoritative too, so Johnny would believe Matthew could handle whatever the issue was. Even if Matthew himself didn't believe it.

The water sounded much closer now, as if Johnny were wading in the surf. "Athena organized the entire honeymoon. Did you know that?"

"No," Matthew said flatly.

Non. Nonna. Nano. Nanny.

Suddenly restless, he threw back the sheet, left his bedroom, and closed the door behind him to preserve the coolness from his window AC unit. Then, without thinking too closely about where he was going or why, he climbed the stairs and wandered into his third-floor home office.

It was dark, of course. And although he hated the dark, he kept the room unlit before looking through the open window at . . . another dark, open window.

Athena's evenings usually ended in her library nook, but maybe she was asleep already. She should be.

"She researched for months," Johnny told him. "She found us hotels that weren't too expensive but put us right next to the beach.

She booked our flights, made restaurant reservations, rented cars, and flagged all the sights she'd wanted to visit for two decades, ever since her parents came back from a conference on Oahu and showed her photos of their trip."

Matthew had no doubt she'd planned the hell out of that honeymoon. Athena didn't seem to do anything by half measures.

"She wanted a vacation so badly. She needed time off, because she worked herself to the bone in that school. Longer hours than we work, even, and for way less pay." Johnny paused. "I told her I'd . . ."

He trailed off with a weird sort of choking sound, but it didn't matter. Athena had already filled in the rest of the sentence for Matthew. Johnny had told her he'd support them both while she recovered from burnout and found a livable path forward. The promise hadn't stopped him from leaving her broke and jobless and never looking back. With Matthew's unwitting encouragement.

Any words Matthew spoke would hurt both of them, so he said nothing for a long time. He simply mouthed *nana* to himself over and over again and rubbed his forehead.

After a minute or two, the squawk of an oceangoing bird pierced the silence between them, and Matthew took that as his cue. Because maybe he didn't need to hear it, but Johnny needed to say it. To face it.

He prompted, "You told her you'd . . ."

"Never mind." The gentle crashing of waves almost drowned out Johnny's quiet sigh. "I stood on a mountaintop the day after I arrived and watched the sun rise, and it was . . . otherworldly. Indescribably stunning. That Haleakalā tour was probably the thing on Maui she was most excited to do. Whenever she'd talk about it, she'd get giddy."

Giddy. He'd like to see Athena giddy someday.

It wasn't ever going to happen. Not with him anywhere nearby.

"It's like the surface of Mars up there, and she could have told me why. Because she's curious and Googles everything, and because . . ." Johnny's breath audibly hitched. "This was her dream. You paid for our trip, but she planned every bit of it. She needed it. And I took it. I took her dream. I realize that now."

Matthew bowed his head, his own throat tight, and marveled. This was the most self-reflection his brother had ever done. The most ruthlessly honest he'd been with and about himself. And if something in Hawaii was helping him face facts at long last . . .

"I know it's asking a lot, Matty, and I'm so sorry." Johnny sounded entirely sincere. "But I need more time to figure out what I've done and what I need to do next, and it's easier to think here, away from . . . everything."

What I need to do next. About work? About Athena?

Because there was nothing more Johnny could do for or about his ex-fiancée. She wouldn't take him back even if he begged, and she wouldn't accept money from him either. As far as work . . . well, there was definitely room for improvement on Johnny's end. And if two more weeks helped cement whatever self-awareness he'd achieved, maybe approving the leave might be worth the hassle. It might even be worth pissing off his best friend yet again.

Nunnery, nan, nin.

"I'll share your request with Yvonna tomorrow, and I'll do my best to advocate for the extra time away," Matthew said wearily.

"Thank you. Really." A long pause. "Um . . . how's Athena doing? Have you had the chance to talk to her again?"

He frowned at his phone. "Not recently."

Across the alleyway, the woman in question appeared as if summoned.

The third-floor light came on and illuminated her approach. Easily visible through the two sets of open windows, she collapsed into the embrace of her library nook's oversized chair. When she yawned and stretched, her thin tank top stretched across her breasts, and those loose boxers rode up on her charmingly dimpled thighs. Stretching accomplished, she produced a paperback with a black and red cover and curled into a comfortable little ball.

He could see the outline of her nipples.

It wasn't right to sit here in the dark and covet his brother's ex-fiancée, much less spy on her like a creep. He forced himself to look away and think about something other than soft breasts. Other than velvety areolae, drawing up tight beneath his tongue.

Desperate, he stared down blankly at his phone, then registered the time.

She was definitely up too late, given how early a morning she'd had. Luckily, though, her first shift at the library seemed to have gone well. According to Yvonna—who'd received a midday report from Jackie—Athena had fit in like a lifelong employee.

"I don't understand, Matthew. Why won't you let Jackie tell her your role in all this?" Yvonna had asked that afternoon. "Doesn't Athena deserve to know? Don't you *want* her to know?"

He'd sighed. "She despises me, Yvonna. If she'd known I helped find her the job, she might not have taken it. If she found out now, she might still quit."

"That's one possibility. Here's another: If she knew you'd helped, she might no longer despise you."

Shit, that would be . . . miraculous. Enough to make him fall to his knees in gratitude to an unexpectedly kind universe.

But the universe wasn't kind to anyone, in his admittedly non-comprehensive experience. At best, it was indifferent and chaotic, controlled by chance and forces still only dimly, incompletely understood by humankind. Which was why it required such careful, unceasing attention to stave off potential disaster.

People were kind. Or they could be, anyway. That had to be enough.

"Hmmm," he'd said, unwilling to argue with his best friend.

She'd left his office shortly thereafter. Which was something he hadn't done himself until almost nine that evening, given the patients he'd seen after normal business hours. Johnny's patients, for whom there'd been no room in the schedule. Until Matthew made room.

After a hasty dinner eaten at the kitchen counter, he'd showered, pulled on some pajama bottoms, and headed for bed. He'd fallen asleep.

Then Johnny had called.

Called and shared the amount of thought he'd been devoting to his ex-fiancée. *Lots* of thought. More thought than he'd given her during their actual engagement.

And now he was asking about her. Again.

Was this evidence of newfound emotional maturity, or something else entirely?

Ninny-ninny-ninny-ninny-fucking-ninny.

"How does she seem?" Johnny persisted. "Happy? Lonely?"

All at once, Matthew's last dregs of patience evaporated.

He slammed his office window shut, stalked into the hallway, and kicked the door closed behind him before speaking.

"I'm neither Athena's friend nor her confidant." Dad Voice had left the building, replaced by a near snarl Matthew didn't even recognize. "If you're so eager to know what she wants or how she feels, ask her yourself once you're home. Assuming she'll talk to you, which she *won't*."

Several seconds of absolute silence seemed more like a year.

Dammit. What was wrong with him?

"It's after midnight there, isn't it?" His brother didn't sound offended. More . . . regretful, surprisingly. "You're exhausted from covering for me, and you were sleeping when I called. I didn't even think about it. I'm sorry. Again."

Yes, that was it. The best explanation for Matthew's outburst. Exhaustion.

Johnny gave a little half laugh. "I seem to be apologizing a lot today."

"I owe you an apology too," Matthew forced himself to say. "Sorry for snapping at you."

A few strained pleasantries later, and they said goodbye. For a while, Matthew simply stood in the hallway with everything in his body clenched tight. His fists. His gut. His jaw too, because no number of *ninnies-nanas-nunneries* would suffice at this moment.

Then, already knowing what he'd find, Matthew opened the door and went back into his office. From across the alleyway, the library nook had gone dark once more. Her window was shut for the first time since she'd moved into the Spite House.

Athena was gone.

7

Matthew attended the college library's book sale every year. Teeming with endless piles of paperbacks, hardbacks, and even audiobooks—some donated, some culled from the collection—the event was a great fundraiser for the institution. It was also a key source of board, picture, and chapter books for his practice's exam rooms and waiting area.

Thus, he hadn't driven to the Ladywright College campus in hopes of seeing Athena on her last day at the library, and he certainly wouldn't skip the sale to avoid her either.

Her presence was immaterial.

Yet somehow, despite the crowds picking over the sale tables like bibliophilic vultures, Athena was the first person he noticed when he pushed open the heavy entrance door.

An elderly woman had amassed a huge pile of books, and Athena was transferring them into a red plastic basket. After positioning the chunky handles in the crook of her left elbow, she offered her right to the frail patron as a means of support. Together, the woman's hand clutching Athena's arm, they slowly walked toward the nearest cash register.

She wore scarlet lipstick and her distinctive cat-eye glasses. He would have recognized that honey-gold hair and that hip-twitching walk from across a sold-out stadium. From a mile away. A continent.

In an easy movement, she swung the heavy basket atop one of the checkout tables and gently patted the elderly patron's hand.

Smiling, she made sure the woman could fully support herself on the sturdy wooden table, then walked to a nearby shelving cart.

Athena was alone for the moment. She was also a librarian, however temporarily, and he was a patron, was he not? If he had questions—and he did, very valid and pertinent questions—he should ask her. All the other employees were so busy. Too busy to help him.

And maybe, while he was discussing various official library matters with her, he could also mention one other concern. Not that it had been, say, interfering with his sleep or anything, but as long as he was already talking to her, why not?

Since that night when Johnny had called to ask for more time in Hawaii, he hadn't seen her reading in her library nook even once. In fact, that window, and only that one window, had remained shut ever since, its shade drawn down.

That couldn't be an accidental oversight. No, that was a *statement*, and he knew why she was making it. His proximity and attention had made her uneasy, and now she was avoiding one of her favorite spots in her own home. But if someone's window needed to be closed and covered, it should be his, not hers. And so he'd tell her, without further delay.

As soon as she noticed his approach and began to look up at him, he blurted out the words, because if she gave him that wide rictus smile again, it might kill him.

"I'm sorry." In his agitation, he scrubbed a hand through his hair, and it was probably sticking up in clumps now. So be it. "I promise I didn't intend to make you uncomfortable. I can keep my window shut and the shade down in my office from now on, and you can keep using your library nook in peace."

She simply stood there looking at him with her brow crinkled.

He tried to pat his hair back into place while he waited for her response but was pretty sure he only made things worse.

"I . . ." She rolled her glossy lips between her teeth for a moment. "I wasn't making *you* uncomfortable?"

He frowned at her. "No. Of course not. Why would you think that?"

"I don't know, Matthew." Her small hands settled on her hips. "Maybe because the last time I tried to read in the nook, you immediately slammed your window shut and left your office?"

"Oh." Huh. That did seem like a plausible interpretation of events, assuming she considered him an asshat. Which she did, so . . .

She tapped her tennis-shoe-clad toe. "I wasn't even making any noise, so your abrupt departure seemed like a pretty clear indication I was bothering you with my *mere presence*."

Fuck, why did everything always go so horribly, horribly wrong with her?

"That wasn't why I shut the window and left." He sighed, rocking back on his heels. "I had a phone call, and I didn't want to disturb you."

. . . or talk to my brother about you as you listened to the entire conversation. Which would have been spectacularly awkward. Even more awkward than our present conversation, if you can believe it.

Her doubtful expression lingered. "It doesn't bother you when I read in my chair?"

"Athena." He bent down close, held her stare, and spoke firmly. "You can do literally anything you want in that chair, and it won't bother me."

A tide of pink color washed from her sweetheart neckline up to her neck and cheeks, and he wanted to trace its path. Lick it.

"Um . . ." Her scarlet lips quirked. "That sounds like a dare."

Oh, heaven help him. Now he was imagining her in the damn chair, doing things he hadn't ever previously contemplated— filthy, *filthy* things—and there was no unringing that particular bell. Every time it rang again, every time he saw that chair from now on, he'd salivate like one of Pavlov's famous dogs. He'd *sweat*.

He tugged at the collar of his tee. "It wasn't a dare. Trust me on that."

"So you thought I closed the window because you were bothering *me*?" She sounded amused by his interpretation of events, but it really wasn't any more absurd than hers.

He nodded. Then remembered the ostensible reason he'd sought her out.

According to Jackie, via Yvonna, Athena's final shift in the circulation department ended at three that afternoon. She should, co-incidentally enough, be getting off work just about the same time he was leaving the library—but only if he started scanning the sale offerings now.

He scratched his freshly shaven chin. "Um, could you show me the tables with children's books? I want to buy some for my practice."

"Turn around." Her dry tone told him precisely what he would see.

He sighed and didn't bother looking. "It's the section directly behind me, isn't it? Literally five feet from where I'm standing."

"Mmm-hmm."

If that tip of her lips was a smirk, it contained more friendliness and true amusement than her previous iterations of the expression. He would almost say her eyes were sparkling with humor, but . . . well, her glasses had become sadly smudged, so he couldn't confirm that.

An easily fixable problem at last. *Huzzah*, as they exclaimed at Historic Harlot's Bay.

"Here," he said. "Let me . . ."

Carefully, using both hands, he removed the frames from her face while she stood motionless, hazel eyes wide and bewildered. The cleaning cloth he used for his sunglasses was back in his car, so he huffed out a breath to fog one of the lenses, lifted the hem of his tee—clean and soft, so he wouldn't scratch anything—and polished that lens, then repeated the process for the other side.

He studied her face as he rubbed away the smudges. Studied her face and worried.

Her cheerful dress and bold, playful makeup might silently inform onlookers, *I'm confident. I'm happy. Would a sad woman wear winged eyeliner and scarlet lipstick? I think not.* But even the world's brightest red lipstick wouldn't be enough to light the shadows in and under her eyes, shadows now readily visible without her glasses on.

He almost wished she still seemed angry. Her anger, however uncomfortable, at least gave her a temporary hard shell. Without it—under it—she was soft. So incredibly, alluringly soft. Since her move to Harlot's Bay, he'd been chasing that remembered softness with every conversation they had, willing it to the surface with compulsive fervor, for reasons he preferred not to contemplate too closely.

Unprotected, though, she was much too easily injured. And he didn't think she could afford another wound right now.

Put the strongest substance in the world—graphene, a sort of lattice of carbon atoms; she'd inspired him to keep a list of his own random questions to research at night—under enough pressure, and it broke. How much more pressure could Athena survive intact? How much of that pressure could he divert or bear for her, with or without her knowledge?

A quick check against the overhead light revealed one last smudge he'd missed, so he kept fussing over that bit. Her gaze dropped to where he'd raised his tee's hem and lingered there, maybe to check whether he was being sufficiently cautious with her lenses. Once he'd finished the job to his satisfaction, he again used both hands to lightly settle her glasses back onto the bridge of her nose. The temple pieces slid easily into the fine hair above her ears. Except . . . one strand got caught, so he teased it free with a gentle fingertip.

A tiny pulse at her temple throbbed, and a rosy flush tinted her cheeks once more, warming her skin. He wanted to chase the heat with a stroke of his thumb or the press of his mouth.

Reluctantly, he dropped his hands and stepped back.

The tip of her tongue wetted her lips as she stared at him, and he started babbling, because it was either that or kissing her, and only one of those things was a conceivable option for him, now or ever.

"The other place I get books for my exam rooms is the local used bookstore. Have you been there yet?" Without waiting for an answer, he kept rambling. "It's called Bluestocking, and it has a pretty good children's section. The grandfather of one of my patients is the owner. He has an emotional support chicken he keeps in the store."

Behind her glasses, her slightly magnified eyelashes fluttered as she blinked.

"An . . . emotional support chicken?"

"Yes. She's a second-generation ESC, so Hill calls her Roberta Downy Jr."

"Downy?" she repeated slowly.

He knew she'd appreciate that. "Downy. Without the *e*."

"I see." She ducked her head, her shoulders trembling. "Well played."

A heady rush of pride expanded his chest.

He'd made her laugh. Humorless, too-solemn Dr. Matthew Vine the Third had made this complicated, spectacular, troubled woman *laugh*.

And somehow, words were still tumbling from his disobedient mouth.

"I was planning to go to the bookstore after I left the library sale," he heard himself tell her. "It's open until five on Saturdays, and Hill would let you pet Roberta. Care to join me?"

Where had his vaunted self-control gone? His ability to bite back words he didn't wish to say aloud? Because his invitation was a damned stupid idea. The last thing he needed was the temptation of her continued proximity, especially when everything about her already preoccupied him far too much.

Luckily, though, there was no way in hell she'd ever say—

"Yes." She looked as shocked as he felt. Still, she didn't take it back.

"Yes?" He needed confirmation, because maybe lack of sleep finally had him hallucinating. "You'll come with me to the bookstore?"

She bit her lip before nodding. "I'm done here at three. Let's meet in the alleyway between our houses at half past. Does that work for you?"

"It does," he told her, then fled to the sale tables before either of them could come to their senses.

BLUESTOCKING HADN'T CHANGED much from Matthew's visit last month. If anything, it had deteriorated further. The shelves sagged in the middle, the books all had cracked spines, and most attempts at alphabetization within genre had apparently ceased.

On the shelf beside him, Sadie Brazen's *My Mothman, My Mate* had been placed next to a Nora Roberts book, and it was making him twitch. But he understood why it had happened.

Being unexpectedly thrust into the role of full-time caretaker-grandpa had taken every ounce of Hill's energy and strength. With his entire heart devoted to his beloved, grieving granddaughter Lily, he didn't have much left for the store.

Thus the dust on the shelves. Thus his emotional support chicken.

Not that Athena had noticed dust or cracked spines or probably even the presence of books or shelves. No, her entire focus remained on Roberta. Who, Matthew had to note, somehow resembled a miniature llama more than ever today.

"As you can tell from her plumage, her blue earlobes, and her five-toed feet, Roberta's a silkie," Hill was telling Athena, his absurdly fluffy white chicken nestled against his thin chest. "They're the calmest, friendliest chickens around."

"She may be a silkie, but she looks like a dang Muppet," countered Athena with a laugh. "How many toes do most chickens have? And do her feathers live up to her breed name?"

His palm smoothed lovingly down Roberta's back. "Four. And as far as her feathers, feel for yourself."

Roberta's wings shifted a little as Hill transferred her into Athena's waiting arms, but otherwise . . . no reaction. Good. Still, Matthew hovered nearby, ready to spring into action if any agitated pecking might occur. At least Athena's glasses would protect her eyes, should the worst happen and Roberta take a turn for the Hitchcockian.

"Oh. My. Heavens. She's so light! And her feathers feel like silk!" Athena's nose wrinkled in self-mockery, even as she beamed. "Thus the name, I suppose."

She cuddled Roberta closer . . . in her mostly bare arms.

Which was another concern of Matthew's. Exposure to chicken feces could cause various unpleasant diseases in humans. How could he tell if Roberta was poised to poop on Athena?

"Do chickens . . ." Dammit, he already knew how this was going to sound, but he couldn't let that stop him. "Do chickens have an equivalent to a human child's potty dance? Do they flap their wings a certain way, or make recognizable pre-evacuation noises, or follow some other ritual before they . . . ?"

Athena's murmured cooing as she petted that lucky, lucky chicken abruptly ceased. Roberta's beak turned his way in unison with Hill and Athena's heads, and all three of them stared at him incredulously.

"Pre . . . evacuation noises," Athena echoed faintly, then bit savagely into her lower lip, all shadows temporarily banished from her dancing eyes.

"For the most part, they kind of move their butt fluff aside and shit wherever and whenever they want." Hill resettled his baseball cap on his thinning hair. "Must be pretty freeing, I've always thought."

Athena snorted. "No potty dance, then?"

"No potty dance," Hill confirmed, his voice quivering just the slightest bit.

It was funny, and Matthew didn't mind laughing at himself, but— "Chicken feces is full of harmful bacteria, right?"

Better to ask that as a question than state it as a fact, since a statement could very easily sound accusatory. Like he was saying to Hill, *You have given this wonderful woman a very cute creature to hold that might, nevertheless, shit all over her and make her very ill, you absolute monster.*

Okay, so maybe he was feeling a little accusatory. He'd thought Hill would let Athena pet Roberta, not *hold* the bird.

Hill immediately sobered to address the valid concern. "Yes. Which is why I wear long sleeves and pants when Roberta accompanies me to work, even though she generally doesn't poop while anyone's holding her. I also take her out back twice an hour to prevent accidents."

Athena's sleeves were too damn short.

Shit.

Literally. Shit was the problem, and Matthew needed to make sure no vulnerable skin remained exposed to said shit.

After he'd brought his library-sale haul home, he'd donned a loose, open button-down over his tee to protect his arms from the sun as they walked to Bluestocking. Yanking the shirt off, he presented it to Athena.

She studied the offering but didn't reach for it. "First of all, my arms aren't free to put that on. Second of all, no way in hell your shirt's going to fit me. So I appreciate the thought, but there's no need to channel Walter Raleigh and fling your shirt over a puddle of bird poop."

Oh. The first problem Hill could easily solve. But the second . . . hmmm.

Matthew's new mini-notebook and its attached pencil resided in his back pocket. He dug them out and made himself a note about Walter Raleigh.

Then he turned to Hill. "May I borrow a pair of scissors?"

"Matthew, what . . ." Athena trailed off, looking entirely befuddled.

While Hill ducked behind the register, Matthew studied exactly where Roberta came into contact with Athena's arms. And when the store owner handed over some sharp-looking shears, handles first, Matthew didn't hesitate.

His steady hands could have made him a surgeon, as Athena had once suggested, so his cuts along the back of the shirt's arms emerged straight and clean. Another long vent following the line of the spine all the way to the hem, a couple shorter cuts over the shoulders, and . . . done.

The altered shirt unceremoniously tossed on the checkout table, he cautiously lifted Roberta from Athena's unresisting hands and transferred the silkie to her owner.

"Arms back," he told Athena, and she slowly obeyed.

He eased his shirt over her hands and up to her shoulders, then fastened the cuffs and the top several buttons in front to keep things in place. Three steps back allowed him to scan his work and check for issues. As far as he could tell, none existed.

He allowed a slow, smug smile to emerge as he looked at Athena.

There. Problem solved. She was covered in the essential spots, and Roberta could shit at will. As long as the poop didn't go projectile. Did chickens projectile-shit? Should he ask?

Lips twitching, Athena fingered one of her arm slits. "I look like I'm wearing a piece from the Freddy Krueger collection at New York Fashion Week. Either that, or I Hulked out very precisely."

Once more, Matthew's notebook and pencil emerged from his back pocket. The Hulk reference he got. Freddy Krueger, though . . . wasn't that a grocery chain?

"I, uh . . ." Hill shifted Roberta in his arms. "I'd gladly give Bertie here back to you, Miss Athena, now that you're"—he cleared his throat—"properly attired. It's past time for her break, though. I need to take her behind the store for a few minutes."

In other words, Athena probably wouldn't hold the chicken again.

Matthew returned the mini-notebook to his back pocket, the tips of his ears aflame. Dammit. What kind of fool cut up his own shirt for no good reason?

Athena's small hand clasped his now-naked forearm and squeezed comfortingly. When he raised his head in startlement, she offered him a gentle smile.

"Your sacrifice isn't in vain, Matthew. I'll bring this shirt every time I visit Roberta from now on." Her nose crinkled adorably. "Which will probably be often, because apparently I too require an Emotional Support Extremely Cuddly Chicken."

Even after she let go of his arm, he could have traced the exact outline of her fingers. He was only surprised they didn't leave char marks around the edges.

"Could you two keep an eye on the store while I'm outside with Bertie? Just poke your head out the back door if anyone comes." Hill's face drooped. "Shouldn't be an issue. I don't get many customers these days."

Roberta quietly clucked and butted her head against the underside of his chin, and he murmured in response, tenderly scratching a spot above one of her wings as he disappeared into the private back room.

Athena set her hands on her generous hips and surveyed the store. "Let's shop, shall we? What do you like to read, Matthew?"

Evidently he hadn't been sufficiently embarrassed yet today.

"I like reading, of course." He paused, idly rotating a half-empty spinner of paperbacks. "I just haven't had much time to do it."

Her eyebrows drew together. "Recently?"

"Ever."

A woman who loved books as much as she did . . . she must consider him a barbarian. Or worse, an incurious dullard.

Visiting the children's section would help him escape this conversation, so he fled down the far aisle. "Mostly I read medical journals. Sometimes the continuing education classes I take for licensure assign reading too."

There. He'd reached the end of the row. Surely she wouldn't yell at him from across the—

"What about fiction?" she yelled at him from across the store.

Dammit. "What about it?"

The only two board books on display had once belonged to a teething infant, or possibly a pissed-off barracuda. The picture book selection was only slightly less dire.

"You've never read books just for fun?" Shouted as they were, he couldn't quite read the tone of her words. Pitying? Condemnatory? "Because you wanted to get lost in a world entirely different from your own?"

That would have been a luxury he couldn't afford. His actual world had required his full attention at all times. But maybe, back before Johnny was born . . .

"Ships," he recalled suddenly. "I used to like books that had tall ships in them. Adventure stories."

"Did you pretend to be a pirate?"

"Not really?" He absently flipped through a chapter book. "I more imagined myself a shipboard doctor."

In his boyhood fantasies, he'd sailed the seven seas. Traversed scrubbed wooden decks barefoot, the sun hot on his shoulders. Stitched up his bloody captain after a vicious buccaneer's cutlass attack. Stopped the navigator's pretty daughter from being swept overboard during a violent storm, using nothing but a bit of rope and sheer triumphant heroism.

Also, he'd had a peg leg and a parrot named Squawky and

sometimes a dashing eye patch. What had happened to his various missing body parts, he didn't remember, but it seemed the life of an imaginary shipboard doctor was both unpredictable and dangerous.

He'd forgotten those stories. The sort of expansive life he'd once imagined for himself.

The ship's doctor had become an infant's caretaker, then a land-bound pediatrician, and he couldn't regret any of it. Had never regretted any of it, because a healthy, happy brother was worth any sacrifice he had to make.

"I see." Her voice sounded thoughtful. And closer. "I wonder which section has adventure books for adults? They're not thrillers . . . not westerns . . . maybe just general fiction?"

She appeared at the head of his aisle, mouth pursed in dismay. "Things here could really be organized a bit better. There should be hanging signage and a map at the end of every row illustrating the store's layout and where to find each section."

All true. Also all rather amusing, coming from a woman who'd yet to fully empty a dozen boxes after a month and a half in her new home.

She wandered off again, disappearing down a different aisle. "Better alphabetization would help too. Good gravy." After a brief silence, she spoke again. "However, the store's collection of Sadie Brazen books is undeniably impressive. And if I'm not mistaken . . . yup. All the cracks in this one's spine indicate where the spicy scenes are. Very convenient."

Spicy = erotic? he printed carefully in his notebook.

"Bertie and I are back inside," Hill called from behind the curtain. "We'll be there in a minute."

Carrying the small armful of picture and chapter books he'd

managed to scavenge from the depleted children's section, Matthew joined Athena near the register. She had a novel tucked under her arm and was staring at another, looking pained.

"I should only get one, but . . ." she murmured. "Heaven help me, the fins. I want to know about the *fins*."

Was that . . . a guppy on the cover? With visible abs?

"What in the . . ." Hold on. Did he really want to know? "Never mind."

When Hill returned, carrying a sleepy-looking Roberta in a cloth-lined wicker basket, Matthew plucked the guppy paperback from Athena's hand and added it to his pile of children's books on the checkout counter.

She grabbed for the book. "No, I—"

He gently nudged her hand away. Then did so again when she made a second attempt at reclaiming the paperback. Looking vastly entertained, Hill began scanning barcodes and depositing books in the canvas tote Matthew handed to him.

Athena turned to gape at Matthew. "Did you—did you just *shove my hand*?"

"No." He frowned down at her. "I *nudged* your hand. There was zero shoving involved."

Her fists returned to their natural home, her hips. "You have no nudgery rights where I'm concerned, Dr. Matthew Vine the Third!"

"Did I hurt you?" He didn't think so, but he wanted to be certain. "If so, I sincerely apologize."

"No," she said sulkily. "You didn't hurt me. But you can't just—"

His credit card took only a moment to shove into the appropriate slot, and the matter was settled. "I think you'll find that I can. Besides, I desperately wanted to read . . ." Oh good lord.

"... *Desire, Unfiltered: An Erotic Monster Romance*. I suppose you can have it once I'm done."

"You're full of more shit than our feathered friend over there, Matthew."

"Hey." Hill snickered and handed over the receipt. "Keep Bertie out of this."

"I think I'm offended," Matthew informed Athena. "Just for that, you'll have to carry the book yourself."

He passed it over to her, with no intention of taking it back. Ever. Ever-ever.

"You *think* you're offended?" Placing her remaining book on the counter, she plunked down several crumpled ones. "Keep the change, Hill."

"Wait." Matthew scratched his chin. "Now I know. I'm definitely offended."

Her eyes rolled to the water-stained ceiling. "Like hell you are. Smartass."

Then she—

Was this a fever dream? Because he could swear she'd just . . . she'd . . .

She'd *smacked him in the butt with the book*.

She was now staring at her own novel-laden hand as if it belonged to a stranger, and his ass stung faintly and pleasantly in one guppy-abs-paperback-shaped spot, so all indications were: He hadn't imagined the whole thing.

"I . . ." Her mouth worked. "I . . ."

That was where she ran out of words. He sympathized. He wasn't any less confused. Probably significantly more aroused, though.

"Well, it's been real interesting, folks, but I'm closing now." Hill came out from behind the register to flip the sign on the door and douse the lights. "Visit again soon, will you?"

Within moments, he'd ushered Matthew and Athena out, leaving the two of them standing on the sidewalk in extremely fraught silence.

Eventually, she sighed. "I'm . . . sorry?" After zipping both books inside her oversized, cross-body purse, she plucked at the hem of his cut-up shirt. "I think I blacked out for a moment there. Or entered a fugue state. Or had an out-of-body experience. One of those things. Definitely one of those things."

"It's fine. Don't worry about it." A throat-clearing felt right, so he did that. Then fumbled for further areas of non-ass-smacking-related discourse. "Uh . . . what did you think of the store?"

Athena turned on her Ked-clad heel and began walking toward their homes, and he fell into step with her. For a block, she said nothing, but he could almost hear the wheels turning as she focused her sharp mind on Bluestocking.

"It has lots of potential," she finally said. "It badly needs a thorough cleaning, some redecoration, and better organization, though. And if business has been slow, I get why Hill's been accepting books in terrible condition, but that needs to end. Their presence in the store makes everything look shabby."

That was true, now that Matthew considered the matter. He'd never thought about it, but yes, all those battered, water-stained books made Bluestocking seem a bit . . . downscale.

Athena was warming to her subject. "Once he's fixed his stock issues, he can move on to other initiatives. It's like I told Karl: Compliance strategies are key." When Matthew hummed encouragingly, she elaborated. "Hill should put a cart of really cheap, overstocked books in front. If he can get customers to buy one, they're more likely to keep spending afterward." She spread her hands with a flourish, sounding very much like the teacher she'd once been. "Voilà! The foot-in-the-door phenomenon at work."

Compliance strategies, Matthew wrote in his notebook, smiling to himself.

Beside him, she slowed. When he glanced over to see what had happened, he was stunned by the change in her. Slumped shoulders. Pinched, downturned mouth. Her luminous curiosity and enthusiasm had gone dark, as if she'd suffered a one-woman eclipse.

"Never mind," she said, sounding . . .

Not just tired. That wasn't a strong enough word. Drained, maybe. Hopeless.

Concerned, he stopped walking, and she drifted to a halt beside him.

"No one should listen to me." She gave a listless shrug. "I know nothing about success."

Head downturned, she picked at her cuticles.

One by one, he was gathering words of comfort and reassurance, words that hopefully wouldn't make her hate him again, when a gleaming droplet of blood welled up alongside her thumbnail. The small injury had to hurt. She kept picking.

He immediately laid a hand over hers, pressing lightly until she stilled and spared herself further damage.

"Stop," he said, his voice pitched low for privacy. "Please."

She yanked her hand away from his, the blood smearing across her thumb and over her fingertips in a livid crimson streak.

"I'm so sorry, Doctor." The acid-soaked words could have peeled the flesh from his bones. "Am I too gross for you? Too messy?"

They were back to that, then. Back to anger and hurt and antipathy.

He swallowed past the thickness in his throat.

Inside his wallet, he always kept disinfectant wipes and a bandage or two tucked away, just in case. He removed what he needed, opened the wipes' packaging, sanitized his hands, then gently clasped her wrist to hold her in place. Through some miracle, she didn't pull away from him a second time.

He didn't glance up at her. He didn't have to. He already knew how she looked when she hated him.

Carefully, he cleaned and dressed the little wound. Wrapped the sticky arms of the bandage around her thumb tightly enough to contain the bleeding but not tightly enough to cause discomfort. Tucked the discarded packaging in his front jeans pocket.

He didn't let go for a moment. A bystander might have thought Matthew was simply holding her hand now. Might have thought he was her lover, not her enemy.

"You were hurting yourself," he told her quietly, "and risking infection with an open wound. You hadn't washed your hands since holding Roberta."

He'd fixed the only injury he could access at the moment. There was nothing more he could do. He relinquished her hand, letting it drop before she could yank it away from him again.

Her exhalation shook. "I'm sorry. I keep trying to peg you as Lawful Evil, but you don't fit that slot very neatly, do you?"

The snap and sarcasm in her voice had reverted to simple fatigue.

Someday, he might understand every word she spoke, every gesture she made, every shift of her emotions. Not today, though.

Lawful evil, he printed in his notebook, then back into his pocket it went. Her stare followed his movements, but she didn't ask what he was doing.

They began walking again. Not fast, although it wasn't a relaxed stroll either. He'd classify it more as a trudge, at least on her part.

"Today was your last day at the library, correct?" When she nodded, he asked, "So what's next for you?"

Because he hadn't discovered any new work possibilities for her, and he was hoping she'd located an opening he knew nothing about.

"Not much," she said, after a long hesitation. "More unpacking, I guess."

No job, then. Fuck.

An uneven brick tripped her up, but she recovered before he could assist. "Is your brother coming home soon? Jackie said something about that today."

They'd reached the alleyway separating their two buildings.

Matthew stopped. So did she.

"He gets back the first of October." Oh. Wait. "Which is . . . tomorrow, I just realized."

Good thing she'd reminded him, since he was supposed to pick Johnny up from the airport absurdly early in the morning.

Did Athena want to see his brother? Was that why she'd asked? Or did she want to avoid him at all costs, as she'd previously claimed?

She nodded. "Okay. Thanks for the warning."

Apparently the latter, then.

"Bye, Matthew." Her smile was small and sad and quickly gone. "I appreciate your taking me to Bluestocking."

With a little wave, she turned into the alleyway and walked to her front door.

She was still wearing his sliced-up shirt. At the sight of it, a certain satisfaction warmed his gut. That is, until he got home and began washing off all remaining traces of Hill's cute little ESC-slash-disease vector.

Nudging the faucet handle upward with the back of his wrist, he started the water running in the sink and looked down. Then hesitated, deeply uneasy for reasons he couldn't quite pinpoint.

There weren't many smears, really. Only a few, small and dried and no longer vividly red. And he'd already disinfected and bandaged her very small wound.

Still, Athena's blood was on his hands.

He hadn't noticed.

8

*F*rankly, Athena had hoped to avoid Johnny for at least a few days. Maybe a few weeks.

It wasn't an unreasonable goal. They might be next-door neighbors, but a nice, thick brick wall separated their homes, and since she remained involuntarily unemployed, she could run any necessary errands during the normal business hours of the Vine brothers' workplace.

Another reason for optimism: If her ex-fiancé saw her, he might experience guilt over his actions, and he'd want to avoid that however he could. Which meant he'd avoid *her*, and she was a big fan of that impulse.

If she actually encountered him again, she had no idea what she'd say or do. Maybe yell until her vocal cords gave out. Or cry from frustration, which he would wrongly interpret as grief at their failed relationship—and if that happened, she thought she might go Full Rumpelstiltskin, throw a fit, stomp her foot so hard it sank waist-deep into the earth, then seize her other foot and violently tear herself in two.

She preferred her body un-bifurcated, so if he stayed away from her, she'd gladly return the favor. Forever, if at all possible.

Given her presumption of mutually assured avoidance, when her doorbell rang around lunchtime on Sunday, she figured it was just another rando wanting an impromptu tour of her home. That happened sometimes, and she generally just stared stonily at them until they left.

But no. She opened the door and there he stood, hands tucked awkwardly into the pockets of his jeans. Her ex-fiancé.

What the fuck? Why wasn't he dodging her as long as possible?

"Athena." His Adam's apple bobbed as he swallowed. "Hi."

He was as handsome as ever. Maybe even more so after six weeks on vacation, basking in the Hawaiian sun. He looked well rested. His Henley and skinny jeans clung to a broad-shouldered body assiduously maintained at the gym. His skin had turned a slightly deeper shade of gold, and the sun struck reddish highlights in his straight brown hair.

Right now, his dark eyes resembled Matthew's more than ever before. They contained no humor, no playfulness. Only grave wariness.

Still, he looked a million years younger than she felt.

"Johnny." She didn't move from the doorway, and she didn't invite him inside.

No yelling, she reminded herself. No crying. No Rumpel-stiltskin-ing. Nothing that would mislead him into thinking she'd grieved his absence from her life.

She missed her savings account and her old condo, her sense of security, her hope for a bearable future, but not him. At least, not in the way she'd have expected. Not in the way an ex-fiancée probably should.

He shifted his weight under her pitiless scrutiny. "May I come in?"

"Nope."

So he could get an up-close-and-personal view of the damage he'd caused? As if.

"Okay." He nodded a little. "Okay. I understand."

"I honestly don't care whether you do or not," she told him.

Maybe his flinch should have elicited her sympathy. It didn't.

"Then I'll say it here." Removing his hands from his pockets, he straightened to his full height, maybe a couple inches taller than Matthew, and made direct eye contact. "I'm sorry, Athena. I shouldn't have made promises I would've had trouble keeping even if we'd gotten married. I should have relied on my own judgment when it came to our engagement, instead of my brother's. And most of all, I should have checked on you after I called off the wedding, because I never wanted you to suffer for having known me. For having loved me."

Shocked beyond words, she couldn't do anything but stare at him blankly.

He bit his lip. "You deserved better from me. I know that, and I'm very sorry."

The apology was gracious, comprehensive, and completely un-expected. Truly, she hadn't thought him capable of it. And she was grateful for the gesture, really she was, but it didn't change her current situation, and it couldn't drain months' worth of anger in one fell swoop.

"I appreciate that," she finally managed to say.

He stood on her doorstep and looked at her expectantly, but he'd heard her entire response. Maybe once she had a normal-sized home and a regular paycheck again she'd be more inclined to tell him he was forgiven, if that was what he wanted. For now: nope.

"I wasn't sure you'd even be willing to see me." Dropping his gaze, he scratched the back of his head. "Matthew said—"

Oh, hell no. They weren't going down this particular road again.

"I'm sure your brother has a lot to say, but I don't need to hear it." She paused for emphasis. "Again."

His cheeks turned ruddy. "Yeah. I get that, and I'm truly very s—"

"You want to mend fences with me. Is that correct?" When he dipped his chin in mute affirmation, she continued, "Then let me be clear. The best way to earn my forgiveness is to keep your distance. Maybe not forever"—that was a lie; definitely forever—"but for a while. Okay?"

He exhaled slowly. "Okay. If that's what you want."

"It is."

She'd already stepped back, ready to close the door on him both literally and metaphorically, when he spoke again in a near whisper. "I've missed you, Athena."

Then he was down her steps and gone from the alleyway. But she was almost entirely certain he'd be back, wheedling and ingratiating himself to earn her stated forgiveness, far sooner than she'd prefer. Johnny was accustomed to getting what he wanted and disregarding the consequences for everyone around him. Notably her, but also . . . his brother.

It had only occurred to her last night: Johnny had been gone *a month and a half* from a practice with only three doctors. No wonder Matthew looked so freaking exhausted every time she saw him. And she could only assume he was living in a home without central air-conditioning—even though he was a *doctor*, and not a newish one like Johnny—because he'd spent a good chunk of his savings on his brother's solo honeymoon.

Didn't Matthew cover half of Johnny's student loan payments every month too? For that matter, when her ex-fiancé had blithely described the renovations he'd like to undertake once they owned the Spite House, who exactly did he think would pay for them?

Matthew. He'd been counting on Matthew.

She wouldn't be seeing much of *him* anymore either, now that Johnny was back home. Which was kind of a shame. As long as they stuck to uncontroversial topics, he was a damn good conversationalist, with an understated but keen sense of humor.

She might actually . . . miss him? Unlike his brother?

Didn't matter. She planned to avoid Johnny, and when both brothers were home, the two were usually a package deal. That had become clear during her engagement. So . . . *goodbye, Johnny* also meant *goodbye, Matthew*, unfortunately.

Or so she thought. Until, that is, Matthew showed up on her doorstep later that day and *wouldn't fucking leave*.

She'd gotten undressed and was stepping into her small-ass shower when the doorbell rang. No one had mentioned visiting her, and darkness had already fallen over Harlot's Bay, so she had no intention of answering that summons. Not even after a second peremptory *ding-dong*.

Then came the firm knock. Another *ding-dong*. More knocking.

If this was Johnny again, she was going to drop-kick him into the sun. Muttering to herself, she threw on her silk robe— last year's Christmas gift from her parents—belted it around her waist, and stomped to the door.

Through the peephole, Matthew stared back at her, brow predictably furrowed, hair uncharacteristically rumpled.

Fine. Fine, she'd talk to him one last time before her all-encompassing Vine Brothers Avoidance Policy took effect. Because he'd been so gentle patching her up yesterday. Because she'd misjudged him multiple times. Because maybe he wasn't Lawful Evil after all, or even Lawful Neutral. Maybe he was Lawful Good, as long as she wasn't engaged to his baby brother.

Opening the door, she waved him in without a word. He strode inside, only to come to a sudden, inexplicable halt when he got his first real eyeful of her.

A glance downward didn't reveal anything wrong, though. Sure, she wasn't wearing a bra and the robe gaped a little, but she didn't have a tit hanging out.

"What?" She shut the door behind him. "Why are you looking at me like that?"

"Do you need a minute to, um . . . ?" His gesture indicated her berobed state. "Do you want to change? I can wait here."

Holy macaroni, what a prude. "I'm about to shower, so you'll have to say whatever you came to say with me in my robe. If that's a problem, please feel free to leave, and I'll let you know the next time I've donned my nun's habit."

"No." He sort of shook himself, then dragged his eyes back to hers. "No, it's . . . totally fine. No need to change. You're—perfect."

Very convincing.

"In that case . . ." Eyebrows raised, she waited for him to get on with things.

"Listen, Athena." Arms akimbo, he let out a long breath. "I'm sorry my brother visited you. I told him he shouldn't, but—"

"We've already discussed this," she interrupted remorselessly. "You can't apologize on Johnny's behalf. He's a grown-ass man, and he can express remorse for his own actions. Which he did today, with surprising grace. I was impressed, frankly."

At that, he blinked. Then stepped closer, studying her face with an odd intensity.

"You were . . . impressed." His voice had turned sort of rumbly.

"Yes."

"Hmmm."

When he didn't add anything, her limited patience came to an end. "Matthew, if that's all—"

"He wouldn't tell me about your conversation." A decision that clearly bothered Matthew. "I didn't even know he came to see you until half an hour ago, although I should have guessed. He was quiet and withdrawn all afternoon."

"Was he?" A better person would probably feel bad about that. Alas.

"Yes." Matthew's intensity had somehow ratcheted upward yet again, and she couldn't seem to look away from his grim scrutiny. "Which I don't understand. If you forgave him, why does he seem so down?"

She snorted, genuinely amused. "Oh, I didn't forgive him. I told him I appreciated his apology but wanted him to stay away from me for the foreseeable future. Still, he gave good remorse today. He apologized for breaking his promises and hanging me out to dry. He even apologized for listening to your opinion of me instead of his own."

At the reminder of that whispered fraternal conversation in a cold museum hallway, her stomach soured, and this conversation no longer seemed entertaining to her. At all.

She directed a meaningful glance at the door. "It's late, and I need to wedge myself into my tiny shower, so—"

"Why aren't your parents helping you?" Another step toward her, and he was so close she shivered at the heat of his live-wire, lean body. "From what Johnny said, they have the resources to take care of you until you're back on your feet, so why move to Harlot's Bay? Why live in this house, next door to a man you'd ostensibly prefer never to see again? What's your endgame here, Athena?"

Ostensibly?

Was he . . . was he implying she'd lied about that? Did he think she *wanted* to live near her ex-fiancé? Oh, dear heaven, did he imagine she'd willingly take Johnny back? Ever?

"I want to be clear about this, Dr. Vine." She set her fists on her silk-clad hips, ignoring how her robe gaped wider with the movement, and rose to her tiptoes to get right. Up. In. His. Stupid. Face. "I owe Johnny zero explanations, and I owe you even fewer. If negative explanations existed, that's what you'd deserve from me. But I have my pride—"

"Boy, do you," he muttered.

"—so I can't say nothing and let you think . . ." The words almost choked her. "I can't let you think I'm living here because I still want him. Cripes on a cracker. What bullshit."

He hadn't moved an inch. Hadn't backed away from her challenge. If anything, he edged closer, until her breasts almost brushed him with every agitated breath.

"Yes, my parents would take me in if I asked," she told him. "But I won't."

"Why not, Athena?" he asked, dark-eyed and severe. "If you don't want to be near Johnny, why the hell not?"

"My parents—" She dropped back to her heels, her calves burning. Her heart aching. "My parents went straight from university to med school to residencies to fellowships, and then into private practice. They're internationally recognized for their work, they love what they do, and they've never wavered. Never doubted what they wanted to accomplish or who they wanted to be. And then there's me."

The contrast was hilarious, honestly. A children's morality tale. One of Aesop's fables. The industrious ants and the profligate grasshopper, and sure enough, look who was heading hungry into a long, desolate winter?

She laughed, the sound brittle and bitter enough to make him wince. "I'm thirty-seven years old, Matthew. I have no job. No savings. No idea what I want to do. They've already paid for two graduate degrees, neither of which I'm actually using. They sank good money into an engagement party that didn't result in an actual marriage and lost substantial deposits for a wedding that didn't happen."

The words were chunks of flint, and they drew blood as she dredged them from deep, deep down in her mind. Where she'd hidden them from everyone, including herself.

"Somehow they haven't realized it yet, but I know it. So do you." She held his stare, granting no quarter to either of them. "Their daughter is a fuckup."

He closed his eyes, as if pained, but she kept talking. He'd wanted to know, so he was damn well going to hear everything she had to say.

"You can mock my pride all you want—"

"I wasn't—Athena—" His eyes had flown open in shocked denial, but that was a sham. He knew what he'd said only moments before.

"—but it's all I have right now, and I can't admit this level of failure to them. I just c-can't." Biting her lip, she waited until she could speak without her voice cracking. "I can't ask for more when I've already wasted everything they've given me before. So I told them I was excited about a fresh start in Harlot's Bay and charmed by my unique fucking house and overwhelmed with all the help I'd gotten for the move. I let them assume I'd get my Maryland teaching license and substitute until that happened. I bought myself more time before they finally realize who I am. What I am. An utter disappointment to everyone around me."

With his flush of anger gone, his face looked more gray than pale.

He lifted a hand. His fingers hovered near her upper arm, then landed, light as butterflies. "Athena, please—"

She shook them off. "So no, I didn't move to Harlot's Bay to win back a man who promised me the world then abandoned me—not because he realized he'd made a mistake, or didn't love me like he should, but because *his big brother told him to*. I'd rather die alone than take him back. I might have nothing, and I m-might"—she choked on a sob—"I might *be* nothing, and maybe you were right that I'd make a terrible wife, but even *I* can do better than that."

Of course, Matthew had thought the opposite. Thought his brother deserved better than a woman like her. She'd heard the words from his own mouth.

Last December, she'd entered that deserted museum hallway in search of an unoccupied bathroom, in need of a sanctuary while she grappled with her alarmingly intense reaction to her fiancé's brother. And there they were. The two brothers, arguing about . . . her. Matthew, ripping her character to shreds. Johnny, defending her even as his doubts seemed to grow with every charge Matthew laid against her.

The next morning, she'd told Johnny what she'd overheard, and he'd claimed his older brother would come around. He'd said Matthew simply didn't know her well enough yet.

She hadn't believed him.

She recognized the merciless voice of judgment. She heard it in her own head, every single day, every single hour, unless she kept herself too busy to think. Her verdict never changed. Matthew's wouldn't either. She'd known that down to her marrow.

But maybe . . . maybe she'd been wrong.

The brothers' horrible hallway conversation had happened almost ten months before. What felt like half a lifetime ago. Matthew had been kind to her, repeatedly. He seemed to enjoy her company. And that expression on his face now, tonight . . .

She couldn't quite read it, but it wasn't disdain. Disdain was cool, removed. Right now, Matthew was so close, he could claim her mouth with a simple bend of his neck. Close enough that an inch farther would press her inexplicably hard nipples against his chest. And the color might have fled from his face, but the heat of his body seared her.

So yes, maybe Johnny had been right for once, and Matthew had simply needed more time and contact with her. Maybe now that he knew her better, he'd declare her not guilty of all the charges he'd laid against her, all the charges she'd laid against herself.

Maybe she'd believe him if he did.

"Athena," he began again, his voice gentler than she'd ever heard it. "Please don't—"

"You want to hear what my endgame is? Surviving until I figure out my next step, then selling this fucking house and moving on with my life. That's it. That's the entirety of my devious master plan." She tipped her chin high. "Which means you know everything now, Matthew. All my secrets. So tell me something, and be honest."

She had to ask. She had to find out for certain before she slapped her palm on his plasma globe and invited the current her way. Before she cracked his protective glass and discovered whether all that power would set her alight or simply electrocute her.

If she didn't know better, she'd say he was scared too. The pulse at the base of his neck beat frantically, but he didn't interrupt her. He simply stood there as she laid everything on the line.

"Tell me," she repeated hoarsely. "If you could go back, would you still convince Johnny to leave me?"

He started to speak, then fell silent. Once. Twice.

Her knees turned watery, and so did her eyes, because he didn't need to say a word. She had her verdict.

Guilty.

She forced him to answer anyway, just so she wouldn't waver again. Wouldn't forget exactly who he was, and exactly who she was, and exactly why she should never, ever allow him anywhere near her heart.

"Say it." The order came accompanied by her biggest, brightest, fakest tooth-baring of a smile, and she reveled in his flinch. "Would you still tell him to leave me? Yes or no?"

His head bowed, and he stared at his pristine sneakers for a moment. To his credit, though, he raised his eyes to hers before answering.

"Yes."

One word. All she needed.

She had two for him, as it happened.

"Get out," she said.

AT FIRST, ATHENA did her best to forget the confrontation with Matthew.

After closing her windows and drawing the shades, she watched an HGTV marathon until three in the morning, then read until her eyes wouldn't focus anymore.

Sadly, though, her usual techniques to avoid thinking her

thoughts and feeling her feelings until she collapsed into an exhausted slumber didn't work. When she flopped onto her mattress at dawn and closed her stupid leaking eyes, sleep was nowhere to be found.

In its place, there he was behind her eyelids. Matthew. Telling her no, he hadn't changed his mind. He still thought she'd make a terrible partner; he still thought she was irresponsible and spoiled and far too messy to be loved.

It was foolish, so foolish, to feel betrayed by him. But she did. Somewhere over the past month and a half, against her better judgment and despite her best efforts, she'd grown to . . . like him. She'd thought he might even like her in return.

He didn't, though.

He didn't fucking *like* her, much less respect her.

All his efforts on her behalf, all his concern, all his interest—they were just Responsible Older Brother Matthew doing his duty and attempting to clean up the mess Johnny had left behind. He probably figured the more he helped her, the faster she'd get back on her feet, and the sooner she'd leave the Vine brothers' vicinity.

It hurt to admit that. It hurt to acknowledge she'd misjudged him when she should have known better. It hurt more than she could even understand.

She finally slept in fitful snatches. And when she woke, she was done trying to forget. Instead, she remembered every ugly detail. She reminded herself of the many reasons she despised Dr. Matthew Vine the Third and let herself steep in her rage. Let it overtake the sadness and confusion. Let it give her newfound purpose.

Now she had a project she could really sink her sharp, sharp teeth into. Her goals: first, making sure he minded his own fucking business from now on instead of keeping tabs on her; second, living down to his expectations of her, because she was a contrary little bitch like that; and third, avenging herself in the pettiest ways possible against the asshole who'd repeatedly contributed to her current misery.

She didn't intend to limit herself to wreath adjustment and Rick-rolling anymore. Those pranks were mere amuse-bouches compared to the hearty entrées of spite she'd soon be dishing out.

No need to be a mature adult about all this. He didn't expect it from her anyway.

Producing a lined notepad, she labeled the top sheet in her messiest possible handwriting, because didn't they always say to start as you meant to go on?

PROJECT: ANNOY THE LIVING FUCK OUT OF DR. MATTHEW VINE THE FUCKING THIRD.

Satisfied by her magnificent scrawl of a header, she began to make her list.

9

Matthew's first sign of new and unexpected trouble: when he involuntarily spent a long autumn evening listening to a limber, extremely broad-minded woman fuck a Sasquatch.

Sasquatches apparently boasted prehensile, pulsing tongues, ridged penises, and the ability to use both assets effectively with their human lovers. Good for them. Matthew simply hadn't anticipated hearing about their impressively athletic sexual exploits as he was sitting in his home office and attempting to reconcile his receipts and bills with his bank account.

Because of the unseasonable October heat, almost everyone on their street had opened their windows. Including him. Including Athena. In the past, she'd been careful not to make much noise under those conditions. But now . . .

Frankly, it was difficult to concentrate on his bills as Dakota and Ugg discovered her G-spot together.

"Oh, no. No, you mustn't, not while my entire family is hunting you," she gasped unconvincingly. "And surely your tongue can't reach all the way inside my—"

His tongue could. It did.

Matthew accidentally signed up to receive newsletters from the county's water and sewer department while she was noisily, ecstatically coming. When the immediate confirmation email arrived in his inbox, he hurriedly clicked the "unsubscribe" link—only to sit wondering tiredly what "products and services" they could possibly advertise to him. He was already pretty sold on the concept of running water and indoor toilets.

Out of sheer morbid curiosity, he resubscribed.

Then he sat at his office desk and waited for Athena to notice how very loudly she was playing her erotic audiobook. Whenever she got out of the shower or stopped whatever noise-muffling activity she was doing, she'd surely turn it down.

Only . . . he spotted a hint of movement right then. Not in the unlit library nook, where Athena's laptop lay on the side table next to her reading chair, barely visible in the gloom. Thanks to that laptop's speakers, he now knew Bigfoot lived up to the old stereotype about big feet. But she wasn't there. She wasn't in the shower, either.

"Oh god, oh god," Dakota breathily, deafeningly chanted. "That big Sasquatch cock . . . the ridges—Ugg, I'm about to—"

Athena was, if he wasn't mistaken, hiding just out of sight beside one of her open fourth-floor bedroom windows. Or, rather, hiding where she *thought* she was just out of sight. Those generous breasts and the sweet swell of her belly would cause difficulties for her, should she ever decide to take up spycraft for a living.

"Then she heard a noise," the narrator said, "and saw a furry face that seemed . . . oddly familiar. Ugg's sexy Bigfoot BFF? Why was he there too? And why did the sight of him stroking his own monstrous cock, a bottle of homemade Sasquatch lube in his free paw, as he approached them—"

Matthew's brows rose. Plot twist!

"—make her scream in pleasure, convulse, and come harder around that pumping ridged dick than she even knew was—"

Athena's bedroom remained dark. Her blond hair, though . . . as she edged closer to the window, it glowed like a beacon in the moonlight. With a subtle twist of his neck, a subtle glance out of the corner of his eye, he could watch her watching him.

Everything became clear in that moment. The recent, mysterious instability of his house numbers and wreath. The occasional 180-degree reversal of his welcome mat. That confusing radio dedication.

He knew now why the audiobook was so loud. Why her laptop lay beside the open window directly across from his office. Why she was attempting, with a somewhat hilarious lack of stealth, to spy on his reaction.

She thought listening to a Sasquatch ménage à trois would bother him. This was retaliation. Her latest and most ambitious punishment for his manifold trespasses against her.

She wanted her pound of flesh? Fine, then. She could have it, and maybe giving it to her would help ease the hollowness in his chest.

Probably not, though.

He kept telling himself the confrontation two nights ago had been inevitable. Johnny's absence might have allowed Matthew and Athena to skirt their fraught history for a time, but the honeymoon had to end eventually. And no matter how firmly he advised his younger brother to stay away from her, Johnny wasn't going to listen. Not when he wanted Athena's forgiveness.

And perhaps . . . perhaps more than that.

So Johnny's decision to corner Athena right away, in hopes of expiating his sins, didn't shock Matthew. What had shocked him: the apparent gracefulness of his brother's apology, and how Athena had openly *admired* Johnny's efforts.

When she'd praised that damn apology, somehow everything in his mind had collided. Her scarlet lipstick in a dim museum corner. Her arms and chest covered by his shirt—*his*—as she softly caressed the fluffiest chicken alive. Her breasts in that silky robe, with its easily undone knot of a belt and its ever-widening V of a neckline.

Johnny, arm slung carelessly around her shoulders, drawing her away from Matthew's side and smiling down at her at their engagement party, handsome and charming and so very young. Johnny, whispering over a phone call from Hawaii that he'd fucked up when it came to Athena. Johnny, who always, always got what he wanted.

In that moment, as need and resentment and fear crashed into one another, Matthew had felt something within him strain under the impact.

His self-control, he presumed.

If that fucking robe had opened another eighth of an inch, he'd have snatched her to him and found out just how soft those half-covered breasts felt pressed against his chest. He'd have taken her mouth and backed her into the nearest wall.

Instead, roiling with emotions he refused to parse, he'd pressed against her another way, pushed for answers, and she'd cracked before his control had.

Because of him, she'd wept. She'd raised bleak, red-rimmed eyes to him and called herself a failure with complete, resigned conviction, assuming his agreement. In that moment, the destructive maelstrom enveloping him had blown away, leaving him awash in horror.

If his blood would have erased the utter self-loathing and hopelessness inscribed on her sweet face, he'd have found a scalpel and bled himself dry for her. He'd been about to offer whichever inadequate words he could gather in his panic, and then . . .

Then she'd asked a question he didn't want to answer, for so many reasons.

Before meeting her, admittedly, he'd thought she sounded irresponsible. He'd thought she sounded like someone he'd eventually have to support and whose problems he'd have to solve. He'd thought she sounded—well, like Johnny, frankly. And if Matthew was laboring under the burdens he'd already assumed, what would he do when a woman with so few resources became almost entirely dependent on his brother?

In the end, she'd turn into Matthew's albatross, and he didn't want to bear her weight. Didn't want her anywhere near him or his brother.

Until, of course, he'd met her. Fifteen minutes of conversation, and wanting her near him was no longer a concern.

Correction: It was, but only because he wanted it too much.

She wasn't at all as he'd expected. Messy, yes. Troubled. Running from something and using the wedding to do so, unless he missed his guess.

Not careless in the same way as his brother, though. Not in the slightest.

She was incredibly warm, thoughtful, bright, funny, and beautiful. So very, very beautiful. And she and Johnny were an absolutely terrible match. After meeting her, Matthew was more committed than ever to making sure the wedding would never happen.

Only fifteen fleeting minutes together had shown him the fundamental issue: She was more than Johnny could handle in almost every way. A woman like her required someone with steady hands, metaphorically speaking. Someone patient. Someone who'd pay her the attention she needed and deserved. Someone who could truly appreciate that quicksilver wit and exacting intelligence of hers.

Johnny wasn't that man. He'd only disappoint her and break her heart, although he wasn't self-aware enough to realize that. Even if he did, he was devoted to his own interests first and foremost. He wouldn't end the engagement for her sake, only his own. So Matthew didn't bother trying to convince Johnny of his wrongness for Athena. Instead, Matthew doubled down on his previous criticisms of her, added a few new ones to discomfit his brother, and then, increasingly desperate, threatened to move away.

Voilà. At long last, no more engagement.

In his own perverse way, he'd been trying to protect her, protect all of them, and maybe he had. But he'd also inadvertently hurt her, much more deeply than he could ever have guessed.

And he'd done it again the other night.

If you could go back, would you still convince Johnny to leave me?

The only honest answer was yes. Matthew would still tell Johnny to end the engagement for the very same reasons he'd done so after the engagement party. Not because Athena was messy or struggling or uncertain of what she wanted, as she assumed, but because his brother could never give a woman who was all those things the life and love she deserved.

Johnny needed easy. Athena was anything but.

When she'd asked the question, his full explanation had rested on the tip of his tongue, and it would have comforted her. It would have allowed her to interpret their history and his behavior with more accuracy.

It also would have tempted him to confess, *I've never had easy, and I don't need it. I just need you*. Heaven help him, his resistance to her splintered more with each minute in her presence. To preserve his remaining control, he'd required distance. He'd required time apart.

Yes, he'd said, without further discussion.

Then watched her flinch away from him. Watched whatever warmth had flared to life between them simply . . . extinguish.

Gutted, he'd halted a step from her door and almost told her everything. Which was when he'd heard a *thump* through the far brick wall. Johnny, doing—something.

His brother. His fucking *brother*.

He'd left without another word.

After a sleepless night spent contemplating how to ameliorate the damage he'd caused, he'd risen at dawn on Monday and done some research to identify Athena's mortgage company and their payment address. Later that day, he'd mailed them a money order without his return address on the envelope.

He'd hurt her again, and he couldn't seem to find her steady work, but he didn't mind a few lean weeks. He could at least make sure she didn't fall behind on her house payments.

There'd be hell to pay if he offered help more directly, though, which meant . . . that was it. That was all he could do to assist her, and it was killing him.

So yeah, if it made her feel better, she could sabotage his wreath and Rickroll him and play erotic audiobooks about sexually adept Sasquatches at top volume for years to come. And if she wanted to inadequately hide and actually *watch* him suffer, no problem. He didn't have to change anything, except how openly he showed her what he already felt.

"Come inside me, Ugg! Give me your Bigfoot baby!" Dakota

pleaded with remarkable clarity for a woman currently accommodating two Sasquatch penises. "Fuck, yes, Gar, take me harder with that cryptid cock!"

A glance at the clock told Matthew he should have been in bed five minutes ago, but he still had receipts to scan, bills to look over, and misery to convey. With an especially loud, heavy sigh, he tapped at his keyboard to reactivate his screen, then took a minute to rub his aching jaw.

He kept his movements as big and obvious as possible. Easily seen from four feet and one floor away. If he'd ever taken part in an amateur theater production, he imagined it would have felt very much like this.

Several minutes later, Dakota, Ugg, and Gar had all experienced transcendent orgasms, and Matthew was ready to get his work done during the more boring bits of the story. Surely Sasquatches had refractory periods too?

"To her shock, both Ugg and Gar were still ridged and rigid," said the narrator. "And Dakota remembered all at once that when Sasquatches found their mates, they entered a sort of rut. A temporary state of insatiability, in which they might take their fated love dozens of times in one night."

Shit.

"Gar passed the cavemade deer-fat lube to Ugg, and the two men switched places," the narrator continued. "Dakota moaned, then moaned again at an unexpected sensation. Was that Gar's tongue pulsing against her clit from so far away? Was the agile appendage actually . . . extendable?"

Jeez. How could mere human penises and tongues compete with that?

At least I can speak in complete sentences, he comforted himself. *That's something.*

"Oh, Gar, don't stop!" Dakota begged. "Don't ever stop!"

Matthew ostentatiously rubbed his knuckles against that aching spot in his skull. And when he faintly heard gleeful feminine snickering, he angled his face so no one—including, say, a would-be spy from across the alleyway—could see his pained smile.

ATHENA, AS MATTHEW soon learned, boasted an impressive repertoire of tactics for irritating him, and she apparently had no intention of stopping anytime soon.

The volume of campaign donation requests he received had increased exponentially in recent days. In another awkward development, eager local representatives of several multilevel marketing companies had been disappointed to learn that he did not, in fact, wish to host parties to sell makeup, herbal supplements, or Tupperware.

"I'm not sure how the mix-up occurred," he unconvincingly lied each time. "Thank you for your time, but there's no need to check in with me again in a week, as your caller helpfully indicated you should do. I am content without a—what did you call it?— *side hustle*."

As another means of revenge, Athena had created absolute chaos in her home and ensured it was readily visible through their windows. She'd begun leaving her boxes and bins scattered all over the floor, instead of pushing them against the walls, and their contents now littered almost every surface not already occupied by dirty dishes and empty Diet Coke cans.

He didn't care about any of it.

Okay, that wasn't entirely true. It didn't look safe or sanitary for her, and involuntarily witnessing such an egregious mess pained him. A lot. *A lot.* Which she clearly understood.

Still, he could overlook mess. Kind of. What he couldn't overlook: his marrow-deep guilt and loneliness. If he'd ever felt worse in his last three decades of existence, he couldn't remember when. All those calls from Avon representatives were fine by him, because at least they were a kind of contact with Athena. A sign she was thinking of him, however angrily.

He preferred the erotic audiobooks, though. They provided not only proof of his presence in her thoughts, but also company in the evenings. A temporary distraction from his misery.

Even when the weather cooled a bit, his window stayed open, because otherwise, how was he to know whether Dakota's money-hungry family finally captured Ugg and sold him to a shadowy government agency for imprisonment and possible dissection?

His neighbors' windows also remained open, he'd noticed. During the scene where Ugg reunited with Dakota, Matthew could swear he'd heard a loud sniffle from elderly Mrs. Jennings next door and a muffled whoop from Kenny, the carpenter across the street.

Honestly, he'd begun to think of the audiobook performances as an informal community event. Like a deer-lube-intensive block party. One that was free for all involved, since Athena wasn't paying for the audiobooks.

Your girl came by for more Sadie Brazen the other day, Karl texted one evening, not long after Athena had begun playing a new story. Guillaume—he was a French gargoyle, complete with a credible Gallic accent—had spent the previous evening demonstrating how many different parts of his body could be used as a makeshift dildo. The answer: countless. Matthew could only hope the sculptors had polished that stone *thoroughly*, because otherwise . . . yikes.

Karl's next text popped up before Matthew could finish typing that Athena was not, in fact, his girl or his . . . anything. Currently, she wasn't even someone who spoke directly to him, unless erotic tales of Gothic statuary counted.

Heard her and Bez snickering out front. Sounded like they wanted to make you suffer using the audiobooks. Don't know why, don't care how.

Matthew deleted his half-written message and started fresh. *So you didn't give her more?*

If the audiobook recitals stopped abruptly, he expected riots in his neighborhood.

Gave her extra, Karl texted back. *Half my stash.*

He blinked. *What?*

Couldn't say no. A brief pause. *Didn't want to say no, either. Enjoy, Vine.*

Matthew could picture Karl's smirk. *Jackhole.*

His so-called friend sent a middle finger emoji, then added, *You ever visit Reddit?*

What? He frowned down at his phone. *Is that a restaurant, or a town, or . . . ?*

AITA mean anything to you?

Karl might as well have been speaking in tongues. *No. Should it?*

Nope. Don't worry about it. Just online bullshit. Another pause. *K-pop stuff.*

K-pop?

Jesus, Matthew, even I know what K-pop is, and I'm a cranky-ass hermit, Karl texted, then terminated the confusing exchange without an actual farewell.

So Athena wouldn't be running low on erotic audiobooks anytime soon, and despite Matthew's feigned outrage and frustration, he didn't mind that in the slightest.

But then . . . but then. He made a terrible mistake.

The starlit night started pleasantly enough. Athena had dragged a chair in front of her usual fourth-floor spying window and sat there, forearms on her sill, chin propped on her folded hands, moonlight reflecting off her hair.

She must have thought he was the least observant human being ever born. She wasn't even attempting to hide anymore. Sure, her window was dark, and he very deliberately never glanced in her direction, but *really*. How incredibly dense did she think he was?

His pride would sting, if only he had pride when it came to her. He didn't, though. Duties and desires and conflicting, constricting ties of loyalty, yes. Pride, no.

So he sat at his desk and sighed extremely loudly and rubbed his forehead and jaw in sweeping, extravagant gestures and glared in the general direction of her house, but not at her directly. After about half an hour, the gargoyle book—*Rock-Hard Lover*—ended happily, whereupon the sound of faint clapping drifted from their neighbors' homes.

His frown deepened in severity, the better to hide his lips' telltale twitch.

At that point, Athena began playing *Loch Ness Master.* The story featured a seductive, dominant Scottish lake monster and a wide-eyed American named Dani who lost track of her tour group and stumbled into the cold loch . . . only to encounter a scientifically improbable and unceasingly horny creature of the deep. So far, so good. Nothing out of the ordinary.

Well, Sadie Brazen's ordinary, anyway.

Then Ms. Brazen unexpectedly included a scene written from the point of view of Nessie's nemesis, the resident monster in a neighboring lake. One intent on snatching Dani, dragging her beneath the surface of his own loch, and keeping her there until she was dead.

As Matthew listened with increasing alarm, the lake monster antagonist stalked Dani from the shallows, all the while imagining in vivid detail how he'd capture, torture, and then drown her. It was horrifying. So horrifying, in fact, Matthew lurched to his feet and fled his office, slamming the door behind him.

Halfway down the hall, he already knew he'd fucked up. He'd shown her his genuine uneasiness when it came to scary things, and Athena would make him pay for that mistake.

Sure enough, he woke early the next morning, opened the shade on a window facing the alleyway, and—

Holy shit! Holy shit!

Quickly, he slammed the shade back down. Then opened it again, much more tentatively, to ensure he hadn't been hallucinating.

Nope. No hallucinations. Just . . . Murder Dolls.

Overnight, Athena had somehow installed a half dozen Murder Dolls in the windows facing his bedroom, their little arms reaching out to snatch him, their mouths gaping obscenely.

Back down went the shade, clattering to the windowsill with all due speed. But it was too late. He'd met the Murder Dolls' beady, malevolent eyes, so they knew him now, and they knew where he lived.

He was doomed. The last thing he'd see before his inevitable violent death at their tiny, horrifying hands? Their discolored, cracked faces and half-closed lids and creepy smiles and ragged tufts of hair, and—in one especially horrifying case—chillingly sharp teeth.

And even if Matthew miraculously survived the Murder Dolls, he was *still* doomed. Athena had been stationed at her usual window, damn her, just waiting for him to wake up and see what she'd done. His reaction would have told her everything she needed to know. He was now a marked man. Murder Dolls were just the beginning.

Over the next few days, gory decorations appeared in all the other windows that faced his home. A skeletal monster whose eyes glowed red at night. A mask with dead eyes and a smile that stretched terrifyingly wide. A fake-blood-stained ax.

One night soon thereafter, she made her next move. Only an hour into Nessie and Dani's adventures, Athena unexpectedly stopped the story—and devoted her second hour to the audiobook of *In Cold Blood*.

Some of the neighbors didn't like that, their distant grumbles cutting off abruptly as they closed their windows. But the next night, they were back again for Brazen's tale, and most stayed for both books.

Not him. Shit, he'd never sleep again if he did. Each night, as soon as Athena switched to true crime, he bolted immediately. Because while he wanted her to exact whatever vengeance she felt necessary, he also wanted to close his eyes sometime in the next decade.

Worst of all, he was entirely certain she wasn't done with him yet. The woman was not only angry as hell, but also extremely creative—and in possession of far too much free time.

Another job, he couldn't help thinking, would keep her both solvent and occupied. By something other than murder and mayhem and demon-possessed dolls, preferably.

It was time to prioritize finding Athena some damn work. Yesterday, if possible.

FIRST THING ON a Monday morning, about two weeks after Athena's payback efforts had begun in earnest, he tapped at Yvonna's office door.

"Sorry to bother you," he said quietly. "I was hoping you had a minute to talk. Not about the practice."

His best friend's voice was civil but cool, and she didn't look up from her laptop. "Yes?"

The thaw in their relationship had abruptly refrozen a month ago, when he'd argued for Johnny's continued absence from Strumpet Square Pediatrics, and even his brother's return from Hawaii hadn't improved matters much. Her willingness to speak with him about personal matters was nearly nonexistent right now, so he'd keep this conversation brief.

He stepped through the doorway but remained standing. "Did Terence hear anything about the Historic Harlot's Bay position?"

A few days ago, Yvonna's brother had alerted her to an unexpected opening at HHB, a full-time job leading group tours through the historic area. She'd forwarded the email to Matthew without comment.

He'd responded immediately. *Can Jackie possibly tell Athena about the opening without mentioning my involvement?*

I still think you should come clean, but fine. An hour later, she'd written again. Jackie had sent Athena a link to the listing, and Athena had said she'd apply that night.

Sitting back in her chair, Yvonna finally made eye contact. "Lots of applications. None from Athena. The listing closes next Monday, so she'd better not wait too long."

"Shit," he muttered, and massaged his jaw.

Nine ninny nuns nunning nunnily.

Why hadn't Athena applied? Did she object to something about the actual position? Or was something else going on?

He shouldn't ask another favor of Yvonna, but here he was, about to ask another favor. No wonder she was pissed at him.

"Uh . . ." He scratched the back of his head. "I don't suppose you or Jackie would have time to drop by Athena's house this week and discreetly offer some help with the application?"

Yvonna skewered him with a hard, merciless stare.

"Let me get this straight. You want me or my wife to visit your brother's ex-fiancée, a woman for whom I've already expended un-usual effort, given that I've only spoken to her"—she raised an elegant forefinger—"one time. And during that visit, you want us to offer help in completing the HHB application, even though she's a grown woman with multiple degrees and therefore more than capable of applying for her own work. Is that correct?"

He squeezed his eyes shut for a moment, ears aflame with em-barrassment.

Then he met her stony gaze and nodded.

"Your favor well has run dry, Matthew." Her fingers formed a perfect steeple. "Even though none of the favors you've requested have actually been for you."

The cool wall behind his back supported his sagging frame. "I understand. I'm sorry."

"So if I do this, it won't be for you," she said flatly. "It won't even be for Athena, although I liked her when we met. It'll be for

Jackie. She considers Athena a friend. She wants her to stay in the area, she wants her in that bizarre book club, and I want my wife happy, so Johnny's ex needs a job. Especially since Jackie and I both appreciate Athena's taste in sapphic monster-fucking literature."

His breath emerged in a *whoosh* of sheer relief. "Thank you. I know you won't be doing it for me, but *thank you*."

"The demoness book . . ." She trailed off, her gaze unfocused. "I haven't seen Jackie that revved up since Valkyrie frenched Lady Sif in *Thor 6: That Bridge Is Rainbow and Contains the Prefix 'Bi' for a Reason*."

She shook herself a little, as if emerging from a pleasant daydream.

"I wouldn't rush to offer gratitude, Matthew. Close the door." Once he had, she continued. "We need to talk about your brother."

"Okay," he said, already knowing whatever she told him would be both well deserved and unpleasant to hear.

"Ever since Johnny asked for more time in Hawaii, I've been trying to figure out how to say this to you." Yvonna straightened in her chair, her shoulders square. "I know having him as a doctor in our practice has made your life harder, Matthew. But he's made my life much harder too, and I could say the same for every other employee of this practice. That's eleven of us suffering for the sake of one grown man."

She let that sink in for a moment. "He's your family, not ours. I won't speak for the rest of our colleagues, but he's not even my friend. I require more from my friends than a good smile and some easy charm."

That he knew. If smiles and charm had been her prerequisites for friendship, she'd have cast Matthew aside two decades ago.

"We've been covering for him for a long time now. It hasn't helped him become a better doctor or a better colleague, and my willingness to make allowances for him has reached an end. I've given you and your brother two years already, and I'm done." Her mouth was a thin, determined line. "The next time you support him as he screws the practice over, I don't know what I'll do, but leaving isn't off the table."

He scrubbed his hands over his face, lead-limbed and defeated.

Failing to advocate for his baby brother or disciplining him like any other employee seemed wrong on a gut-deep level. But the thought of losing his best friend from the practice they'd built together . . . *fuck*.

Or maybe he couldn't even call her that anymore. Did she still consider them best friends, or friends of any sort? Even if she did, after everything he'd asked her to bear over the past two years, hadn't he forfeited the title?

"You need to do some thinking, Matthew," Yvonna said. "And in the meantime, let's both hope Johnny returned from Hawaii a changed man. Otherwise, you may need to find a new business partner."

He wished he didn't believe her. But he did.

10

*Y*et again, answering the door had been a mistake. One Athena had no intention of repeating anytime soon.

The lesson had been learned too late, however, so now she was standing on her doorstep only inches away from neat, lovely Jackie and her gorgeous, impeccably groomed wife, Yvonna. The couple stood hip to hip, their fingers intertwined, their devotion obvious. They might as well have been posing for the cover of a glossy magazine: *Success and Love Monthly*. This issue's lead article: "What These Women Have That You Never Will, Athena Greydon."

Couldn't a bitch peacefully wallow in slovenly unemployment? It had only been three weeks since her temporary library job ended, after all. Far too soon for her grasshopper to be confronted by additional industrious ants.

"Hi, Athena." Jackie smiled at her. "I hope you don't mind our dropping by."

"No, it's—" When Athena rubbed her eyes, they were crusted from sleep. It might be four o'clock on a Saturday afternoon, but a woman who stayed up all night had to rest sometime, right? "It's good. Good to see both of you."

The hand Matthew's business partner extended for shaking had gleaming, perfect nails painted in crisp chevron stripes. "Lovely to meet you again, Athena."

Slowly waking up, Athena dutifully shook. "I feel the same. I really enjoyed our conversation at the museum, and Jackie's said so many wonderful things about you."

After letting go of Yvonna's hand, she discreetly checked whether her tank top and boxer shorts were stained. They were. Splatters of canned spaghetti sauce; the orange and thin type, unbeatably cheap and impossible to remove from clothing. Not that she'd tried.

Well, this was awkward.

"I think your spam filter is eating some of your emails." Jackie was looking at her far too closely. "It doesn't seem like you've been getting the book club notifications or any of my recent messages. Or Victoria's, for that matter."

Maybe her spam filter *was* misbehaving. Athena wouldn't know, as she hadn't inspected her inbox for a while. No calls or texts had disturbed her solitude either, since her cell had needed charging for several days. She'd even managed to dodge her parents, who knew her landline number, by calling them during their work hours, leaving chipper messages, and ignoring the phone when they called back.

Other than a few grocery and thrift store trips, she'd been blessedly alone and invisible. Until now.

"I'll have to check. I'm so sorry I've missed your messages," she lied, then offered an apologetic smile—wince combo. "I'd love to invite you in, but . . ."

My house is filthy, because I'm trying to irritate Yvonna's business partner and best friend with my mess. As any mature adult would do, hahahahasob.

Okay, so maybe she wouldn't have had the energy to clean even if she wanted to, but she *didn't* want to. Cleaning was for suckers, and she didn't mean Hoovers.

Oh goodness. Had she stopped talking mid-sentence? Jackie and Yvonna were staring at her expectantly, their brows creased in confusion, so . . . yeah, probably.

With effort, she regathered her thoughts and tried again. "I'd love to invite you in, but things are a little chaotic in there right now. I'd rather have you see my home at its best, especially for a first visit."

The two women exchanged glances.

"No problem," Jackie said, her voice soothing. "We were just walking in your neighborhood, and I happened to notice your amazing Halloween decorations. Which all seem to be, uh, facing . . . one way."

Toward Matthew's house. For obvious reasons.

She couldn't afford to buy anything for the rest of the house, and without spite spurring her on, she couldn't motivate herself to care about the other sides anyway.

"Do you need help putting up anything else?" Yvonna asked. "Or did you decide just to specialize in that one area?"

"I'm a specialist." Athena braced her hands on her hips. "Less is more. Except on that one side, where more is more. Especially when it comes to creepy-ass dolls."

Yvonna bent over in a sudden coughing fit.

"I see," Jackie said blandly, thumping her wife's back in a helpful manner. "Fair enough. If you change your mind, let us know."

"I will." Athena wanted to offer them a real smile, she truly did, but had to settle for fake and forced. "Thank you so much for stopping by, both of you. I'm delighted to finally meet you again, Yvonna."

"We won't keep you." But before Jackie could leave, a thought seemed to strike her. "Wait. I almost forgot. I meant to ask whether you were having any issues with your HHB application. Like I told you, Yvonna's brother Terence works there, so I have a bit of insider knowledge as to what they're looking for, and I'd be happy to help."

Another smile Athena had to dredge from the murky depths of her being. "I'm good, but thank you, Jackie. I appreciate the offer."

She had the online application open on her laptop. She'd had it open for over a week now. It was pretty straightforward, so every day she told herself to get going. To complete the damn form. To pull up her fucking big-girl panties and do what was necessary.

It was maybe an hour's work, max.

She couldn't seem to do it.

What kind of lazy bitch couldn't fill out one fucking application? Her kind of lazy bitch, evidently, because it was too much. Every day, it was too much. Unpacking was too much. Cooking was too much. Washing dishes was too much. Checking her email was too much. Talking to her parents was too much. Canceling her absurdly expensive landline was too much.

Thinking was too much as well, and she didn't want to do it. So she read obsessively, and when she wasn't doing that, she was watching television. It kept her a state of comfortable detachment, and she liked it there.

Well, maybe not liked. She found it bearable, which was basically the same as liking if she squinted. Which she did a lot recently, because finding her glasses in the absolute chaos of her home? Too, too much.

Even without vision correction, though, she couldn't miss the alert sharpness of Yvonna's gaze. The other woman's scrutiny felt like it could penetrate to the broken, bitter heart of her.

"Athena," the doctor said after a long pause, her rose-gold hair shining in the afternoon sun, "have you seen the letter of recommendation Matthew wrote for you? The one he sent to the library and HHB? I imagine he was too shy to share, but I think you should have a copy."

What . . . the . . . actual . . . fuck?

Athena opened her mouth, then found herself both unable to close it and unable to speak.

"Vonna, you told M—" Jackie began.

Her wife held up a finger. "Hold on. By sheer coincidence, I think I may have the letter in my purse."

Jackie's eyes rolled to the wispy clouds above, as Athena's continued to bug out.

A moment later, Yvonna produced a folded, stapled document and essentially shoved it into Athena's limp hands.

"Here you are," she briskly declared. "Personally, I'd have that framed. I've never heard him talk about anyone in such glowing terms, and you know he wouldn't lie. He can't, not without blushing and stammering and flagellating himself in penance. Compared to him, Pinocchio is basically Mata Hari."

Guilt, Athena told herself numbly. *He did it out of guilt, not because he believes what he wrote. And I'm sure it's just a basic, pro forma letter. Not* glowing, *by any means.*

Still, she was holding the printout so tightly now, the paper crinkled and bent around every finger.

"That man is . . . well, you know how he feels about you, after the whole mortgage thing." Yvonna dismissed the subject with a breezy wave, even though Athena would have welcomed more information. Much, much more information. "Anyway, he was so excited when that temporary library position opened up, he practically sprinted from my office to call Bunny and tell her how great you'd be at the job. Her grandniece is his patient, you know. He wrote the letter of recommendation on his lunch break and took it to Bunny after work that day."

With a sigh, Jackie added, "Matthew also had Terence tracking any openings in the historic area and asked me to tell you about that new listing."

Athena stared at the two women blankly as she grappled with what they'd just said.

It explained everything. Everything and nothing.

No wonder the temporary library position had simply fallen into her lap. Matthew had orchestrated the job offer anonymously, just as he was attempting to do with the HHB opening. And she supposed she now knew why the mortgage company, when she'd called to ask for an extension, had told her she was good for the next two months. She'd wondered if she'd somehow paid extra previously without realizing it, or if her parents had intervened, but . . .

No. It was all Matthew.

But *why*? Why had he done it? Would even a rigidly honorable man go to those lengths for a woman he considered a mere responsibility, or could he possibly—

"He's a good man, Athena," Yvonna said softly, "and a good friend to have."

No. No, she couldn't believe it. She *wouldn't*.

The last time she'd believed in his essential kindness and hoped for his approval, he'd gutted her and left her bleeding out in her own house.

"I'm sorry, but you don't—you must have misunderstood something. We—we're not friends, Matthew and I. He thinks . . ." She blinked away the sudden, unwelcome wetness in her eyes. "He doesn't think much of me, honestly."

Yvonna shook her head. Then, when Athena nodded, shook it again.

"I hate to contradict you," Yvonna said, "but—"

Jackie snorted. "That's a lie. She loves to contradict anyone and everyone. You, me, Matthew, the people on TV, strangers on airplanes, occasional inanimate objects—"

"—that's not true in any sense. He thinks a lot of you, and he thinks of you a lot. As in, *a lot*." Ducking her head, Yvonna forced Athena to make direct eye contact with her. "If you didn't know that, you should. Read the letter, honey."

Then she took her wife's hand, offered a bright farewell, and hustled them both away before Athena quite knew what was happening.

"Matthew's going to fucking *strangle* . . ." she heard Jackie say faintly, her voice growing more distant word by word, until it was entirely inaudible.

Then they were gone, and Athena was alone again, the only evidence of their visit clutched in her sweaty hand.

It didn't matter what they'd said. Weighed against her previous experiences with Matthew, the conversation was a mere featherweight. A worthless bit of fluff. Furthermore, a simple letter couldn't change what Athena knew about her neighbor and nemesis.

Still, by the time her door shut behind her, she was already reading it.

IN SUMMATION, MS. *Greydon would be an incredible asset to Historic Harlot's Bay*, he'd written toward the end of his lengthy and—yes—astoundingly glowing letter of recommendation. *Both bright and kind, she is well-liked by everyone around her and can function beautifully both in a group setting and individually. Her background as a social studies teacher would be invaluable in the tour guide position, as would her previous living history museum experience. Her studies in psychology would allow her unusual insight into the decisions made by Harlot's Bay's original settlers, as well as the beliefs and actions of modern-day visitors to the historic area.*

Even disregarding her relevant knowledge and experience, Ms. Greydon is curious, committed to accuracy, and quick to pick up anything she needs to learn. She's also a very hard worker, one fully committed to the good of her workplace and all its inhabitants. HHB would be very fortunate to have her as its newest employee, and I can wholeheartedly recommend her for the open position without a single reservation.

If you have any questions, please feel free to contact me via—

Athena went back to the beginning and read it again. And again.

This wasn't a pro forma letter written out of guilt and an overactive sense of responsibility. Not one word reeked of obligation or reluctant necessity.

Instead, it seemed to be . . .

Somehow, he'd written . . . oh, for Pete's sake.

Impatiently, she knuckled away the tears before they could fall on the paper.

Heaven help her, the letter was a full-throated defense of her as both a person and an employee. No, not even a defense, a *celebration* of who and what she was, of where she'd been and what she'd done, and—and—

And she didn't understand. Not a sentence of it. Because how could a man like Matthew write this letter about *her,* of all people? Why would a man like Matthew have intervened on her behalf so many times, with such generosity of spirit, if not out of obligation?

Unless a man like Matthew . . . wasn't actually a man like Matthew.

Or at least, not the Matthew she'd believed him to be. Not the Matthew she'd damned and punished him for being.

And if he wasn't a rigid, judgmental asshole, if he was instead a genuinely good man who maybe even liked her but simply didn't believe she'd make a good spouse . . . could she blame him for that? After all, he wasn't wrong, was he?

So how in heaven's name could she have gotten *him* so completely and utterly wrong?

Motivated and alert for the first time in days, she set down the letter and went searching.

A few minutes digging in her third-floor detritus produced her trusty AP psychology textbook. She popped open a Diet Coke despite her persistent heartburn, sat down at her kitchen table, and flipped to several relevant sections in the hefty tome.

As it turned out, more than a few AP psych concepts explained her total misjudgment of Dr. Matthew Vine the Third.

After overhearing that terrible conversation at the museum, she'd assumed dismissive harshness must be part of his basic personality, rather than the result of a specific, stressful set of circumstances in his life. Namely, his brother's impending marriage to a totally unsuitable failure of a fiancée. As the textbook might put it, she'd overestimated the impact of person factors on someone else's behavior and underestimated the importance of situational factors. A classic case of *fundamental attribution error*, plain and simple.

But she'd made no allowances for that common mistake, and due to *overconfidence*, she'd overestimated the accuracy of her judgment when it came to him. Which was hilarious, because her excellent judgment had also led her to get engaged to a man she was pretty certain she'd never actually loved, then purchase a fucking *spite house* out of . . . well, spite.

Her judgment was shit. She shouldn't listen to it. Ever.

Because she'd deemed him rigid and hypercritical and intimidating and believed that verdict infallible, she'd figured everyone else must feel the same, which was an obvious case of *false consensus effect*. Hell, she'd even assumed his patients would be terrified of him, and had hurt his feelings by telling him so.

Fuck, what a bitch. And she knew—she *knew*—why she hadn't seen the truth earlier.

Confirmation bias. It explained her endless search for evidence that supported her Matthew-is-a-judgy-jerk theory and willful dismissal of anything contradictory. Every time a situation could be interpreted several ways, she'd chosen whichever interpretation made him the undisputed villain. Only to discover that—for instance—her cuticle-picking didn't gross him out, but simply worried him, because he didn't want her self-inflicted injury to become infected.

Considered objectively, he wasn't the villain of this particular play. She was. The woman who'd been deliberately tormenting the story's beleaguered hero for weeks now.

Shit, she couldn't even begin to list the various defense mechanisms she'd employed throughout their acquaintance. *Denial*, obviously, but *projection* too. She'd firmly believed he felt hostile toward her, simply because she'd felt hostile toward *him*.

She'd acted on that hostility too. Tried to inconvenience and discomfit him. More than that, she'd deliberately *frightened* him, and when had she become a person who'd do *that*?

In retrospect, it was all so excruciatingly obvious. So incredibly shameful.

He might have been unkind at times, but he'd also been right. About everything, including the engagement.

When Johnny ended that engagement, her heart hadn't broken. Or, rather, *he* hadn't broken her heart. She'd been lost rather than lovelorn, unsure what to do or where to go next, her pride wounded.

How could she have agreed to freaking *marry* a man whose absence from her life she hadn't especially missed? Could she honestly claim she'd ever truly loved him? Or had he been a pleasant-enough diversion from her inner turmoil and a convenient deus ex machina when it came to her work woes? And if so, what did that say about her?

Even if she'd loved Johnny as she should have, it *still* wouldn't have worked between them. Because, as Matthew had seen from the very start, she was too unsettled, too troubled, too misguided. Johnny simply hadn't noticed yet, since they'd spent so little time together. For a few months, she'd managed to fool him into thinking she was a functional human being worthy of a relationship, but she couldn't have maintained the façade forever. Sooner or later, her authentic self would have emerged, and he'd have understood the truth the same way his brother had.

She was too messy to be loved. By him. By anyone.

But instead of acknowledging that, she'd aimed all her self-directed rage at Matthew. She'd blamed him. She'd provoked him. She'd scared him.

If he did in fact like her to some degree, as the letter of recommendation seemed to indicate, she didn't understand how.

The tears on her cheeks cooled and turned sticky as she considered the matter.

Finally, tipping back her head, Athena drained her can of Diet Coke and set it alongside the others on the table. The weighty textbook thumped decisively when she slapped it closed, and she stared at the cover without seeing a thing.

When it came to work—or, hell, life in general—she had no idea what to do next. After only a minute or two of thought, though, she did know what to do about Matthew. It would be the easiest thing in the world.

She couldn't go back in time and erase her previous mistreatment of him, but she could do better from now on. Namely, by making sure he never had to see or deal with her again.

AFTER THAT SATURDAY, Athena simply didn't leave the house anymore.

It wasn't as if she had a job to report to, and groceries could be delivered. No need to venture outdoors. Better yet: The weather had turned cool enough for closed windows, and with her shades down, she couldn't be seen inside either.

Since all the residents of Harlot's Bay seemed tied to Matthew somehow, and she was removing her presence from his life entirely, she continued not talking to them. People unconnected with Matthew and Harlot's Bay, including her friends from Virginia . . . well, she didn't want to talk to them either. So she didn't.

When she couldn't avoid her parents any longer without them descending upon Harlot's Bay to investigate, she picked up the landline, offered them cheerfully vague proclamations of happiness and references to entirely fictional substitute teaching stints, then turned the conversation to their lives and hung up as soon as politely possible.

Easy-peasy.

Not thinking about her mistakes and failures proved less

challenging than anticipated too. During meals, the Food Network and HGTV kept her mind sufficiently occupied. The rest of her day she spent with her nose planted in a book, because if she immersed herself in someone else's life, she didn't have to consider her own.

Nothing in her reading roused her curiosity enough to warrant research, so Professor Google got some well-deserved rest too. Good for him.

Each night she went to bed later and later, reading until she literally couldn't stay awake any longer. No lying in bed and agonizing over poor choices for her, no sirree. She went straight to sleep, no matter when she collapsed on her mattress.

Her bedtime shifted about an hour daily. After several days, she was crawling under the covers when most other people were grabbing lunch at their workplaces.

She stopped checking the status of her rapidly dwindling bank account, even though she suspected—when a stray worry happened to sneak past her defenses—that one or two more COBRA payments would drain her savings entirely.

Since she wasn't seeing anyone, she also stopped bathing every day. Or every other day. Besides, washing up required so much effort, and she couldn't read in there. So what if she went maybe four or five days between showers? It was fine.

She cried a lot, but that was fine too.

Things would be so much easier if I could just disappear entirely, she thought sometimes in a vague sort of way. *God, what a relief.*

It usually occurred to her in the damn shower, where everything was too quiet, and whenever she had that thought, something deep inside her twinged.

Pay attention to this, a tiny, tiny voice faintly insisted. *Isn't that an odd thing to think?*

But then she'd dry off, pick up a book, and manage to disappear without actually going anywhere, if only for a few hours, and it didn't matter anymore.

For six days, *nothing* mattered, and nothing changed except her ever-later bedtime.

On the seventh day, though . . .

Heaven help them both.

On the seventh day, Dr. Matthew Vine the Third—known acrophobe; the most cautious of souls—climbed through her fucking *third-floor window*.

11

*T*his was a terrible idea. Truly terrible. Still—

"I don't have a choice," Matthew reminded himself, then leaned over the windowsill to contemplate the brick alleyway far, far below. "I have to do this."

He double-checked—more like centuple-checked—his knots and makeshift harness, making absolutely sure they matched what he'd seen after consulting Professor Google. The search query *strongest knots rock climbing* had proven very informative, especially once he added *-fishing* to exclude knots for anglers, because he wasn't a damn trout. Sadly, he wasn't even a guppy-guy with washboard abs. He was just a normal, adult-sized man.

A normal, adult-sized man who was going to perch several stories in the thin air, climb from one window to another in the dark via an old, disused ladder that was secured only on his side, and try not to die. Or vomit in terror.

No choice, he told himself sternly. *No choice*.

He tested the sturdiness of his metal ladder yet again, checking for any rusty or weak spots. It seemed solid enough, but what the hell did he know?

The third floor. The fucking *third floor*.

Matthew scrubbed a sweaty hand through his hair, working to regulate his breathing.

For about a millisecond that evening, he'd considered calling the police and asking them to check on Athena instead. Sure, she'd never forgive him for it, but she wasn't going to forgive him anyway. He didn't trust law enforcement to deal capably with whatever the issue might be, though. Far too often, people in distress—even those who'd called for assistance of their own volition—ended up dead after police intervention.

Besides, he needed to do this himself.

Because he wouldn't inflict a stranger on Athena, especially if she were ailing somehow. Because suffering through his terror of heights felt like penance for hurting her so many times, in so many ways. Because doing this would silently make the same statement he'd withheld during their last conversation—*I care about you far too much*—and she deserved to know it. He needed to show her, since he simply couldn't bear for her to go on thinking the opposite.

He also couldn't bear his continuing uncertainty about whether she was okay.

Maybe she was simply taking some time to herself, and maybe she was regularly in touch with her parents or her friends in Virginia. But sometime last Saturday, she'd taken down the Murder Dolls and her other horrifying Halloween decorations, then closed all her shades for the first time since she'd moved in—and as far as he could tell, no one in Harlot's Bay had seen a glimpse of her since.

Starting that weekend, her windows had remained stubbornly shut during her normal Sadie Brazen story times, much to the disgruntlement of their neighbors. And on Monday, after the deadline for the Historic Harlot's Bay position had passed, Terence had confirmed her lack of a completed application.

That was when Matthew rang her doorbell the first time. She hadn't answered. Not the second time he'd visited either, or the third, or the tenth.

At that point, he'd recruited people Athena actually *liked* for assistance: Victoria, Jackie, Bez, even Karl. But she didn't respond to their knocks, didn't pick up when they called, and didn't answer their texts, their DMs, or their emails.

Her car remained parked beside the curb. The usual gossip chain of their small town reported that she'd had groceries delivered at least once. She was *there*. She was just . . . isolating herself. To an alarming extent.

"Did something else happen when you talked to her that day?" he'd asked Yvonna countless times. "I know you told her about my role in her job hunt and shared my letter of recommendation, but did anything apart from that seem to be troubling her? Was she ill?"

Yvonna had been remarkably patient with the repeated questions. She'd finally, thankfully forgiven him, maybe out of guilt, or maybe because Johnny had actually been doing his job. Nevertheless, Matthew got the same answer each time he asked. She couldn't tell him anything new. Athena had seemed sleepy and unkempt and stunned by what they'd said to her. Unhappy, but not in any sort of acute danger and not sick.

So, yes, maybe she was merely taking a staycation, as Bez had tentatively suggested. But maybe she was in crisis somehow. There was no way to know.

He'd been anxious about the situation all week. Then, as soon as he'd gotten home today, he'd noticed the newly cracked-open window across the alleyway.

Thank goodness for another unseasonably hot day, and thank goodness he hadn't gone with his first instinct: climbing directly from his window to hers without any safety precautions, like some sort of aged, not-especially-limber, doomed-to-splatting Spider-

Man wannabe. Instead, he'd done his research, and any moment now, he would be crossing from his office to her library while three floors in the air, good sense be damned.

His heartbeat seemed to echo in his skull, and he was still breathing much too fast.

It didn't matter. His time had come.

He'd already secured the ladder on his side as best he could and used it to nudge her window as high as possible. There was absolutely nothing left to do except climb aboard.

"Here I go," he choked out, and heaved himself onto his makeshift bridge. It shifted beneath him slightly as he knelt, which wasn't at all alarming, and definitely didn't make a trickle of sweat roll between his shoulder blades. "We who are about to die salute you."

Without further hesitation, he began slowly, slowly crawling.

IN THE END, Matthew made it across. Barely.

It all went well enough at first. His tunnel-vision stare remained trained on either her window frame or the knots anchoring his makeshift harness to the ladder, knots he had to reposition one at a time as he moved.

Because if everything went wrong and he fell off the ladder, those internet-guided knots would save his life. Assuming he'd created the harness correctly. And the knots connecting that harness to the ladder. And the knots connecting that ladder to the radiator in his office.

Professor Google better know what the fuck he's doing.

Halfway through, though, Matthew made the mistake of looking down at the bricks below, and shit. *Shit.* Vertigo crashed over him like a tidal wave, and he clutched the ladder beneath him with clawed, shaking hands as he swallowed frantic gulps of air.

His hands cramped, but he couldn't let go. Couldn't move.

Athena. He had to think of Athena. Her blood on his hands. Dried and dark.

That memory, and only that memory, returned him to shuddering motion. Sick with fear, crying with it, on the verge of hyperventilating, he moved one inch. Then another.

Minutes later, when he finally reached the other end of the ladder and scrambled off, desperate for solid ground, his knees collapsed beneath him. He landed on a paperback and an empty, now-crushed Diet Coke can.

Holy fuck.

Improbably enough, he'd *done it*. He might be spent and racked with uncontrollable tremors, but he was kneeling safely inside Athena's library nook. He clung to her window frame for a few moments, panting, before recovering himself enough to undo all the knots holding him to the ladder.

He ran a sweaty forearm over his equally sweaty forehead and tried to determine his next step. Frankly, he hadn't even considered what to do once he made it across the ladder, because his imagination had stalled in the thin air over that alleyway.

On some level, he guessed, he hadn't expected to survive the crossing.

A thick blanket of silence smothered the stale, musty house. The entire third floor was dark, as were all the other spaces readily visible to him.

It was eight in the evening, though, too early for bed. Athena should have easily heard his clanking progress and can-crunching arrival and reacted somehow.

Earphones, he told himself. *She could be wearing earphones . . .*

Even though she's alone. With almost all her windows shut.

No more speculation. It was time to know for sure what was going on.

When he turned on the lamp beside her window, he scanned the third floor and saw nothing ominous, just scattered books and papers and cans. But the light didn't bring her running either, which was . . . troubling.

Since he'd only invade her bedroom if absolutely necessary, he trudged downstairs next, anxiety a leaden weight in every step. The second floor was as messy and silent as the third, although it smelled somewhat more strongly of trash. The TV on the wall was turned off. The loveseat contained nothing but a few paperbacks, a tangled blanket, and yet more Diet Coke cans. The bathroom at the far end of the floor could have used a good scrubbing but stood empty.

The garbage-smell intensified as he took the narrow stairs to the first floor. A flick of the light switch revealed dirty dishes piled on her countertops, lots of them. Cans and boxes thickly covering the dining room table. An overflowing trash container, which explained the odor.

No Athena.

Once again, he had no choice. Breaching the sanctity of her fourth-floor bedroom would constitute such a terrible violation of her privacy, but . . . he needed to see her. He needed to be certain he didn't fail her as he'd failed Adrian. If someone had only noticed what was happening and intervened in time—

He sprinted up the stairs, three flights of them, and slammed the fourth-floor light switch upward with the edge of his fist.

There. *There.*

Involuntarily folding in half, he braced his hands on his knees and fought tears of relief. Because there she lay, only steps away, atop her bed. Curled up on her side under a single sheet, hair a dark-honey tangle against her white pillow, brow puckering as she shifted and blinked dazedly.

Alive. Conscious. Not in any immediate danger.

"What . . . the fuck?" she murmured, her voice drowsy and thick. *"Matthew?"*

She half raised herself on an elbow, the movement jerky and uncoordinated, squinting at him through the lank bangs flopping across her forehead and into her eyes.

Crumpled tissues lay scattered all over her bedside floor. Her eyes were reddened and swollen, she appeared disoriented, and— why wasn't she screaming at him to *get out*?

Gingerly, he sat on the edge of her bed, near her hip. Expecting to be slapped away at any moment, he reached out and smoothed her hair off her forehead. Then he laid the back of his hand there. Not overly warm, but he should confirm that with a thermometer.

"Athena," he said quietly. "Have you been ill?"

Her breathing was steady and unlabored, and she didn't appear or sound especially congested. When he took her pulse at her wrist, it was within normal range. A quick press of his fingertips suggested the lymph nodes in her neck weren't swollen.

Once he'd finished the quick exam, she sank back onto her mattress and curled up a bit tighter, her hands clasped and tucked beneath her chin. Her lids drooped, and she turned her head to yawn into her pillow.

"I'm fine. Just tired." Her forehead creased a tiny bit. "What time is it? And why are you here?"

"I've been worried about you." He glanced at her bedside clock. "It's a bit after eight."

"Night or morning?"

With her blackout shades drawn, time of day could be hard to determine. Still, her confusion on the issue didn't bode well.

"Night," he said, running light hands over her skull in search of bumps or bleeding. "Have you hurt yourself? Fallen, maybe?"

She shook her head, the movement slight. It didn't seem to pain her, though.

Still— "Any dizziness? Headaches?"

As best he could, he visually scanned the rest of her, but couldn't find any obvious signs of injury. Should he remove the sheet to check more thoroughly? Would she rouse herself enough to murder him if he did?

"Uh-uh. Matthew . . ." With a breathy sigh, she settled herself more comfortably. "I don't really get why you're here, but I only went to bed, um . . ." She paused, evidently to do the math. "Two hours ago. Can I just go back to sleep? Please?"

"Only if you promise me you haven't been sick or injured." Shit, he hoped she'd tell him the truth about that. "No one's seen you for days, and we've all been concerned."

"Promise," she murmured, her eyes closing as she spoke. "Cross my heart and hope to die."

He recoiled. "Don't *ever* say that. Please."

"Okay." She smiled a little, but then her brows drew together, and she shifted restlessly. "You're a good man. Sorry for what I did to you."

A good man? What the fuck?

Another quick check of her skull didn't reveal any overlooked cranial trauma, so he was stumped. But he supposed his answers could wait until after she'd slept more.

"You don't owe me an apology." He wanted so many things

from her, so few of which he could have. Contrition was not and would never be one of them. "Not after what I've done to *you*."

"Hmmm." Her frown remained, even as her words turned increasingly slow and indistinct. "Thanks for . . . checking on me. Tell everyone I'm . . . fine, okay? Lock up when . . . you leave . . . please."

Until he'd gathered all the information he needed to determine whether she was all right, he was going nowhere. She'd discover that for herself soon enough, however.

She pried one eyelid slightly open, peering at him through her lashes. "Probably good . . . you have a spare key. Just . . . in case."

Wincing, he prepared to confess everything. His, er, *unconventional* means of entry. The gouges his ladder had left in her window frame. How Joaquin and Wade had reclaimed all their spare keys before moving out of the Spite House.

Matthew had no key and no excuse for breaking into her home. Nothing except his anxiety and his . . . feelings . . . for her.

Then a faint snore drifted from her pillow. Carefully, he rose to his feet, trying not to jostle the mattress or wake her. All his confessions would keep until later. They'd have to.

While she was sleeping, he had work to do.

YEESH, WHAT A bizarre dream.

Why Athena's subconscious had chosen to imagine Dr. Matthew Vine's presence at her bedside, his gentle touch on her face and neck, his dark gaze soft and studying her with such concerned care, she had no idea. Sure, maybe Joaquin or Wade had given him a spare key at some point, but even a good man's sense of responsibility to his brother's ex had its limits. And thank goodness it *was* just a dream, because right now neither she nor her home had been cleaned in a while, and neither smelled particularly good.

Rolling to one side, she checked the time. A bit after midnight.

Six hours of sleep. Good enough. She could always nap again later.

Heaving herself to her feet, she yawned and stretched, then padded down to the bathroom. After peeing, she washed her hands and decided to go back upstairs. She could read in bed for a while before scrounging for something to eat in her depleted cabinets and empty refrigerator.

As always, she had to turn slightly sideways to fit within the narrow, spiraling stairway, which she kind of hated. So much about this house made her feel awkward and oversized, when her body had never been a real concern or hindrance to her in the past.

Once she got upstairs, though, the fourth floor was her tower. Her impregnable sanctuary, equipped with her best and truest companion, the bed. Grabbing a paperback, she propped herself against the headboard and prepared to think about other people's lives for as long as possible.

The wife had definitely murdered her husband at the campsite. Ann Rule was drawing out the matter, but Athena had no doubts, and honestly, what else did they expect when they went camping? They were privileged, well-to-do Americans. Without indoor plumbing and electricity, of *course* someone was going to lose their shit and start stabbing people.

"Um, Athena," came a tentative male voice from somewhere downstairs, and she'd like to say she didn't jerk violently and shriek and instinctively throw her paperback across the room, but that'd be a lie, because she totally did all those things. "Fuck. Sorry. I'm so sorry, I didn't mean to scare you, but I heard the water running and realized you were awake, so—"

"*Matthew?*" She knew that voice, but— "Cheeses *Pete*, what in heaven's name are you *doing* here?"

"I—I apologize." He spoke hurriedly, tripping over the words. "I'm very sorry, Athena. I know I shouldn't have entered your home without permission, but I was concerned, *everyone* was concerned, and I had to—I had to know if you were okay. May I come up?"

"Just . . . wait." Taking deep, calming breaths, she covered her legs with the sheet and reminded herself that she wasn't angry with him anymore. That she did, in fact, owe him recompense of some sort, or at least all the politeness and patience she could currently muster. "Okay. You can come up."

His footsteps thumped softly on the stairs, and then he was there. In her bedroom. Navigating the obstacle course of her floor, standing beside her mattress, and studying her with deep creases above his inner brows.

She couldn't locate words sufficient for the situation, so she just clutched a pillow to her chest for reassurance and waited for him to explain himself further.

Silence. Awkward, awkward silence.

He opened his mouth, only to pause before he finally spoke. "I invaded your home without your permission, and you're not angry. Why aren't you angry?"

There was no point in pretending she was okay. It wasn't as if he could have somehow missed the current state of both her hygiene and her house, so why bother?

"Anger requires energy. I have none to spare." Her dismissive wave lasted only a moment, and then her hand dropped limply onto the sheet. "Also, I'm done being mad at you. That's the other reason I'm not, uh"—she paused, searching in vain for greater eloquence—"mad at you."

More silence. She stared at his bloodshot eyes, wondering numbly why he looked so terrible, and how much longer it'd be before he left and she'd be alone again.

"Okay. That's . . . good? I think." His frown deepened. "Athena, I asked you this before, and I apologize for repeating myself, but—have you been ill? Injured? Maybe you changed medications recently?"

She shook her head.

"Then I don't understand." He perched on the edge of her mattress. "Why haven't you been answering your door, your cell, or your messages?"

Fine, so maybe she was done pretending to be okay, but did she have to *explain* her lack of okay-ness? Couldn't he just accept it as fact, given what he'd already seen?

She hitched up her knees, an embarrassingly self-protective gesture. "When did you get here? You were around earlier, right? That wasn't just a dream?"

Not the slickest change of subject in human history, but whatever.

"A bit after eight." With a sigh, he raked his fingers through his dark hair, leaving it rumpled. "I have a confession to make, Athena."

Her brows rose, and a spark of interest lit within her.

"I don't have a key to your home." Ruddy color climbed his cheeks. "Well, I *didn't*, anyway. I do now. I took it from your kitchen drawer."

Then how the heck had he gotten inside? She kept all her doors locked, and until yesterday, every single one of her windows had been— "Wait. Wait. No way."

"Yes way. I think. Depending on what just occurred to you." Listing tiredly to one side, he braced himself with a hand on the mattress. "If it helps solve the mystery, I didn't break anything or procure a lock-picking kit, so . . ."

She stared at him in astonishment. "I must have opened a first-floor window without realizing it. Because as far as I know, the only open window was on the third floor, and you're clearly terrified of heights and a very cautious man, so there's no way in hell you climbed across from up there."

"Um . . ." His attempt at a smile looked more like a grimace. "Surprise?"

"No," she whispered. "You couldn't have."

For her? He'd done that for *her*? And if so, why? Neighborly concern and a sense of responsibility vast enough to dwarf the solar system, or . . . something else?

"I did what I needed to do." It was a simple statement, spoken without a hint of self-congratulation, and it stunned her.

"But . . . you're acrophobic."

"Eh." He shrugged. "I only dry heaved once. I barely even hyperventilated."

Her chapped lips curved the slightest bit, because he really was funny, in his own dry, understated way. Then she pictured the drop from the third floor, the unmerciful bricks below, and that flicker of amusement died.

She shoved aside the pillow in her lap, suddenly filled with restless energy. "You could have *killed* yourself, Matthew. What the hell were you *thinking*?"

Another dismissive lift of his shoulder. "I used a ladder. I didn't just leap from one window to the other, like a . . ." He pursed his mouth in thought. "Like whatever sort of animal could success-fully do that. A mountain goat, maybe?"

"A worthy query for Professor Google." The first she'd wanted to research in days. "But even with a ladder, crossing from window to window was still incredibly dangerous, and trust me, I am *not* worth that kind of risk."

He glanced down at his lap then. After a moment, he gave a little nod, but it didn't look like agreement. It looked like . . . recognition.

"Athena." His eyes lifted to hers, and they were so warm, so clear, so sad, she couldn't seem to look away. "You didn't answer my earlier question."

She knew which one.

No matter how hard she blinked, the room blurred in front of her.

"I'm not your doctor or your lover, and I'm sure you don't con-sider me a friend. I won't press you if you don't want to talk about it, but . . ." Something blotted away her tears. It smelled clean and felt soft against her cheek. "Why haven't you left the house or talked to anyone all week? Can you tell me?"

She bit her lip. Bowed her head.

The man apparently carried around an actual freaking hand-kerchief. Of course he did. But she couldn't even laugh about it, because . . . god.

That low, tender voice *hurt*.

Like the concern in his soft brown gaze, like his ludicrously brave journey between their windows, it was a weapon. One he'd deployed at exactly the right spot to weaken the wall she'd erected between her and . . . everyone. Everything. Her own thoughts.

The feelings that could sweep her into oblivion if she didn't keep them dammed safely away.

The acknowledgment she'd been avoiding for a long, long time now.

She licked her cracked lips, and the moisture stung. "Matthew . . ."

No. She couldn't speak the words. She wouldn't, because if she did, that would mean she'd have to relinquish the only thing she had left. Her pride. She'd have to admit that nothing, absolutely nothing, was fine, and she'd have to do something about it, and she was so fucking *tired* all the time.

Tired and sad. So horribly, unendingly sad.

He'd cradled her against him at some point, supporting her as she shook, and his lips rested against the crown of her head. Her nose was running, and he blotted that too, and something about the gesture, its intimacy, its pragmatic kindness, broke her.

She closed her eyes and let the wall crumble. "Do . . . do you think I'm depressed?"

"Yes, sweetheart," Matthew said quietly, then gathered her closer, and she sobbed in his arms until she could barely breathe.

12

When Matthew handed Athena a cool, wet washcloth, she pressed it to her eyes and sagged against the bathroom sink. "I guess I should find a therapist that takes my insurance. Make an appointment with a doctor, too, to talk about antidepressant options. God, what a pain in the ass."

As carefully as possible, he'd already asked her about suicidal ideation, and she didn't seem to be in any immediate danger. This might constitute a crisis, but not one that required a trip to the ER. Come Monday, he'd make some calls, and hopefully therapy and meds would eventually help, as they did for most people.

In the meantime, she needed a friend, someone she could trust. She might consider him neither of those things, but he was both. From now on, he would always, always be both, no matter the consequences. He was done hurting this woman.

She was still sniffling from her crying jag, still hiccupping every so often, and the few remaining uncracked bits of his heart broke with each forlorn, half-stifled sound of lingering grief.

"If absolutely necessary, I could write a prescription for your medication." Grime ringed her sink, and he tried not to wince when she draped her washcloth there. His cleaning efforts hadn't yet reached the second floor before she woke up, which was a shame. "But I'd rather you get it from someone more objective, and someone who deals with adult patients on a regular basis. I can arrange for you to see an excellent local doctor on Monday, if you'd like. I could probably help you find a good therapist this week too."

A number of people in Harlot's Bay owed him favors. The time had come to collect.

Another gut-wrenching sniffle. He handed her a tissue, since his handkerchief had no more dry corners, and she blew her nose.

"I—I would appreciate that. Thank you." With a listless flick of her fingers, she dropped the tissue into the trash. "Everything has felt kind of . . . overwhelming . . . for a while now, and I could—I could use the help. Thank you, Matthew."

I don't want your gratitude.

"You're welcome, but I'm happy to do it." More than happy. Honored. Relieved.

"Which reminds me . . ." The washcloth had begun dripping onto the tile floor from where she'd laid it over the edge of the sink, and she wrung it out and repositioned it with a sigh. "I know you're the one who paid my mortgage for two months."

He sighed too. "Dammit, Yvonna."

"I owe you." Her shoulders drooped. "I'll pay you back as soon as I can."

"I'm not worried about that," he told her, leaning against her bathroom doorway.

"I a-am."

Her voice betrayed her, undercutting the firmness of her response with a quaver. Her eyes were swimming with tears again, and hectic color—embarrassment?—had flooded her cheeks.

His thumbs were cleaner than that damn washcloth now, so he used them to carefully dry her wet cheeks, then cupped her sweet face in his palms until she was willing to make eye contact.

"I think right now is a good time not to worry about anyone but yourself, love," he said gently. "Let the people who care about you worry about everything else."

But that only elicited more heart-cracking tears, and he couldn't kiss them away, so he dropped his hands and fumbled for both a clean tissue and a change of topic.

"Speaking of people who care about you," he said as she blew her nose again, "you have some choices to make. Here's the first: Either you let me or someone else check on you regularly until you're feeling better, or I'll have to contact your parents."

Johnny would have their number. If forced to do so, Matthew would get it from him, even though he'd rather his brother remain as distant as possible from the current situation.

As she began to protest, he raised his hand. "I don't want to do it, Athena, but I will. You might be a fully independent adult, more than capable of taking care of yourself, but you're too important not to have someone watching over you while you're going through a rough patch. So who's it going to be? Your parents, one of your local friends, or—"

"You." She hesitated, even as he blinked at her in pleased shock. "If that's okay. It's just . . . I hate having anyone see me this way, but you've already witnessed the worst of it, so . . ."

At that, he deflated a bit. But what had he expected, anyway? That holding her through a single bout of crying would make her declare him Her Favorite Person Ever, and she would anoint him her knight-protector because she trusted him above all others?

Idiot.

"Understood." He nodded. "I'm happy to check in with you, and I'll keep this private unless you tell me otherwise. But, Athena,

I genuinely think you should let your friends support you while you're struggling. They care about you. They'll *want* to help. Why don't you text Victoria? Or someone from Virginia?"

She narrowed her reddened eyes at him, and the stubborn set of her jaw wasn't hard to read. He had significant experience with that defiant jut, unfortunately.

"Fine. That's up to you," he conceded. "May I at least tell your local friends that you're not sick or injured, and you'll contact them when you're ready?"

After thinking for a moment, she exhaled hard. "Okay. Fine."

"Thank you." That would considerably relieve the concerns of various people around Harlot's Bay. Did she even realize how much goodwill and affection she'd already earned in her new community? "Three more choices."

She rolled her swollen eyes. "Oh, goody."

At the welcome reappearance of her usual sarcasm, he couldn't help it. He had to touch her. Had to brush a forefinger over that beauty mark high on her left cheek and smile down at her. When she gazed back up at him, her breath hitching, he could have sworn he saw something more than grief and embarrassment in those tired hazel eyes. Something warmer.

Clearing his throat, he lowered his hand. "I know you haven't had much energy lately. May I help you straighten up your house a little?"

A lot. *A lot.*

"I'm sorry it's such a disaster in here. Even before I was like"— she swept a hand, indicating her current state—"this, things were already messy." She paused, then added, "In part because I was deliberately trying to needle you, Mr. Everything-in-Its-Place."

Ah, so she was admitting it. In that case, he might as well congratulate her on the thoroughness of her efforts to bother him and the impressive results she'd achieved.

"Successfully, I might add." Propping his shoulder against the doorframe, he crossed his arms over his chest and kept his tone solemn. "Your support of my MLM *side hustle* ambitions was very gratifying, by the way. Thank you for that."

She snickered, and the glowing pride he took in that sound could have lit the entire state of Maryland.

"In case you didn't notice, our entire neighborhood enjoyed your nightly Sadie Brazen Story Hour." He winced a little. "I'm sure most of them liked *In Cold Blood* too. Not to mention your Halloween decorations."

Murder Dolls. Gah, *Murder Dolls*.

He hoped she'd disposed of them safely. I.e., under several feet of packed earth, encased in an unbreakable tomb of some sort, with the assistance of an exorcist.

Her smile had died. "Please forgive me, Matthew. Once I realized scary stuff bothered you, I used that knowledge in the cruelest possible way. I'll understand if you can't forgive me, but I want you to know I'm sincerely very, very sorry."

You don't need to apologize, he almost said again, echoing what he'd told her earlier that evening. *I understand why you did it*.

But in her current state of mind, she wouldn't accept that. She'd simply feel guiltier that he wasn't angry at her. What she needed was a form of penance, however unnecessary.

And he knew just the thing.

"I'll forgive you," he said, "if you'll let me clean and organize your entire home."

She actually gasped. "*No*, Matthew. Watching you work in here, when I left everything dirty and messy specifically to bother you, would make me feel terrible."

"Yes. You'd feel terrible."

"Oh," she said slowly. "That would be my punishment."

"Your *penance*," he corrected, "will be keeping me company as I clean and doing absolutely nothing to help me."

Her brow puckered. "But wouldn't that hurt you more than it hurts me?"

"I like cleaning." He found it relaxing. Meditative, almost. "So what do you say?"

"Okay." She exhaled slowly. "Okay, you can clean and organize my house. As long as you promise to forgive me."

"I promise." Perfect. "You should know that you've earned one floor of absolution so far. It would have been two floors, but you woke up earlier than I expected."

"Oh, for . . ." She gripped the back of her neck and squeezed. "What have you done, Vine?"

"You'll see. Two more choices, Athena."

She gestured for him to get on with it.

Hopefully she was still feeling guilty. "When you have a bit more energy, may I help you find work? Something offering benefits and a living wage that you wouldn't mind too much?"

It took her a minute, but she eventually nodded. "Yes. Please. And thank you for landing me the library job and making sure I knew about the HHB opening. That letter of recommendation you wrote was . . . very kind."

Not kind. Truthful. But he wouldn't interrupt his current string of successes by arguing with her.

"Last choice." He kept his voice gentle, because this wasn't a demand. It was an offer. "Are you willing to talk to me about what's troubling you?"

He had his suspicions. But he certainly didn't understand everything, and he wanted to know. He wanted an accurate rendering of her sorrows, so he could study the map, help her navigate through treacherous waters, and watch her make landfall once more.

She needed some solid ground beneath her. And until she had it, she could use a companion with a steady hand, as he'd often thought. Not to take her wheel, because she was her own captain, but to keep her balanced and strong as she righted her ship.

"No," she whispered. "Not yet. I'm sorry."

He wished to hell she'd stop freaking *apologizing* to him. He got why she didn't want to share her innermost thoughts with a man she'd loathed until very recently. But in that case—

"Athena . . ." Once more, he gathered the visual evidence of her time spent in misery and isolation. The tear-blotched face. The dirty hair. The stained clothing. "Who do you talk to about everything? When you're hurting, who do you call?"

Because whoever they were, he'd make certain they were ready to support her.

She bit her lip, her eyes filling, but she forced out her heart-rending answer. "N-no one."

In lieu of the sort of solace he wanted to offer, he pressed another tissue into her hand.

A few deep breaths later, she managed to regain her equilibrium. "That was the last choice, right? Can we go downstairs now? I'd like to eat."

Sudden anxiety tightened his gut, because what if he'd miscalculated? What if the meal he'd prepared only reminded her of his past transgressions, the pain he'd caused, rather than showing her how clearly he remembered what brought her pleasure?

He wasn't a man who gambled, but this was a reckless shove of his chips to the center of the table, and his nerves jangled as he led them both downstairs, into her now-sparkling kitchen.

"Holy *fuck*," she said, mouth agape as she surveyed her transformed first floor. "You—you did my dishes. You scrubbed the floor. You gathered all the recycling, all the trash, and—wait. Where are the boxes? Did you . . . did you unpack all my kitchen supplies too?"

He couldn't quite read her tone. Was that an objection, or simply confusion?

"Um, yes." He shifted uncomfortably. "You can rearrange them to your liking whenever you want, obviously. But until then, everything should be easier for you to find this way, and you'll be able to walk around without tripping."

"Holy fuck," she repeated. "Matthew, I—I don't know how to thank you for this."

Enough. "Then don't, please. No more thank-yous and no more apologies. Consider that the second and final part of your penance."

"Dammit, Vine." She propped her fists on her hips, aggrieved and wet eyed. "That's just mean. Plus, we'd already reached an agreement about forgiveness."

He raised an unimpressed brow. "Don't play the true crime if you can't do the no-apologies-or-gratitude time."

"Hmph." Turning her back on him, she headed for the fridge. "Well, if I can't thank you, I should at least feed you, but I don't know if I have—"

She opened the refrigerator door and stopped dead at the sight of the packed shelves.

"I swear to all that's holy," she said, fervent sincerity in every word, "if you keep being nice to me and don't let me express my gratitude, I will murder you, Dr. Matthew Vine the Third. And I've been reading a lot of Ann Rule recently, so I'll probably get away with it too."

For the first time ever, when she called him that, it didn't sound like mockery or sarcasm. More like . . . a sort of nickname, just between the two of them.

"Penance," he reminded her. "Speaking of which, I already made food for us both, and you can't thank me for that either."

Athena didn't seem to have noticed the platter on her countertop yet. Bracing himself for her reaction, he lifted his offering and carefully placed it on her freshly cleared table.

The potato chips lay in neat rows, each topped by a small dollop of crème fraîche, little bits of chives he'd cut with scissors, and a thin slice of smoked salmon.

He'd taste-tested what he'd assembled. It wasn't quite the same, but it was close.

"I hoped . . ." Swallowing over such a dry throat hurt. "I thought about how happy this dish made you, and I . . . hope this is okay."

She didn't say a word. She just kept staring at the loaded potato chips.

"I know the caterers did it better. They probably fried their own potato crisps, for example, and—"

"Oh, damn," she whispered, then sniffed loudly. "You *remembered*."

Shit. She was tearing up again.

"I'm sorry." He reached for the platter, intending to remove it from her sight, from her house, and preferably from her memory and all of human existence. "I shouldn't have—"

"D-don't you touch those p-potatoes, Vine." Her voice trembled, but she'd darted between him and the table, fists planted on her hips. "I l-love them."

Then she bent in half and started crying in earnest. He opened his arms, and she fell into them.

MUCH LATER THAT morning, Matthew called his brother.

Exhausted by her weeping, Athena had gone back to bed not long after they'd polished off the potato chips. Taking advantage of her absence—because he didn't truly want her to suffer through watching him clean—he'd tackled the second-floor bathroom, then surrendered to his own fatigue for several hours.

Luckily, Yvonna had already been scheduled for their Saturday hours today, but he needed to make arrangements for the following week. Discreetly, and without revealing anything Athena didn't want known.

"I apologize for the late notice, but I'm taking time off this week," he said without preamble. "Every day after two, I'll need you to cover for me, and you'll have to take my after-hours on-call shifts as well. Right after I hang up with you, I'm phoning the front-desk staff and letting them know to reschedule those afternoon appointments and transfer them to you. I don't want Yvonna doing any of this."

None of that was a request. Of all the people in Harlot's Bay who owed him favors, Johnny remained the deepest in debt by far. As recently as yesterday, Matthew would have denied that debt's existence or sworn he'd never collect on it, but things had changed. After holding a sobbing Athena in his arms, *he'd* changed.

His determination to remain by her side had nothing to do with his brother or the broken engagement. Nothing to do with responsibility or obligation or honor. It was simply an . . . imperative. A nonnegotiable demand originating from somewhere much more deep-seated, much more atavistic, than his conscience.

His prefrontal cortex could go fuck itself. Less enlightened parts of his brain were hereby in charge.

"Matthew, what—" Johnny's voice was shocked. "You never take time off, especially not at the last minute. Are you ill? Do you need me to come over there? Just let me get dressed, and I'll—"

"No." When his brother began to protest, he said with firm authority, "There's no need to come over. I'm fine."

"Then what—"

"I'm tired, Johnny. I've worked incredibly hard over the past several months, and I'm tired." All true. All a deliberate attempt to play on whatever guilt his brother might feel over that extended trip to Hawaii, which wasn't very brotherly of Matthew, but so be it. "I need time off, and I need it now."

"Okay." After a long pause, Johnny repeated, "Okay. Don't worry about calling the front-desk staff. I'll do it myself, and we'll work out the logistics for next week. Are you sure you don't want to leave during the lunch break, instead of at two?"

That was . . . a surprisingly thoughtful question, albeit one that showed his brother's ignorance when it came to their practice. "I can't. If I leave then, you won't be able to fully cover my appointments, even by coming in early and staying late. No matter what, I don't want Yvonna taking a single extra patient."

If he intended to stay her best friend, he needed to act like one. No more hanging her out to dry. Certainly not for the sake of his brother's desires, or even his own.

"Understood. I'll make sure that doesn't happen," Johnny said resolutely.

"Thank you." He meant that. His brother could have objected, could have insisted on an explanation or whined, but he hadn't. He'd simply . . . stepped up. Like a loyal sibling. Like a loyal colleague. Like an adult.

"Matty, are you sure you're okay?"

Matthew closed his eyes and let it soak into his parched bones. For thirty years, he'd been trying to replace the family his little brother never had, and now . . .

God, he'd forgotten how it felt for *him* to have a family. One where responsibilities and obligations and worry and love didn't always flow in a single direction. One not entirely comprised of Yvonna, who'd been his sister in every way but blood for a long time now.

"I'll be fine." Better than fine, if Johnny was finally becoming the man Matthew had always hoped his brother would be. "But thank you for asking, and thank you for taking on the extra work."

"I love you, bro." Johnny's voice had turned a bit hoarse. "If you need me, call or text or just come over."

That wouldn't be a lengthy trip, since Matthew would be spending most of his afternoons and evenings only a single brick wall away from his brother. Thank goodness very little sound made it through that thick barrier. Occasional thumps, but no voices. No conversation.

"Love you too," he told Johnny, and hoped like hell his brother never discovered just how Matthew intended to spend his time off.

13

When Matthew let himself inside Athena's house that afternoon, he couldn't hear any sounds from the fourth floor, so he figured she was still sleeping. Which was good, since she needed her rest, and he needed a couple hours to tackle the remainder of the second floor.

By the time her footsteps came creaking down the two flights of stairs to the bathroom, he'd finished cleaning that level of her home and was stretching his back, sore but content.

Groggily, she surveyed him and their surroundings.

"I can't thank you or apologize," she finally told him, her lips curving slightly upward. "So I won't express either my heartfelt gratitude or my immense guilt at all the work you've done and how tired you must be. Feel free to compliment my considerable restraint."

"It's remarkable," he said obligingly.

It really was. The way she battled through her obvious misery and dug deep to offer him a small, sweet smile. How the brightness of her wit couldn't help but shine through, even in her darkest hour.

"My house and I no longer match." She trudged into the bathroom, and the closing door muffled her next words. "It's much cleaner than I am now."

He'd been thinking about that issue. Her un-showered state bothered him, although not for the reasons she'd probably assume.

While she didn't smell fresh as a daisy, she didn't smell *bad* to him, and he honestly wouldn't care if she did. But people usually got itchy after a few days without bathing, and she seemed self-conscious about her state of dishevelment. If she washed up in the shower, she'd probably be much more comfortable.

When she emerged from the bathroom a minute later, he chose his words carefully. "I know you've been really tired and over-whelmed. Sometimes, when I'm exhausted, even taking a shower can feel like a lot."

She eyed him askance. "You mean I smell."

"No. Not really." After more side-eyeing from her, he conceded, "A little, but not in a bad way. It's just—I think you'd feel better if you were clean."

"I know, but . . ." She spread her hands in a sad, helpless gesture. "It's hard to make myself do it. My shower is so freak-ing small, I have to contort myself to reach various parts of my body, and I hate how quiet it is. I can't distract myself from my thoughts while I'm in there, and my brain is *not* a good place to be right now, Matthew."

"I understand." He shifted from foot to foot, then made him-self say it. "I was wondering if maybe you might let me help. Since it's a tub-shower combination, you could just sit, and I'd handle whatever feels too difficult for you. I wouldn't—I wouldn't take advantage of the situation. I wouldn't even look at you unless absolutely necessary."

She was poised to refuse him. He could see it in her expression.

Before she could say no, he kept talking. "I understand why you might be too shy or uncomfortable to say yes, but I won't hurt or embarrass you. I promise, Athena. I swear it on my"— he had to pause, if only for a moment—"on my brother's grave."

Her eyes went wide with shock.

Had Johnny truly never told her about Adrian? Or was she simply stunned that Matthew had invoked his lost brother's name in this context?

Maybe it would seem blasphemous to most people. But he didn't know how else to convey the gravity of his promise to her, or how else to make her trust him with both her body and her feelings when he'd hurt her so many times before.

What he was asking from her was as intimate as lovemaking. He wouldn't badger her into an answer, so he merely stood there and waited for her verdict: trustworthy or not.

Her voice was a fragile thread of uncertainty. "You won't hurt me?"

She wasn't talking about physical damage.

"No." He held her worried gaze. "I won't."

"I . . ." After studying his face for a moment, she nodded. "Okay. Let's do this."

It was a kick to the chest, in the best possible way. He could barely breathe.

She turned and walked back into the bathroom, and he followed her to the doorway. She plugged the drain and started the water running.

Then she reached for the hem of her grimy tank, and he drew in a harsh breath and swiveled to face the other way. Out of the furthermost corner of his eye, he could see the tank hit the floor. Then boxers.

Water splashed.

"I'm in," she said.

Which meant she was naked. Naked and wet and waiting for him to touch her.

He dug a knuckle into the hinge of his jaw. *Non. Nein. Nannies gnawing a 'nana.*

"It's okay." Athena sounded tired but matter-of-fact. "You don't have to do this. In fact, I can't believe I even agreed to *let* you do it. My being a lazy bitch isn't your problem, so why don't you—"

Fuck it. If he got an erection, he'd simply make sure she couldn't see it. Somehow.

He bent to press an admonishing kiss to the top of her head, trying his best not to look at anything else. "Not lazy. Not a bitch. Depressed."

Bracing a hand against the tiled shower wall, he reached for the tiny shelf at the back of the stall, where she kept her shampoo. At the same moment, she sat up straighter in the tub.

Which meant he'd shoved his jeans-clad, half-hard dick in her face.

He jerked away, lost his balance, tried to catch himself on the way down, and landed with one hand on the bath mat, one hand in the water.

Dazedly, he registered the current position of that waterlogged left hand. His palm rested against smooth, slick porcelain. His wrist and forearm, however, were surrounded by something much warmer and much, much softer.

So apparently he'd now thrust his entire hand between her inner thighs, which was somewhat of an improvement over force-feeding her his be-jeaned penis, but still not great.

No amount of nuns and ninnies could help him now.

Getting his hand between her thighs might be a secret wish of his, but not like this. Fuck, definitely *not like this*.

His entire face was aflame. Cheeks, ears, everything. And dammit, he'd promised not to look at her, so he couldn't check her expression. Was she offended? Angry?

A long, complex silence filled the steamy confines of the bathroom.

"Did I hurt you?" he finally forced himself to ask.

"No."

More silence as he knelt beside the tub and carefully removed his hand from between her legs, which she spread farther in an effort to assist him. Jesus.

He cleared his throat. "I apologize for . . . that. What just happened."

"It's fine," she said, her voice unsteady.

Was she crying?

"Athena." He kept his eyes on the tiles directly in front of him. But in his peripheral vision, he could see movement. Her shoulders quivering? Fuck. *Fuck.* "It wasn't intentional. I swear."

"I-I know."

"If it's still okay with you, I want to do this, but . . ." Another throat-clearing helped matters not at all. "Things may get a bit awkward. At times."

There was an odd snorty sound. A sniffle, or—

"You think?" she said faintly.

Then she was laughing so hard, the sound echoed off the tiled walls and rang in his ears. She jackknifed forward as she giggled, clutching his upper arm as she shook with hilarity.

He laughed too then. In relief that she didn't hate him. In joy at *her* joy.

"Maybe . . ." Levering herself back upright, she patted his shoulder. "Maybe I should reach for the shampoo, conditioner, and soap from now on."

"You think?" He imitated her dry intonation exactly, and she giggled again.

Blindly, overcome with affection, he reached down to stroke her damp hair back from her forehead. He was relatively, but not entirely, certain he didn't poke her in the eyeball while doing so. In response, she took his hand and nuzzled her smooth cheek into his palm for one brief, heart-stopping moment.

When she let go, he nearly begged her to keep touching him. But he'd promised not to take advantage of the situation, so he didn't. He wouldn't.

"Ready to try again?" he asked, once he could speak coherently.

"Oh, Dr. Vine," said Athena, and he didn't have to look to know she was smiling. "I simply can't resist. I *must* know what you intend to do for your encore."

SADLY, THAT ENDED the portion of Athena's bath that could be considered—by the ungenerous, anyway—lecherous.

Matthew couldn't have been more careful. More careful or more tender.

When he shampooed her hair, he tipped her chin back to make sure she didn't get bubbles in her eyes. As he lathered every strand, he kept one hand steady and warm at the back of her neck, supporting the weight of her head, and she leaned into his strength. Trusted it not to falter.

Not a drop of water ventured below her eyebrows when he used the handheld shower head to rinse away the shampoo. And when he massaged in her conditioner—the cheapest she'd found at the grocery store, vaguely fruity in scent—his strong fingers rubbing along her scalp melted her spine, even as they raised gooseflesh everywhere else.

As soon as he noticed, he made the water warmer, which solved nothing. Her reaction wasn't about temperature. It was about conduction, arcs of power no longer safely contained behind a sphere of glass. It was about the terrifying vulnerability of this moment. It was about the way his controlled, deliberate, damnably gentle hands on her brought nothing but pleasure.

So many men had been careless with her.

For so many years, she'd been careless with herself.

She closed her eyes then. Closed her eyes and pretended this wasn't about how pathetic she'd become, or how kind and responsible Matthew was. No, this was a man ministering to her out of love and need, desperate to touch her any and every way he could.

Somehow, her brain kept giving that nameless, faceless, devoted man Matthew's austere features. Matthew's forearms, with their shift of lean muscles and tendons beneath pale skin. Matthew's competent, caring hands; the hands of a could-be surgeon who'd chosen to tend children instead, watching over them as they fumbled toward adulthood.

Her brain was dumb. Why would someone like him want her, of all people?

The very idea should make her laugh, but instead it hurt like a raw wound.

After rinsing the conditioner, he drained the tub and added fresh water, continually checking to make sure the temperature wouldn't burn or chill her. As far as she could tell, he didn't glance at her nakedness even once, although she wouldn't care if he did. Her body was the least of her worries.

He washed her face then, using a clean washcloth to remove every slippery streak of cleanser. With her head tipped back once more, he cradled her skull in his palm as he worked, and she didn't want him to release her. Ever.

He did, though, once he'd patted her eyes and face dry with a towel, and she tried not to ruin his efforts by crying.

Somewhere around the time he eased her forward and began washing her back, she heard herself speaking slowly, thickly.

"I'm a failure in every aspect of my life," she said, slumped and boneless, hands limp in her lap. "As a daughter. As a friend and lover and would-be professional. As a human being. I've been given every privilege, and I've achieved nothing. Built nothing. I'm thirty-seven, and after almost two decades as an adult, I have nothing to show for it but a ten-foot-wide house where I barely fit on the stairs. I almost married a man I don't think I ever loved. I did my best to torture a man who showed me more kindness than I deserved. I got fired from a minimum-wage job after less than three weeks. I've taken thousands and thousands of dollars from my parents, and they might as well have tossed it in a dumpster."

His hands paused on her back before resuming their gentle circles.

"It's all just a waste." Her tears dripped into the water, and they didn't even make a ripple. They didn't matter, and neither did she. "I'm a waste. Of time, of potential, of effort, and I'm just so fucking tired, Matthew. I'm tired of trying so hard and getting nowhere and fucking it all up even if I do get somewhere."

He set aside the soap. Using his cupped hands, he began rinsing her back clean, patch by patch.

She slapped away her tears. "This past week, I kept thinking what a relief it would be to disappear. Not hurt myself. Just . . . dissolve into nothingness for a while, because I'm sick of me."

With little touches, each feather-light, he checked for any remaining soap on her back. When he didn't find any, he took her hand in preparation for washing her left arm.

"You wanted to know what was troubling me." She dragged in a hitching breath. "Those are the highlights. I mean, lowlights."

She kept waiting for him to reclaim the soap, but he simply knelt by the bath and held her hand. *Please don't leave*, she thought desperately. *You must be so tired of me, but please don't leave me here.*

Then he let go and rose to his feet, because of course he'd had enough. She was too much for anyone, just like he'd told his brother.

She couldn't track him through the blur of tears, with her head bowed to her chest, but she waited for the sound of footsteps on the stairs and the thud of a door closed forever.

Instead, she heard small splashes. She felt feet slide beneath either side of her butt as a careful but inexorable hand scooted her forward a few inches. Her knees bent higher as she basically formed a miserable human ball, and then he somehow squeezed in behind her, fully dressed, and wedged his jeans-clad legs above her hips, because there was no room anywhere lower than that in such a small bathtub. Water slapped against the sides of the tub and spilled over the side, and he made no attempt to mop it up.

It couldn't be comfortable for him—it wasn't all that comfortable for her either—and she had no idea how he intended to get either of them out, but he hadn't left her. He hadn't left her, not even for a moment.

His arms closed around her shoulders and settled her back against him. His now-wet tee was soft along her spine, his chest hard and supportive. Exhausted, spent, she let him position her however he wanted, because she was done fighting him for the sake of her pride.

"I have a lot of things I'd like to say," he told her. "Will you let me say them? All of them, even if you disagree?"

He'd promised not to hurt her, and she was trying to trust that he meant it. But even if he did hurt her, either by accident or on purpose, she deserved the pain. It could constitute another part of her penance, she supposed.

"Yes," she whispered.

He took both her hands in his, interlacing their fingers, and his cheek rested on top of her wet head. When she lifted his arms and crossed them over herself, he tugged her tighter against him.

"We both know you can't always trust your thoughts when you're depressed." His voice was quiet and calm, each word selected with care. "I understand that everything you just said to me feels like the truth right now, but it's not, sweetheart. It's not. It's the unkindest possible interpretation of your life, and it only makes sense if you ignore all context."

She hoped the last thing she heard on this earth was Matthew Vine calling her *sweetheart*.

He lightly tapped a finger against her shoulder, dislodging a water droplet. "You have an MA and an MS. If a stranger came up to you and proudly told you they'd earned their second master's degree, would you think it was nothing? Would you tell them it wasn't a real achievement?"

She shook her head, her hair rubbing against his tee. Of course she wouldn't think it was nothing. She wasn't mean, and graduate degrees took a lot of work. Getting one—or two—*was* an achievement.

For other people. Not her.

"Let's talk about your work history." He planted another hard kiss on the crown of her head, the gesture somehow both tender and chastising. "Does leaving the classroom erase all the time and attention you gave your students? Does it wipe you from their memories and reverse any impact you had on their lives? Does quitting retroactively invalidate all the work you did and make it meaningless?"

Well, when he put it that way—

"For that matter, does leaving your other jobs mean you weren't good at what you did, or that you didn't make a difference to anyone? Because I can't believe that." Sounding less calm and more outraged, he squeezed her until she was breathless. "I *don't* believe that, because I know better. After two weeks at the library and less than three weeks at the bakery, you made countless friends. You also forced a crusty, curmudgeonly hermit to pick up his phone and voluntarily call me—not text me; *call me*, with his actual hands, using actual, out-loud words—because he was concerned for your well-being and upset he couldn't keep you as an employee."

"Karl shouldn't feel bad about that." Athena used their joined fingers to scratch the tip of her nose. "I know he didn't have a choice. Bez told me about Charlotte's kids, and under the circumstances, I'd have fired me too."

"Okay, then. So why should *you* feel bad about it?"

That was a fair question, and she thought about it for a minute.

"Because I do," she finally whispered. It was the only answer she could give him.

That earned her another fierce squeeze.

"Who have you hurt, Athena?" he demanded. "Other than yourself, who exactly have you hurt?"

Hallelujah. Finally an easy question. "You."

"Yeah?" He made a surprisingly rude noise. "I hurt you too. We're even. Who else?"

She bit her lip. "I've wasted so much of my parents' money."

"Have they said that to you? Do they resent the money they gave you?"

No. Her parents had offered it freely and never lamented how little practical usage she'd gotten from it.

After another shake of her head, he asked, "Did they have that extra money available? Did transferring it to you hurt their quality of life in any significant way?"

Her parents were internationally renowned pediatric cardiologists without expensive hobbies. Paying for her degrees, her engagement party, and her cancelled wedding had maybe removed the equivalent of a single cotton ball from their financial cushion. Possibly two.

"They have plenty of money," she admitted.

His next breath was deep enough to lift her and drop her back down again, as if she were floating atop an unsettled ocean. When he spoke, he was back to choosing words carefully.

"Getting engaged to Johnny was a mistake." Another swell of breath beneath her. "Given what I did and said, given what happened, I obviously won't argue with you about that. But it wasn't a mistake you made alone. And even if you didn't love him, even if you were together for the wrong reasons, you *thought* you loved him. You *wanted* to love him. You got engaged in good faith."

His tone betrayed no doubt. No condemnation.

"Half of all marriages end in divorce, and most relationships that don't lead to marriage end too," he said. "So what if you picked the wrong person? At some point, so has almost every other adult on the face of this planet."

It all sounded so sensible when he explained it. So inarguable. Somehow, though, her brain *did* keep arguing. It told her he didn't truly understand. It insisted if he knew her better, he would think as little of her as she thought of herself.

"If your personal history belonged to a friend, and they sat down and cried to you about it, we both know you wouldn't think, 'Wow, what a failure. What a waste her existence has been.' So why can't you be that kind to yourself?" He jostled her a bit in his arms, emphasizing his point. "Why do you have to be perfect, Athena? Why can't you make mistakes, or take a few detours as you figure out where you want to go?"

Of course everyone made mistakes. But not everyone made such *terrible* mistakes, or made them so frequently. And other people's mistakes always seemed a lot more understandable and forgivable than hers, which maybe had something to do with the depression, but—

"You know, I've spent a lot of time this week thinking about all those jobs you've had, about how they all suffocated you sooner or later, and do you know what I finally realized?" His chin settled atop her head, a bit too sharp for her comfort. "I'm not the slightest bit surprised. After Johnny met your parents at that pediatrics conference, when he came over to their house and they introduced him to you, they told him you were valedictorian of your high school class, graduated summa cum laude from undergrad, and kept a four-point-oh in both your graduate programs."

No doubt Johnny had shared the information with his brother as a way of justifying the engagement, but she wished he'd kept it to himself.

She squirmed a little, embarrassed. "I hate when they tell people about that. It's so . . . smug. That stuff means almost nothing in real life. Even if it did, it would only make my failure to succeed less comprehensible and more egregious."

"You could interpret things that way." His legs trapped her knees and squeezed. "*Or* you could think to yourself, 'Of course she switches jobs. She's incredibly intelligent and curious, and her brain requires new challenges to stay happy and avoid boredom. And at non-boring jobs, she expects perfection from herself and doesn't have anyone who tells her to slow the hell down and take care of herself, so she works to the point of burnout.'"

Frankly, she hadn't known such a positive interpretation of her job-hopping was even possible. Bravo to him, because coming up with it must have taken considerable mental effort.

Still, he should really acknowledge at least a corner of the ugly truth. "Most people have to stay at work that bores them, Matthew. My ability to flit from job to job is unbearably privileged."

"I won't argue with that." His shoulders shifted beneath her in what felt like a shrug. "But if they had the necessary resources, don't you think all those bored people would quit and try to find work they liked better? If they did, would you begrudge them doing it?"

Evidently, her one-man cheerleading squad hadn't yet run out of pep, and she didn't know whether to kiss him or shake him until he remembered his common sense.

"And let's look at the issue more broadly. Why is professional success the best measure of your life's meaning? If you never worked again, would that make you worthless as a human being?" He waited for her to think it over, then said firmly, "Your value doesn't lie in how productive you are. Your value lies in *who* you are."

"Who am I?" she whispered.

She had to ask, because she wasn't sure she knew anymore. She didn't feel like the person she used to be, and she certainly didn't feel like the person she'd intended to be.

He didn't hesitate. "You're Athena Knox Greydon, cherished daughter of Doug Greydon and Juno Knox-Greydon. Lifelong learner. Devoted student of Professor Google. Beloved friend. Hardworking employee. Whip-smart and intensely curious. Witty and kind. Beautiful. Funny. Prone to overworking, and way too damn hard on yourself in every way."

What he considered being too hard on herself, she'd describe as facing reali—

Wait. Did he just call her *beautiful*?

"As far as I can tell, your only real crime is that you're sometimes unsure what would make you happiest personally or professionally, and if that's a capital offense, I'm afraid most of us should be locked away or guillotined."

Not guilty. He was declaring her not guilty.

Her hands trembled, and she clutched his more firmly.

"You're exploring, trying to find the best path forward, and sometimes exploration gets confusing and messy." Carefully, he maneuvered their upper bodies until he could meet her tear-glazed eyes. "Remember the *Maryland Virago*? The informational sign on the dock quotes an eighteenth-century German writer, Gotthold Ephraim Lessing. When I visited the ship on my lunch break last week, I read his words and thought of you."

He tenderly cupped her cheek in his palm, and in those bright, warm brown eyes she saw the boy who'd once loved tales of adventure. She could picture him, standing rock-steady on an undulating deck, his cheeks flushed in the bone-baking sun, his linen shirt whipping in the wind as he traversed the seas, doctor's kit in hand.

Caring for people. Saving them. Because that was what he did.

"'They make glorious shipwreck who are lost in seeking

worlds,'" he quoted softly, his smile a slight, sweet curve of his mouth. "I know you're lost right now, Athena. I know you're damaged. But you're seeking new worlds, sweetheart, and sometimes that's what happens. It doesn't mean you'll never set sail again. And no matter what happened before, no matter what happens next, you couldn't be anything less than glorious if you tried."

Matthew gently stroked away a tear from her jaw.

Then he leaned down and kissed her.

14

The next day, it felt like a hallucination. A fever dream, brought on by excessive water temperature in the bathtub.

Matthew—Dr. Matthew Vine *the Third*—had kissed her, Athena "Shipwreck" Greydon, while she lay naked and cradled in his arms, her cheek cupped in his careful hand.

For a fleeting heartbeat of time, his lips had caressed hers so warmly, so sweetly, so lightly, it might have been a brush of velvet instead of a kiss. It might have been a ray of sunlight flickering over her mouth, melting everything inside her that had been cold and dark.

The kiss hadn't lasted long. That didn't matter. It was still the best kiss of her life, maybe because it was the least selfish kiss of her life. It offered gentleness and caring but made no demands of her. It certainly wasn't an attempt to persuade her into further intimacy, because right after that, he'd carefully climbed back out of the bathtub, dripping everywhere, and begun washing her left arm.

Or maybe it was the best kiss of her life because . . .

Well, because it was *Matthew's* kiss. His, specifically.

Afterward, she'd sat stunned and silent in the water. He'd soaped and rinsed her arms, her lower legs, his gaze firmly trained on the bathroom tiles, and she'd let him rearrange her however he preferred while she stared at him in confused wonder.

Somehow, he was both men at once: the one whose kiss had sent a heart-stopping bolt of voltage arcing through her body, and the one who grounded her, protecting her from damage.

After a while, he'd quietly asked whether she wanted him to wash the rest of her. Her breasts, she dimly realized. Between her legs.

"No," she'd said at last, shaking off her daze. "Thank you, but I'll get it."

He'd nodded and stood.

"The floor's wet." With a nudge of his foot, he'd positioned the bath mat closer to the tub. "Be careful when you step out."

Then he'd left the bathroom, closing the door behind him with a tiny *click*. By the time she was done in there, he was fully dressed again in dry clothing, and it was as if the joint bath had never happened. It was as if the *kiss* had never happened.

She had no idea what it meant to him.

To her, it was a tether, temptation and danger twined into a single rope and tugging her toward him. Or a lovely little campfire, offering light and heat and comfort. Singeing the unwary. If allowed to burn out of control, threatening cataclysmic damage.

Not that she'd ever been camping. That was how people got stabbed.

Had he even thought about the kiss since it happened? Or was it a simple gesture of comfort to a grieving woman, kind but essentially meaningless?

That had to be it. He might like her as a person, but she already knew how he felt about her as a potential romantic partner.

Two thumbs down. Zero out of ten, would not recommend.

"I had an idea." Standing at her kitchen counter, he grabbed a handful of chips and deposited some on his plate, some on hers. "You're obviously a fan of Halloween."

"Obviously." Well, kinda. Mostly she'd been a fan of bothering him.

"Right." The sandwiches he laid on their plates didn't skimp on the fillings: thick slices of cheddar, innumerable paper-thin layers of rare roast beef, and lots of dijonnaise. He'd put the whole shebang on potato bread too, because he was a prince among men. "So, for the last few years, Harlot's Bay has held an annual Halloween event. There's trick-or-treating, a costume contest, face-painting, and whatnot, but also a competition for downtown businesses. They put Halloween displays in their front windows, and whichever one wins first prize gets a pretty nice check from the city."

Huh. Sounded cool.

It also sounded like it would draw crowds, and crowds were exhausting.

He carried their plates to the table, and she followed. "Anyway, it's this Thursday, and the mayor asked Yvonna to be the MC and judge for the decorations contest. But she said she'd be happy to have you do it instead, since you're into Halloween and don't mind public speaking, and I told her I'd ask you. What do you think?"

Mostly, she thought: *What the fuck?*

She hadn't left her freaking house in a week. Just yesterday, the man had been forced to help her *bathe*. And he considered her ready to stand in front of the entire town and cheerfully yammer at them about Halloween decorations?

"Why in the *world* . . ." Sitting down, she cleared her throat and began again. "I mean, please thank Yvonna for me, but I think that's a bit more than I can handle right now. Sorry."

"No problem. I'll let her know." When she filled his glass from the pitcher of water, he offered her a small nod of gratitude. "Instead of being the competition's MC and judge, then, how would you feel about helping me with Bluestocking's decorations tomorrow afternoon? Hill desperately needs some assistance. He doesn't even have any props to use, so I thought you might be willing to loan him your, uh"—he cringed a little—"very memorable dolls, and all the other stuff from your windows, and we could work together to make the display."

It wasn't that she didn't want to help, but that seemed like . . . a lot.

Head down, she folded her napkin in half very precisely. "I don't know."

"He really needs the money, Athena. The only way he can pay himself for the month of October is if he wins the cash prize, and the only way he'll win the cash prize is if you assist. I'm no good at choosing or arranging decorations. Please help me."

He was looking at her pleadingly, his brown eyes clear and warm and hopeful, like a spaniel begging for a treat. It was an effective look.

Since breaking into her home Friday night, he'd spent all his waking hours either with her or doing things for her comfort. He'd shopped, cooked, cleaned, consoled, made phone calls to find her a doctor's appointment, and even offered to assist with another bath.

Dammit.

"Fine." After taking a resigned bite of her enormous sandwich, she put a hand in front of her full mouth, her words garbled. "I'll do it."

"Fantastic," Matthew said, his smile full of affection and approval, and she wanted to stretch beneath that smile like a cat sprawled in sunlight. "I'll text Hill right now to tell him."

About five minutes after that text got sent, Athena noticed her AP psychology textbook perched on the far edge of the kitchen table. It was open.

In fact, it was open to the section discussing compliance strategies. Which included, just to pick two at random, *norms of reciprocity*—the tendency to feel you should pay back someone's kind gesture with a kind gesture of your own—and the *door-in-the-face strategy*. As she'd explained the latter to her students: "If someone refuses a very large request, they're more likely to agree to a follow-up request that seems more reasonable."

Why, that sneaky, shrewd bastard. He'd used her own knowledge against her!

Later that evening, as she dried a dish he'd just washed, she nodded to the textbook and told him, "I know what you did."

He offered her a look of such confused innocence, he might have been a choirboy. More specifically, a choirboy who'd never learned to lie convincingly and had recently set the altar cloths aflame with a thurible, then doused the conflagration with the church's entire supply of holy water.

Wow, that man could blush.

But it was too late. It didn't matter that she'd uncovered his secret plot to get her out of the house. She'd agreed to help Hill, and she was a woman of her word.

So the next day, there she was: out in the wide world once more on a Monday afternoon, thanks to Matthew's machinations. In an effort to spare him unnecessary Halloween trauma, she'd put all her decorations in a big trash bag, which he'd slung over his shoulder to carry. The whole walk to the bookstore, he kept glancing over at her, looking pleased with himself and pleased with her too, and his uncharacteristic self-satisfaction was so adorable, she couldn't even puncture it by complaining about his treachery.

Earlier in the day, she'd had a virtual appointment with Matthew's own doctor and received a prescription for antidepressants.

Matthew had picked up the medication on his way home from work and handed her the water to wash down her first pill. As she'd swallowed, she'd mentally put a checkmark next to the first daunting item on her endless to-do list.

She'd even forced herself to shower before his arrival, which he hadn't seemed to notice. But then, right before they left for the bookstore, he'd reached out and captured a strand of her clean, soft hair, letting it slide slowly between his forefinger and thumb while he beamed down at her.

He'd noticed. He'd noticed, and he was proud of her. And maybe it was stupid and pathetic, but she was a little proud of herself too.

Along the walk to the bookstore, they studied the rival window displays they'd have to out-decorate. Karl had created oversized cookies shaped like knives and axes and iced them accordingly, complete with blood spatters. They were now hanging in the front window of Grounds and Grains, along with an enormous, old-fashioned hockey mask made out of puff pastry.

Ah, Jason Voorhees. Yet another stabbing-related reason to avoid camping at all costs.

Truthfully, Athena was unsure whether Karl had created the display for Halloween. Maybe he'd simply wanted to express his murderousness in a new medium and gotten lucky with his timing.

Matthew paused in front of the window, brow furrowed. "Why is there a hockey mask?"

She could tell him, but . . . "You don't want to know. You'd never be able to go camping again."

"Camping?" His aristocratic nose wrinkled. "I don't go camping. If I wanted to sleep on the dirt and lack access to necessary sanitation, I'd . . . go camping. Which I don't. Because I don't want that."

She had to laugh. "Fair enough, Dr. Vine. I assume you're not much of a movie buff either?"

"Never had time." He lifted a shoulder. "Johnny and med school and work have fully occupied three decades of my existence."

Before the engagement, Johnny had mentioned in passing that Matthew essentially raised him, and they were both estranged from their parents. "They weren't able to care for us the way they should have" was his only explanation, and she hadn't pushed, because his open, cheerful face had turned stony and closed upon mentioning them.

She hadn't even known about the third Vine brother. At least, not until Matthew had vowed upon his late sibling's grave not to hurt her. Since then, she'd occasionally considered asking him what happened or using Professor Google to unearth the lost brother's story, but that felt too invasive, even for her.

If Matthew wanted to tell her more about his family, he would. If not—as seemed to be the case—she didn't need to know.

They started walking again, past the bakery and down the street, until they came upon another contest competitor. The yarn store had somehow created the cutest crocheted guillotine ever, complete with amigurumi severed heads lying in a knitted pool of blood.

"Vive la fluffy révolution," she murmured, and he snorted.

The downtown grocery store had used ketchup and several hams very creatively in its display, while dangling skeletons outside Strumpet Square Pediatrics danced a jig in the waterfront breeze.

Her steps slowed. "Please tell me—"

"Plastic," he affirmed. "And I know it's a lackluster display, but that's one hundred percent my fault. Out of kindness to me, Yvonna indulged her love for Halloween decorations at home, rather than our workplace."

From the outside, his practice looked tidy and welcoming. What would it be like inside?

"Could I visit you here someday? I know nothing about how doctor's offices work behind the scenes, and I'm curious."

He turned his head toward her, lips tipped up in a private smile. "I'd like that. Just let me know when, and I'll . . ." Twin creases appeared above his inner brows, and the happiness in his expression faded into his accustomed solemnity. "You realize, of course, that you'd most likely encounter the practice's other doctors during your visit."

Oh goodness gracious. How had she managed to forget Johnny?

"Of course," she echoed weakly.

Well, so much for that idea.

After several more minutes of awkward silence, they arrived at Bluestocking. Cradling Roberta Downy Jr. in his too-thin arms, Hill welcomed them into the store with weary warmth and a heart-felt gratitude both she and Matthew did their best to deflect.

Together, all four of them stared thoughtfully at the empty front window.

"Whatever you decide to create will be better than nothing." Hill stroked Roberta, who butted her head beneath his chin affectionately. "Do anything you'd like, as long as it's cheap."

Mentally, Athena took stock of their supplies, arranged them in a tableau, then disassembled everything to explore another option. Then another.

In the end, there was one clear winner.

"What's your vision, Athena?" Matthew asked. "How do you imagine the display?"

Her eyes met his. "Are you sure you want to hear this?"

"No." He sighed. "But tell me anyway."

"Brace yourself, Dr. Vine." Laying a light hand on his upper arm, she gave him a comforting squeeze. "We're going to make it look like possessed demon dolls attacked, murdered, and consumed a hapless bibliophile while he sat reading in his rocking chair. Some of the dolls will be chewing on the bones of his partially disassembled skeleton, and we'll position the blood-stained ax beside a doll that's been cut in half, since the victim put up a valiant defense before being overcome and eaten. We can keep the skeleton's head and torso in the chair and put some reading glasses on the poor guy. Matthew, do you have a set?"

He groaned faintly. "I can probably find some, but . . . why the dolls, Athena? Why must we embolden the Murder Dolls? It's only going to intensify their already insatiable bloodlust."

She and Hill looked at him, then at each other.

"You're joking, right?" she asked cautiously.

"Sure," said Matthew.

"I'll protect you from the Murder Dolls. I promise." His arm beneath her hand had gone rock-solid, and she squeezed again. "But if we want to win the contest, I think we have to use them."

He muttered something, and it sounded remarkably like *I guess I've had a good run.*

Struck by inspiration, she exclaimed, "Oh! I just had the best idea!"

This time, Matthew's groan was considerably less faint, and she let go of his arm so she could swing behind him and massage his warm, iron-knotted shoulders.

"We should totally stack some fake books on a side table next to the rocking chair. *Where the Red Fangs Grow. What to Expect When You're Expecting Half a Dozen Murder Dolls to Disembowel You. Oh, the Places You'll Go When the Murder Dolls You Foolishly Bought Drag You to Hell with Them.* Whoever's the artsiest can make the covers." Getting on her tiptoes, she peered over Matthew's right shoulder and grinned at Hill. "And on the bookshelves surrounding the scene, we'll put all the store's best stock, cover-out, so everyone will see what amazing books they could buy from Bluestocking."

Hill smiled back at her. "If you can make that happen, I'll be thrilled."

"If you can make that happen, we'll all die horribly," Matthew said under his breath.

Yeah, massaging his neck accomplished nothing. She might as well have been massaging a chunk of petrified wood, instead of petrified man. Giving up, she returned to his side and glanced at his face.

Greenish. Deeply unhappy.

Somehow, he mustered the will to ask, "What do you need me to do?"

"Why don't you focus on the procurement of necessary supplies?" She could easily keep the dolls in the garbage bag until he'd gone elsewhere. "We'll need the rocker from the children's section, a side table, and sturdy bookshelves to define the display area, as well as one of the skeletons from your practice."

He sagged in immediate relief. "God, *thank you*." A slight pause. "I mean, yes, that sounds like the most reasonable distribution of labor. I'll gladly find what you need. In fact, why don't I do that now? Right now."

It was a shame he'd probably been too busy to run track in high school, because his sprint to the door was a thing of beauty.

SOMEWHERE AROUND THE time they began making their first fake book covers—Hill was quite a talented artist, as it turned out—everyone else arrived.

Matthew hadn't asked them to come; Athena confirmed that with several people. Harlot's Bay was simply a small town. Whispers of her weeklong descent into hermit-dom had spread, and once she'd been spotted outdoors once more, texts were sent, plans got made, and the Nasty Wenches swung into action.

They didn't crowd her. But somehow, there was always one of them nearby as she worked, drawing her into undemanding conversation and making her laugh.

Victoria wandered up first, greeting her as if they'd seen one another only the day before, and together they brainstormed other book titles.

"*War and Pieces of Flesh*!" Victoria held up her hand for a high five, which Athena returned. "Wait, I know! *She Stoops to Conk Him*!"

"You dug deep for that one," Athena informed her dryly.

Victoria only grinned, then ran a gentle, comforting hand along Athena's upper back as she left to get more paper.

"We chose another theme for our next meeting," Jackie said a few minutes later, as she helped Athena select Hill's best books. "Monster-fucking can wait until you're ready. No hurry, honey. Take your time."

Athena's eyes blurred. "What d-did you decide on?"

"Femdom." Jackie looped an arm around Athena's shoulders and tugged her close, discreetly ignoring an occasional sniffle. "It's been quite instructive. Out of curiosity, do you think Sif would top Valkyrie? Or the other way around? Because Yvonna and I now have a running argument about that."

"Valkyrie tops Sif." Athena blew her nose and cuddled a bit closer to Jackie. "No doubt in my mind."

"Dammit, Greydon."

Shortly after that, as Athena prepared to cut a doll in half,

Bethany appeared with a flutter of her flowered skirts. "I brought you my favorite gargoyle romance," the older woman whispered. "*Stone-Cold Dick: Falling for My Boss*. Get it? Boss?"

Athena blinked at her.

Bethany tucked a stray hair back into her bun. "Bosses are purely ornamental gargoyles, but also supervisors in the human world, so theirs is a love doubly forbidden and taboo."

"I had no idea." Athena's previous cathedral tour guides had clearly been holding out on her. "You've broadened my horizons today, Bethany, and I thank you for it."

"You'll thank me even more when you get to page one eighty-two." She winked, pressed the book into Athena's hand with a little bonus squeeze, and left to talk to Hill.

Other library coworkers came up for brief chats and gestures of silent support. Bez strolled in with several bakery boxes full of doughnuts, as well as a loaf of still-warm potato bread. The scrawled sticky note attached to the steam-filled plastic bag read, *Now you can stop being a pain in my ass about goddamn potato bread, you tuber-loving freak*. A bold, irritated-looking *K* identified the note's author, as if she wouldn't have already known.

No one prodded her to confess her woes or explain her pro-longed absence from the world. No one demanded apologies for all the messages she'd failed to return or all the concern she'd dismissed. They just . . . stood by her and offered her as much affection as she'd accept.

They didn't seem angry. They didn't seem disappointed or pitying or disdainful.

And if they hadn't lovingly forced the issue, she'd have avoided them for weeks, months, maybe forever. Because she was ashamed. Because she was afraid of their judgment.

Somewhere along the way, her thinking had gotten fucked up in ways she couldn't yet untangle, but she now knew one thing for certain: She wasn't giving the people who cared about her enough credit.

A scan of the room revealed Hill sitting on a stool by the register, holding Roberta.

"I'll be out back for a few minutes, if that's all right." Athena held up her phone. "I have a call I need to make."

Hill nodded. "Use the exit from the back room, hon. No need to walk all the way around."

The patch of grass behind the store contained a small fenced-in area for Roberta. Just beside the fence sat a wooden bench, and Athena settled there in the sun and voluntarily called her parents for the first time since moving to Maryland.

Both of them had semiretired from their pediatric cardiology practice several years ago, although they still saw some longtime patients, kept up with the latest research, and gave seminars and talks at conferences. Generally, they finished up before late afternoon, so Athena figured they'd be home.

"Hail to the thief!" her father boomed, and she put him on speakerphone. Sooner or later, he'd be forced to admit he needed hearing aids, but it hadn't happened yet. "How are you doing, sweet pea?"

She'd stolen his stethoscope once. *Once*.

"I was six, Dad," she told him for the trillionth time. "It's the first and last thing I ever burgled, and I gave it back to you a day later."

To her vast disappointment, she hadn't been able to hear the heartbeats of her favorite stuffed animals, and their homicidal cat had scratched the hell out of her forearm when she'd tried to use the stethoscope on him. She still had the scar.

No wonder she wasn't afraid of the Murder Dolls. She'd already gazed long enough into the abyss, and the abyss had glared back at her, licked its butthole, and clawed her for a can of tuna.

"Wait a second, lovebug. Putting you on speaker." There was a rustling sound, and then she had both parents on the line. "You called at the perfect time. Your mother is bored out of her ever-loving mind now that all the major cycling events are done for the year."

For some reason, her mom had gotten into televised competitive cycling over the summer. They'd had countless dinnertime conversations about pelotons and domestiques and what determined the "most aggressive rider." Sadly, the answer didn't involve a bunch of guys on bikes punching each other, because that would have really livened up the flat stages.

"I think she's in yellow jersey withdrawal." A faint smacking noise came over the line as Doug kissed his wife. "It's pitiful, really."

Juno harrumphed. "Douglas P. Greydon, do you or do you not spend most of your free time watching various blond women discuss which walls are load-bearing? Because—"

"Wait," Athena interrupted excitedly. "Dad, do you watch that show where homeowners try DIY renos and completely screw it up, and then—"

"A blond woman arrives to tell them they tore out a load-bearing wall?" Juno sighed. "Yes, he does watch it. Frequently. Loudly."

"I want it known that I'd never mess with an electrical panel, like that guy did last week," Athena told them. "If I set my house on fire, it'll be because I'm committing arson for the insurance money or because I finally burned those cucumber-melon candles I got twenty years ago and fell asleep at exactly the wrong moment."

"Very reassuring, sweet pea!" her dad shouted. "How are you doing?"

Dammit. Athena had been half hoping they could banter long enough that her parents would need to leave for . . . something. Maybe one of those art classes they'd decided to take together, in hopes of finding a common hobby before semiretirement became maxi-retirement.

"Ummm . . ." She bit her lip. "Not great?"

It was the first time in her adult life she'd ever admitted that.

Silence echoed down the line, and Athena could almost hear the gears screeching as her mother and father transformed from delightedly bickering spouses into a united parental team.

"Tell us," her mother said.

"Please," her father added.

A few sentences in, she began crying, but they didn't interrupt. They let her get it all out. Her guilt over the money they'd wasted on her. Her shame at her failed engagement and her lack of professional achievements. Her burnout as a teacher. Her current living conditions. Her depression, and what she was doing about it with Matthew's help.

That was the only point where they interjected.

"Matthew Vine?" her mother asked tentatively. "As in, the older brother of your ex-fiancé? The man who was a total prick to you during your entire engagement?"

Athena bristled at that, oddly enough. "He apologized."

"I should hope so," her father loudly declared.

They didn't understand, and she couldn't let them go on thinking that way about Matthew. Not after everything he'd done for her. Not after the way she'd begun to feel about him.

"He's horribly afraid of heights, Dad. But when I didn't leave the house for a few days, he climbed through my third-floor window from across an alleyway, since that was his only way to get inside and check on me." Athena sniffled. "Then he brought me groceries, cleaned my house, and put smoked salmon, crème fraîche, and chives on potato chips for me."

Her mother grunted. "Was it good?"

"Very."

"Hmph." Juno considered that for a moment, then asked, "Is that everything, honey? Is there more you want to tell us?"

All this nose-blowing was beginning to chafe like hell. "I'm done."

Hopefully they'd be gentle with her. As much as she adored her parents, and as much as they adored her, they were pediatric cardiologists, and pediatric cardiologists had a certain reputation. They knew what to do, always, and they knew what you should do too, because they had a bit of a god complex.

Her parents, heaven love them both, fit that stereotype, and Athena didn't know what they'd think of her. She hadn't followed their firm advice. There was no way in hell she was getting licensed in Maryland and returning to the classroom. Worse, she had no ideas of her own about what to do next, and how could they even begin to comprehend that?

Lack of certainty baffled them, and right now, she was composed of ninety-nine percent doubt and one percent potato products.

"Sweet pea, why didn't you tell us all this before?" Her father's voice somehow managed to be both incredibly loud and incredibly gentle. "Did you think we'd be angry at you? Or disappointed?"

"I—I didn't want you to know, because . . ." She swallowed back a sob, but couldn't help her hitching breath. "I thought maybe you'd finally r-realize what a failure I am. You gave me love and money and an education and everything I n-needed to s-succeed, and I've done *nothing* with it."

Suddenly, there was a soft handkerchief in her free hand and a warm, hard thigh pressed against hers on the bench. Without saying a word, Matthew wrapped his flannel-clad arm around her shoulders, and she leaned into him gratefully.

He made eye contact, then pointed to himself and the store in silent question, but she didn't want him to leave. She shook her head, and he settled more firmly onto the bench.

Her mother spoke slowly. "Athena, my dearest child—"

"Your only ch-child. Technically, I'm also your least d-dear child."

"Hush." Juno began again. "Honey, we love you. We want you happy, and we want to help you however we can while you're figuring out how to get there. That's all. Unless you plan to murder kittens, whatever you do is fine by us."

"Not even one kitten? What if it's an evil kitten?"

Matthew huffed out an amused breath.

"Stop being a smartass." Her mom's Voice of Maternal Authority still had the power to snap Athena's mouth shut, after all these years. Impressive. "And stop worrying about that money. Right now, Athena Knox Greydon. We have more than we need, and it brings us joy to spend it on our favorite—and also, simultaneously, least favorite—child."

She deserved that. "Ha-ha."

"Sweet pea . . ." Her father paused, probably in search of the right words. "No education is ever wasted. No experience is ever wasted. Your degrees and your jobs helped make you the woman you are, and as far as we're concerned, you're absolutely wonderful."

Sincerity rang from every overly loud syllable, and she didn't understand why kindness seemed to make her cry so much, but it did. She dabbed at her chapped nose with the handkerchief, helpless to stop her eyes from watering yet again.

Matthew slid a caressing hand up and down her arm, gathering her closer.

"Once the path you expected to follow vanishes beneath you, it can take a while to decide where you want to go next." Juno hesitated, then added, "You were a wonderful surprise, Athena, but you *were* a surprise. When your father and I realized I was pregnant, we had to recalibrate a bit. We got married, when we hadn't previously intended to. We'd pictured ourselves working all over the world with medical charities, but instead we made a home here in Bethesda, put down roots, and never looked back."

The math had been clear to Athena years ago—her birthdate was way less than nine months after her parents' wedding—but she'd always assumed they'd anticipated their vows, not gotten married *because* of the pregnancy. And their plans to do charity work around the world . . . she'd known nothing about that either.

She wished they'd told her long ago. But how could they have known she needed to hear these stories, when she hadn't shared her insecurities with them?

Juno placed special emphasis on what she said next. "We didn't fail, just because the life we'd envisioned and thought would make us happy didn't come to pass. We merely—"

"Recalibrated," Athena whispered.

"Exactly." Her father sighed. "Look, sweet girl, here's the bottom line: No one with a good heart is a failure. You have a good heart. You've always had a good heart. You always will. Even with your unfortunate predilection for larceny."

"We know hearts, honey," her mom said. "Trust us."

Athena managed to laugh, groan, and cry, all at the same time.

Juno continued, "So you never have to worry about our disapproval or wonder whether we'll turn our backs on you, because we won't. We'd cut out our own hearts first."

"Exactly." Athena's father cleared his throat. "And now that we have the important bits settled, let's talk logistics."

Juno jumped in. "Do you want to stay with us for a while? Until your house is sold, or until you figure out what you want to do next?"

"Or forever? We'd be good with forever." Poor Dad sounded a bit stuffed up. He'd always been the more sentimental of her two parents.

Matthew's body had gone stiff against hers. She raised her head from his chest to see what was wrong, but his face didn't give anything away.

"I think . . . I think I'd like to stay in Harlot's Bay," she said. "At least for now."

He visibly relaxed, and his thumb swept over the cap of her shoulder in a small, slow arc.

She had no idea what that meant. Probably not what she wanted it to mean. "I have the beginnings of a community here. I know I have ties in Bethesda too, but returning there would feel more like a retreat than a recalibration."

"Okay." Dad sounded a bit unhappy. "I hear what you're saying, sweet pea, but let me be blunt: How exactly can you make a fresh start as the filling in a Vine brothers sandwich?"

Uh, wow. That was an image she really didn't need in her head. The thought of further intimacy with Johnny . . . no.

In class, she'd taught students about the Garcia effect: the way even one instance of illness after consuming a certain food or drink could cause a powerful learned taste aversion. Turned out, Johnny dumping her on his brother's say-so was the equivalent of vomiting after a meal of raw-bar oysters. She would never, ever again consume him in any way, shape, or form.

Beside her, embarrassment had Matthew throwing off heat like a furnace, poor man.

"Well, Dad," she eventually said, "to belabor a truly unfortunate metaphor, one slice of Vine brothers bread has promised to stay away from me until I tell him otherwise, and so far he's kept that promise. So it's more of an open-faced sandwich situation, and I'm okay being spread over the other slice of Vine brothers bread."

Oh hell. Rubbing her free hand over her face, she muttered, "So to speak."

At this point, Matthew's body temperature indicated he was experiencing spontaneous human combustion. No doubt that should summon some guilt within her psyche, but she was too busy dying of mortification to care.

A very long, very fraught silence ensued.

"I . . . see," her mother eventually said. "In that case, we're going to need your banking information, because no child of mine is living on canned spaghetti while we have money in our accounts. From now on, we'll be calling more often, and we'll expect you to answer, Athena Knox Greydon." The Voice of Maternal Authority brooked no argument, and Athena didn't try to offer one. "We'll also be visiting sooner rather than later. And once you've recalibrated, let's talk about your new path and how we can make it a bit smoother, okay?"

The pride Athena had to swallow went down easier than expected, probably because an enormous serving of love surrounded it. "Okay. Thank you, Mom and Dad."

"All right, then." By her father's tone, he considered the subject closed. "We love you, sweet pea."

"Athena dearest, we need to go now, but we love you very much, and we'll talk to you later today or tomorrow," Juno told her. "If you need us before then, promise me you'll call or text. Please."

Athena promised, her throat thick with tears and gratitude. Then her parents said their final goodbyes and swept off to whatever they were doing next.

She put her phone back in her purse. Gradually, Matthew's arm dropped from around her shoulders, and the autumnal breeze suddenly gave her goose bumps.

"Those are definitely your parents. No doubt about it." His voice was as dry as the fallen leaves crunching beneath their feet. When she raised her brows, he clarified, "I meant that as a compliment to all three of you."

Good. Because her fondness for his particular slice of bread wouldn't save him if he insulted her family. "Thank you."

He stretched his legs out in front of him, exhaling slowly. "I apologize for intruding on your privacy, but we need you inside. Everything else is ready, so it's time for the final positioning of the"—either a shiver or a shudder rolled through his frame— "dolls."

Definitely a shudder, then.

"Great." Newly energized after her phone call, she stood. "Let's go make everything perfect."

He frowned. "The display doesn't need to be perfect, Athena, and I don't want you to feel guilty if Hill doesn't get the prize. You volunteered your time and energy and made something wonderful, creative, and entirely you. In the process, Hill had fun. Your friends did too." Rising to his feet, he braced his hands on his narrow hips and regarded her steadily. "What about you, Athena? Did you have fun? Because if you did, that's already a win for everyone."

So fierce. He was so damn *fierce* in his defense of her.

"Yeah. I did. I had fun, and I reconnected with the world." Rising up on her tiptoes, she kissed his now-cool cheek. "Because of you, Matthew."

His lips parted on a sharp, shaky breath.

She made herself take one step away, then another. Turning on her Ked-covered heel, she headed toward the store, knowing she had Matthew at her back the entire way. And when he opened the door for her and laid a gentle, guiding hand on her lower spine, she wondered yet again: What did the contact mean to him?

Was he touching her out of politeness—or hunger?

She had to know, and she had to know soon. Because, heaven help her, she'd just realized she wasn't simply hungry. She was starving. She had been since late last December.

And she wasn't sure how much longer she could stay polite about it.

15

On Tuesday, Matthew convinced Athena to leave her house, venture into the cool autumn afternoon, and stroll to the waterfront with him. With what he considered vast shrewdness, he did so by taking advantage of her soft heart. No AP psychology techniques necessary.

"I'm lonely," he said, urging her upstairs to change into outdoorsy clothing. "I'd appreciate your company on my walk. Please, Athena."

It was the truth, albeit one he hadn't confessed to anyone before now. He *was* lonely—except with her. Whenever she accompanied him, everything was better, brighter, and easier. Even though *she* wasn't easy, and she likely never would be.

After another walk on Wednesday, he invited her to spend Halloween evening with him, and she agreed without even asking whether Johnny would be there too. Which he wouldn't, because he was going straight from work to a friend's party. Otherwise, Matthew would never have issued the invitation. Just as he wouldn't have gone on those walks with her if Johnny weren't safely occupied at work.

Athena wouldn't welcome an appearance by her ex-fiancé. Even if she would, Matthew didn't intend for his brother to discover how much time he was spending with her. Whatever he and Athena were creating, he instinctively wanted his sibling as far from it as possible.

And if Johnny saw them together, he'd know. He'd know how Matthew felt.

He'd accuse Matthew of betraying him, and probably he'd be right.

Maybe that should have stopped Matthew from basking in her companionship, from touching her in any way he could plausibly defend as platonic and several ways he couldn't, from watching over her as she took her first shaky steps toward dealing with her depression. It didn't. Right now, he wasn't sure *anything* could tear him from her side, not when he wanted her so desperately and she needed so much loving care.

The best he could do was not kiss her again.

Jesus fuck, he needed not to kiss her again.

Easier said than done, unfortunately. Tonight, as they poured Halloween candy into a large glass bowl, he could hardly drag his eyes off his witch companion. The most adorable witch in this entire universe, and any other universe too.

The black, flowing gown matched her black, flowing wig and black, pointy hat. Her black lipstick emphasized the plumpness of her lips. Her cackle—which she'd demonstrated for him several times already, soliciting his input as to whether it conveyed sufficient menace—rang through his home, loud and clear and powerful.

"I mostly chose this outfit because it was easy, but I also wore it for you, you know," she told him, emptying another bag into the bowl. "I have a scary costume I could have worn instead. Frieda Krueger: invader of dreams, murderer of innocent children, despiser of nail clippers. Second only to Waldo in her devotion to horizontal stripes."

Aha! He knew that reference, thanks to Professor Google!

Other than the Waldo bit, but he could look that up later.

He nodded sagely. "You're referring to Freddy Krueger, the fictional homicidal maniac, rather than Kroger, the national grocery store chain."

"This is true." Her lips twitched, but her voice was dead solemn. "I do not, in fact, own a Halloween costume that anthropomorphizes an existing business franchise."

"I know you're mocking me, and I don't care." Lightly, he flicked the end of her cute nose. "Any conversation where I can mostly keep up with you I consider a moral victory."

She laughed. "Well, if you're the moral victor, I have your spoils. Here."

Straightening, she walked over to the bag she'd left just inside his front door, then handed it to him. The paper crinkled as he opened the top.

The bag contained an eye patch and a tricorn hat, both black. She intended for him to dress like a pirate captain, evidently. Only . . . instead of a cutlass or blunderbuss, she'd included a large leather purse as well, brown and vaguely rectangular.

"I know you didn't intend to wear a costume tonight, but . . ." She poked at the purse. "If you squint, this makes a decent medical bag, and I know you have a white button-down shirt. If you wear it loosely tucked into a pair of dark pants, we can roll up the legs so they look like breeches, and voilà! One passable old-timey shipboard doctor's outfit, made to order."

This wasn't an attempt to make him a captain, all-powerful and authoritative. No, she was offering Matthew his boyhood dream. The one he'd all but forgotten until she'd coaxed the memory from him.

He'd never wanted to be in charge of everyone. He'd only wanted to feed his curiosity by exploring the world and help people along the way.

"We could put a fan by the door and aim it in your direction, so your shirt would flap in the shipboard breeze," she continued, still discussing his costume. "Also, let's discuss guyliner."

In the end, he agreed to everything, because his agreement allowed him to flee to the third floor in search of a fan while she left to fetch makeup for him. Right then, he needed to impose some distance between them. As much as possible.

It was either that or kiss her. Again.

LATER THAT NIGHT, after he'd posed dramatically for the umpteenth time, shirt rippling in the wind as Athena passed out candy, they collapsed side by side on his slipcovered couch. He dropped his tricorn and eyepatch on the coffee table, grateful for the reprieve.

"That was the last of the candy." She sounded tired but satisfied. "Your light is off, and the official town hours for trick-or-treating are over. We. Are. *Done*."

With a pleased sigh, she tugged off her hat and wig, tossing them toward the door.

"Yes. We. Are." He groaned and stretched. "Remind me never to become a male model. Posing and preening is more grueling than I'd ever imagined."

"When the next talent scout approaches you and promises runway stardom, I'll be sure to mention this conversation." Her hand covered her mouth as she yawned widely. "At least you have good reason to be tired. You worked most of today, while I was being lazy and reading in bed. I have no excuse."

She was so fucking hard on herself, and Matthew hated it.

Gradually, she was normalizing her sleep schedule. She'd done her best to stay up as long as possible every night that week, since they'd decided it would be easier to stretch her bedtime five or six hours later instead of moving it over twelve hours earlier.

So that was one good reason for her fatigue, but she had others. Like, say, serious depression that was only now getting addressed. Even if her new antidepressant worked to lift her mood—which wasn't at all a guarantee, since brains were finicky—it would still take at least three or four weeks for her to feel a real change.

Plus, Athena's first meeting with a psychologist had occurred yesterday. People's therapy experiences were probably all different, but when Jackie was talking to a counselor regularly, Yvonna had taken time off after every session to care for her wife.

"Digging up all those painful emotions wears her out," Yvonna had told him. "Once she's done, she always wants a cool cloth for her eyes and a nap. She calls it her post-therapy hangover."

When he'd knocked on Athena's door yesterday afternoon, he'd brought a refrigerated gel eye mask. One look at it, and her already red-rimmed eyes had filled and spilled over.

"My head hurts," she'd whispered after thanking him, and he'd helped her back into bed, where she'd dozed until dinnertime.

In deference to her privacy—and in cowardly fear the question might make her cry again—he hadn't asked about the appointment before now. But if he needed to find her a different counselor, he wanted to know that as soon as possible.

Unable to stop himself from touching her, he covered her nearest hand with his. "How did therapy go? Do you want to try someone else, or does Dr. Solomon seem like a good fit?"

"It's kind of hard to tell after just one session? But so far, I like her. She has a sense of humor, but she's also willing to call me out—nicely—when I try to deflect a hard question by being funny." In a restless movement, she flipped her hand over and twined their fingers. "Before our next meeting, she asked me to pay attention to my thoughts about myself and track how many are negative versus neutral or positive."

"How's it looking so far?" Not that he didn't already know.

"I, uh . . ." Her teeth chewed a corner of her lower lip. "I'm maybe a little harsh sometimes."

More like *definitely a lot harsh all the time*, but it was a start.

Angling herself to face him, she asked, "Have you ever seen a counselor, Matthew?"

He closed his eyes. *Dammit.*

He'd spent decades not talking about this, but turnabout was only fair. She'd bared her underbelly to him, both literally and metaphorically, trusting him to treat her with care despite their shared history. And she didn't seem to need invulnerability or infallibility from him. Pretending he had his life and emotions perfectly in order at all times only made her feel worse about her own troubles.

So he might cry and he might hurt, but he'd tell her the truth. Because he couldn't and wouldn't lie to her. Because she deserved it from him, and Adrian deserved someone like Athena holding him safe in her heart too.

"Yes. I've seen a counselor." He forced the words through a constricted throat. "A, uh, long time ago. When I was a kid."

Her thigh suddenly pressed warmly against his, and her shoulder nudged his upper arm. At the first sign of a chink in his armor, she'd scooted closer to him. Very metaphorical, that.

"My parents were lawyers. Busy ones. They lived in this house, and my maternal grandmother lived in Johnny's house. All our other family was across the country." The moisture had evaporated from his mouth, and it hurt to swallow. "Like you, I was a surprise, and they waited a while before having more kids. Adrian was born when I was seven, Johnny when I was eight. There were eleven months between them."

He allowed himself to turn clinical for a moment. Academic, rather than personal and grief-stricken. "Kids aren't simply little adults. Their physiology is different, and certain medications we can use safely have dangerous side effects in children. Over-the-counter cough and cold medicines, for example, don't actually help children under six years old, and they can cause rapid heart rate, convulsions, or death, especially if a child is given too much."

A quick glance at Athena's expression revealed a mouth down-turned in sadness and absolutely no confusion. She understood now. She knew where this story was going.

"Johnny was only two weeks old when Adrian died, so he has no memory of what happened, obviously." His palm had turned sweaty against hers, but when he tried to pull away, she held on tighter. "I do."

During Johnny's early childhood, Matthew had relived the devastation over and over in his restless dreams. When Athena vanished from view the previous week, that old nightmare had returned, and only climbing through her window had banished it once more.

His voice kept cracking, but he pushed out the words while he still could. "I caught a cold at school and passed it to Adrian. He got it worse than I did, and his breathing sounded a bit labored, so my mom called the family doctor late at night. Something in the conversation got muddled, and he thought I was the main sick kid in the household, instead of Adrian. He suggested a medication with pseudoephedrine, a nasal decongestant. My dad picked it up at the pharmacy and didn't notice it was theoretically meant for me."

Athena covered their interlocked fingers with her free hand.

"Things might still have been okay, but—" He cleared his throat once. Again. "Between work issues and having two infants in the house, my parents were exhausted, and they were fighting a lot and barely talking to one another. They each thought they were the only one giving him medicine. He ended up getting two separate doses at the minimal interval, in the amount appropriate for an eight-year-old."

After Adrian's birth, their mom told Matthew to watch over his baby brother. To protect Adrian, because whenever Dad was working or absent, Matthew was the man of the house. After Johnny's birth, their father clapped Matthew on the shoulder and said a big brother always took care of his younger siblings, but he wasn't worried, since Matthew was already such a good brother. Such a responsible kid.

He was responsible. Praise and warning both, encompassed in a single word.

He wanted to make his parents proud, so Matthew generally changed diapers and prepared bottles as soon as he woke up, because Mom and Dad needed their sleep. That morning, he took care of the infant, then crept into Adrian's quiet, dark room, surprised that his other brother wasn't fussing and impatient already.

"I found him dead in his crib." The words were stark. Unemotional, unless you could hear the decades of silent sorrow embedded in each syllable. "Pseudoephedrine intoxication."

"Matthew." Her voice was as gentle as her fingertip on his cheek, sweeping away the wetness he hadn't quite managed to blink back. "I'm so very sorry."

He licked dry lips. "Afterward, we went to family counseling for a while. So yes, I've seen a therapist before."

Unearthing a clean tissue, she handed it to him. "Did it help?"

"She made me feel less guilty about Adrian's death, but otherwise . . . not really." There was no patching their family back together at that point, no matter how good a son and brother Matthew tried to be or how good a counselor they found. "My parents blamed each other for what happened and eventually got divorced."

Once he'd set aside the tissue, Athena lifted his arm and positioned herself beneath it, her body warm and giving, her hand sliding into his once more. "Did you stay with your mom? Or did they have joint custody?"

"Joint custody." But Adrian's death had broken both his parents, so joint custody looked more like joint neglect. His mother threw herself into her estate-planning practice, worked ludicrously long hours, and kept herself distant from her remaining sons. His father grieved too hard to care adequately for anyone, including himself. "We spent most of our time with Granny, though. She had emphysema and needed our help."

From that point on, Matthew spent many, many years being very careful about absolutely everything. Trying to keep Granny and Johnny safe. Trying not to upset his parents further.

Athena cuddled even closer. "Are she and your parents . . ."

"My parents are alive, but we don't see them much. When Johnny started college, my mother moved to California, and my father left for Arizona. They gave me this house"—out of guilt—"and when Granny died a couple years later, they gave Johnny her house."

"Johnny said you basically raised him."

"Yes," Matthew said curtly.

When he and Athena were together, he didn't want to think about Johnny. Not about her past with his younger brother. Not about how that past precluded any possible future with Matthew.

Non. Nein. None. No.

She asked quietly, "Is Adrian's death why you became a pediatrician?"

The question didn't demand. It coaxed sweetly, and he so longed to be known by her.

"Yes and no. Even as a kid, I always pictured myself as a doctor of some sort. But yes, losing Adrian probably had something to do with my choice to treat children." He smoothed his thumb over her knuckles. "There's no recording of the phone call to tell us what was said or what exactly happened that night, so I've never known how to apportion the blame for his death."

There was plenty of blame to go around, Matthew had eventually concluded. They were all awash in it, other than Johnny.

Johnny, his only remaining brother. The infant who essentially lost his entire immediate family on that awful day, with one lone exception: Matthew.

His voice ragged, he kept explaining. "That said, I do think general practitioners aren't always as careful as they could be when it comes to children and medications. As a pediatrician, I can make damn sure my patients and parents don't come to grief because of negligence on my part. Besides, helping parents and watching their children grow up feels . . ." *Like I have a family again too. Almost.* "It feels good."

He liked kids. They were honest and straightforward with their emotions. A bit mischievous too, which he found endearing in both children and—he glanced at Athena—adults. Evidently.

"I can imagine," she said with a small, sad smile.

"Young children in particular are . . . indescribably vulnerable." When he closed his eyes, he could still picture just how small his brother's body looked in that crib. Still see Adrian raising his arms trustingly, reaching for Matthew with total faith that his big brother would keep him safe. "They're entirely dependent on their caretakers for everything they need to survive. Nutrition. Shelter. Loving touch and attention. Intervention when they fall ill. *Everything*. I want to be their advocate, Athena, because they can't do it for themselves, and sometimes their families can't do it for them either. So I became a pediatrician."

Athena blotted his right cheek with something soft.

He blinked back the remaining tears and lifted her hand to his mouth, pressing a kiss of gratitude into her warm, cupped palm.

"When you lose a patient, it must destroy you," she whispered, and she wasn't wrong.

It was rare, but despite his best efforts, his kids sometimes became sick in ways he couldn't fix. They had accidents. They met with violence or ended their own lives. They died, and he grieved them more than anyone knew, except maybe Athena.

In his heart, all of them still lived. They were safe and loved, and they would remain that way always. Sometimes he pictured his baby brother keeping them company, and he wondered how Adrian would look now, at thirty-two years old. Like Johnny, he imagined.

He nodded jerkily. "Yes."

Her arms closed around him, and she cradled him as he dropped his head to her shoulder and sank into her embrace. When their cheeks brushed, hers was cool and wet. She was crying, this time for him, and he didn't know what to do with that kind of gift.

"Thank you for telling me," she murmured, and clasped him tighter. "Thank you for trusting me with that."

He'd made her weep again, and she was thanking him for it.

The remaining shreds of his control slipped from his grasp, and somehow he was telling her things he shouldn't. Not everything, but enough. Enough to damn him.

"You don't understand. I didn't explain it." He spoke into her neck, into the hair curving around her jaw, and if heaven existed, it would smell fruity and warm. "What I said hurt you, and I'm sorry. You need to know."

When she stiffened, he tugged her closer, and suddenly she wasn't holding him. He was holding her. Clutching her.

"What? Matthew—"

These words required no dredging. They'd rested on the tip of his tongue for months, swallowed back again and again, bittersweet and dangerous. "It was different before the party. I was worried about Johnny. About myself. But after we met, after I followed you to that corner, I knew. I *knew*."

Fuck, he shouldn't be telling her any of this. It was disloyal to his brother. It revealed too much about his own obsessive longing for her.

Didn't matter. The words kept leaping from his mouth in a desperate rush, because he'd said he was done hurting her, and he'd meant it. She was struggling for so many reasons, most of them beyond his control. But this—*this* pain he could fix. He had to, because he couldn't bear inflicting it any longer.

She'd gone very still. "You knew what?"

"You were lovely beyond words, whip-smart and funny and totally lost, and he couldn't make you happy. He couldn't give you what you needed. He's so fucking *young*, Athena. He hadn't grown up enough to be your partner, and he would never have realized that, never admitted it, and you wouldn't have either until it was too late for everyone."

He'd have watched her walk to the altar and commit herself to a man who'd only bring her disappointment, then watched from across a narrow alleyway as his brother failed her again and again. In the end, Matthew would have taken care of her instead. Taken care of her, given her whatever she needed, and sent her back into his brother's home, into his brother's arms, into his brother's bed, night after night after fucking night, and he couldn't let that happen.

It would have broken him. It would have broken all of them.

A mere month before the wedding, despairing and afraid, he'd told his brother he might have to leave Harlot's Bay if the wedding took place. He'd intended the words as an enormous, desperate bluff—but once they actually spilled from his mouth, they sounded like nothing more than the raw truth. A confession, rather than a threat.

"The engagement had to end, I ended it, and if I could go back, I would end it again. Just like I told you." Lifting his face from her neck, breathing roughly, he pressed his forehead hard against hers, willing her to listen. To believe him. "Not because there's something wrong with you. Not because you wouldn't make the best fucking wife on the planet. Not because you didn't deserve my brother, but because you *both* deserved more."

No one else would have recognized his voice like this, raw and fevered and harsh. Not his patients, not his parents, not his brother. But Athena knew it now. She knew him. She knew he contained wildness within him, so carefully controlled he hadn't even acknowledged its existence until she stood before him, a bee-studded curve of honeycomb, at her engagement party to his fucking *brother*.

Forehead to forehead, she was too close to see clearly, but he couldn't look away. Her eyes held him in place. And before he said another word, her mouth crashed into his.

His world caught fire.

When Athena Knox Greydon committed to something, she committed every molecule of her being, and right now she was committed to destruction. Total incineration of the man he'd believed he was, the man he'd tried so hard to be.

For all the plush softness of her mouth, it claimed his like an occupying force, marching under the command of her war goddess namesake. Her palms cupped his cheeks and held him still for pillaging, and she tilted his head exactly where she wanted it, exactly where she could inflict maximum damage. Her lips clung to his. They captured his own lips, one at a time, top and bottom, and tugged lightly. The sly, subtle flick of her tongue along the seam of his mouth was the advance scout testing his defenses, and he opened to her helplessly. Fell before her, conquered.

He was panting. Shocked. Awed.

She tasted like the peanut butter cups she'd snitched from his trick-or-treat bowl, and the inside of her mouth slid like hot silk beneath his tongue. Need twisted inside him, turning him restless and impatient, and he no longer wanted to surrender.

He wanted to claim his own spoils.

Firmly, carefully, he pushed her back into the couch cushions with shaking hands and moved to stand between her legs. He bent over her, buried his fingers in her hair, and—

Johnny's ringtone. His brother's favorite song as a preteen, "Hate to Say I Told You So" by The Hives, all strident guitar and cacophonous feedback and bratty confidence.

What the hell was he doing?

In an uncoordinated rush, his skin prickling with shame, he extricated his hands from her hair, heaved himself upright, and stumbled a step away from the couch. Two. Three.

His refusal to hurt Athena didn't mean he intended to hurt his brother instead. If Johnny ever found out about this, maybe he'd forgive Matthew, but maybe he wouldn't. Matthew hoped they never had to discover the answer.

Even if Johnny *did* forgive him, or even if Johnny never found out, what about Athena? How could he justify this kind of carelessness with her? Right now, her thoughts and emotions were muddled, and he didn't want her in his arms for the wrong reasons. If she ever regretted intimacy with him, he'd crumple to dust.

Did she truly desire him? Or was this only misdirected gratitude?

She stared up at him from the sofa, hazel eyes dazed and wide, cheeks flushed. Hair rumpled by his hands. Lips swollen from his mouth on hers.

Well, hers on his, technically. Either way, she wouldn't be in this state without him, so he'd be the one to guide them both back to safety.

The phone rang itself into silence, then dinged with an incoming text message.

He extended a hand to help her up. Slowly, she accepted the offer of assistance, and he helped ease her to her feet. Then he dropped her hand like it had scorched him.

Because it did. He had no idea why blisters weren't rising from his flesh.

"I should probably find out what's happening." He nodded toward his cell phone, then stretched and yawned far too ostentatiously. "Hopefully I won't need to see a patient tonight. I'm really tired."

Her daze had vanished, leaving her gaze sharp on his face. His body language. Her brow puckered at whatever she saw, and she pushed her glasses to the bridge of her nose with her forefinger.

He'd smudged the lenses. His fingers twitched at his sides, wanting to fix the mess he'd made, but he wasn't a fool. If he got that close to her again, he'd make an even bigger mess. Maybe one he could never fully clean.

"Me too," she finally said. "I guess I should . . . go."

He walked her to her door and waited until she locked it behind her, then returned home and read the text from his brother.

Apparently Johnny and his friends had trooped downtown for the Halloween celebration. He knew Matthew often visited Blue-stocking, so he was sharing the news of Hill's window-decorating victory.

Hill and Athena's friends must have kept that afternoon in the bookstore to themselves. If Johnny knew his brother and ex-fiancée had worked together on that ghastly, prize-winning window, he'd have said something. Or possibly punched something, such as Matthew's jaw.

So, in the end, everything had worked out perfectly. Hill could pay himself for another month. Johnny remained happy enough, or at least not angry and betrayed. Athena had seemed confused but not hurt by Matthew's loss of control and subsequent withdrawal. Matthew had somehow kept both the trust of his brother and Athena's friendship.

Win-win-win-win.

Funny. It didn't feel like a victory. At all.

16

*I*n early December, Athena finally felt her depression begin to lift.
It wasn't a huge difference. She didn't transform into the same
person she'd been three or four years ago: energetic, focused, determined, optimistic. She wasn't suddenly humming show tunes as
she jauntily scrubbed her home and twirled her mop like a dance
partner, before declaring loudly what a beautiful, sunny day it was
and carpe diem–ing that shit.

But one morning, she was sitting at her breakfast table, eating
her cereal and watching people totally fuck up their home renovations, and she realized the world seemed a bit more manageable.
She didn't need to escape her thoughts quite as assiduously, since
her head was no longer a total hellscape of self-hatred. It had become a heckscape of self-doubt instead, which wasn't great, but
certainly an improvement.

It was as if she finally had a safety net beneath her, stopping
her from dropping quite so far into despair as before. She still
cried a lot. She still had occasional days where she did nothing but read. She still had nasty thoughts about herself and her
choices. But her vague—and terrifying, in retrospect—desire to
disappear had vanished, because she knew she mattered. To her
parents, her friends, and herself.

It was mid-December now, and she'd finally begun thinking
about her future again. Contemplating her life and her needs and
evaluating her options.

Things were definitely, definitely better. Not great, but okay.

The meds and therapy were helping, but so was her return to regular work. Soon after Halloween, Bunny had called from the library about another temporary position, substituting for a circ employee on maternity leave for three months. So starting in mid-November, she had a paycheck once more, and between that and her parents' financial support, she was eating foods from the outer edges of the grocery store these days. She was keeping a relatively regular sleep schedule. She was seeing friends every workday.

Even better: She couldn't find a single bit of evidence that Matthew had finagled the job offer for her. She'd earned it on her own, based on her previous good work, and that made her return to the library all the sweeter.

Nevertheless, she couldn't have upgraded from hellscape to heckscape without him. While they never quite recovered their former intimacy after she forced that stupid kiss on him, he'd kept coming around afterward. Checking in, fixing meals, cleaning as necessary, coaxing her into occasional walks.

In return, she'd conducted a twice-weekly Remedial Memes Bootcamp for his benefit, so the next time he saw three Spider-Men pointing at each other or Sith Lord Kermit encouraging bad decisions, he would be *ready*, dammit.

Ever the dutiful student, he sat down at her kitchen table one afternoon, placed his coffee mug on the table, and announced, "This is fine," completely straight-faced and unprompted. Whereupon she deemed him an honored graduate of her bootcamp and bestowed upon him the certificate of completion she'd created earlier that week, then threatened to take it back when he failed to get why she kept yelling, "You get a certificate! You get a certificate! *Everybody gets a certificate!*"

"*You* didn't get a certificate," he pointed out, brow creased in sincere, adorable concern. "Do you want me to make you one? Because I can."

Just for that, she let him keep his alumnus status.

The entire month of November had cemented his place in her life as her friend. A good, loyal friend, and that would have to be enough for her.

So what if he'd kissed her? In retrospect, maybe that brief, gentle press of his mouth on hers in the bath was just kindness, or an automatic reaction to a naked woman, or a momentary signal-crossing of responsibility and attraction.

And maybe, on Halloween, she'd thought she read need in his eyes and his body. In the revelations he'd offered and the way he'd allowed her to comfort him. In the intensity of his grip and voice when he'd insisted she wasn't too messy for love and marriage and told her she was *lovely beyond words*.

But after his phone rang, he'd reverted to scrupulous politeness and become a perfect gentleman again. Openly caring, but not hungry for her. So apparently she'd been wrong.

Only . . . she'd begun to wonder about that.

Her therapist kept saying Athena should trust herself and her own judgment more. She was doing her best to follow that advice, and her judgment kept telling her the same damn thing, over and over.

Dr. Matthew Vine the Third was full of shit.

He'd dry heaved in the open air for her, thirty feet above unforgiving bricks. Washed her naked body with care and reverence. Gripped her greedily to his chest. Told her his secrets.

He watched her mouth and marked her words as if she were an oracle poised to pronounce his fate. Put those careful, capable hands on her, given the slightest excuse. Forced himself to drag his gaze from her tits whenever she wore a tank top without a bra.

He wanted her. He wasn't letting himself have her.

Yeah, it was weird that she'd been engaged to his brother. She got his hesitance. She didn't share it—Johnny was a grown-ass man who'd dumped her of his own free will, and he'd get over any damage to his ego sooner or later—but she got it.

If she could in fact trust her judgment, Matthew Vine didn't know what to do with her, given their complicated history. Didn't know what to do with how he felt about her.

No worries. If he truly desired her, she could show him *precisely* what to do.

That very night, as a matter of fact.

THESE WERE THE shortest days of the year, and darkness had fallen hours ago. Matthew ate his dinner alone, his back turned to Athena's kitchen window. Soon, he would finish his sandwich, wash his dishes, and head upstairs to his office. And once he did . . . well, Athena was still figuring out what she'd do.

What was the best way to discover whether a cautious, controlled man like Matthew considered her a platonic friend—or a woman he desperately wanted in his bed?

Partial nudity. Whatever strategy she chose to employ, partial nudity would help.

Girding her loins for the battle ahead would, paradoxically, involve putting as little fabric over her actual loins as possible.

Her hands shook as she opened her dresser drawer, but she refused to let self-doubt prevent her from going after what she wanted. *I'm unstoppable*, she told herself as she changed into her thinnest, tightest, shortest tank, then tugged off her panties and pulled up her skimpiest pajama shorts. *A woman on a mission. A tigress on the prowl. A Mountie after my man. Uh . . .* Rumours-*era Fleetwood Mac hunting down their cocaine dealer?*

That last one . . . probably wasn't the *best* analogy, but whatever.

By the time she finished getting ready, Matthew had moved into his office. The rumpled state of his dark hair kept drawing her eye, maybe because he'd finally let it grow long enough to curl. He'd rolled up the sleeves of his shirt, as he always did at night, and unfastened its top two buttons. Heavens to Betsy, those *forearms*, and that triangle of pale skin below his neck . . .

She wanted to follow his veins with a fingertip. Trace that triangle with her tongue.

One hand absently rubbing his stubble-shadowed jaw, he sat in front of his computer and peered at the screen. Innocent. Solemn. Unprepared for what was about to hit him.

Showtime.

She knelt on a cushion in front of her library nook's window and raised it. The resulting groan of wood must have carried through the night air, because he immediately looked in her direction. She smiled and waved, doing her best not to visibly shiver.

Rising to his feet, he opened his own window and bent down to speak. "It's thirty-four degrees outside, Athena. You're going to freeze like that."

Oh, that severe frown. It did nothing but spur her on.

"I wanted to ask you something." Also show him something. Namely, her big, barely covered tits and their chill-hardened nipples. "I thought about calling"—no, she hadn't—"but then I saw you through the window, so . . ."

She lifted her shoulders in a huge, helpless shrug, as if she'd had no other choice but to parade herself half naked in front of him. Her breasts shifted beneath the tank top, which was *just* short enough to flash some of the goodies if she raised her arms high. But she was saving that revelation for later.

He seemed to be having trouble with eye contact, poor lamb. After a long pause, he cleared his throat and directed his resolute gaze above her neck.

"What . . ." He pressed two fingers against his forehead. "What's going on? Do you need me to come over?"

"That all depends, Matthew." Idly, she trailed her fingertips across her upper chest, drawing his eyes there again. "If you wait a second, I'll . . . hold on."

"Hmmm?" He sounded a bit distracted, maybe because she'd turned around and lowered herself to her hands and knees, arching her back as she reached for the book on her chair. "I, uh—"

"Got it!" Swiveling back around, she brandished the paperback in feigned triumph.

Now her butt was an icicle too, because those pajama shorts didn't even fully cover her cheeks. What exactly he'd seen from his window, she couldn't say. Definitely a generous amount of ass, but maybe a peek of pussy too.

This might not be *the* moment of truth, but it was *a* moment of truth.

A platonic friend would cut off this conversation to save them both embarrassment or warn her she was inadvertently—or so he thought—flashing him. And even if that platonic friend were too polite for either option, he certainly wouldn't keep staring at her tits and thighs like he could devour her body in a dozen greedy gulps.

But that was exactly what he was doing. Staring, a starving man at a banquet. Slashes of hot color on his cheekbones, eyes heavy-lidded, hand rubbing slowly across his mouth.

"Here." She thrust the book through the window, cover facing his way. "I checked this out for you yesterday."

His vocal cords produced a sound, but it wasn't a word she'd ever heard before.

She continued as if he hadn't just emitted a garbled groan. "I was looking for stories I thought you'd love, and I kept coming back to this author. Have you seen the movie *Master and Commander*?"

He shook his head. Then did it again, randomly.

"We'll have to watch it one night soon." Preferably cuddled up together in bed. "Anyway, it's based on a series by Patrick O'Brian, all about an English naval captain during the Napoleonic Wars and his best friend, the shipboard physician. I've heard the books are great. This is the first in the series, and if you're interested, I'll pass it along."

He blinked at her for a while.

"I'm . . . uh, interested," he finally said, his words hoarse but intelligible. "Thank you for thinking of me, Athena. I haven't . . ."

He trailed off, watching her with his brow furrowed.

The heat in his dark stare hadn't disappeared, but it was now accompanied by seeming bewilderment. Had no one ever catered to his interests before? Ever?

She spoke gently. "If you end up liking it, I can get you the rest of the series too."

"Thank you," he repeated, then shivered.

If she kept this window open much longer, he'd be courting hypothermia, and her nipples would freeze solid and crack like grapes in liquid nitrogen, so this conversation had to end. The problem: She hadn't yet established his desire for her—specifically *her*, not simply a nearly naked woman thrust into his sightlines—beyond a reasonable doubt.

She'd just had an idea, though. A reckless, possibly disastrous idea. But her therapist had said to trust her instincts, right? And if she was a glorious shipwreck, as Matthew had claimed, she needed to brave the ocean again. She'd spent enough months ashore.

Maybe she'd never skim over the waves with as much blithe confidence as before. Maybe there'd always be jagged edges and jutting beams in place of once-smooth decks. But she'd been pieced back together, and she might not be perfect, but she was sturdy enough.

It was time to unfurl her sails, and to hell with possible storms on the horizon.

"Dr. Vine . . ." *Bon voyage.* "You once told me I could do literally anything I wanted in this chair"—she patted its seat—"and it wouldn't bother you. At midnight, Matthew, I'm going to test that. Close your shade, and I'll know you don't want to watch. But if your shade stays open . . ."

His lips had parted, and she could see his chest expand in a sudden, deep inhalation.

Her slow smile was a promise. A challenge. "I'll know you do."

Raising her arms high, she lowered her window and drew her own shade down to the sill. That final flash of her tits should serve as fair warning, she figured.

In the quiet darkness of a new day, she intended to explore deep, deep waters.

AS BEST ATHENA could tell, all their neighbors had gone to bed already. If they hadn't, though, that was fine too. Only one person had windows facing her library nook. Only one person could see her.

If he wanted to.

Thirty seconds to go.

In a corner of the room, two of her old cucumber-melon candles flickered, providing just enough illumination to reveal what she was doing, but not enough to make her feel spotlighted or self-conscious. The tank top and cheeky shorts remained perfectly inadequate in their attempts to cover her plentiful curves. She'd dragged her oversized chair right up to the window, where it overlooked the silent night, and all she had to do now was open her shade. Open her window.

Open her legs.

Her entire body trembled with every rapid heartbeat, but she refused to surrender to fear. At the stroke of midnight, she opened, opened, opened, and saw.

His office was dark as pitch.

But his shade . . . his shade was as open as her thighs. So was his window.

Leaning against the far wall of his room, he was a half-glimpsed silhouette at best, but it didn't matter. As soon as she raised her shade and window, the current between them snapped to life, electrifying her in an instant. It told her everything she needed to know.

Dr. Matthew Vine the Third was watching. Waiting.

He wanted her.

In an unhurried, deliberate movement, she bent her right knee high and propped her bare foot against the windowsill, offering him a better view. Giving herself an easier reach.

Normally, she closed her eyes when she touched herself. Not this time.

Staring straight into the shadows, she slid her left hand under her tank top, cupping her breast. Squeezing. Rubbing and pinching her nipple. The shirt snagged against her wrist, her forearm, dragging upward moment by moment, until the cold air washed unimpeded over her tits and stiffened her nipples even more.

The darkness before her didn't shift, but a ragged breath punctured the hushed night.

Not hers. His.

In the blackness of midnight, she could imagine anything. Everything.

They reclined in liquid warmth once more, pressed hard and tight against one another. This time, she contained no shame. No defeat. Only triumph, because he'd slipped into her bath for one reason and one reason alone, and it wasn't charity. It was carnality.

His chest braced her back, radiating tense heat as he settled her between his legs. As he encircled her body with his arms and sent those strong, careful fingers in pursuit of her pleasure.

Ever so slowly, she slid her right hand down the center of her body, caressing the bare, generous curve of her belly, slipping beneath the waistband of her tiny, tiny shorts. Her palm was his, broad and smooth. Her fingers were his, long and nimble and unhurried. Her moan was his, because he'd earned it with that initial stroke, so sweet and slow, coaxing her open to his touch. Parting her folds so he could slide through them and discover every sensitive inch of flesh.

She moaned again.

God, he was a tease. That gentle rub through the slick furrow of her pussy, that gentle slip of his thumb over her vulva, that gentle tease of his fingertip at her entrance . . . they weren't enough, and he knew it. He knew where she needed attention and friction.

She braced her foot and raised her hips, legs taut and straining, but he wouldn't yield to her mute demands for haste. In lazy little forays, he'd caress close to her clit, but never close enough. His open mouth hot against her neck, dragging along the curve of her shoulder, he murmured, "Stop fighting, love. Let me take care of you."

That voice could melt glaciers. It melted her, turning her slippery and soaked. And once she relaxed back against his hard chest, into his protective arms wrapped so firmly around her, he gave her what she needed.

"Matthew," she breathed, and a sharp, strangled sound drifted from the shadows of his office. "Oh . . ."

She was so wet now, his leisurely glide around her clit became a smooth, frictionless circle. Bit by bit, his fingertips edged closer, sweeping over the hood, tenderly worrying the sides of that swollen, needy bit of flesh.

He was so careful with her. Far more careful than she'd ever been with herself.

When he tugged lightly at her nipple, she exhaled in a harsh pant, rocked by a momentary sunburst of pleasure. He circled her clit around and around, concentric loops tightening and tightening again, adding more pressure a featherweight at a time, dragging a thin, desperate whimper from her throat.

She wasn't the only one panting now, the only one frantic. He pressed harder, tugged harder, and she rose up against his knowing hands, lost.

"Please, Matthew," she begged, her eyes drifting shut at last, and somewhere in the darkness, a rough grunt ripped from the throat of polite, quiet Dr. Matthew Vine the Third.

He stroked her clit, firm and sure, and she came.

The orgasm swamped her, crashing into her and tipping her sideways. It tore through her in waves, and all she could do was keep stroking herself, shudder after shudder.

The pleasure receded gradually. Reluctantly.

Eyes still closed, she withdrew her hand from her pajama shorts and took a minute to reorient herself. Then she looked at that faint silhouette of a man across the alleyway, removed her foot from the windowsill, and stood on shaky legs.

"Now you know," she said. "And now I do too."

Then she closed her window, walked away, and let him make his decision.

RIGHT BEFORE SHE went to bed, Athena composed her email to Matthew: an invitation to the pre-Christmas Nasty Wenches book club meeting happening later that week. The group had kindly delayed tackling the monster-fucking theme until she felt able to come, and that meant Matthew could participate too. After all, he'd listened to several Sadie Brazen stories through their windows, however unwillingly. He wasn't precisely a master of the monster-fucking oeuvre, but he was no innocent either.

The email served several purposes. It was a genuine invitation to an event she suspected he'd reluctantly enjoy. With the message's casual, breezy tone, it was a reassurance that no matter what happened next, she wouldn't get overly dramatic or make things hard on him.

It was also an implicit request for him to render his verdict.

Would he deny himself yet again? Or did he want her too much to resist?

Sent. Done.

The rest of the night she spent reading and periodically checking her inbox, because she couldn't sleep. Luckily, she didn't have to work the next day.

The darkness surrendered to dawn. The sun climbed, then began to lower again.

No response appeared in her inbox. He didn't text. He didn't call. He kept his windows closed and his shades drawn.

It was a no, then. No, he didn't want her enough to upend his careful life. No, he wasn't willing to risk his relationship with Johnny to have her.

That evening, she cried to her therapist, Carole, who reminded her that cautious people needed time. Even cautious people who might want something—or someone—very much. Together, they worked on coping techniques to help Athena through whatever might happen next, and she kept waiting.

The second day after she sent her email, she stumbled through her library shift in a sad daze. Until, that is, she remembered Bez and Karl. More specifically, she remembered Jackie's promise to take Athena to the local tearoom for mini-scones and triangular sandwiches if she managed to get her hermit-like former employer to the book club meeting.

No sweat. Athena had zero problem employing guilt to meet her mini-scone needs.

Hey, Special K, she texted. *This is your freaking delight of an ex-employee. Remember how you fired my very fine ass?*

He answered almost immediately. *Don't fucking call me that. What do you want, Greydon?*

I want you to remember the moment you told me I would no longer have a paycheck or health insurance, despite having done nothing wrong . . . Special K.

Three dots appeared and vanished. Once. Twice.

I repeat, he finally wrote. *WHAT. DO. YOU. WANT.*

Later this week, the Nasty Wenches book club is meeting. I'll send you the details shortly. They're discussing monster-fucking books, and we both know you're the biggest monster-fucking enthusiast in Harlot's Bay, so I want your ass there, Special K. I'm asking Bez too, but you're the only one whose presence will win me tearoom mini-scones.

You fucking BET on me?

Is that a no?

More dots came and went.

I supply those mini-scones. Could give them to you directly.

Ah, but do you supply the triangular sandwiches too?

. . . GODDAMMIT.

So are you coming to the meeting or not?

A long pause. Then his answer appeared, and her confidence proved justified.

Fuck you, Greydon. Yes.

Ta-ta, Special K. Love you too! 😏 See you there!

At that point, she was pretty sure he'd crushed his phone to shards in one meaty fist whilst trying to set enormous stand mixers aflame using only the fiery intensity of his homicidal glare. Just picturing it made her smirk the rest of the afternoon, despite her empty inbox.

The third day after she sent her email, she was walking to Bluestocking when her phone dinged with another text. Probably Bez. Or maybe Karl, who was fretting over what to bring to the meeting in the tersest, most obscenity-laden manner possible.

His latest texted missive had read, *You motherfuckers like cookies?*

Yes, she'd answered. *We motherfuckers like cookies.*

He hadn't bothered to respond, so she could only assume every motherfucker in the book club would either be voluntarily eating cookies or having said cookies forcibly shoved down her throat by a maddened, possibly murderous baker. Honestly, Athena couldn't wait.

But—hold on. This text wasn't from Karl. It wasn't even from Bez or Victoria or Jackie.

I'll be at the meeting, Matthew had written. *I apologize for taking so long to decide. Please put me down for potato chips on the snack form. See you there, Athena.*

Oh. My.

17

After Yvonna waved Matthew into her office, he closed the door behind him and collapsed into the chair in front of her desk. Propping his elbows on his knees, he buried his face in his hands and scrubbed roughly.

A pointless gesture. No amount of scrubbing would remove the memory of Athena, gilded by candlelight, splayed and arched and shaking with pleasure, breathing his name. *His.*

He shouldn't have watched from the shadows. He had.

While he watched, he shouldn't have stroked himself over his boxer-briefs. He had.

And maybe he could argue that sheer curiosity had compelled him to discover what she planned to do in that chair; that at least he hadn't let himself come; that nearly anyone attracted to women would have done the same, assuming someone as gorgeous as Athena sat there in front of them and fingered herself to orgasm in plain sight.

But there was no use pretending anymore. He wasn't *anyone*, and he wouldn't have watched anyone else. He didn't want anyone else.

Which meant he shouldn't have agreed to attend the book club meeting. He had, though.

He'd held out for three of the most terrible days of his life, but in the end, desperate for her to the point of madness, he'd said yes.

Because he could resist his own needs and desires, no matter how he might suffer for it, but he couldn't keep resisting hers.

"Matthew?" His best friend rolled her chair around her desk and laid a hand on his shoulder. "You all right?"

He sighed and lifted his head. "I don't know what the hell I'm doing, Yvonna."

"Tell me," she said, so he did. Without violating Athena's privacy more than absolutely necessary, he explained what she'd done. What he'd done. What he'd agreed to do later that very night.

Namely, discuss monster-fucking at a book club meeting with the one woman in the world he shouldn't want and couldn't have, all the while knowing his attendance implied surrender. A relinquishment of arms as he fell into hers.

After that meeting, he'd walk her home in the dark. What he'd do once they got there . . .

He didn't know. The right choice was clear to him, but he was so fucking, *fucking* tired of making the right choice when it *hurt* so much.

"Help me." It was a raw, choked plea. "Please, Yvonna. Help me do what I need to do. Talk me out of going to the meeting. Talk me out of going to her."

Yvonna didn't answer for a long, long time. Then she took his face between her cool palms and studied him gravely.

"Matthew . . ." she finally said. "Do you blame yourself for your brother's death?"

The unexpected mention of Adrian was a sucker punch of grief he hadn't braced himself to absorb. But she was still cradling his face, a silent support as he recovered. And when he could speak again, he told Yvonna the truth.

"No. Not really." For a long time, the answer would have been yes, but he'd made his peace with his brother's passing by now. Mostly. "Do I wish I'd checked on him during the night? Yes. Do I wish I'd been in charge of the medicine, or at least tracked who was giving it to him and when? Of course. But I was eight years old. Saying I was responsible would be saying I was in control of everything, and I wasn't. I couldn't be."

Letting go of his face, Yvonna sat back in her chair and steepled her fingers. "Okay, then. If you don't blame yourself for Adrian's death, I guess I don't understand."

"Understand what?" he asked, lost.

"Why you're not allowed to be happy."

He winced. "I'm allowed to be happy. Just . . . not at my brother's expense."

"Because his happiness is more important than yours," she said flatly. "Even though he's a grown man in his thirties."

What could Matthew say in response to that accusation? It sounded ridiculous, and he should probably deny the charge, but his life to this point certainly seemed to confirm its essential truth.

Something inside him had shifted, though. Every time he saw Athena, spent time with her, dreamed about her, a box he'd allowed to rust shut decades ago strained at the seams. In a dark room at midnight, the lid had groaned open, and he didn't seem able to close it again. Need and chaos and heedless, selfish desire kept pouring out, no longer safely contained.

And—wait. There she was.

At that very moment, she appeared on the sidewalk outside the practice, as if placed there by divine providence, and his breath hitched in surprise.

She scanned the building as she walked. The tinted windows

didn't allow her to look inside, but he could see every beautiful detail of Athena Greydon. The cool sunlit afternoon glowing in her honeyed hair and limning the soft lines of her body. Her slick of red lipstick. Her sockless Keds.

Together, he and Yvonna silently watched her stroll past the window . . . only to hesitate near the entrance to the practice.

Was she coming to visit him, as she'd once suggested? Even knowing Johnny would be there too? If so, how could he possibly hide how he felt from his brother?

But she didn't move closer. Instead, she looked at the door, where all the doctors and CPNPs were listed in white painted letters. In theory, she could have been staring at anyone's name on the list. Yvonna's. Akio's. Even Johnny's.

But he knew. He knew.

As she looked at DR. MATTHEW VINE III on that door, her lips curved slowly. Sweetly.

It wasn't a smirk or a defensive baring of teeth, but a small, true smile. It lit her from the inside out, brighter than the jealous sun above. Softer than the gentle breeze tugging a tendril of hair across her cheek. Lovelier than his childhood visions of heaven.

She looked . . . happy. Hopeful.

If anyone tried to take that away from her, including himself, he'd gut them with his steady, could-have-been surgeon's hands.

He loved her. He *loved* her.

With that one smile, there was no going back. His happiness might mean less than Johnny's, but hers trumped all. And now that he'd slotted his priorities in their proper order, his path forward became clear.

For however long she wanted him, she could have him.

It might be a matter of months, or even a matter of weeks. Her temporary position at the library would end soon enough, and with her parents' support, a universe of options had now opened to her. Eventually she'd leave to explore them, because she'd never wanted to be stuck in a ten-foot-wide house and a small town without many job prospects.

At this point, Harlot's Bay was merely a way station for her, a place to rest and gather herself before she left to tackle a brilliant future. Not her permanent home.

He was a way station too, and that was fine. He'd give her what she needed and let her go, even if watching her walk away would feel like clawing at his own chest and tearing out his needy, lonely heart. Because there was no way she'd willingly live forever in the same town as her ex-fiancé, and no way a man like him—cautious, charmless, her ex-fiancé's goddamn *brother*—could tempt her into staying.

Since limited-time relationships didn't require public acknowledgment, Johnny never had to find out, as long as both Matthew and Athena committed to discretion.

Everyone would get what they needed . . . except him. He was third on his priorities list, though, and that was fine too. When she was gone, he'd simply make a new box. A stronger one. He'd keep his love for her safe there, where it couldn't hurt anyone but him.

Outside the window, Athena swiveled on her tennis shoe's heel and kept walking, probably toward Bluestocking. When she'd completely vanished from sight, he blinked and remembered where he was. What he'd been doing.

He turned back to Yvonna.

"I don't know how to interpret that look on your face." A line etched itself between her eyebrows. "What are you thinking, Vine?"

"I'm thinking I have preparations to make, potato chips to buy, and patients to see." He rose to his feet. "Thank you for listening, Yvonna. I appreciate all your help and advice."

"Hmmm." Her wary gaze followed him to the door. "Am I going to like whatever decision you just made?"

"Probably not," he said, and left her office.

"NOT SAYING BRAZEN isn't creative with dicks," Karl argued, "but vibrating cocks only get you so far."

"Far enough," Victoria murmured.

"Getting that far is one of my new life goals," a gray-haired woman with a perm whispered loudly to her neighbor.

Matthew did his best not to blush or laugh, with only limited success.

"The audiobooks' spectacular narration is the key to the stories' appeal. Not weird dicks with ridges and fins and whatever the fuck." Karl sat back in his chair, arms folded across his thick chest. "If you disagree, you should shove a cookie in your piehole—"

"Cookie-hole," Athena muttered, leaning far too close to Matthew. "Otherwise, it's just weird. But then that raises the question: Are there separate holes for different baked goods? And if so, wouldn't yeast infections become an issue?" When he choked on his Danish, she paused. "Okay, that made it even more weird. Forget I mentioned holes. It was a mistake, I see that now."

Desperately, he gulped down some sparkling water as she patted his back.

Was he having an actual hot flash? Was this what menopause felt like? Because Athena's proximity had always seared him from the inside out. But now, knowing what might happen later that evening, her nearness necessitated an industrial fan aimed directly at him. Or maybe a meat locker he could visit.

And that was before she started talking about . . . er, holes.

"—and think about how fucking bad your life choices are," Karl finished.

Victoria waved a hand. "If life choices leading me to a pulsating dick with a G-spot teaser and a clit-flicking fin are bad, I don't want to be good. Also, I think you're understating Brazen's anatomical creativity. What about the tongues, Karl?"

"Yes, Karl." Athena snorted. "Will no one think of the extendable, agile, textured tongues?"

Jackie's voice was bone dry. "Truly, they require an advocate to speak for them, because they're otherwise occupied."

When Bez laughed, she sprayed out a mouthful of semi-chewed cookie.

"As part of our tongue discussion, let's talk about sapphic monster-fucking." Jackie held up a copy of *The Lady Orc's Lover*. "Because I don't think you fully comprehend the vast array of exciting bonus features orc warrior-maidens' tongues offer to human vaginas."

"That sounds great, babe." Yvonna smiled at her wife, then cast Matthew a sidelong glance. "But first, I have a question for Dr. Vine over there. I know he's listened to several of Brazen's books, and surely he has an opinion about them."

As far as he knew, his best friend had never before attended a Nasty Wenches meeting. But when he'd showed up a few minutes late to Victoria and Akio's condo, delayed by an appointment that ran over, Yvonna was sitting by Jackie, a plate of snacks on her lap.

She'd winked at him. He'd known then he was probably going

to regret *his* life choices, for reasons entirely unrelated to dick-fins.

Athena had already been seated too, but she'd saved him a place at her side. He'd walked to her like a man hypnotized, sunk into the loveseat cushion, and immediately begun sweating at the sensation of her thigh nuzzling against his.

As the meeting began, she'd handed him a plate with a streusel-topped cheese Danish—his favorite flavor—and an orange-caramel crunch scone. Also a favorite. From a coaster on the floor, she'd passed him a can of strawberry-flavored sparkling water.

His favorite. Again.

Because it reminded him of the dress she wore the first time they met.

"What are your thoughts, Matthew?" Yvonna asked in a tone of innocent interest.

He thought no one had ever paid him the sort of close attention Athena evidently had. No one had ever catered to his preferences as she did, hoping to please him.

He thought her bright, happy hazel eyes were lovely enough to start a war, and sharp enough to end one. He thought her gloss-slicked, candy-apple-red lips could launch a thousand lust-driven ships, but she only wanted his. She only wanted *him*.

He thought this was, and would be, the best night of his entire life.

But he didn't intend to share any of that with the Nasty Wenches, so he'd talk about dicks instead. "I think Brazen's readers may be disappointed by human penises and their lack of special accessories." He smiled wryly. "Sadly, we really can't compete."

Athena turned to him, a worry line between her brows.

"Well . . . there's fantasy, and then there's reality. I think you need to trust that we can separate the two." The gentleness in her tone stripped the statement of any admonishment. "No shadow-creature has ever cooked our favorite foods. No lake monster has ever comforted us when we cried."

Things he'd done for her, as very few people in the room knew.

She was offering him reassurance, and he needed it. Boy, did he need it.

"And no guppy-man will ever bring us pleasure as he warms our beds"—she frowned in thought—"even assuming he's warm-blooded, which he probably isn't. Since he's part guppy."

"Coulda used a cold-blooded guppy-man in my bed about fifteen years ago," the lady with the perm informed her neighbor. "But no, I just got estrogen instead. Damn you, Dr. Welinski."

"Anyway, my point is this: You don't need to worry about Sadie Brazen's readership being disappointed in our lovers for not sporting monster-dicks." Athena's lips twitched. "Especially when there are so many *other* reasons to be disappointed with them."

"Amen, sister," Bez said.

Matthew had to laugh, along with everyone else in the living room. Everyone except Karl, who appeared to have disassociated so he could better contemplate upcoming murders.

"Besides, there are always toys." Bez pointed at Matthew. "You might not have a Sasquatch penis, but with the right accessories, you could be Sasquatch penis-adjacent."

Matthew hesitated. "Thank you?"

"Ah, toys," Athena mused. "The great penile equalizer."

Holy fuck. Holy *fuck*.

He unfastened another button on his shirt. When that didn't

help, he drained his can of sparkling, strawberry-flavored water and heaved a heartfelt mental sigh.

Times like these, he too could use a cold-blooded guppy-man.

WHEN THEY WALKED home together, Matthew didn't trust himself to touch Athena.

Her state of mind no longer concerned him. She was less desperate for comfort these days. Less likely to confuse gratitude with desire. Which sounded patronizing as hell, because she'd always been an intelligent adult, even at her lowest point, but still. If he'd pursued intimacy with her before now, even a month ago, he'd always have wondered whether he'd taken advantage of her vulnerability.

What did concern him: If he touched her, he might not be able to stop, and before they took things any further, he needed to make absolutely sure she wanted that. He needed to make absolutely sure she wanted *him*. He needed the words.

As they approached her door, his heart thumped so hard, he wondered if it might beat its way out of his chest and offer itself to her. And then—

And then she patted a moonlit hand over a tiny yawn.

Dammit.

"You need more sleep," he told her. Told himself. "I know you like to wind down from the day by reading awhile, but maybe you should just go to bed tonight."

"Says the man who starts each day with a vat of coffee, since he works late into the night and doesn't sleep enough," she told him, utterly unimpressed. "Tell you what, Dr. Vine. I'll go to bed ASAP if you promise to do the same."

He supposed he wouldn't get much work done anyway, between gut-deep disappointment and grinding sexual frustration. "Fine. Done."

Not that he'd sleep. But maybe he could do . . . other things.

"Fair warning." A quick turn on her be-Kedded heel, and they stood face-to-face. "I know you sometimes get restless and end up working again." The intensity of her stare allowed him no quarter. "Tonight, Matthew, if you go to bed but don't stay there, I'll join you and *make* you stay."

With those words, an entire school of guppy-men couldn't have stopped him from catching fire.

"Come here," he said, and produced his keys with rock-steady hands.

She followed him into his home, and the heavy door shut behind them with a quiet click. He turned the deadbolt. Turned to her in the near dark.

With one step, he was close enough that her skirts brushed his legs. So close, the heat of her body merged with his and the tips of her breasts brushed his chest.

They were hard. So was he. "Is that an offer?"

"Yes." Then she offered him an entirely new smile, slow and confident and hot. "Also a promise, Dr. Vine. If you have trouble sleeping, I'll wear you out. Gladly."

The words were spaced for emphasis. *Wear. You. Out.*

"You want me?" His voice hoarse, he clenched his hands against the need to seize her right then and drag her into his arms.

She laughed, as if the question were absurd. "Oh, yes."

An icy flicker of reason stole into his fevered brain, and he forced his fists to stay where they were, tight to his sides.

"What we have . . ." How could he explain this in a way she'd accept? In a way that wouldn't hurt her? "I don't want to share it with other people right now. I don't want to offer explanations or justify anything to anyone. I just want *you*."

That gorgeous, provocative smile faded. "You want to keep this a secret?"

"I want to keep this *private*," he emphasized. "For now."

Because he wasn't going to hurt Johnny unnecessarily. Not when Matthew's relationship with Athena would only last until she didn't need him or Harlot's Bay anymore.

She hesitated, hope battling wariness in those expressive eyes. "Just until we know it'll work?"

Or until she left, which he figured was way more likely.

He nodded. "Exactly."

"Okay." After a moment, her smile regained its wattage. "I can do that. For now."

Almost boneless with relief, he exhaled in a rush. With her agreement, he wouldn't be forced to pit his love for her against his love for his brother. Which meant—

"What do you say, Dr. Matthew Vine the Third?" She traced her forefinger down the side of his neck, the gesture thrillingly intimate and possessive. "Shall I join you in bed tonight and make sure you stay there?"

"Yes." He'd never wanted anything more in his entire damn life. "Yes, please."

She immediately kicked off her Keds and shucked her jacket and cardigan. When he took longer than she preferred to remove his own peacoat, her nimble fingers quickly undid the buttons for him. She tossed the heavy wool garment atop her pile of discarded clothing, propped her hands on her hips, and waited as he bent down to unlace his Oxfords and set them aside.

He straightened. Carefully, using both hands, he slipped off her glasses and set them on the entryway console table. Sliding his fingers into her silky hair, he stroked her cheeks with his thumbs and simply looked at her.

Athena Knox Greydon was so damn lovely. Lush and warm and *his*, finally. If only for now.

With uncharacteristic patience, she waited trustingly under his gaze, her hands loosely curled atop his chest. When he bent to kiss that tempting beauty mark on her cheekbone, her skin bloomed with heat under his touch. From there, he let his lips graze over her beloved face, pressing light kisses to her hair-draped temple, her fragile eyelids, her stubborn chin.

He nuzzled her in that shadowy seam between her cheek and ear, and she giggled. He smiled against her jaw and continued to explore. Burying his nose in a soft, fragrant patch of flesh below her earlobe, he inhaled slowly. Deeply.

"I can afford the good grocery store shampoos now." Her fingertips delved into his hair, gently scratching his tingling scalp. "No more fake fruit. I'm all herby instead."

Her bright gloss had disappeared sometime during the meeting, so her lips were pale in the moonlight, pale and plump. Salty on the tip of his tongue, like the potato chips they'd both eaten. But inside . . . oh, inside her mouth, she was so damn sweet, she dizzied him. Her tongue twirled around his, playful and seductive, and he slanted his head to kiss her harder, deeper, before resuming his exploration.

With his knuckles, he traced from cheek to chin, then tenderly down her vulnerable throat, following his hand with his lips. Between her neck and shoulder, he softly sucked, his teeth a whisper-graze over her trapezius, and her silent gasp pushed her harder against his mouth.

Vaguely, he registered the movement of her own hands. She was unbuttoning his shirt, tugging it free from his trousers. Ever so carefully, she trailed her nails up his bare, hot back, and he shuddered under the deliberate provocation.

His palms slid up her sides, then cupped her heavy, incredible breasts through her dress. They were just as warm, just as giving, as he'd always imagined, and when his thumbs swept over her stiff nipples, it was her turn to shudder.

He needed them closer to a bed. Now.

Lacing together their fingers, he drew her upstairs and into his bedroom. Earlier, before leaving for the book club meeting, he'd lit a bedside lamp, and it cast a warm glow over the room and over her.

She paused just inside the doorway, and he stopped too.

"Matthew . . ." Her halting steps took her to the nightstand. With her forefinger, she rubbed a petal from the purple-and-cream hellebore bouquet he'd placed there at lunchtime. "These are absolutely lovely."

Her voice sounded husky, and the smile she directed his way quivered a bit. But there was no sadness in her eyes, only pleasure.

He sagged in relief. She liked them. He hadn't screwed this up already.

He'd considered roses, and dismissed them as too common an offering for a woman like Athena. But hellebores bloomed in the chill of winter, stubborn and hardy despite how fragile they seemed. That felt fitting to him. Plus, some varieties were apparently poisonous, and only a fool would consider Athena harmless.

"They're yours." Gently, he clasped her shoulders and turned her to face him. "Athena, sweetheart . . ."

Boosting herself to her tiptoes, she planted a kiss on his chin. "Yes?"

How would a man of vast experience say this?

"Lift your skirt," he said, low and quiet. "Please."

Slowly, her eyes holding his, she bent and gathered her hem. Inch by inch, she raised it. Over curved, strong calves. Over dimpled, adorable knees. Over gorgeously thick thighs. Until . . . holy fuck. Holy *fuck*.

His brain shorted out. Went dark and still and quiet.

"I always wear long dresses, and I hate laundry, so . . ." She glanced down, her teeth nibbling at a corner of her lower lip. "Surprise?"

The hair between her legs was dark amber. The other night, he hadn't been able to see that. It shone in the lamplight, a beacon guiding him closer.

She widened her stance, parting those luscious thighs, and his next breath audibly shook. "Do you want to touch me, Matthew?"

Dazed, he lifted his stare to meet hers. He couldn't say a word, and he didn't have to. Evidently his expression told her what she needed to know. With one hand, she still held her skirt high. Her other hand guided his between her thighs, dropping away once he carefully cupped her.

Crisp pubic hair framing skin softer than a hellebore's petal. Heat. Dampness.

Only days ago, he'd watched, mesmerized, as she stroked herself to orgasm, but this moment eclipsed that memory. All there was, all there had ever been, was Athena's rosemary and saline scent. Her open legs, and his thumb gently parting her vulva, stroking down the intimate seam of her body.

He dropped to his knees before her, and she inhaled sharply.

Wrapping an arm around her hip, he pressed his forehead against the velvety swell of her bare lower belly. Her hand tunneled through his hair in a soothing caress, even as his fingertips rubbed slowly up and down, learning the intimate geography of her most vulnerable flesh. When he smoothed his thumb lightly over her clitoris, she made a small, needy sound deep in her throat.

Her knees began to tremble unsteadily, and slickness coated his fingers.

Good. Good.

"Lay back, love," he eventually whispered against her stomach. "Stay near the edge."

Bending down, she pressed a fierce, lingering kiss to the crown of his head, then settled her upper body onto the mattress. He didn't let himself think about it a moment longer. He simply glided his palms up her legs, then urged them over his shoulders.

His head would be a tight fit between those legs, and he was glad. He'd wanted to swamp himself in her for months.

He nuzzled against one pillowy inner thigh, then the other. "I won't be able to hear you well. If you like something I do, pull my hair. If you don't, tap my head or push me away. Okay?"

"Matthew." Propping herself on her elbows, she looked at him, her breasts rising and falling with her rapid breaths. "Forgive my crudeness, baby, but please. *Please* hurry up and eat me."

This time, his brain didn't go dark. It flashed white, the blinding white of total blankness.

"I'm sorry, sweetheart," he murmured once he'd regathered himself. "I don't intend to hurry."

He didn't want to rush anything about this. And Athena might sometimes be impatient with herself, but he refused to follow her lead. She deserved all his time and attention, and she'd get both, right now.

With one hand, he stroked the silky skin of her leg. With the other, he spread her vulva for his tongue. Leaning forward, he let her thighs block out the world. The only sound was his own heartbeat, his own harsh, excited breathing. Her scent filled his lungs, and he licked her in an unhurried, deliberate sweep from her vagina to her clitoris.

She wasn't sweet. She was salty and tart, and he wanted to devour her whole.

With his second ravenous lick, he moaned against her, and her entire body jerked. Her fingers tangled in his hair, not quite pulling. Close, though. Emboldened, he dragged his tongue through the folds of her vulva in measured strokes, then drew the delicate pleats of flesh between his lips and tugged gently. Moving upward, he hummed softly against her clit. Her legs spread wider at that, her hips rising to meet the vibration.

He was throbbing for her, hard and ecstatic, so happy it felt like pain.

Slowly, he began to learn. She didn't like teeth, not even a gentle graze. She did like when he tenderly sucked her stiffening clitoris. She shivered when he dipped his tongue inside her. And for all her impatience, it wasn't until the tip of that tongue traced a leisurely, lingering circle around her clit that her fingers in his hair curled into fists. The sharp pull detonated down the length of his spine, and he could have come from that alone.

As her vulva turned puffy and swollen under his attention, he teased her entrance with a fingertip, swirling around and around until she was straining against the slight pressure. Gradually, he pressed two fingers inside her, rubbing against her inner walls as he sank deep. An easy pump of his hand, a slight twist of his wrist, and she turned molten around him, grinding against the penetration.

He thought—he hoped—he'd learned enough about her preferences that he could make her come in another minute or two of focused effort, but he had all the time in the world for her. She was so slippery and so fucking delicious, he was becoming increasingly convinced that when the ancient Romans referred to ambrosia, they meant pussy.

When his jaw began to hurt, he could not have given less of a shit. But eventually, he wasn't sure how much longer he could hold on to his control. Besides, the sooner Athena had her first orgasm, the sooner he could start working on her second.

When he scissored his fingers inside her vagina, she jolted, her legs restlessly moving over his shoulders. Another unhurried, measured suck of her hard little clit. Another relaxed tongue-tip circle, around and around again, as she squirmed. Another stroke against the spot on her vaginal wall where she was most sensitive, where firm pressure made her quiver against his knuckles.

He laid the flat of his tongue against her clitoris and rubbed slowly, and Athena went rigid, her thigh tensing under his caressing palm as she arched and trembled. Her fingers in his hair tightened, setting his scalp ablaze. Then she exploded into climax, her vagina clamping around his fingers as she twitched against his gliding tongue. Even with his ears covered, her hoarse cry vibrated through them both.

With fierce hands, she shoved him harder against her pussy as she came, fucking his face like the goddess she was.

He couldn't breathe, he was pretty sure he'd pulled something in his neck, and his jaw burned like fire, but even in his dreams, he hadn't imagined this glory.

He couldn't wait to do it again. And again. And, yes, please god, again.

18

*A*thena literally saw stars when she came. Bright plumes of light flashing behind her eyelids, like she was a cartoon character who'd just had an anvil dropped on her head.

Her anvil was named Matthew. He didn't drop on her head.

He did, however, *give* phenomenal head.

She lay sprawled on his mattress, every muscle limp, as he gently licked her through the last few pulses of orgasm. Absently, she petted his head as she scrambled for sanity.

How? How had he done that?

A lot of guys managed to get a woman off once using a particular technique—spelling the alphabet with their tongue, humming "Chiquitita" against her clit, whatever—and sort of decided, *Welp, that's it, I guess. My One True Oral Technique. No need to experiment further.*

Every woman thereafter got the same treatment. The same trick employed in pursuit of her climax, over and over again, until the whole experience became a routine, rather than a joint exploration of what gave them both pleasure. Rub Tab A over Slot B, suck like Roomba C, and voilà! Cunnilingus: achieved.

But Matthew . . . he tried everything and anything she might enjoy, then paid attention to her responses. One tap to the side of his head, and he made sure his teeth stayed far, far away from her pussy. One pull of his hair, and he understood at basically the same time she did that those dawdling, agonizing circles around her clit fucking *destroyed* her.

So he'd rubbed her leg soothingly as he wrecked her in super-slow-motion with his tongue, like a horny sloth who really loved the taste of pussy, until she'd nearly ripped out his damn hair when she came.

His longer, curly hair was *really* fun to pull. In silent apology, she petted him again, and he rumbled contentedly against her inner thigh.

"Matthew." She managed to raise her head an inch, then dropped back to the mattress in defeat. "I can't compete with that. You are the undisputed Champion of Head, long may he reign, and long may he lick. But I'm happy to go down on you, if you'd like. Or you can grab a condom and get inside the pussy you now own. Congratulations, by the way. The owner's manual will arrive in your inbox shortly."

After one last kiss to her inner knee, he stood with a slight groan and peered down at her, his talented mouth wet, his brown eyes bright and happy. "You . . . you enjoyed that?"

"Enjoyed is such a pallid word, baby." She scooted back like an inchworm, then grabbed his shoulders and tugged him up and onto the mattress. "If a normal climax is a jalapeño, that was a ghost-pepper-intensity orgasm. Or . . . wait. Maybe a Carolina Reaper?" She frowned. "Whichever one is higher in Scoville heat units. Remind me to check with Professor Google about that later."

He was kneeling between her legs on the bed, a slow grin spreading across his face. He looked damn good there.

"Okay." Sadly, he was still wearing his pants, so he actually took out his notebook from a back pocket and scrawled a reminder. "Done."

"Time to get naked, Vine." Clambering to her own knees, she whipped her dress over her head and wrestled off her wireless bra. Entirely nude, she piled a few pillows near the headboard and reclined to watch the show. "I've spent the last several months contemplating the bitable curve of your ass inside those suit pants you always wear, and it's unfair to tease me with it any longer."

His cheeks darkened with a flush. "I . . . all right."

With meticulous care, his eyes fixed on his task, he unfastened his cuffs, then tugged at them to remove the shirt, keeping it right-side-out. After folding it, he leaned over to place the neat bundle on his nightstand, beside the flowers.

Sparse dark hair sprinkled his hard chest and arrowed down the center of his torso, pointing toward his abdomen. Since he'd begun feeding her, he'd filled out some. He was still lean, but those surprisingly broad shoulders seemed sturdy rather than angular, and his entire upper body looked slightly, delightfully thicker. As far as she was concerned, the more of him she could hold on to as he fucked her, the better.

Exhaling quietly, he reached for his pants placket, cheeks still ablaze.

Wait. Was he shy?

"On second thought, why am I outsourcing the pleasurable process of getting you undressed?" Athena smiled at him comfortingly. "Come over here, Matthew."

By the time she climbed off the bed, he was standing in front of her. While she unbuttoned his pants and carefully lowered the zipper over his erection, he ran a caressing fingertip over the back of her hand, his gaze following her every movement.

"What do you think?" She slid her fingers beneath the waistband of his boxer-briefs, preparing to tug them down with his pants. "Blowjob or PIV? Or did you have something else in mind?"

His stomach muscles shifted and tensed against her knuckles. And when she pushed his remaining clothing down to his calves, she finally caught a glimpse of everything Dr. Matthew Vine the Third had been hiding beneath those unassuming dark pants of his.

"I want to bury myself inside you, Athena," he told her, his voice quiet and gravelly. "As deep as I can get."

Good. The sooner the better, especially given what she'd just seen.

She crouched to help him step out of his remaining clothing before straightening again.

Then there they were. Facing one another in the golden lamplight, entirely unprotected by clothing or pride or pretense. He lifted a hand to cup her cheek. Resting his forehead against hers, he eased closer, until they stood belly to belly.

Tenderly, she clasped his wrist and rubbed it with her thumb.

"We can do this however you'd like," she whispered, afraid to fracture the moment.

"How would I know what I like?" His lips curved in a small, wry smile, and he nuzzled the tip of his nose against hers. "It's my first time."

She froze.

Oh . . . my.

She cleared her throat. "You'd . . . you'd gone down on someone before, right? I mean, you're not some sort of cunnilingus savant."

Because if that was his baseline level of talent without any actual hands-on—tongue-on?—experience, he was a prodigy. The Mozart of head-giving.

"I consulted Professor Google," he said simply. "*Cosmopolitan* magazine in particular seems to specialize in lists of advice concerning oral sex. To be fair, though, they're mostly about fellatio." His brow wrinkled. "And grapefruit, oddly."

She bit her lip, smothering her smile. Should she explain?

Nah. This early in his sexual awakening, he didn't need to picture himself swinging citrus fruit around his dick like an oversized bangle.

"I'm also a doctor. Human anatomy isn't exactly a mystery to me." With his free hand, he gently rubbed her bare butt cheek. "Honestly, most of the advice came down to paying attention to your partner. Whenever you're in my vicinity, every last cell of my body is focused on you, so I didn't find that an issue."

He *was* a prodigy, then, as well as a total sweetheart. Well, damn.

She leaned back a couple inches to see him better. His color was still a bit high, but he didn't look embarrassed or nervous. Good. There was no reason he should be either.

Besides, she understood exactly why he hadn't had sex with anyone else. Casual affairs and one-night stands wouldn't suit such a cautious man. And when would he have had the time to form a substantive romantic relationship before now, between raising his brother, becoming a pediatrician, and opening his own practice?

She was honored by his trust. Also, however wrong it might sound, more than a little turned on by the prospect of planting her flag in him and claiming his virgin lands for the sovereign nation of Athena Greydon. Although she supposed it was more him planting his flag in her, really.

Whatever. Flag-planting of some sort was happening, and she was *into it*.

When she inhaled, she smelled herself on him, and it made her smile widen. "Fair enough. If you don't know what you like, let's find out, shall we?"

"I—" He audibly swallowed. "Yes."

With a single fingertip, she nudged him back onto the bed and made sure he was comfortably positioned with a pillow behind his neck. Then, using the same care he'd shown her, she knelt beside him and began to explore that lean, strong, overworked body of his.

His small, neat ears were exquisitely sensitive. Blowing on them made him squirm, and a tongue flick around the rim or against his lobe shortened his breath.

His pale throat bobbed under her open-mouthed, wet kisses. If she nibbled at a certain spot just above his collarbone, he moaned.

"Good?" she murmured, and he wheezed out an enthusiastic *yes*.

Before moving any lower, she took a minute to massage his jaw, because she hadn't missed his ongoing TMJ issues, and he'd certainly put that area to hard use tonight.

Under her kneading fingers, he didn't squirm or moan. Instead, he lay entirely still and stared at her with such pained longing and affection, her sinuses prickled. Even though she didn't understand why he seemed so stricken when she was right there, naked and eager to flag-plant.

Eager to erase whatever thoughts were hurting him, she skipped a few steps after the massage and veered straight to his nipples. Gentle tweaks didn't do much, but a firm rub made him shift restlessly. A stroke of his bobbing, silky-hard cock forced a low grunt from his throat, and she gripped him tightly and kept pumping as she moved lower still. Trailing her mouth down his belly, she psyched herself up to give him the best citrus-free blowjob in human history.

Before she could do more than breathe on the damp, hot tip of his dick, his hand clasped her upper arm and eased her away. Startled—because at no point in her existence had any penis-bearing individual interrupted what was clearly oral-to-be—she sat back upright and looked inquiringly at him.

That flush over his upper chest and neck, burning bright along his cheekbones and the shells of his adorable ears, wasn't shyness anymore. It was arousal. Physical need. The sadness in his gaze had vanished entirely, transformed into fiery desperation and determination.

"Let me touch you again." His voice had turned gritty. "If you keep going, I'm going to come, and I need to get you ready."

What? He'd already given her an incredible orgasm, so . . . "I am ready, baby. And if you come now, no problem. We have all the time in the world to start over."

He blew out a frustrated breath. "I want you close to another orgasm before I get inside you, because I won't last long. Lie down, sweetheart. Please."

If the man was committed to making her multiorgasmic, who was she to argue?

Obediently, she flopped onto her back and starfished on the bed. At this point, he could do whatever the hell he wanted to her, and she trusted his native talents—along with *Cosmo* and Professor Google—wouldn't steer him wrong.

That man dove for her vagina like she had a stash of streusel-topped cheese Danishes hidden down there. But then, despite the urgency of his hold on her thighs pushing them wide, despite the searing heat radiating from his needy body, he began licking around her clit as if he had hours to kill.

Her fists clenched in his hair, and she whimpered.

She could actually feel him smile against her. Circle, circle, circle. Circle . . . circle . . . cir . . . cle.

Was he actually slowing down each time? Because it felt like he was, the too-patient bastard, and she didn't know whether to applaud or tweak his ear in frustration.

His fingers pushed back inside her, inch by inch, in a leisurely, relentless penetration, and he squeezed her right breast with his other hand, tugging lightly at her nipple. She was starting to pant, starting to ride his face, starting to sweat. If he kept going, she would in fact come again, but she'd do it before he even got inside her.

Time to run a little experiment.

Nudging his hand aside, she cupped her own breasts. Arched her back, pinched her nipples just hard enough, and gasped as the pleasure arrowed from there to the exact spot where his talented tongue was tracing those small, infuriating circles.

Although he couldn't see what was happening, he obviously knew something was going on. He paused for a moment, and she began talking.

"When we were in the bath, did you look?" Pinching her nipples again, she exhaled in a breathy moan. "Even then, as bad as I felt, I wanted you to see me. I wanted you to want me, Matthew. I wanted you to wash my tits, tease them until I couldn't stand it, and pinch them like this. I wanted your hand between my legs, slick with soap, stroking me clean, and then I wanted you to fuck me with those strong fingers of yours."

After only a few words, he'd raised his head to hear more clearly. His always-steady hands were shaking now, and it was her turn to smile.

Her voice was languid. Husky. "Did you, Matthew? Did you look?"

He shook his head, which he kept bowed. All the better to watch those trembling fingers press inside her over and over again, twisting and rubbing and crooked just right.

"Did you think about how easy it would have been? I was already in your lap. You could have just unzipped your jeans and planted me on your dick, baby. You could have made me take every . . . single . . . inch."

His hand stilled.

"I would have moaned so loudly for you, Matthew. I would have cried and begged you to fuck me. I would have come on your cock, baby, and squeezed you so hard—"

"*Enough.*" It was a near snarl, and suddenly he wasn't facedown over her pussy anymore. He was on his knees and reaching into his bedside table, fumbling for a condom. She helped him roll it on, and he hissed at the lightest touch of her fingers, his dick as flushed as the tips of his ears.

"This first time, I want you on your back." His hair at his temples was damp, his jaw like stone. "I want to see your face. I want to give you pleasure, rather than having you take it from me."

Oh good. She'd fantasized about his weight pressing her down. Dreamed about him fucking her deep into the mattress.

She beckoned to him with her arms. Spread her thighs wide and raised her knees high. "Come inside me, baby."

Strained patience in every careful movement, he climbed between her legs and lowered himself to his elbows. She reached down and helped position him at her entrance.

His hands still shaking, he framed her face with his palms. Pressed fervent kisses to her forehead, her cheek, her mouth. Whispered her name like a prayer.

Then, his fierce gaze pinning her in place, he slowly pushed inside her.

Her eyes closed for a moment, and she breathed shakily, trying not to come as he stretched her wide and sank so deep, she wanted to weep in joy.

Finally, she thought. *Finally*.

When she looped her legs over his thighs, he pressed even deeper. She made a choked sound as he bottomed out, and he paused, his body vibrating with tension.

"Okay, love?" It sounded like he had to drag the words from the depths of hell.

Opening her eyes, she smiled up at him and slid her hands down his spine to that tight, tempting butt. "You feel so good, Matthew."

With how ready he'd made her, how fucking *perfectly* he filled her, if she lasted more than a minute, it'd be a miracle.

He managed a half-strangled laugh. "You feel better. I can't even . . . *god*."

His hips rocked, a tentative, testing motion. She exhaled sharply, and he swallowed a groan and did it again, studying her face as he moved. Her fingers bit into his ass, and he nodded a little and found his rhythm inside her.

A slow, firm thrust, followed by an agonizingly drawn-out retreat. He sank into her each time as if he intended to mark every inch of penetration, to memorize the way she had to stretch around him, stroke after deliberate stroke.

The first time she raised her hips to meet him, the tendons in his neck strained, and his leisurely slide ended in a hard little jolt. When she moaned, he repeated the split-second of balls-deep force with his next stroke, that small shove as he made her take his last inch, only to draw backward again even more slowly. Again. Again.

A glow of heat grew deep, deep inside her, and she hitched her legs higher, feeling the telltale twitch of her pussy as he forged into her once more, but she didn't want to come yet. She didn't want this to end.

Still, she squeezed his cock tightly as he left her each time, refusing to make it easier on either of them, and he stared into her eyes, both of them panting now.

"You. . . ." He kissed her chin, still fucking her open slowly, thrust after thrust. "You are . . . so damn . . . *beautiful*."

A slight shift of her hips, and . . . there. Pressure on her clit, the endless slide of his dick, the firm command of that final, forceful bit of penetration, and the glowing heat within her exploded outward, turning the night incandescent as she blindly convulsed beneath him.

She was sobbing out little cries, her pussy throbbing and clamping down on him, trying to hold his cock inside her. But he kept fucking her through her orgasm, pushing inexorably past her trembling inner muscles, giving her no choice but to stay spread wide for him.

"There you are, love," he murmured in a strained thread of sound. "Fuck, Athena . . ."

Her nails dug into his ass, and she ground herself against him desperately, still quivering and coming. His hands left her face at last and clutched her hips, holding her in place as he shoved deep one last time, threw back his head, and came along with her.

He shook so hard, she wrapped him tightly within the cradle of her arms and legs in an instinctive attempt to keep him together.

His orgasm wasn't loud, but he kept panting out soft, broken noises for a long, long time, his expression agonized. Until, that is, he collapsed down onto her and began to laugh almost soundlessly.

"Oh my god. Oh my god, Athena." He stamped a fierce kiss on her nose, still laughing, then buried his face in her neck. "It's actually ridiculous, how fucking good that felt."

If she could have breathed, she would have laughed along with him.

"Shit," he finally gasped, carefully pulling out and flopping down next to her. "Sorry. Didn't mean to crush you."

Immediately after he took care of the condom, he urged her onto her side and back into his arms. They were both sweaty, and their skin stuck together, and she really should pee as soon as possible, but right now she didn't even care.

Face-to-face, he scrutinized her expression, his normal frown back in place. "Was—"

"Don't you dare ask if that was good for me." She yawned, not even bothering to cover her mouth. "Choirs are singing in the depths of my vagina. My clit already went online to nominate you for the Nobel Prize in Sexing, and my vulva have started a grassroots fundraising campaign to bronze your dick for posterity. You know the patron saint of really incredible head?"

He was grinning now, his face bright pink.

She didn't wait for his answer. "Well, I saw his heavenly face tonight. He goes by the name Matthew, really likes orange caramel-crunch scones, and eats pussy like it's his damn *job*."

"I . . ." He snorted. "I'm happy to hear that."

"Not as happy as I am to say it." She planted a smacking kiss on his mouth. "Do you think there really is a patron saint of oral sex?"

"We should consult Professor Google," he said. "After."

She crinkled her nose at him. "After what?"

Before she quite knew what was happening, she was on her back once more, his head buried between her thighs. It took longer that time, but when she came on his tongue again, she clenched so hard she almost pulled a muscle.

Afterward, he rested his head on her belly, and she played with his curls and massaged his jaw for a while.

Athena kept her voice dry as the Mojave. "You're really into that, huh?"

"I really am," said Matthew.

LATE THE NEXT morning, Athena woke in Matthew's bed. In Matthew's arms.

Sometime during the night, she'd flipped onto her side, and now the hard warmth of his body molded against hers from behind. He had one arm under her neck, one circling her middle, and his breaths ruffled the hair at the crown of her head.

In a tiny, almost imperceptible movement, he was stroking her belly.

He was awake too, then. Good. She smiled and stretched a little, ready to show him exactly what they could do in this position, when she remembered.

Dammit.

"I'm visiting my parents over the holidays," she said, her voice rough with sleep. "I have to leave later today, unfortunately."

His hand paused, then continued stroking. "When?"

He didn't sound drowsy. He sounded weary but alert, like he'd been awake for hours or hadn't slept at all.

"Theoretically, whenever I want." Depending on the traffic

around DC, getting to Bethesda could take her anywhere from an hour and a half to . . . way longer than that. But it was fine. The Beltway held no mysteries for her. "I could go after dinner, if you'd like?"

He made an unhappy noise. "I don't want you driving in the dark."

"Then I should probably leave between two and three." She glanced at the clock on his bedside table. "In about four hours or so."

"Hmmm." Lowering his nose to her neck, he inhaled deeply. "Will it take you long to pack?"

She shook her head. "No. Not long at all."

His arms tightened around her, but he said nothing.

"I'm sorry." She meant that. They'd taken a huge leap forward in their relationship, and she didn't want her near-immediate departure to sour something so ineffably sweet and promising. "Normally I'd just go a day or two later than planned, but Mom and Dad have been worried about me. They wanted to come here to Harlot's Bay weeks ago, but I asked them to give me time."

They hadn't been happy about it, but they loved her and were trying to respect her wishes, so they'd agreed.

He kissed her nape. "You don't have to apologize, Athena. Of course your parents want to see you over the holidays."

Did his estranged parents ever invite him to visit over Christmas? And if they didn't, how did that make him feel? Lonely, she'd imagine. Abandoned. As if he and his brother were orphans, for all that their parents were still alive.

Carefully, she asked, "Are you traveling too?"

"No. Someone needs to cover on-call duties for the practice, and I volunteered, since I wasn't planning to go anywhere." His tone was unconcerned, but she couldn't accurately gauge its truthfulness without seeing his expression. "When will you be back?"

Since the college library would remain closed for over a week, she'd intended to return either New Year's Day or January second, but . . . "New Year's Eve."

Maybe he already had plans, but if he didn't, she hoped they could count down to midnight together. As a sort of vow to the universe: *This year will be different. This year, we'll handle whatever may come as a team.*

When she turned in his arms, his warm brown eyes studied her face. "Would you like to spend New Year's Eve with me? You probably have other plans, but—"

"Yes." She traced his hairline with her forefinger. "I'd love that."

His lips curved in a soft, private smile. "Good."

When he edged closer, his breath a sweet, cool caress, she jerked her head back. "Dr. Matthew Vine the Third, you dirty, rotten cheater!"

He froze. "What? What did I—"

"You got up and brushed your teeth," she accused. "And now you intend to kiss me without giving me the same opportunity for minty freshness!"

When she scrambled out of bed, headed for the bathroom, he reached out to her in vain, then collapsed onto the mattress.

"I don't care whether you're minty fresh, sweetheart," he called after her. "And I sincerely hope my mouth won't taste like tooth-paste much longer either."

She paused at the door, looking at him over her shoulder. "Are you implying what I think you're implying? Because I'm surprised you don't have lockjaw by now, baby."

"I won't remain the Champion of Head for long if I don't work to retain my trophy," he told her solemnly. "It's an honor, but also a responsibility."

When she giggled, he grinned.

"Give me five minutes." Backing into the bathroom, she winked saucily at him. "Then we'll see who claims the crown today. I have tricks, Dr. Vine. Moves that Professor Google couldn't even begin to comprehend, or his algorithms would implode. Techniques that would make *Cosmo* squirm in longing as it fellated a grapefruit-bedecked dick."

He snorted. "Far be it from me to deny a challenger her shot at victory."

In the end, he deemed the contest a draw, but she knew better. Once she could muster the energy, she applauded and plucked flowers from the bedside vase to toss over his spent body. His blush was well worth the admission of defeat.

"See? No more mint," he murmured, kissing her lazily as they lay wrapped in each other's arms. "Just the sweet, sweet taste of victory."

"That's pussy, baby," she told him, and his shout of laughter ringing through the quiet house was her own private victory.

EVENTUALLY, SHE GAVE Matthew one final lingering, non-minty kiss, then dragged herself from his embrace to shower and pack at home, while he walked to his office and caught up on charting. Luckily, Johnny was working that Saturday, so she didn't have to worry about dodging him as she left his brother's house in a well-fucked daze.

Keeping her relationship with Matthew a secret didn't please her. But she understood why he wanted to avoid the towering awkwardness of that conversation with Johnny, and hopefully it wouldn't take Matthew long to realize . . . this was it. She was his, he was hers, and there was no point in delaying the inevitable.

Their one night together had told her everything she needed to know.

She wanted him with her forever—and not just because of the sex, although heaven knew that was a powerful incentive to keep him by her side. She wanted him because she'd never even imagined that kind of emotional intimacy. Never offered herself to someone who understood absolutely everything about her and still seemed to adore her. Never curled up next to a lover and known for certain she could depend on him, no matter what challenges lay before them. Never trusted anyone with this sort of bone-deep faith in his essential goodness.

She'd never loved a man this way, without caveats or fear.

He made her laugh. He made her think. He made her come. Like, a lot.

He made her believe in a future full of love and joy and possibility.

And if she could in fact trust her own judgment, he loved her too. So yes, she wanted to settle things between them and publicly claim him as hers, despite the complications posed by her history with his brother, so they could get started on that bright future together as soon as possible.

Maybe she could broach the discussion on New Year's Eve, if the moment seemed right.

And as long as she was thinking of her future, she should probably check the local job listings one more time before she left for

Bethesda, just in case Historic Harlot's Bay was hiring again or a position had finally opened up at the public library. If she intended to be with Matthew—and she did, obviously—that meant she'd be staying in Harlot's Bay, and *that* meant she had to find more permanent work somewhere.

The search took five minutes. Maybe less. At which point, she sat back in her chair and offered her laptop a pleased grin.

Earlier that day, HHB had posted a new listing. They needed someone to work in costume and give tours inside the buildings.

She could do that job. No problem.

One click, and the application that had seemed like such an in-surmountable obstacle only two months before appeared on her screen. Today, she filled it out in thirty minutes. Another click, and the completed form was winging its way across the interwebs.

No need for help from anyone. Not Jackie, not Yvonna, not even Matthew. She could do it on her own, and she had, and it felt *good*.

After she shut down her laptop, her other travel preparations only took an hour, so she had plenty of time before leaving to complete the project she'd been working on for a couple of weeks: Matthew's Christmas present.

Putting everything in place took another hour, and then she packed her car with her suitcase and gifts for her parents. After locking the Spite House's door behind her, she walked to Matthew's side of the alleyway and pressed her back against the brick façade of his house for the best view possible.

Designing the custom clings had required time and considerable consultation with Professor Google, but she'd had just enough extra money in her checking account to decorate every window facing Matthew's home.

Across from his kitchen, she'd positioned clings of scones and cinnamon rolls and Danishes and potato chips. Across from his office, various sexy monsters lounged enticingly, including a guppy-man with ripped abs and fins. And across from his bedroom . . .

The ocean. Rippling aquamarine waves topped with white foam. Clear blue skies. Sunlit sails, puffed and flapping in the sea breeze, above the pristine wooden decks of an eighteenth-century British warship. Atop those decks stood tiny sailors, an equally tiny captain, and the small figure of a man with a peg leg, a dashing eye patch, and a parrot named Squawky perched on his strong, capable shoulder. The man held a medical bag.

Even if they'd never become lovers, she still would have done this for him. As an apology. As a tribute to the man he was and the boy he'd been.

Matthew's childhood dreams had been stripped from him far too young. And although she longed to be his heartfelt adult dream, she couldn't be everything to him. She didn't *want* to be everything to him, because he deserved the world. Endless dreams, all coming true.

She might hope those dreams included her, but they should never, ever be limited to her.

If he wanted undulating seas and sunbaked decks and adventure, she'd give them to him as best she could. If he wanted her body, she'd give him that too.

And if he wanted her heart . . .

She didn't have to give it to him. He already held it in his hands.

19

The morning of New Year's Eve, Matthew claimed he was too tired to stay up until midnight and urged his brother to make plans without him. Which, much to Matthew's relief, Johnny promptly did. Apparently he was meeting friends at a waterfront bar for some pool and the town's annual fireworks display.

Perfect. If Matthew was careful enough, his brother would never need to know what he'd done and be hurt by it. And when Athena returned to Harlot's Bay, to him, he didn't want to wait for a private reunion.

The entire week she'd been gone, he'd *pined* for her. There was no other word for it. Now that he'd finally had her in his bed, the sheets felt cold without her. The house seemed to echo with silence.

Also, his hands and wrists might never recover from all the constant texting. Unlike A—as he'd discreetly dubbed her in his contacts—he'd never learned to type with his thumbs, and pecking out messages with a single forefinger took a painful eternity. Especially if he used proper punctuation and capitalization, which he couldn't seem to stop himself from doing, even during their most wonderfully distracting exchanges.

Impressive grammatical clarity under pressure, Dr. Vine, Athena wrote after their first awkward but ultimately satisfying attempt at long-distance sexual gratification. *Never imagined sexting anyone who'd remember the Oxford comma in the heat of the moment.* A short pause. *Can't say it didn't turn me on.*

I never imagined sexting anyone, period.

Period? There you go again with your punctuation foreplay. She sent him several fire emojis and, inexplicably, a kitten. *Give a woman a bit of recovery time, won't you?*

Oh. *Oh.* A kitten!

All right, then. Time to bring out the big grammatical guns and demonstrate his retention of her meme bootcamp lessons.

Can't stop; won't stop, he painstakingly typed out. *Using correct punctuation during sexting: 23/10, would grammar-sext again.*

You'd better, mister, she immediately replied. *Don't tease me with a semicolon unless you mean it.*

So they'd had extensive contact during her absence, but he'd missed her terribly anyway, and he kept wishing there were some way to see her face whenever his loneliness overwhelmed him. Why the hell didn't he have a single picture of her he could access without Johnny's knowledge or assistance? And how did a woman as versed in modern culture as Athena not have a single social media account?

He'd ask her to send him a selfie, but it was too risky. Someday, his brother might borrow the phone and spot the damning evidence of Matthew's devotion, either while Athena still remained in Harlot's Bay or after she'd moved on—to a more permanent job somewhere else, to a town that didn't contain her ex-fiancé, and to a man who could match her bold, brilliant charm. So selfies were out as well.

Eventually, Matthew had found a digitized image from an old newspaper. Athena Greydon, high school valedictorian, her blond hair lighter and longer, her grin undimmed by shadows. She wore a shiny white gown and held a rolled-up diploma, and he could have stared at that picture for hours.

He did, in fact, stare at that picture for hours. Like a damn weirdo, but . . . desperate times, desperate measures. When he wasn't doing that, he was staring into space and remembering how sex with her had surpassed even his wildest fantasies. And when he wasn't doing *that*, he was staring out his windows and marveling at *her* windows. At how much thought and effort she'd devoted to him. At her generosity of heart.

At how very, very much he adored her.

Every time he looked at those window clings, the ocean breeze ruffled his hair like Athena's fingers. The air smelled like salt and tasted like Athena on his tongue. The sun warmed his shoulders, like Athena's arms draped over him from behind.

Before she left Harlot's Bay, he needed a photo of her. A recent one. He'd print it and hide it somewhere in his home. Memorize it so it would remain safe in his heart, always.

And in the meantime, he wanted her safe in his house. She would be arriving in the early evening, even though he'd urged her to wait until morning, so she could travel in daylight and avoid any drunk drivers who'd pre-gamed—her word—New Year's Eve.

She hadn't listened, and a tiny part of him was glad of that.

In preparation for her arrival, he changed his sheets. He showered and shaved and ran a comb through his newfound curls. They tangled easily, but she'd obviously liked gripping fistfuls of them as he worshipped between her legs, and he'd liked how those sharp tugs felt. Those curls weren't going anywhere while Athena remained in his life and his bed.

Around five, he began looking out his window in anticipation of her arrival. By eight, when she finally parked at the curb, he was coming out of his skin with anxiety. As soon as he saw her, he hurried from his house directly to her car. And when he heard her locks disengage, he yanked her door open and took his first deep breath in hours. Maybe days.

"Matthew?" She looked and sounded tired, but he couldn't see any signs of injury. "Is everything okay?"

Now it was. He nodded, his throat tight.

Peering up at him, she asked gently, "Are you sure?"

"Yes, love." Leaning into the car, he unbuckled her with hands that weren't entirely steady. "I'm sure."

"I'm so sorry I worried you." With a groan, she swung her legs out of the car, and he helped her stand. "The Beltway traffic was awful, Matthew. People were driving like maniacs. My phone fell under my seat when I stopped short, and I didn't want to take my attention from the road long enough to retrieve it. But I should have pulled off somewhere to tell you I'd be late. I apologize."

"You don't have to apologize to me," he told her, not for the first time, and then he gathered her into his arms, buried his face in her neck, and let the scent of her skin and shampoo fill his lungs and ease his concern.

"Sometimes I do," she murmured. "Did you like your Christmas gift?"

"*Like* is such a pallid word, baby," he told her in a deliberate echo of what she'd said the one night they'd spent together. She snorted in recognition, and he tugged her even closer. "I love it more than I can say. Thank you."

He loved *her* more than he could say.

"It's cold out here." Reluctantly ending their embrace, he rested his palm at the small of her back and guided her toward his house. "Come inside, sweetheart. If you give me your keys, I can unload your car while you warm up and relax."

"I would be very, very grateful." She shivered a little as they stepped inside. "My bladder and I have been in a grudge match for the past hour or so. I won, but only through sheer force of will."

After she rushed into his powder room, he removed the small suitcase from her back seat, along with a cherry-red cashmere blanket, still neatly folded in its upscale packaging. Thick. King-sized. A Christmas present from her parents, he presumed.

Once he'd set the blanket carefully atop her suitcase, he opened a kitchen drawer and removed two printouts. When she emerged from the powder room, he handed her the papers.

"Oh, cheeses Pete. That feels *so* much better." She glanced at the printouts, then at him. "What's this?"

"Part of your Christmas gift." He'd thought hard about what to give her, then went with his gut. Or, technically, her gut. "Read the letters."

His gifts weren't exactly a diamond necklace or even a cashmere blanket, but Athena didn't wear much jewelry and ran hot at night, so . . .

Her delighted gasp relieved his doubts. "Matthew. *Freakin'*. Vine. There's such a thing as a potato chip of the month club? How did I not know about this already? Were people *keeping* it from—wait. *Wait*. There's an organic potato sampler of the month club too? That's . . ."

She trailed off, seemingly speechless. Then she tossed aside the papers, flung her arms around his neck, and squeezed him until he grunted.

"Thank you! I love it! Both *its*, not just one of them!" Planting a smacking kiss on his mouth, she jiggled them both in a happy dance. "Merry potato-y Christmas to me!"

Smiling now, he told her, "There's one more present. It's in my bedroom, near my fireplace."

"Oh, really?" She raised an eyebrow. "Is it you, spread naked on a fluffy rug by the flickering firelight?"

He looked down at his fully dressed body. "Uh, no."

"A pity." Her fake sigh gusted across his chin. "Still, I'm sure it's a wonderful gift, even if it's not"—she leaned back and leered ostentatiously at his jeans placket—"*the* most wonderful gift."

No one had ever considered his penis a gift before. This truly was a red-letter day.

He followed her upstairs, and as soon as she saw the large box, she squealed and dropped to her knees beside it. Making claws of her hands, she tore away the paper in gleeful, enthusiastic rips, rather than neatly separating the gift wrap at the seams as Matthew did.

When she revealed the item's packaging, she smiled happily at him. "You got me a window AC unit. Thank you, baby."

"I want you to be comfortable here when the weather gets hot again." Only that was presuming way too much, wasn't it? She'd probably be gone by next summer. "Or if you move somewhere else that's hot, maybe you can use the unit there instead."

Her mouth opened. Then she bit her lip, squinting at him with an unreadable expression on her lovely face.

After several moments, she said firmly, "Let's clear this up right now."

Oh shit. That sounded ominous.

"Sit down, Matthew." She pointed an imperious finger at his mattress.

Gingerly, he perched on the edge of the bed. "Okay."

"Here's what you need to know." She hitched backward until she sat braced against the wall, facing him directly. "I've been periodically checking the job listings for Historic Harlot's Bay, and a tour guide position opened up last week. I've already sent in my application. If I get the job, the training will start in March, not too long after my temp work at the library ends. Just to be clear, no one told me about the position. I found it and applied on my own." Pride suffused her expression, radiating from her straight spine and squared shoulders. "I assume HHB still has your letter of recommendation, but if they don't, may I get another copy from you?"

He nodded, afraid to interrupt.

She wasn't moving away and leaving him behind? Truly?

"I might not want to stay at HHB forever, but the job seems like a good fit for me right now. It would give me plenty of time around other people and a definite end to my workday. Which I need, since my brain won't supply a finish line for me. Since I'd be giving tours at quite a few sites, I'm hoping the work would keep me interested long-term." She took a deep breath. "But if it didn't, if I got restless and needed a new challenge, I'd do my best not to hate myself for it. Like my dad said, no experience is ever wasted. And no matter what, I'd leave knowing I was the best employee I could be while I was there."

God, he was so damn impressed by her progress over the past two months. Impressed and relieved and awed by her strength.

"Just now, you talked about the possibility of me moving, so let me be absolutely clear." Rising to her knees, she shuffled to his bedside. Her hands rose to cup his cheeks, and her stare demanded his full attention. "Even if I left that job, I wouldn't leave Harlot's Bay. As long as you want me, I'm not going anywhere. I love you, Matthew."

The abrupt rush of joy dizzied him, and her sweet, beloved face turned blurry.

He hadn't even let himself hope she'd stay. Not for a single minute. Not when decades of loneliness had taught him the futility of wanting something—someone—for himself.

But she loved him. *Loved* him. Loved *him*.

If she told him again, maybe he'd allow himself to believe it.

"You do?" he whispered. "Are you sure?"

With gentle sweeps of her thumbs, she wiped away his tears. "I'm one-thousand-percent sure I love you. And you can trust the accuracy of my numbers, since I took far too many statistics courses in college."

He gave a watery snort. "In that case, I'm ten-thousand-percent sure I love you more."

Her breath hitched, and she gave him a smile like the dawn. Like he was the only man she'd ever want for the rest of her life, and their life together began now.

"I don't think so." She shook her head, frowning in faux solemnity. "Sorry, baby. There's no mathematically possible way you could love me more than I love you. The best minds of our generation have tried to theorize how it could happen and given up in despair. There's simply no out-loving me."

Yet here he sat before her, tearstained and exultant, living proof she was incorrect.

Sliding from the bed to his knees, he gathered her tightly in his arms and nuzzled the soft hair at her temple. "We'll have to consult Professor Google about that."

"Yes," she said. "After."

"After what?" he asked obligingly, and she showed him.

He might not own a fluffy hearthside rug, but she had a brand-new cashmere blanket, and it felt damn good against his bare ass as she rode him in the firelight. If the gesture wouldn't have confused and horrified her parents, he'd have sent them a heartfelt thank-you note.

RIGHT BEFORE MIDNIGHT, Athena draped them in that blanket as they sat on the wooden planks of his rooftop deck and waited for the fireworks. His back against the brick wall, Matthew settled her between his legs, wrapped his arms around her, and propped his chin on her shoulder.

It was a crisp, clear evening, and starlight fell on him like a benediction. "Warm enough?"

"Yep. I'm good." She leaned forward a little, and chill snuck between their bodies. "Matthew . . ."

He pressed a kiss to her nape. "Hmmm?"

"I don't want to be a secret."

He stilled.

Once they'd declared themselves to one another, once she'd decided to stay in Harlot's Bay, this moment had become inevitable. Still, he'd hoped to delay it as long as possible, because his brother genuinely cared for Athena. Not in the way Athena needed, and not enough to keep fighting for her despite Matthew's doubts and arguments, but . . .

Yeah. Johnny was going to be hurt. Angry. And if Matthew was right about his brother's post-Hawaii intentions toward Athena, things were going to get very messy, very quickly.

But her voice had contained no amusement, no give he could exploit to buy himself more time. Her statement—*I don't want to be a secret*—had been clear and unapologetic, and the implicit demand it made was clear too.

Matthew had to tell his brother.

Maybe he'd misinterpreted Johnny's intentions. Maybe his

brother had moved on and simply wanted to exorcise his guilt by gaining her forgiveness. After all, he'd been willing to leave her a month before their damn wedding, so how much genuine love could he have borne for the woman in Matthew's arms?

Not enough. Nowhere near as much as she deserved.

Asking her to keep hiding their relationship would hurt her, and Matthew had sworn never to hurt her again.

So he could do this. He *had* to do this. "I'll tell Johnny tomorrow night."

She relaxed more fully into his embrace, the subtle distance between them melting away in an instant. "Thank you. I know it won't be easy. If you need me, I'm here."

There was no mistaking her sincerity or affection. "I know, sweetheart. I appreciate it."

He kissed her ear and tried not to worry. Slowly, the night grew colder around them, and they huddled together for warmth and made idle, sleepy conversation.

The clock wound down to midnight. Fireworks exploded in the sky.

And before their eyes, a new year began.

20

Matthew thrust from behind, slow and firm and deep. Teased her clitoris, his gentle fingers circling and sliding. Clenched his other hand on her hip, holding both of them steady as he fucked her relentlessly.

Athena couldn't hold out any longer. She came hard, her elbows collapsing beneath her, and he followed her down onto the mattress, his heaving chest curved protectively over her back.

Even through his own shuddering orgasm, those capable fingers kept moving, teasing out her pleasure with light strokes, and she turned her face to the side, gasping into the pillow.

When they'd both begun to recover, Matthew eased them into a loose spooning position and ran a caressing hand up and down her spine. "You're okay?"

It'd taken a few minutes to convince him she didn't find getting fucked on her hands and knees degrading, as he'd worried, rather than incredibly hot. Even though she'd told him, several times, that *nothing* he could do to her would feel degrading. Not when he touched her with such tenderness and care.

"I'm great." When she pressed back against him, he wrapped his arms around her. "You're good too?"

"I just lived out one of my fantasies, love." He kissed her shoulder. "I'm *fantastic*."

She patted his forearm in appreciation for the wordplay. "Ha."

As they lay cuddling, her brain slowly came back online.

It was New Year's Day, a holiday from work for both of them. They'd snoozed and made love all morning, but sooner or later they'd have to return to life outside the cozy, preternaturally neat confines of his home. At which time he'd need to talk to his brother, a conversation Matthew was clearly dreading.

Only . . . did *he* really need to talk to Johnny? Or could she do it for him?

Matthew had spent his entire life protecting others and taking on their burdens. His parents. His brothers. His grandmother. His patients. Her. But who protected *him*? Who shouldered *his* burdens when he labored under their weight?

Yvonna, maybe. No one else, as far as Athena could tell.

She wanted to do that for him. She wanted to be his champion and shield.

"Hey, Matthew," she said, turning in his arms to face him. "Why don't I—"

His cell rang, cutting her off.

"Sorry," he murmured, kissing her on the cheek before reaching for his nightstand. "I'm on call today. Let me check what's happening."

As it turned out, the practice's answering service was relaying a message from parents frantic about their toddler's swift-spreading rash. Matthew called the parents back, listened patiently to their explanations and concerns, and directed a silent wince of apology her way before agreeing to meet them at the office in half an hour.

She wouldn't have expected anything else from him. She didn't *want* anything else from him, no matter how much she wished they could have kept cuddling and talking.

He tapped his screen to hang up, then sighed. "I'm sorry, sweetheart. I could have sent them to an urgent care, but the wait would be horrendous today, and her parents don't really trust unfamiliar doctors." After another kiss and glide of his palm over her bare hip, he headed for the bathroom. "The appointment shouldn't take too long. If you want to stay here, you're more than welcome. Or if you want to head back home, I can join you there when I'm done."

"I think I'll go home," she called as he ran water in the sink. "I can unpack and do some laundry."

He emerged from the bathroom, his hair damp and neatly combed. "I'll leave a key for you on the kitchen counter, then. Just lock the door behind you when you leave, and I'll be over at your house as soon as I can."

Her muscles ached as she stretched, and she yawned hugely. "Gotcha."

Within moments, he was dressed in his usual work attire. Looking like a man who'd spent the last twenty-four hours in placid, monkish contemplation, rather than assorted fucking-related activities, he halted by the side of the bed and gazed down at her.

He ran the pad of his forefinger over her cheek. "Keep the key, Athena. You're always welcome here."

"Thanks, baby." Grabbing that finger, she gave it a kiss. "Love you."

"I love you too, sweetheart. So much." After stroking her cheek again, he headed for the hall.

"Doctor like the wind!" she called after him, and he laughed.

His footsteps on the stairs creaked. After another minute, his front door closed with a faint *click*, followed by the distinctive *thunk* of a deadbolt sliding home.

Easing out of his bed with a groan, she gathered her discarded clothing and threw on the dress, cardigan, and Keds. No need for a bra when she was only going next door, and no need to deal with her bedhead. She'd take a shower once she got the laundry started.

A key lay on the kitchen counter, as promised. Her suitcase by her side, she yawned again and left his house. After so many hours spent in a dim room with its shades drawn, the brightness of the early afternoon was blinding. Squinting against the glare, she locked the door behind her and looked up.

Only to find Johnny Vine standing approximately three feet in front of her, his back to the sun. As her eyes adjusted, he remained more a silhouette than a man for a few moments, his dark hair haloed by red highlights, his face in shadows.

Once she could see him clearly, she wished she couldn't. His gaping mouth slowly closed, and his jaw turned stony. He scanned her up and down once, then a second time, his cheeks flushing with livid color.

Fuck. Fuck, why hadn't she checked to make sure the coast was clear before leaving? Why hadn't she put on a bra or combed her hair? There was no mistaking where she'd been or what she'd been doing, and no mistaking the man with whom she'd been doing it. Repeatedly.

"Ummm . . ." She gave a weak wave. "Hi, Johnny."

He braced his fists on his narrow hips, a vein at his temple pulsing. "Athena."

"Good . . . good to see you," she managed to force out, then winced.

No, it was decidedly *not* good to see him. Especially not like this, at a moment when she was essentially—if inadvertently—shoving her sexual relationship with Matthew in Johnny's face and grinding it in a bit for good measure.

Get your shit together, Greydon, she ordered herself.

Okay, yeah, this was awkward and not . . . er, optimal. Still, she could take advantage of the situation, right? She could make the necessary confessions so Matthew wouldn't have to, and that would at least salvage *something* good out of this extremely fraught moment.

"What . . . the hell . . . is—" Johnny began, only to stop when she held up a hand.

"Let's go inside my house for this discussion," she told him, and it wasn't a suggestion.

When she swiveled on her heel and walked into the alleyway, he followed her silently, brooding with all the petulant intensity of a dickish Brontë hero.

He'd dumped her ass a month before their wedding on his older brother's say-so. Dr. Johnny Vine the Unnumbered had no right to brood in her direction. Thus, he was definitely a dick. It remained to be seen, however, whether he fell toward the Rochester end of the dick scale—kind of charming despite all his bigamous, wife-imprisoning horribleness—or the Heathcliff end.

I.e., Abandon Hope All Ye Who Let Him Enter Here.

Sadly, she'd let him enter there. Ugh.

She led the way inside the Spite House. He nudged the door shut with his foot and did so softly enough that it didn't slam. One point toward Rochester-dom.

For a moment, they simply stood in the sunlight streaming through the windows and regarded one another.

He was so—*familiar*. His Hawaiian tan was fading, and those dark circles under his eyes suggested he hadn't been getting enough sleep. But his hair flopped becomingly over his forehead. His jeans molded to his fit frame, and his tee stretched over his impressive biceps, and she felt . . . no tug of sexual or romantic attraction. At all.

Weirdly enough, she didn't feel especially angry either. Sometime over the past two months, had she finally gotten over their failed engagement?

Digging deep, she searched herself and found . . . both more and less than she would have expected. A hint of nostalgic sadness for the hopeful, naïve people they'd been a year ago. Some fondness too; a lingering affection for the man-boy who'd made her laugh and cared for her in his own way. Bitterness—yeah, it was there, but not in any great quantity.

The lion's share of her anger, in the end, hadn't actually belonged to him. Mostly, she'd been angry at herself and unable to deal with her overwhelming emotions. Unwilling to confront just how sad, lost, and ashamed she felt. Eager to paper over all her uncomfortable thoughts and feelings with a thin façade of rage directed at the Vine brothers.

But now she loved one of those brothers, and she no longer hated the other. More importantly, she no longer hated herself. So she had enough grace within her to say this with gentleness, even if her ex-fiancé might have earned a bit of spite.

"Johnny . . ." She took a deep breath. "I'm sorry you found out this way. Please let me explain."

To his credit, he seemed to have retreated from his foray into Brontë hero-dom. His hands were loose at his sides, that vein at his temple no longer ticking away in beats of rage. He was still watching her, but not in narrow-eyed judgment anymore.

In fact, if she didn't know better—

"Let me speak first, Athena," he said quietly. "Please."

Uh-oh. "Okay."

He moved a step closer to her. "You asked for time, so I gave it to you. But what I've wanted to tell you since I got back from our honeymoon is this: I made a terrible, terrible mistake, and I'm so very sorry."

"You've already apologized, Johnny." Why was he doing so again, now of all times? "If you want my forgiveness, you can have it. That said——"

"Of course I want your forgiveness. But I wasn't finished, Athena. Please let me say the rest." His throat bobbed as he swallowed hard, and his eyes held hers. "I'm sorry I listened to Matthew instead of my own heart. I'm sorry I broke our engagement. I'm sorry I let you bear the brunt of my bad decisions. I'm sorry I hurt you. And most of all, I'm sorry you're not in my life anymore, because I miss you, Athena, so very much."

She stared at him in absolute shock.

He took another step closer, and she couldn't do anything but blink dazedly at him.

"I want you back." There was no offended pride or arrogance in the statement. Only a heartfelt plea. "I love you, and I want us to be together again."

Oh . . . heavens. This was . . . oh, this was so fucking *awful* and awkward and . . . *gah*.

"Johnny," she whispered, retreating until her butt hit her counter. "I—I appreciate everything you just said. I really do. But . . . Matthew and I are together now. We grew close after I moved here, and we recently became a couple. I love him."

At that, he trained his gaze on the floor, his jaw working.

"Okay," he finally said, his voice thick with emotion. "Okay."

Another apology rested on the tip of her tongue, but she swallowed it back. She wasn't sorry to be with Matthew. She was jubilant. Proud.

Instead, she said in all honesty, "Neither of us wanted to hurt you."

When he looked up again, his brown eyes blazed with renewed rage, and a wash of ruddy color had begun to spread down his tense neck. His hands had closed tight, knuckles bulging.

Whatever his faults, Johnny wouldn't hurt her. She was certain of that. But his expression echoed Karl's usual murderousness more than she'd wish at the moment.

"I can see you're angry at me—" she began cautiously, and he interrupted immediately.

"I'm not angry at you. Not even a little, Athena." He raised a hand when she opened her mouth to speak. "I broke our engagement and left you high and dry. You had every right to fall in love with anyone you wanted, including Matthew."

Whew. Okay, then.

Her heartbeat began to slow, and she closed her eyes in relief. "I'm so glad you understand. I appreciate that, Johnny."

"Athena. Don't mistake me."

He waited until she opened her eyes again. When she did, she flinched at the seething fury in his flushed, grim face.

In that moment, he didn't look like the amiable man-boy she'd agreed to marry. He didn't even look much like Matthew. He was something new. A complete stranger.

"I'm not angry at you," he repeated. "But I am really, *really* fucking angry at my brother."

Then he turned and stalked away, closing her door behind him with a deliberate, stony precision that was somehow more frightening than a loud slam would have been.

Through her front window, she watched him stride in the direction of downtown.

In the direction of Strumpet Square Pediatrics.

And once she could feel her legs again, she scrambled after him.

Turned out, rage lent Johnny a great deal of speed. His longer legs and lifelong commitment to cardio didn't hurt his pace either. There was simply no way Athena could catch up with him. By the time she emerged from the alleyway, he was already out of sight.

As she hustled in his wake, she kept trying to contact Matthew. Texts. Calls. Even an email containing only a subject line. It read: *CALL ME NOW!!! RIGHT NOW!!!*

Unfortunately, Dr. Matthew Vine the Third was a consummate professional, committed to giving even after-hours patients every iota of his attention. His phone was either in silent mode or tucked in a drawer somewhere.

Just as she arrived, panting, at the practice's entrance, a disheveled man carrying a wailing toddler on his hip pushed open the door. Good. Whatever was about to happen inside that office didn't require an audience.

"Let me get that for you," she said breathlessly.

She held the door for the duo, then hurried inside the office, advanced a dozen steps, and—

Time suddenly reversed itself.

The dimly lit waiting room, with its rows of seating and bins of children's toys, transformed into a chilly museum hallway. The nubby carpet under her Keds became marble, her wrinkled blue dress turned moon-pale and sprouted strawberries, and it wasn't January anymore.

It was late December. This was her engagement party.

And the Vine brothers stood just around a corner, arguing about her.

She should have left. Right then. Either that, or let them know she was a half dozen steps away from them. One of those two options.

She stayed instead. She listened.

Because she wasn't sure either of them would welcome her interruption of a private moment. Because her presence might only make things worse.

Because she was so afraid. So very afraid that history was about to repeat itself, and she had to know. What were they saying about her behind her back? Did Matthew love her enough to defend her, to fight for her, even against his own brother?

Unlike Johnny, did Matthew love her enough to stay with her?

"—*loved* Athena, but you told me to dump her. You told me she wouldn't make a good wife. You told me to end the goddamn engagement and never look back. When she came to Harlot's Bay, you told me to stay away from her." Bitter rage had turned her ex-fiancé's voice to grit. "And then you fucking took her for yourself? Who *does* that, Matthew? What kind of terrible fucking brother would even *dream* of doing that?"

Matthew didn't say a word.

"Did you want her for yourself all along? Was that it? Were you sabotaging our relationship and waiting for it to die so you could swoop in like a fucking vulture and snatch her up?" Johnny's rapid breaths were audible, even from around the corner. "Well, guess what, asshole. Athena and I were meant to be together, and I intend to win her back, so step out of the fucking *way*, bro."

Matthew finally spoke, his words barely audible. "There's no winning her back, Johnny."

"Bullshit. Once you're out of the picture, I can convince her, and fuck you for even trying to deny it." A *thud* reverberated through the office, the impact of a hand slamming against the wall. "She might have thrown a pity fuck your way, but she loved me enough to agree to marry me. If you hadn't poisoned everything, she *would* have married me, you fucking liar."

"She wanted to marry you for the wrong reasons. If you asked her, she'd tell you that too." Matthew sounded unutterably weary. "I'm sorry, Johnny. She cared about you, but not in the way she needed to. Not enough to marry you and have a happy life together."

Johnny responded immediately. Angrily. "I don't believe that. I don't believe *you*."

In the hush that followed, Athena's pulse thudded in her ears. The silence stretched and stretched again, turning unbearable, and she waited to hear the words.

Any moment now, Matthew would say he loved her.

Any moment now, he'd tell Johnny he wasn't giving her up. Not for anyone. Not even for his brother, and *especially* not for a brother who'd willingly broken an engagement to her. Which was, as it turned out, the right decision, because she didn't belong with Johnny. She belonged with Matthew, and only yesterday, he'd committed himself to her.

He, unlike his brother, honored his commitments. So he'd spurn Johnny's demands, gently but decisively, and he'd do so . . .

Soon.

Any moment now.

"This is my chance, Matthew." During that extended silence, some of Johnny's anger had dissolved into grief. His words were thick with tears and so wracked with emotion, they hurt to hear. "This is my chance to finally have my own family. You had eight years, and I know that's not enough, but I had two fucking *weeks*. That's it. And then everything was gone. Everyone was gone. All before I was old enough to fucking *crawl*."

Her heart broke for both brothers, even as her entire body began vibrating with dread. Because Johnny had done it. He'd finally found the thinnest, most tender stretch of skin his brother had, the wound that had never entirely healed, and taken a scalpel to it.

Matthew wouldn't give her up for the man Johnny was.

But for the boy Johnny had been . . . the child Matthew had raised so carefully, so lovingly, so fearfully . . .

She didn't know.

"I want to make a family with Athena," Johnny declared brokenly. "So whatever she needs, whatever she wants, I'll fucking *give* her. I won't break my promises. I won't ask you to keep them for me. I'll do it myself, because I love her."

Sadly enough, she believed him. Now, when it was much too late.

"Even if you're right, and she won't take me back . . ." The sound of his muffled sob echoed strangely. "You're my only family, Matthew. The one constant in my entire existence. But if you're with the woman I love, how can I keep you in my life? How can I live next door to both of you? How am I supposed to move on, when my own brother took everything I want?"

Athena's ragged fingernails scored her palms.

"I tr-trusted you." The words were a grief-stricken cry. "I *trusted* you, Matty. How could you do this to me?"

I'm so sorry, Johnny, Matthew was going to say. Any moment now. *I love Athena, and I won't let her go. I know it'll take time, but you're my brother, and I love you too, and we can get past this.*

Another agonizing silence stretched her conviction to its limits, but she grappled for purchase and held on. She had faith in Matthew. She had faith in his commitment to her.

Up until the very second he spoke again.

"All right," he finally said, and it was the resigned, desolate sigh of a broken man. "I'll walk away. I'll end things."

Through the roaring in her ears, she didn't hear Johnny's response, but she did see his shadow moving back toward the waiting room. Back toward her. Her eyes dry as a tomb, she ducked behind a row of seats, and he didn't look her way. He simply walked to the door and exited, a man who'd gotten what he wanted. Temporarily.

She wasn't Matthew. She couldn't be manipulated by guilt. Johnny would never, ever have her again, especially not by *winning* her like a wonky-eyed stuffed squirrel at the county-fair ring toss.

Slowly, she rose back to her feet in the dim, after-hours waiting room.

Of course Matthew let you go. What man fights to keep a girlfriend who's too fucking lazy and damaged to take a fucking shower? What rational being would lash himself to an anchor?

Who would want you, Athena, for anything other than a temporary bout of madness?

No, those were just thoughts. Ungenerous thoughts passing by like dark clouds. It might be easier to focus on those clouds than the bright warmth of the sun, and it might be easier to believe ungenerous thoughts than words of kindness and self-forgiveness.

But she knew the truth, and she had to remember it.

No matter how thickly the clouds gathered or how darkly they shadowed the horizon, the sun shone above them. They would pass, and the sun would remain.

Just as the anchor would sink, but it would rise again, muck be damned.

Closing her eyes, she drew on everything she'd learned in therapy. She pretended everything that had just occurred, everything she'd done and said and been, had happened to a beloved friend instead.

She would never, ever call her friend lazy or an anchor. She'd hold that friend and pass her tissues and make her tea, and then tell her she was trying her best, she always tried her best, and she deserved happiness. She deserved commitment and devotion. And if neither of the Vine brothers had loved her enough to stand by her side, that wasn't a problem with her. It was a problem with them.

Then, pissed on her friend's behalf, she'd probably start contacting MLM companies and political campaigns, but . . . been there, done that.

Johnny's version of love wasn't good enough for her.

Matthew's version of love wasn't good enough for her.

She deserved better.

Her eyes were open now. The insistent prickling behind her lids, the desperate urge to weep, had come and gone, and it would probably come again. Soon. But before it did, before she could go home and send an SOS email to her therapist, she had one last task to complete.

It wasn't hard to find Matthew's office. When she approached his doorway, he was half standing in front of his desk, slumped onto its edge, his head bowed and his hands over his face.

Seeing him like that tore at her heart, but comforting him was no longer her responsibility or her privilege, so she simply knocked on the doorframe.

When he dropped his hands and looked up, his expression was terrible. Defeat and grief had carved every austere line on his face into a canyon, and warmth had fled his skin, turning it so pale it was almost gray. The shadows in his eyes matched the pits beneath them.

The moment he registered her presence, his breath shuddered.

"I wasn't careful when I left your house." She kept her voice neutral. "I apologize."

He shot to his feet and shook his head so violently, he courted whiplash.

"Don't. Don't." His eyes were bright with tears. "Athena . . . I didn't . . ."

"It's fine." No need to extend his misery. Or hers, for that matter. "You don't have to explain, Matthew. I heard, and I get it."

"What—" He dashed away the wetness on his cheeks with his knuckles, studying her through red-rimmed eyes. "What do you get?"

"You love me, but not enough to fight for me. Not enough to stay with me." She mustered a tiny, wry, genuine smile. "Just like your brother."

His mouth opened then, but he didn't seem able to find words. So she pictured the sunlight above a blanket of dark clouds, an anchor slowly rising from the ocean's depths, and she found hers.

"I know I deserve better." At least, she was trying very, very hard to believe it, which was good enough for now. "Thank you for helping me get to that point."

Her voice rang with both sincerity and finality, and he appeared to recognize both.

He simply looked at her, grave and weary and miserable, as she turned to go.

"Goodbye, Matthew," she said, and walked away.

IMPATIENT AS A puppy, Johnny was waiting outside her alleyway door. Apparently she had yet another task to complete before she could email Carole and tell her, *Being the filling in an open-faced Vine Bros sandwich blows. Please therapize me ASAP!*

"Athena—" he began.

"Once your student loans are paid off, you should take Matthew on vacation," she told him. "Somewhere he can try sailing on an old-fashioned tall ship. And during thunderstorms, you need to get him indoors and have him wear noise-canceling headphones."

"I . . ." Johnny hesitated. "What?"

She waved an impatient hand. "Your brother likes old-timey ships, and he's scared of lightning. You didn't know that?"

Johnny's lips pressed into a thin, resentful line. "No, but he's terrible at communicating. You must have realized that at some point."

"Maybe that's true. Or maybe you just didn't pay attention." She shrugged. "The two possibilities aren't mutually exclusive, of course."

After a moment, Johnny regrouped and managed to remember the ostensible purpose of this conversation. The anger in his expression faded, and he drifted closer. "I don't want to talk about my brother, Athena. I want to talk about us."

His voice was so warm. So persuasive. But she'd been inoculated against that particular fever in July, when he'd called off the wedding, and she now had lifetime immunity to his charms.

"There is no *us*." She enunciated each word very, very clearly. "When you ended our engagement, *us* became Johnny Vine and Athena Greydon, two separate individuals who will never—and I mean *never*—be in a romantic relationship together ever again."

His mouth twisted. In sadness, in regret, in denial. She didn't know which. She didn't care.

Meeting his eyes, she willed him to understand. To believe what she was telling him. "There's no going back, Johnny. If that's why you forced your brother to break up with me, all you managed to accomplish was hurting the one person in your life who's always put you first, not to mention the woman you claim to still love."

"You . . ." He swallowed. "You heard that?"

"Yes, I heard your argument at the office. All of it." Removing her glasses, she pinched the bridge of her nose and ignored her growing headache. "Now please hear me. I've moved on, and you need to do the same. If you truly love me like you say you do, you'll accept that and leave me be."

His face was crumpling in grief, maybe even in heartbreak, but if she hadn't softened for Matthew, she certainly wasn't softening for Johnny.

"I wish you luck, and I wish you well, but that's as far as it goes." She put her glasses back on. "Thank you for loving me enough to ask me to marry you, and thank you in advance for loving me enough to let me go. Goodbye, Johnny."

As she turned on her heel, unlocked her door, and closed it firmly behind her, she thought, *I've walked away from both Vine brothers in the last half hour. I now have the complete set!*

She snorted out a hysterical giggle, which turned into a sob.

Through her tears, she called her parents and told them she was finally agreeing to stay with them while she put the Spite House up for sale. Through her tears, she managed to leave a coherent message for Fawn, who'd seemed like a very capable real estate agent. Through her tears, she emailed her therapist.

Finally, through her tears, she closed her window shades.

Not all of them, though. Not this time. Only the ones on Matthew's side.

The rest she left open to the streaming sunlight.

21

*I*t didn't take Matthew long to suspect he'd fucked up. Even before Athena had appeared in his office doorway, the doubts had sprung to life and multiplied, their growth exponential rather than linear.

If he thought about it, he could probably trace their genesis to the very moment he told his brother, *I'll walk away.*

But it was too late. He'd given his brother his word, and keeping his promises to Johnny had been the occupation of his entire lifetime, with the exception of eight short years. So instead of breaking his word to his brother, he was breaking faith with Athena. And appropriately enough, he felt broken too.

Yesterday, she'd closed the shades on his side of the house before he made it back from his office, so he had no way to track how or what she was doing. Which was only fair. She deserved her privacy, and he didn't deserve a glimpse of what he'd willingly relinquished.

Despite those drawn shades, though, he could still see her, and not just when she left the house for groceries or work. Whenever his salt-seared eyes closed, she greeted him with her small, glowing smile. She arched to meet the slow slide of his hand over her soft, soft skin. She cried in his arms, she held him in his own grief, and she stroked his hair in comfort. In gratitude. In affection.

Yeah, he still saw her all the time. The only woman he'd ever loved in almost four decades of existence. The woman whose love for him he'd held carefully cupped in his palm, only to turn his hand over and spread his fingers wide.

Despite Matthew's agreement to leave Athena, Johnny hadn't spoken to him since their argument, so maybe that relationship was irrevocably damaged too. Which would be ironic and probably well deserved.

His younger brother was quiet this morning, and not just with Matthew. As they sat in the employee lounge and Yvonna shared necessary information for the upcoming day, Johnny stared blankly down at his notebook, his shoulders rounded, his pen unmoving.

Maybe he was distracted by his plans to lure Athena into his arms once more. Or maybe he'd launched those plans with his typical impatience and already been rejected, because Matthew hadn't lied to his brother. Athena wouldn't take Johnny back.

Athena wouldn't take either of them back.

"Do you agree, Matthew?" Yvonna asked, in reference to . . . something.

"Yes," he said, because whatever. It didn't matter. If they needed him to take an extra on-call shift or visit the hospital nursery or assist a CPNP with a particular patient, fine. He had no reason to go home. Athena wasn't waiting for him there, and he could access her behind his own eyelids whenever he wanted.

Yvonna was watching him now, her scrutiny sharp.

That didn't matter either. Atop the wholesale agony of his memories from yesterday, he barely noticed the additional sting.

Over a sleepless, ink-black night, he'd replayed the entire, disastrous confrontation. He'd listened to himself acquiesce to his brother's demands, to his brother's needs, over and over. And right before dawn, he'd tried to nail down the reasons he'd done it.

In part, it must have been simple reflex. Matthew had become

Johnny's true father a long, long time ago, and a father's instincts twitched beneath his skin. *My kid is unhappy. I need to fix it however I can. Immediately.* Those instincts, combined with long, long experience in sacrificing himself for his brother's happiness and giving Johnny whatever he wanted, must have guided Matthew through his impenetrable labyrinth of emotions to the nearest exit. The most familiar one. The easiest one, although not easiest for him.

Easiest for Johnny. Matthew's son, in fact if not in blood.

The pale morning light had begun to wash through the windows of the staff lounge, illuminating Johnny's face without pity. For the first time, Matthew noticed crinkles at the corners of his brother's eyes. Crow's-feet born of tiredness, yes, and maybe grief too, but also . . . age.

His brother wasn't a child anymore. Not even a young adult.

Johnny was over thirty years old. At thirty, Matthew had already raised a kid old enough to legally drink. And while that wasn't right—it had never been right; Matthew had deserved a childhood too, and they'd both deserved real parents—the contrast in what the two brothers had done by that age, what had been expected of them and what they expected of themselves, was . . . startling.

If a stranger were to study the Vine brothers now, would they say *Johnny* was the one in need of extra support?

For every moment of Johnny's life, he'd had at least one family member dedicated to his comfort and happiness. Now he was a grown adult, and an intelligent one. He owned a house, free and clear. He'd earned a medical degree and was well on his way to becoming a creditable pediatrician, especially if his post-Hawaii commitment to his work proved permanent. He'd gathered a large, supportive circle of friends who invited him to Halloween parties and New Year's Eve get-togethers, and Johnny gladly joined them whenever his brother wasn't available. He'd never lacked for girlfriends or friends offering benefits, and he'd been engaged once already. That engagement had ended by his own choice, not his fiancée's.

Then there was Matthew. Before Athena, he'd never had a girlfriend. Never had a lover. Most people liked him well enough, but apart from Yvonna and Karl, who would actually consider him a true friend or confidant?

Until Athena, he'd been so fucking lonely. All the time. Disconnected and lost, even though he'd lived in this town his entire life, known and gotten along with everyone, and never questioned his life path or moved out of his childhood home.

She'd blown into Harlot's Bay like a cyclone and upended everything he thought he knew. Only to settle herself comfortably in the bleak, barren corners of his disarranged life, filling them with joy and purpose and affection.

But that was done now. He'd flipped and flexed his hand. He'd watched her love drop to the bricks and shatter.

If she cried, he couldn't comfort her. If she laughed, he couldn't hear it. If she pursued new adventures, he couldn't accompany her. If she wrecked on the rocks again, he couldn't offer his help as she pieced herself back together.

And he still didn't have one fucking photo of her that was his alone.

A chair screeched, and he dimly wondered whose. Then he was standing. Walking out the employee lounge door, out the practice's back exit, and out from under the weight of a dozen shocked, concerned stares.

He didn't take this particular path daily, or even weekly, but it was familiar. One right turn, and then another. Four blocks of walking, away from the town center and toward more residential areas. Through the creaking gate, which he'd treat with WD-40 the next time he came. Over the grass, brown with the desolation of winter.

There were no flowers at the grave, either fresh or fake. Adrian wouldn't have known what to do with plants, apart from eating them. That kid had shoved anything and everything into his mouth, especially when a new tooth was about to poke through his poor, inflamed gums.

Sometimes, stupid as it felt, Matthew brought one of Adrian's teething toys with him when he visited. A ring of plastic keys, or a nubby circle, just the right size for chewing without any risk of choking. Other times he brought his brother's favorite stuffed elephant, its neck floppy from Adrian's little hands and pudgy arms wrapped tight. He didn't leave those mementos of his brother's too-short life at the grave, but they were offerings nevertheless.

Today Matthew brought nothing but himself.

When he sat, the chill of the damp ground immediately seeped into his bones. Didn't matter. He couldn't stay long. There were patients to see. Duties to fulfill. Routines to follow.

He might have broken his own heart, but life plodded on regardless.

God, he hated visiting here in the winter. His brother would be so goddamn cold, and Matthew couldn't do a single thing about it.

A coat, thick and familiar, covered his shoulders, and someone dropped down next to him. Yvonna, the bottoms of her sharp heels studded with clumps of dirt and grass. She maneuvered him like a doll until he was wearing his wool coat, then stretched out her legs.

"Due to my racing stripes, I have the reflexes and speed of a cheetah," she said, her gaze trained on his brother's gravestone. "Good thing, too, since you took off like a broody rocket."

"Sorry." Aching inside and out, he gathered his legs beneath him. "I'll come back."

She rested a hand on his shoulder, and he subsided. "You're covered. Akio's taking your first few appointments, and Johnny's squeezing in a couple of mine, which I confirmed right before I sprinted out the door."

He nodded, unable to meet her eyes. "I apologize for the disruption."

"Skip the apologies and tell me what's going on, Matthew." She scooted closer, until they sat shoulder to shoulder. "I've never seen you like this before. And we've been friends for a really, really fucking long time, so that's saying something."

His next breath shuddered. "I—I can't."

If he talked right now, he'd cry. And if he let himself disintegrate entirely, he couldn't get up and be the in-control authority figure his patients, their parents, and his employees needed.

"I'm in no hurry," she said imperturbably. "We can stay here as long as you need."

For a while, they sat silently, the warmth of his coat and her nearness beating back some of the chill. Then he told her everything, because he knew his friend. She was stubborn as blazes, and she'd outwait him. Hell, if he didn't surrender before nightfall, she'd simply call Jackie and have a tent and sleeping bag brought to the damn cemetery.

After he was done, they sat silently again, waiting until his tears had dried.

Then she sighed and turned to look at him. "Matthew, I may

need you to explain everything again. I'm having trouble understanding why you'd dump Athena for Johnny's sake, even knowing she'd never take him back."

Dump. He'd always loathed using that terrible word in reference
to Athena, but it was apt. Again. Because he'd tossed her aside like
a bit of refuse, hadn't he? Just like his brother.

"I think . . ." He pressed two fingers to the spot where his head
throbbed worst. "I raised Johnny like a father would, and I think
I got too used to giving him anything he wanted, to make up for
what he was missing."

"What you were both missing," Yvonna corrected. "You both
lost a brother. You both lost your parents, even if they were technically still around."

She never let him get away with anything, and he loved her for
it. Always had.

"Yes. You're right. I lost my brother too. I lost my parents. I lost
Granny." Her headstone was only a row away, and she got fresh
flowers once a month. No teething toys. Although, to be honest,
she'd probably appreciate her dentures more than daisies. "Johnny
is the only family I have left."

And that was the final straw, wasn't it? The last, decisive burden
laid upon his straining back, breaking his will to fight for Athena.

"I was terrified, Yvonna. Panicked." Almost unable to form
words through the fear. "I wanted to tell him, *No, I love Athena
and want to stay with her*, but I was so afraid that . . ."

He couldn't even say it out loud.

"You'd lose him as well." When he nodded, she hiked up her
knees and pinned him with her clear brown stare. "Matthew, do
you genuinely think your brother would cut you out of his life forever if you were with Athena? I mean, he may be the only blood

family you have left, but you're also the only blood family *he* has left."

It was a good question. Too bad he didn't have a good answer.

"Maybe not," he said after a minute. "But if I refused him, I knew things would change between us, possibly for good."

Yvonna spread her hands. "Is that really such a bad thing? Do you really want to keep your relationship exactly the way it is now? You, forever the responsible older brother, Johnny the feckless kid who needs guidance and protection, no matter what it costs you? Isn't that doing you a disservice? Isn't that doing *him* a disservice?"

Those were the same questions he'd begun asking himself in the employee lounge. What did Johnny actually need from Matthew now? What did he deserve? What, if anything, did Matthew deserve from Johnny?

He didn't know. Right now, he was only certain about two things.

He and his brother had both failed Athena, one after the other.

And Johnny would eventually be okay without her, but Matthew wouldn't.

"She won't forgive me, and I don't blame her." His voice was so quiet, he barely heard it himself. "I threw her love away, just like my brother did, and she listened to me do it."

Then he'd let her walk off without trying to stop her. Without even telling her one last time how irrevocably she'd stolen his heart.

If he came up to her now, told her he'd changed his mind and refused to step aside for his brother, and tried to make his case for resuming their relationship, she'd fucking *eviscerate* him. Definitely verbally. Possibly physically.

He'd made his own bed. The sheets might be disgustingly filthy, but he still had to climb between them and lie there.

"You're probably right about Athena. At this point, I imagine she's had enough of the Vine brothers, which is a feeling I know all too well. Trust me on that." Yvonna's manicured finger poked him in the ribs, and he yelped out a protest. "But Matthew, you started raising an infant at eight years old, yet somehow managed to get yourself through medical school and a pediatric residency. Then you turned around and did the same thing for your brother. You're smart, hardworking, and incredibly stubborn."

This time, the pressure of her shoulder against his wasn't a comforting nudge. It was a shove.

"So if you love her, why are you giving up without a fight?" She shoved against him again, even harder, and he toppled over onto his side. "Yes, Athena will probably refuse to take you back. Does that mean you shouldn't even *try*?"

When she put it like that, not trying sounded stupid. Absurd, even. Because what did he honestly have to lose? His pride? He'd never had any when it came to Athena. His brother? Well . . . that was a trickier issue. Johnny already kind of hated him right now, and Matthew's decision to pursue Athena would only make matters worse.

"You genuinely think Johnny would forgive me?" he asked tentatively.

Yvonna lifted a shoulder. "Maybe not for a while, but eventually. If you let Athena leave, though, there'll be no *eventually* with her. The two of you will be done. Forever."

It was true that Johnny had never been much of a grudgeholder, and Matthew really was his only remaining family. And—

dammit, yes, it was past time for their relationship to change. Even Matthew could admit that now.

"You're right." He eyed Yvonna cautiously as he raised himself back to a seated position.

"Of course I'm right." His best friend buffed her shiny nails against her fancy peacock-blue coat. "It's time for you to grovel, Matthew. Grovel like no man has groveled before, outside of Sadie Brazen's novels. Just FYI, Victoria said Brazen's guppy-dude removed a guppy-fin to prove his guppy-regret and guppy-devotion after wronging his fated non-guppy-mate."

At Matthew's look of horror, she shrugged. "It grew back. And when it did, for some reason he got an extra guppy-penis too."

Of course he did. Dammit, Brazen.

"My limbs won't regenerate," Matthew said slowly. "So . . ."

Yvonna stood and swatted dead grass off her wool-clad rear. "Get creative. Just *grovel*, Vine. Guppy-style."

"Got it," he told her, then heaved himself to his own feet. "When in doubt, ask myself WWGMD. What Would Guppy-Man Do?"

Limb removal was a hard no. But almost everything else was up for debate.

For the first time since Athena's departure from his office, a sense of purpose and possibility filled some of the desolate hollowness she'd left behind. And as he and Yvonna walked arm in arm back to the practice, he began making plans. Guppy-style.

22

*A*thena's FOR SALE signs kept disappearing.

It was weird. She'd never had any issues with theft before, and neither had the neighbors she asked. But three damn days in a row, she'd trooped over to Fawn's office in the afternoon, procured another sign from the increasingly exasperated real estate agent, and thumped it deep into the little patch of grass in front of the Spite House.

Only to wake up the next morning to a sign-less yard.

She'd think the universe was telling her not to leave Harlot's Bay, but the universe had also presented her with both Vine brothers, so the universe could get bent.

In less than a week, the disappearing signs would become Fawn's issue, because Athena was packing up her belongings for the second time in less than six months and preparing to peace-out of Harlot's Bay. She didn't need reminders of Matthew everywhere she went, and she didn't need all her best friends so closely tied to him. There was no escaping him in this town, so she was escaping *from* this town.

For the last few days, she'd been crying a lot, but she didn't feel depressed, per se. These weren't tears of hopeless despair. They were simply . . . grief. If she could get the hell out of Harlot's Bay, away from Matthew, her state of mind would improve.

Probably. Almost definitely.

Although she was really going to miss the friends she'd made, despite their associations with him. And Matthew himself . . . he was everywhere around her, but he was everywhere *inside* her too. In a prime example of towering irony, when misery began to drown her and she had ugly, self-loathing thoughts, his was the voice she heard in her head, defending her. Arguing quietly, sincerely, that she was being far too hard on herself. Deeming her a woman lost in seeking new worlds, fractured but not a failure.

Never, ever a failure.

Maybe that was the saddest thing of all. He truly loved her. There was no faking that, and Matthew was a terrible liar anyway. He just didn't love her quite *enough*. Not as much as she loved him.

She couldn't live next door to a constant reminder of that, so she had to go, missing FOR SALE sign or no missing FOR SALE sign. She could only hope the lack of him outside her head would eventually banish him from inside its overstuffed confines too.

The evening of the third replaced sign, the next odd thing happened.

Food arrived to her front door. Lots of it.

By *food*, she meant potatoes. A freaking *avalanche* of potatoes.

She received pulled-pork-topped tater tots from the diner. Peanut–sweet potato stew from the Gambian café three blocks away. An exquisite little mini–pommes Anna, its thin slices arrayed like a flower, from the tearoom. Crisp samosas with a savory potato-pea filling from the town's best Indian restaurant. Poutine. Rosti. Even a fresh loaf of potato bread from Karl.

She could potentially eat nothing but potato products for the next week.

It was the sort of thing her parents might do, but they convincingly claimed no knowledge of the potato tsunami. As did Victoria, Jackie, and Bez, when she texted them.

Baffled, she sat down for dinner and ate her approximate body weight in delicious tubers. It was a volume of spuds unmatched in her personal potato-consumption history, which she considered a true feat.

The next morning, she woke to yet another missing sign and a brief note slipped through her mail slot. Generic paper, Times New Roman font, unsigned. The message read, Open your window tonight. 8 p.m. P.S. Check Reddit.

What. In. The. *World?*

Well, she knew for certain the note wasn't from Matthew, because that man wouldn't know Reddit from a wheel of cheese. When she'd discreetly asked him about the site a few weeks ago, curious as to whether he'd seen her scathing Am I the Asshole? post, he'd frowned at her and said he'd heard of Reddit somewhere. Wasn't it a literacy program targeting teens?

So, yeah, no way it was him.

However . . .

One of the newest AITA posts told the tale of a man—39M—who'd broken off a new relationship with the woman he loved—37F—because his brother wanted her as well. He'd realized his terrible error in judgment and was miserable without her, but he was worried attempts to reconcile with her, despite the encouragement of his friends, would be a dick move.

Her words, not his. He was evidently much more refined than Athena, so he wrote *hurtful and unwelcome* instead of *a dick move.*

His closing statement: *I'd like to convince her of my devotion before she leaves town forever, but maybe it's selfish of me to demand her time and attention after I hurt her so badly through my own cowardice and bad judgment. AITA for trying to grovel my way back into her heart?*

The ages matched. The situations matched. The earnest

humility in the writer's words matched Matthew's demeanor. And someone had slid a note through her mail slot pointing her toward Reddit on the very day the post appeared.

On the other hand: teen literacy program.

On the other other hand: Despite his lack of fluency with social media sites, he was more than capable of consulting Professor Google, and she *had* mentioned Reddit to him before.

Welp, there was nothing for it. She'd need to open her window at eight o'clock that evening to find out what the actual fuck was going on. Just to assuage her curiosity, obviously, since the outcome didn't really matter.

Even if Matthew truly had orchestrated all the recent oddities in her life, and done so out of heartfelt regret and love, the two of them were over. Through. Finito. Kaput. Dunzo.

Maybe if she used enough synonyms, she could force her misguided heart to believe it.

COASTAL MARYLAND IN early January wasn't exactly the North Pole, but it wasn't Hawaii either. Opening her window for mysterious reasons based on an anonymous note seemed like a remarkably terrible idea, now that Athena was sitting in her unlit library nook with frigid air swirling around her and sneaking beneath her thick terry-cloth bathrobe.

The message hadn't specified which window to open, but she wasn't offering ground-floor access to a possible stalker. The third floor seemed safer. Although, to be fair, at least one person *had* previously entered her home through this very window, despite its daunting height.

Whatever. She was here. For what reason, she hoped to discover shortly.

Matthew's windows all had their shades drawn, except in his empty office.

But . . . huh. That was odd.

After plopping down in her comfy reading chair, she'd removed her glasses to scrub her face nervously. Now she slid them back on, because . . . if she didn't know better, she'd have said Matthew had a sign in his kitchen window.

A FOR SALE sign, to be exact. One defaced in thick black letters, which were painted directly over poor Fawn's face and business logo.

The sign now read: FOR SALE: EVERYTHING I HAVE, NOW AND FOREVER. $0.

In his dining room window, there was a different message: FOR SALE: EVERYTHING I AM AND EVER WILL BE. $0.

She clapped her hand over her mouth to stifle a sob as she read the final sign, placed in his bedroom window: FOR SALE: 1 BROKEN ♥. NO NEED TO BUY. IT'S ALWAYS BEEN YOURS. I'M SO SORRY.

The letters on each sign were so squished and small, it was damn hard to read the messages. Her crying didn't help much either. Squinting and sniffling, she leaned forward to make sure she'd gotten everything right, because if she had—

A loudly clearing throat made her jump in her chair, and she jerked her head toward the source of the racket. Matthew's office, still dark. But while she'd been studying the signs and sniveling, the window had been cracked open and a laptop positioned on the sill, facing her, its speakers apparently operating at full volume.

Matthew was holding the laptop in place, easily visible. No longer hiding.

His stare compulsively roamed over her face, her body, as if he could swallow her whole through sight alone. She bit her lip, uncertain how to respond, and trained her eyes on the laptop instead of him.

Wait. Was that . . . Karl's voice booming from the speakers?

"Yes, I'm sure it's fucking recording," he grumped ear-splittingly. "You think I'm going to fuck this up, asshole?"

Matthew's voice made its bone-dry, equally deafening debut. "I apologize for questioning your mastery of recording technology. After all, you're such an enormous enthusiast of selfies and other means by which to preserve your image and words for posterity."

"Fuck you, Vine. At least I knew what Reddit was, dude. I'll bet you think a meme is some motherfucker trapped in a stupid invisible box."

Heroically, Matthew managed to ignore that and get the project back on track. "So you'll know how to cut out this part and any other problematic bits and splice everything together once we're done?"

A long pause. "Sure."

"And you're certain what we wrote sounds like a Sadie Brazen story?"

A longer pause. "Sure."

"Then let's do this." Matthew drew a deep breath, then spoke more slowly, with pristine enunciation. "*Down to Pluck: An Erotic Monster Romance* by Sadie Brazen."

She snorted loudly, unable to contain her amusement. Across the alleyway, a smidgen of the anxiety furrowing his brow seemed to ease.

Not that she was watching him. Except out of the corner of her eye.

"Once there was a chicken-man hybrid named Matthew," he began.

"A *sexy* chicken-man hybrid named Matthew, packing plenty of poultry penis," Karl corrected. "Stick to the script, asshole."

"Once there was a sexy chicken-man hybrid named Matthew, packing plenty of poultry . . . goodness," Matthew began again. "He had ripped abs, two . . . um, appendages, and feathers perfectly positioned for tickling a lover's, uh, fancy."

"Chicken-Man is about right." Karl grunted. "You suck, dude."

"*Fine*," Matthew snapped, finally out of patience. "Once there was a sexy chicken-man hybrid named Matthew, packing plenty of poultry penis. He had ripped abs, two cocks, and feathers perfectly positioned for tickling a lover's clit. Happy now?"

Karl's snicker matched Athena's. "Yep."

Thus began the most bizarre and hilarious half hour of her life to date, and she'd once watched *Manos: The Hands of Fate* during her first and only foray into edibles. According to friends, she'd spent the entire evening shouting, "*Manos* means *hands*! It's really *Hands: The Hands of Fate*! Holy shit!"

Haltingly, through various cranky interruptions by Karl, Matthew spun the heartwarming—and also vagina-warming—tale of a half-silkie, half-human man who fell in love with a fully human woman remarkably similar in appearance to Athena. Her name was . . . Athena, because subtlety apparently wasn't the men's greatest writing strength.

Chicken-Man-Matthew and Thinly-Fictionalized-Athena had lots of improbable, enthusiastic sex, the narration of which was clearly killing Human-Matthew, only to find themselves confronted with Chicken-Man-Matthew's chicken-man brother . . . John.

Karl hooted. "Oh, that right there is some fucking *discretion*, Vine. If Johnny ever hears this, no *way* he'll ever figure out who that *John* motherfucker is."

OLIVIA DADE page 366

After that point, Athena stopped laughing, because Matthew didn't sugarcoat what had happened in the office.

"He saw the hurt in her eyes but let her walk away." His voice had turned raw and cracked, and not simply from the strain of narration. "He sagged against the coop's desk, desolate beyond speech. The moment she disappeared from sight, his feathers began to fall softly to the floor, one by one, like the tears he shed. The emptiness of his wing-arms chilled him from the inside out, and he searched his hollow chicken-soul for answers. Why had he broken his chicken-heart and her heart too? Why had he set her aside for his chicken-man brother, even knowing John and Athena weren't fated chicken-mates?"

Then, using his tortured tale of poultry and pain and true love, Matthew told her what she already knew. He'd been his brother's indulgent father-figure for over thirty years, and he was too used to giving Johnny whatever he wanted. But even more than that, Matthew was a man who'd lost almost everyone he loved as a young boy, and he couldn't stand the thought of losing Johnny too. The last true member of his blood family. The last remaining tie to his lost childhood and his lost brother.

"He'd panicked," Matthew concluded somberly, "and in his panic, he made a grievous mistake."

There was no doubting his sincerity. Every word fairly dripped with sorrow and desperate remorse and—yes, love.

"He wanted to earn Athena's forgiveness and regain her trust. He wanted to tell her the truth: that he would never, ever let her go again. That she could keep exploring new worlds for decades to come, and he'd remain by her side the entire time, his wing-arm firmly tucked in hers. That anytime she got lost, he'd peck at whatever was blocking her view until she found her way once more. That she didn't need to be certain about anything but his love."

Which was the moment she began crying for the thousandth time that day.

He continued, "And most of all, he wanted to ask her to be his chicken-mate forever, because spending every last breath of his life with her would be the greatest joy and honor a chicken-man like him could ever imagine. But Athena was a human woman who'd been hurt badly by chicken-men in her past, and he didn't see how she could ever forgive him. He refused to let her disappear from the coop without at least trying, though."

Well, her first tissue was soaked. On to another, and probably another after that.

"One of Matthew's chicken-friends told him to emulate the groveling of guppy-men," he added, sounding slightly aggrieved. "But it turned out guppy-style groveling wasn't feasible, because his chicken-man limbs wouldn't regrow after being cleavered off, and also he owned neither an underseas guppy-estate nor jewel-encrusted scuba gear. So chicken-man-style groveling— *Matthew*-style groveling—would have to suffice."

He sighed. "So he groveled as best he could, in his awkward chicken-man way, and then he had to wait to find out what would happen next. Because he couldn't force or argue Athena into forgiving him, no matter how much he loved her or how very sorry he was for hurting her. Whatever she chose to do next, he'd accept as his chicken-fate, even if it meant her fleeing the coop and leaving him behind for good."

The narration paused there, as his breath hitched.

"If she did leave," he said slowly, hoarsely, "Matthew wanted her to do so with an unburdened heart, knowing she'd done nothing wrong. The fault was all his. And even if he spent forever without her, he would always be grateful she still existed somewhere in the world and that he'd once had the privilege to be loved by her."

Then . . . silence.

"You really need to write a fucking ending, man," Karl interjected.

Matthew's response drifted from the laptop speakers in a frayed whisper. "I can't. It's not my decision."

Athena buried her sniffle in a tissue.

Dammit. He wasn't going to let her hold even the tiniest grudge, was he?

Through tonight's bizarre display, not to mention the Reddit post and last night's spud flood, he'd more than proven himself. He loved her enough to fight his fears and fight for her. To try to stop her from walking away, but honor her choice if she did. To keep her forever, if she'd accept his apology. How could she stay angry at him?

Sadly enough, she wouldn't be able to use this misstep as leverage in future arguments, either. The reminder of what he'd done would hurt him far too much. In any case, she'd inevitably make mistakes of her own in their relationship. Maybe less grievous ones, but they'd add up, and he'd forgive her readily each and every time, because that was who Dr. Matthew Vine the Third was.

He'd already been crowned the Champion of Head. Like hell she'd let him hog the Champion of Forgiveness title too.

After one last hiccup, Athena accepted the inevitable. Matthew's chicken-heart was as soft as a silkie's feathers. Someone needed to protect it, and that someone might as well be his human mate, because she was much more vicious than he could ever hope to be.

She blew her nose. Loudly. Then she produced her phone from her bathrobe pocket and consulted Professor Google on a key point.

When she looked up, Matthew was still staring directly at her, his beautiful eyes full of stricken, hopeless love.

"An adult male chicken is either a cock or a rooster, you jackass." She slipped her cell back in her pocket, stood, and set her fists on her hips. "Sadie Brazen would never call her hero a chickenman when she could call him a cock-man instead. Duh."

"Oh." He frowned even harder. "I probably should have asked Hill for assistance."

She flicked her wrist in dismissal. "Nah. It was more entertaining this way."

"Athena . . ." His voice turned ragged. "I am so very sorry. Can you ever forgive me?"

Ah, the crucial question. Two days ago, she'd have offered an entirely different response, but now . . .

"I suppose so." She heaved a dramatic sigh. "Which means you'd better come over here, meet me in my bedroom, and start earning it."

His mouth dropped open, but he didn't seem to be breathing. Like, at all.

She threw her hands in the air, exasperated. "What are you waiting for, Dr. Matthew Vine the Third? You still have a key."

He about-faced and fled his office without another word. Knowing she didn't have long before his arrival, she hurried to her bedroom and dropped her terrycloth robe on the floor.

Less than a minute later, his footsteps raced up her stairs, and he burst into her room, breathless and wet-cheeked and overjoyed. Before another heartbeat passed, he'd tumbled into her open arms, then into her welcoming bed. Precisely where he belonged.

Even a chicken-man couldn't have flown to her side any faster.

"Put that beak to good use, baby," she murmured against his mouth, grinning. "I am, in fact, down to pluck."

He laughed, his eyes still bright with relieved tears. "A champion's work is never done."

Then he moved down her body, eased open her thighs, and blew her clucking mind.

GIDDY WITH JOY, exhaustion, and anxiety, Matthew showed up at Johnny's doorstep the next morning and wouldn't leave until his brother appeared. Which Johnny finally did, after three presses of the doorbell.

He hadn't talked to Matthew in days, not even at work. So when he finally emerged from the house, Matthew expected shouting. Obscenities. Maybe a punch or a shove.

Instead, Johnny opened the door and wearily leaned against the frame. For a minute, the two brothers simply looked at one another.

Then Johnny pushed off the doorframe, nudged Matthew's arms wide, and huddled against his older brother like a child. His forehead rested on Matthew's shoulder, and his arms wrapped painfully tight around Matthew's waist.

Stunned, Matthew hugged Johnny close, rocking him a little.

When was the last time his brother had wanted comfort from him like this? Twenty years ago? Longer than that?

"I'm sorry," Johnny whispered thickly. "I'm so sorry, Matty. I shouldn't have asked you to leave Athena."

After giving his brother a fierce squeeze, Matthew forced himself to say the words that might end the embrace. That might end their relationship, full stop. "I'm sorry too, but . . . you need to know that she and I are together. If she's willing, I intend to marry her as soon as possible."

Tensely, he waited for an explosion that never came.

"Yeah. I got that," Johnny said, then snorted wetly against Matthew's shirt. "I do live next door, you know. A-plus job groveling, Chicken-Man."

Matthew sagged in relief, unable to fathom his continued good fortune. Also unable to fathom the evident loudness of his laptop's speakers and the fact that he, of all people, had cowritten such filthy—yet inept—interspecies erotic romance.

It had served its purpose, though. Athena had forgiven him, against all odds.

His next impossible task: salvaging his relationship with his brother.

"If you can't be around me for a while, I'll understand." Matthew pressed a hard kiss to the crown of Johnny's head. "But please believe me when I say I never wanted to hurt you, and I'll always want my baby brother in my life. As much contact as you're willing to accept, we'll have."

"Listen, Matty . . ." Johnny sucked in a hitching breath, then let it out slowly. "I'd already planned to come over later today. To apologize, but also talk to you about other stuff."

That sounded . . . ominous. But maybe Matthew was simply a worrywart, as Athena had alleged a time or two.

"In Hawaii, I decided I wanted Athena back, and for that to happen, I needed to be the kind of man who would deserve her," his brother said. "So I started trying to be better. More responsible. Especially at work, but everywhere."

Ah. That explained the post-honeymoon transformation.

"Right after you and I argued the other day, I waited for Athena and made my case to her. She responded with a resounding *fuck, no*." To his credit, Johnny sounded wryly amused as well as pained. "That's when I finally got it, Matty. I loved her. I still do. But I fucked her over, and there's no getting past that. Which is why I need to get my shit together, Athena or no Athena, so I don't do the same thing to the next woman I love."

Matthew's anxiety unwound another fraction. If his brother was already thinking in those terms—of falling in love with someone else—then he'd be fine, sooner or later. As opposed to Matthew, who'd been resigned to remaining alone and lovelorn for the rest of his Athena-less existence.

This was the right choice. Hard and hurtful, but not wrong.

All humor evaporated from Johnny's voice. "Then I saw how . . . empty . . . you looked the morning after we argued. Just—dead inside. I watched you break down for the first time in our lives and run from your own practice, your own employees, because you were hurting so much, and I was so ashamed, Matty. So fucking ashamed. And the moment you left, everything else fell into place too. Why you'd seemed so happy the last couple of months. How selfish I'd been to ask you to give her up, especially after everything you've done for me my entire life. What I need to do now, for both of our sakes."

Now his brother was crying again. Not over Athena. Over *him*.

"I have to start making my own decisions, Matty," Johnny whispered between hiccups. "I've been leaning too heavily on you for too long, and it's not good for either of us. You need to have your own life, and I need to choose whichever way forward will make me happiest, no matter how you might feel about it."

Matthew was crying too, he realized. From pride in the man his baby brother had become, and pride in himself for raising that man. From ineffable sadness, as he listened to Johnny take his first, faltering step away from Matthew, even as they still held one another.

Johnny cleared his throat. "I think I want to be a pediatric sports specialist. I'm going to give it a little more time before I make any moves. But if I decide to subspecialize, I'll have to leave Strumpet Square Pediatrics for my fellowship program, and you'll have to find a new doctor. I'm sorry."

It all made sense. It really did. But still, Matthew's heart beat out a repeated, grief-stricken *no*.

He took a moment to gather himself, because this was what a parent did. You had to love a child with every ounce of your being, care for them and protect them, and try your damnedest to help them become what they were meant to be, rather than what you might have expected or wanted from them. Try your damnedest to help them become an adult capable of navigating the world in pursuit of their own happiness, independently of you.

Only to watch them become an adult navigating the world in pursuit of their own happiness. Independently of you.

It was a devil's bargain, being a parent. Bound to end in pain, no matter what.

Nevertheless, he'd honor his end of the deal. He'd do what was best for his child. Because letting go was maybe the last great responsibility of parenthood.

He spoke carefully. "My being with Athena . . . I know it'll be hard, but I hate the thought of you leaving because of that."

Johnny shook his head. "I would want this with or without Athena. I promise, bro."

Matthew nodded. An acknowledgment. A surrender.

Okay, then. Okay.

He could do this. He could let go without burdening his brother with his own grief. Athena was in his life now, and she would help him make his way through it.

"Where did you run off to the other morning, anyway?" Johnny let his head rest more heavily on Matthew's shoulder. "Yvonna wouldn't say."

"I visited Adrian."

"I haven't been there for . . . years." Johnny clung tight for another moment, then stepped away from Matthew. "Want to go now?"

Matthew's arms fell to his sides, empty. He swallowed hard. "Sure."

He let his brother lead the way to the cemetery. When they arrived, they sat in the brown, damp grass, side by side.

"Tell me about Adrian," Johnny said. "What did he like to eat? Was he walking yet?"

So Matthew shared stories and details no one else remembered, not even their parents, and answered Johnny's questions. After an hour or so, the brothers ran out of words, but neither of them got up. They simply kept each other company. They kept Adrian company.

Finally, though, Johnny stirred and straightened. "Why don't we split the maintenance fees for Adrian's grave from now on?"

"Yes." Matthew ruffled his brother's hair. "I'd like that."

"Quit it, asshole." With an unconvincing scowl, Johnny ducked away from him. "I meant to tell you earlier, I can handle all of my student loans too, if you'd like."

God, Matthew's brain was too tired for math. "We can talk about that later. Find some calculators and figure out what's fair for both of us."

"Calculators." Johnny snorted. "Old-timer."

"Whippersnapper."

Johnny clambered to his feet with a groan. "Shit. I'm not feeling all that young myself right now. Anyway, I need to head out, Matty. I owe Yvonna a long-overdue apology, and I need to tell her about my possible departure." When Matthew opened his mouth to offer himself as an intermediary, Johnny raised a hand. "It's my responsibility. Not yours. But thank you."

Craning his neck, Matthew looked up at him. "See you soon?"

It was a question. A plea.

"Tonight or tomorrow." Johnny reached down and gave him a noogie, ignoring Matthew's squawked protests. "There's no getting rid of me, bro. Too bad for you."

Then Johnny left, and Matthew sat alone in the silent, cold graveyard. He thought about both his brothers, infants in his arms, small and trusting, and let himself weep.

After a while, Athena dropped down beside him with a thump and a little whimper at the chill of the grass.

"Your brother thought you could use some company," she said, and drew his head into her lap.

They stayed that way, her fingers sliding through his hair, for a long time. When he sat up, she offered him one of her small, genuine smiles, her hazel eyes full of tender sympathy.

Her lips beneath his were soft and cool, and he lingered to warm them. To warm himself.

He stroked her bangs to the side, away from her glasses, and her hair was so silky, it almost slipped through his fingers. At the last possible moment, he latched onto the end of a strand and tugged gently.

"Let's go back," he told her. "I'll make you tea."

She studied him so carefully, so lovingly, he almost cried again. "You're ready?"

"I'm ready."

He stood, offered his hand, and helped her up. And together, they made their way home.

Epilogue

Five years later

Felicity didn't even flinch when Matthew gave her the flu shot.

The ten-year-old might refuse to let anyone else deal with her vaccinations—not the CPNPs; not Yvonna; not even Keely, the third doctor in their practice, whom *everyone* loved—but she never raised a fuss when he was the one wielding a needle.

He probably shouldn't take such pleasure in that. Someday, she'd need to accept shots from someone other than him. But in the meantime, her trust trickled through him like warm, sweet syrup.

"Take care of yourself, Felicity," he said once they were done, and he watched her clamber down from the exam table. No signs of illness, injury, or developmental issues. Good.

She flicked him a jaunty wave on her way out the door. "You too, Dr. Vine. See you at the Halloween festival tonight!"

He smothered an involuntary wince. Yes. Unfortunately, he'd be there. Athena was MCing the window decoration contest, and although she'd told him to stay home, he wouldn't miss watching her shine in front of all Harlot's Bay for anything. Even his own sanity.

"Thank you, Dr. Itchy Butt." Ms. Mortenson smirked at him, then rose from her chair.

He grinned back. "My pleasure."

"*Mom*," Felicity complained loudly in the hallway as her mother rejoined her. "I told you to stop calling him that! It's embarrassing!"

Ms. Mortenson's voice faded into the distance as she spoke. "I'm so sorry, sweetie, but I'm your mom. Embarrassing you is my job. Also my hobby."

Matthew laughed quietly to himself, did his charting, and prepared to leave for the day. Since it was a Saturday, he intended to arrive at Bluestocking before his wife's lunch break. He'd already called the tearoom, and they had little triangular sandwiches and flowerlike potato tarts waiting in to-go containers for him, along with some of Karl's mini-scones.

Right before he turned out his office light, he glanced back at his desk and the dozen or so framed photos he'd carefully arranged there.

"Baby, why do you have thirty bajillion pictures of me cluttering your workspace?" Athena asked almost every time she visited. "Don't they trip your Mr. Clean trigger?"

No. When it came to her, mess didn't bother him. And as far as he was concerned, the more pictures of her he had, the better.

His favorite photo hung beside the door. The two of them with their arms wrapped around each other, sunburned and windtossed and beaming, a Pacific sunset behind them and white sails flapping above. As a wedding surprise, she'd found a company in Hawaii offering sailing experiences aboard a tall ship and booked a slot during their honeymoon, all so he could live out his boyhood dreams of traversing blue, blue waters atop sunbaked wooden decks.

Other than the day Athena married him, that was the best day of his life so far.

He pressed his forefinger to his lips and gently tapped it against the glass covering her lovely, glowing face. Then, ritual completed, he put on his coat and left.

A gusting wind greeted him outside, and gray-edged clouds had begun to gather on the horizon. There was a chance of thunderstorms, he'd seen when checking the forecast that morning. No surprise, really. It had been unusually warm all week, and the heat had to break somehow, ushering them back into autumn.

He quickened his pace as he walked to the tearoom, then the bookstore.

The bell jangled on the door handle when he entered Bluestocking. An older male customer was showing Athena a book at the front counter, but she glanced up to see who'd arrived. As soon as she spotted Matthew, her lips curved in a small, sweet, private smile, and when he held up the distinctive tearoom to-go bag, that smile turned blinding.

She held up a finger, requesting patience, and he nodded.

After spending a couple of years at Historic Harlot's Bay, she'd found herself in need of another challenge, and by that point, Hill was desperate for a real break. So he'd hired her as the store manager, banking on her ability to increase his revenue enough that he could afford her salary.

With her usual all-in enthusiasm, she'd overhauled the place with the help of Hill, Matthew, Johnny, and their friends. It was clean and bright now, the shelves sturdy and filled with shiny paperbacks neatly arranged in alphabetical order within genres. Clear signage informed everyone where to find what they needed. In the back, she'd created an area for book club meetings and author events, and the Nasty Wenches met there monthly.

A plate of free cookies—Karl's cookies—sat on the counter,

because Athena believed very strongly in the power of compliance strategies. The cookies were delicious, but they were also her bid to harness norms of reciprocity.

A cart filled with overstocked books stood near the front counter, topped with a pretty sign telling customers the price: four for a dollar. The foot-in-the-door phenomenon in action.

Nothing in her past was wasted. Her time teaching guided her business practices. Her tour guide experience helped her talk to anyone and everyone. Her work at the library gave her the necessary familiarity with authors and specific books. Her short stint at the bakery and friendship with Karl meant she could convince him to supply the bookstore's treats for free—because, as she'd argued, once people tasted his baked goods, they'd want more.

Begrudgingly, Karl had admitted to a significant increase in sales after Athena reopened Bluestocking. His lips had even twitched into a half smile during the confession, at least until he'd noticed Matthew watching him. Then he'd scowled and told Matthew and Athena to get out of his fucking work area before he threw them in the fucking mixer and served them as the featured fucking muffin of the day.

That big faker. He'd throw *himself* in the mixer before harming a hair on Athena's head.

She had other plans for Bluestocking in the works too, and she had a standing option to buy the store from Hill. If she decided she wanted to do that, Matthew would support her. If the store went under, Matthew would support her. If she got bored or overwhelmed and needed to find a different job, Matthew would support her. Simple as that.

Watching Athena tackle new challenges was one of the true pleasures of his life.

Despite her therapy and her meds, sometimes she still struggled with depression, especially in the winter and when she was restless or uncertain. Sometimes she was still harsher with herself than Matthew would wish, and it hurt to watch her suffer. It hurt to know he couldn't fix everything for her, as he longed to do. But it was a privilege to offer her a steady hand and stand by her side as she inevitably righted her ship.

She handed the sixtysomething customer at the counter a free bookmark. "If you'd rather revisit something you already own, no problem. This will help you mark your place in whatever you decide to read next."

The man looked torn for a moment. Then he pushed the book they'd been discussing toward the cash register. "What the hey. Never hurts to try something new, right?"

Ah, yes. Norms of reciprocity, part deux.

"I think you're going to love the story. But if you don't, and you treat the book gently, you can always bring it back for a quarter of the cover price in store credit," she reminded the man cheerfully as she took his money. "Easy-peasy, Louis L'Amour-squeezy."

The man left the store smiling, the bookmark tucked inside the western he'd bought.

Matthew locked the door behind him and flipped the sign that informed customers of Athena's hour-long lunch break.

By the time he turned back to her, she was already around the counter and ready to throw herself in his arms. With a surprised grunt, he staggered back a little, then caught his balance, wrapped himself around her, and tugged her even closer.

"Hey, baby." She planted a kiss on his neck. "Can you possibly give me five more minutes? I need to call a few customers before it gets too late in the day for them to stop by." She cast a longing glance at the bag by his feet. "Will the food be okay?"

"Yes. But before you do anything else . . ." Tipping up her chin with a nudge of his thumb, he covered her mouth with his and reveled in the warm give of her lips, the sweet slickness of her tongue. Afterward, he rested his forehead against hers. "Now I'm good. Take your time, sweetheart."

Just then, the first peal of thunder boomed in the distance, and he jerked in her arms.

"Come on, Dr. Vine." Her embrace became less about cuddling and more about steering. "The back of the store awaits you."

The children's nook at the rear of Bluestocking was surrounded on three sides by shelving. Anyone sitting in the brightly cushioned rocking chair there could see very little of the remaining store and nothing at all of the front windows.

Athena guided him into that chair as another rumble of thunder jangled his nerves, then darted off . . . somewhere. Moments later, she reappeared at his side and laid noise-cancelling headphones on a nearby wooden table.

"Remember to actually turn on the noise-canceling bit this time, okay?" She tapped a ragged fingernail against the headphones' tiny toggle switch. "While I'm up front, do you want to start the next book in the O'Brian series?"

When he nodded gratefully, she went to grab the paperback from behind the counter.

He slipped on the headphones and activated the noise-canceling feature. After thinking for a moment, he scooted his chair slightly to the side. An inch more, a different angle, and . . . there. He could see the part of the counter where she usually stood, but not the front windows. Perfect.

A moment later, she was dropping his book on the table, planting a kiss on his hair, and ruffling his curls before heading back to the store phone. Idly, he took out his own phone, because he was pretty certain he'd felt it vibrate earlier.

Sure enough, he had a missed FaceTime call from Athena's parents. Most likely, they wanted to badger him into judging who had created the better watercolor during their latest art class. Those two were hypercompetitive about everything. *Everything.*

After the wedding, they'd quickly elbowed their way into his life and Johnny's life too, a couple of semi-retired steamrollers with way too much time and money on their hands. So now the Vine brothers kind of had parents again, for better or worse. Mostly better.

They gave really excellent Christmas gifts—cashmere sweaters!—and even better hugs.

He texted them, *I'll call later this afternoon. Sorry. It was my Saturday to work.*

No worries, came the near-immediate response. *Our pièces de résistance aren't going anywhere and can await your judgment indefinitely. Be good, kiddo.*

Doug insisted on calling him *kiddo*, and Matthew should probably hate that.

He didn't, though. At all.

Johnny had evidently texted earlier as well, checking whether Matthew wanted to meet at the Halloween celebration. *I know scary shit is your FAVE, bro, so let's hang out while Athena is doing her thing and can't babysit you. I'll even buy you a candy apple.*

Will you protect me from the Murder Dolls? Matthew wrote back.

Dude, if those creepy-ass dolls decide your time has come, there's no escaping them.

That . . . didn't help me feel better. At all. BRO.

Really? My bad.

Matthew shook his head with a sigh. Responsible adulthood and a fancy new workplace hadn't curbed that smartass streak of Johnny's. His brother was incorrigible.

Still, he couldn't have been more supportive of Matthew and Athena, especially under the circumstances. Since they'd gotten married so quickly, Johnny hadn't yet left Strumpet Square Pediatrics for his fellowship program, and he'd voluntarily covered the lion's share of Matthew's work duties during the honeymoon.

At the courthouse wedding, he'd even served as one of the witnesses. Both brothers had cried during the ceremony, especially during the ring exchange. And if one or two of Johnny's tears hadn't stemmed entirely from joy, he'd managed to fake it very convincingly.

Love you, Matthew texted.

Seconds later, the reply came. *Love you too. See you tonight. BROSEPHINE.*

When he looked up from his phone again, a cookie had magically appeared on the table beside him. Clearly the work of the world's most adorable witch. So before he rejoined Aubrey and Maturin on their various shipboard adventures, he rose from the rocking chair and braved the front of the store, despite the blue-tinged flashes flickering in his peripheral vision.

Athena was still on the phone, talking with a customer. He shouldn't interrupt her, he knew that, but he really, *really* wanted a kiss. And these days, he'd grown quite used to getting what he wanted. Spoiled, you might call him.

But since that was his wife's fault, she'd have to suffer the consequences.

Just like a brat, he rounded the counter and cut her off mid-word with a kiss of abounding, towering devotion. Of gratitude for how fiercely she loved him. Of awe at how very brightly she shone in his personal sky, day after day.

And just like a brat, he winked as he walked away and left her breathless.

Acknowledgments

At First Spite is truly a book of my heart, and—as always—I couldn't have written it without the support of my family and friends. Thank you to everyone, but especially to Emma Barry, Mel (@melon_reads), Therese Beharrie, Theresa Romain, and Mia Sosa, all of whom read this story at some point (Emma and Mel did so twice) and helped buff it until it gleamed. All my love and gratitude to my husband, son, and mother as well. Your unwavering pride in my work brings me so much joy and strength.

My agent, Sarah Younger, is a stalwart wall of support behind me always. I don't know what I'd do without you, Sarah, and I hope I never have to find out. Thank you, and thank you too for taking me on the nerdiest possible agent-author field trip, to the American Museum of Natural History's gems and minerals collection! #Dioptase5ever!

I am so very grateful to Leni Kauffman. She's an incredible artist, but also an amazing person and a wonderful friend. Thank you for creating such beauty on behalf of my story, Leni. I couldn't be more thrilled.

I'm so delighted that Kelsey Navarro Foster agreed to lend her considerable talents to my audiobook once more. You're amazing, Kelsey!

My former editor at Avon, Nicole Fischer, worked through this story with me from the beginning, and I can't say enough about how carefully she considered the manuscript and how much thought she put into her edits. Thank you very, very much, Nicole.

I also owe a debt of gratitude to Sylvan Creekmore, my new editor. Sylvan came to this book after it was in its mostly final form but didn't hesitate to champion it and support me however she could. I'm so lucky to be working with her, and I know it.

I also want to acknowledge and express my gratitude to everyone else at Avon who shepherded my book from its inception to its final printing, and this is my best attempt at doing so:

Sylvan Creekmore **Editor**
Yeon Kim **Art Director**
Beatrice Jason **Senior Marketer**
DJ DeSmyter **Marketing Director**
Jessica Cozzi **Publicist**
Rachel Weinick **Production Editor**
Marie Rossi **Production Manager**
Pam Barricklow **Managing Editor**
Madelyn Blaney **Editorial Assistant**
Justine Gardner **Copyeditor**
Abigail Nover **Audio Producer**
Liate Stehlik **Publisher**
Jen Hart **Associate Publisher**
Sarah Strowbridge **Proofreader**

Thank you, thank you, *thank you* to all of you.

And finally, to my readers: Every day, I do what I love because of your support. Thank you from the bottom of my very grateful heart.

Praise for Olivia Dade

Ship Wrecked

'[A] smart, stellar contemporary. . . . A banger of a finish, and an absolute joy'

New York Times Book Review

'[A] superbly entertaining, boldly sensual love story. . . . Combine this with wit-infused writing and some love scenes hot enough to keep any Viking couple warm during those cold winter nights, and the result is another impactful romantic triumph from Dade'

Booklist

'A sexy, funny, heartwarming enemies-to-friends-to-lovers romance. . . . The story pulls readers in with well-developed, likable characters, and an unputdownable plot'

Library Journal (starred review)

'We need more representation like this. . . . Filled with banter and tons of pining . . . this emotional romance will fill readers with hope for their own happily ever after'

The Nerd Daily

'Olivia Dade never fails to make me laugh, blush, and feel like I'm being wrapped in a warm blanket. Cannot recommend enough!'

Katee Robert, *New York Times* and *USA Today* bestselling author

'Dade challenges love story norms in *Ship Wrecked* with a wonderfully complex relationship that's years in the making. Sexy and delicious from page one!'

Nisha Sharma, author of *Dating Dr. Dil*

All the Feels

'[*All the Feels*] weaves in sharp wit and dry humor even as it tugs at the reader's heartstrings. . . . A consistently entertaining and often insightful romance'

Kirkus Reviews (starred review)

'[A] charming, sexy contemporary . . . friends-to-lovers, opposites-attract romance. The writing is excellent, with witty, banter-filled dialogue'

Library Journal (starred review)

'After wowing readers with *Spoiler Alert*, Dade returns with another stunning contemporary romance that brilliantly celebrates the redemptive power of love. With a deliciously acerbic sense of humor and endless measures of grace and insight, Dade . . . skillfully develops both the sweet emotional connection and the searingly sensual attraction'

Booklist (starred review)

'An absolutely witty, swoon-worthy behind-the-scenes romp! Delightful from beginning to end!'

Julie Murphy, #1 *New York Times* bestselling author of *Dumplin'*

'Joyful, clever, and full of heart, with two irresistible characters whose connection is both gorgeously sweet and wildly hot. Mixing riotous humor and aching tenderness, *All the Feels* is all the things I love about romance. Olivia Dade has jumped to the top of my auto-buy list!'

Rachel Lynn Solomon, nationally bestselling author of *The Ex Talk*

Spoiler Alert

'Dade delivers and then some. This book frolics through fields of fannish allusion and metatext. . . . It takes a skillful writer to juggle so many elements, yet the emotional through-line shines clear and strong at every point'

New York Times Book Review

'Dade's book is a sparkling jolt of fangirling, body-positive swoons'

Entertainment Weekly

'It's a path of self-discovery, healing, and growth, punctuated by scorching chemistry, whip-smart dialogue, and sidesplitting humor'

Washington Post

'With richly drawn characters you'll love to root for, Olivia Dade's books are a gem of the genre—full of humor, heart, and heat'

Kate Clayborn, author of *Georgie, All Along*